The Curse of the Bailey Women

by

Zenora Knight

Zenora Knight

First Edition

ISBN-13: 978-1-947373-00-6

ISBN-10: 1-947373-00-5

Printed in the United States of America

Deposited in the Library of Congress

Cover Design: Anelia Savova,
https://annrsdesign.wordpress.com

Lexingford Publishing LLC

New York Ottawa San Francisco Hong Kong

www.lexingfordpublishingllc.com

Dedications

I dedicate this book in loving memory of my mother, "G," and my grandparents, Emma and Walter Toone. I know they are in heaven smiling down on me. Where would I be if it had not been for these three people loving me unconditionally?

I pay homage to all my ancestors.

Acknowledgments

Thank you, God, for all your mercy and grace shown to me throughout my life. I am grateful for each day that I am blessed with another opportunity to embrace life, for without you, I am nothing.

Denise, my sister, thank you for the many long hours you spent reading, editing, giving me feedback and suggestions, and support. God chose you to be my sister. But choosing to be a devoted sister and friend, this is your doing. Never stop laughing.

To my son, Javian, thank you for reading chapter after chapter. Many times, I knew you had other things to do, but you read anyway. I knew if my novel hooked you and made you laugh, I was on the right track.

A big shout out to my son LeMar, my daughter-in-law, Afua, and all my beautiful grandchildren: Embrey, Jayla, Asia and Caiden. Thank you, guys, for the love and joy you bring to my heart.

"Stop procrastinating! Finish the book! If the book is great, super-fantastic! If the book is a flop, who cares? Move on to the next one. Stop being afraid of success!" Thank you, Eddie Lopez, my motivational coach and dear friend. I would not be holding this book in my hand had it not been for your teachings. Thank you for helping me to see and live life differently.

Frances Septimo, my dearest friend. You are a true gem. You have been there from my novel's conception to birth. I have nothing but love for you.

Karen Chin Sue, co-worker and friend of thirty years. Thank you for referring me to my first editor and legal services, and for offering support to my family when we needed it most. Our adventures have just begun.

Susan Cook, co-worker and friend. You are one of the strongest women I know. You taught us all that when life knocks you down unexpectedly, one must dig deep, find the strength, and keep on living. "BEAT the BETES," INC, keeping her daughter, Octavia Ocean's dream alive.

In a writing class, someone raised their hand and asked, "How will someone like Zenora ever get published?" I responded, "What the hell!" Now I say, "Like this!" Thank you, David Lieberfarb, for editing my book and for all your suggestions. You are the best!

Cousin Cynthia Harrell for asking me 365 days a year, for many years, "How's the book coming along?"

Cousin Cynthia Doswell, whose eyes popped out of her head when she read the love scenes.

Cousin Darnell Davis for connecting me to David Lieberfarb.

Thank you, Joe Boykin, family friend and musician, for all your encouragement.

"Gone but never forgotten!" Glover Davis, a dear friend who filled the room with his hardy, infectious laughter, and Debbie Travers, a beloved co-worker. Debbie was the first person to read my book.

There is not enough room to mention everyone by name, but you know who you are. It's been a long journey and I've crossed this finish line with your love and support.

 Love you all,

Zenora

Zenora Knight

Table of Contents

Zenora Knight

Chapter 1

Moving Day

"There is no way for a woman born into the Bailey bloodline to ever avoid the Curse of the Bailey Women, not even you." Thirty-three year-old Anabay Bailey Jones was clearly hearing the voice of her soft-spoken mother speaking to her as if she were standing right next to her. Feeling like a ton of bricks had dropped from the ceiling to crush her, Anabay spun around, then quickly exhaled a sigh of relief, realizing her mother wasn't there. The very thought of her mother speaking to her from the grave caused her skin to break out in goosebumps. She shivered. It was almost too much to bear.

"Damn," she mumbled to herself, "Guess I'm having one of those out-of-body experiences I've heard so much about."

After today, she would no longer stand in front of the large bay window in the living room of her four thousand square-foot, ranch-style home on Pine Cliff Way overlooking the Hudson River on the New Jersey side. After all she had been through, she wondered if she would be able to pick herself up and move forward with life. The last thing she needed was a ghost talking to her, even if it was her mother.

It was not every day a black woman, such as herself, could own riverfront property in such a prestigious neighborhood with her very own private view of the sun rising in the east over the river and setting in the west behind the mountains. Having lived here for a short time, Anabay truly loved everything about her home. It had provided her with peace, tranquility, and many beautiful memories, especially of her baby boy, Delbert.

Anabay stood still, reflecting on her life. She had considered changing her name many times throughout her young life before coming to the realization that a name does not make a person. It's what's in the heart. At five feet, five inches tall, most folks back home where she grew up would describe her as light or fair-skinned with good hair. Some even describe her as a cross between Jasmine Guy and Halle Berry, but she didn't know about all of that.

Her heart felt heavy, filled with sadness. At this moment, she had no idea which direction her life would take. Tears streamed down her face watching the twenty-foot, white-box moving truck she hired, backing up in her driveway.

Seeing that vehicle finalized things for Anabay, causing her to sink deeper and deeper into her depression. It wasn't that long ago when she had felt truly blessed because of all the positive things that had unfolded for her. 'Yes,' she thought, 'I am finally living my life according to my plan. I'm so glad I had enough sense not to buy into all that old crap Mama used to preach.'

Ever since she could remember, her mother had been drilling into her head that she was not going to live a happy life because she was cursed, by virtue of being born into the Bailey bloodline. Her mother used to always say, "Anabay, your life will never be normal. Life for you will be filled with pain and hardship. Listen to me, Girl, there is no way around it--you are cursed. Some people are cursed and some are not."

She just figured her mother didn't know what she was talking about. There was no way she was ever going to believe in a damn curse, especially a family curse. As far as she was concerned, the curse on the Bailey women was a myth, a fairytale made up by ancestors strictly for entertainment before there were televisions.

Personally, she felt her mother and all the other Bailey women before her had used the curse as an excuse for the poor decisions they made in their own lives. There was no way she was going to live her life around that shit. She vowed to herself early in life that she would never allow herself to be ruled by the fear of a curse. Her life was going to be filled with love and all things good, she convinced herself.

Anabay had wanted nothing more than a long and happy union with the love of her life, Claudale Jones, her childhood sweetheart. She knew from the moment she laid eyes on him that he was the man God created just for her—to be her one and only true love. The love she felt for him was etched deeply in her heart and soul. She idolized him. They both had been happy about where their lives were taking them. Then there was Delbert, their son, the apple of his mother's eye. She truly adored her baby boy.

Now, she was confused, bitter and angry as she clung to what she knew her life to be. "Why? Why? Why?" she asked herself repeatedly. She certainly was not an evil person who sowed bad seeds and did people wrong. Why then was she reaping such a terrible harvest? She found herself entertaining the possibility that her mother might have been right all along. She asked herself over and over again, "What caused things to go wrong for me? Was Mama right? Has the curse come home to roost?"

The truck came to a complete stop. One by one, three men exited the truck, but all on the passenger side, including the driver. Apparently, the driver's door was broken. The driver immediately started trudging up her walkway, leaving the other two burly men leaning on the fenders of the truck. 'They can't even fix their truck door...what kind of business are they running? Black folks are always half-stepping,' Anabay thought to herself.

Suddenly, she began feeling nauseated and lightheaded, as if experiencing a panic attack. Her legs wobbled and buckled. She quickly plopped herself down onto the bay window cushion seat to keep from falling. "Lord, have mercy on me," she prayed. "You have nothing left. You have nothing left," was the mantra chanting over and over in her head like a scratched album on a turntable. Things rapidly got worse as she tried to steady herself on the window cushion. Her life began flashing in front of her eyes, like they say it does when one is dying. The sound of her mother's voice returned: "Anabay, I warned you. You should have listened to me."

Anabay had forgotten what it felt like to smile, to laugh, to be happy. Today was no different from yesterday, and yesterday was no different from the day before and the day before that. This was her reality. The thought of taking her own life was not too far removed from her consciousness. But, deep inside, she knew ending her own life would be a sin and she didn't want to burn forever in hell for it. Her depression was so bad at times, she felt hell couldn't possibly be any worse than what she was going through on earth. She just didn't have the courage to find out.

Hearing the melody of her doorbell brought back bittersweet memories of Delbert, who loved playing with the doorbell when they first moved in. She flashed back for a moment to how cute he always looked running around the house. It was just one of many wonderful memories.

Feeling emotionally drained and remorseful, she struggled to the door. Every limb ached, like her body was plagued with an acute case of rheumatoid arthritis. This was going to be her last time answering the door at this house, a place she once called "Home Sweet Home."

Anabay choked back tears. It took all the strength she had to just open the door. She wished the past few years were only a nightmare she could wake up from, surrounded by all the people she loved. But reality was reality. What she wanted wasn't going to happen, and there was nothing she could do to turn back the hands of time.

"I'm Big Willie Brown. I'm Big Willie Brown. I'm the best mover in the whole damn town!" There stood a fat dark-skinned man snapping his fingers, gyrating his hips and shuffling his feet to the lyrics of his silly made-up rap. "What's up, Mama? I'm Willie Brown, your mover, owner and operator of Brown's Moving and Storage Company, and in case you haven't noticed, I am a black man who is on time." He emphasized the word IS. Willie had a big grin on his face.

Seeing him standing there acting like a jerk made Anabay smile for a hot minute, although she really felt like slamming the door in his face. She was not in the mood for silly shenanigans.

"You don't have to tell me, I already know. I am quite handsome," he said with a high-pitched chuckle.

Willie looked to be in his mid-forties. He reeked of a cheap, musky cologne, and the smell was so over-powering, it caused Anabay's stomach to churn and her nose to burn. She immediately stepped back from the door to catch her breath. She could not believe what she was hearing, seeing, or smelling. And, to top it all off, this man had the nerve to be calling her Mama.

'Perhaps I heard wrong,' she thought, but she knew her eyes and ears had not deceived her, and her nose was definitely on fire.

Willie was fat but he had a lot of rhythm and was light on his feet. Anabay didn't ask for it, but her imagination painted her a picture that made her cringe, Willie's big ass naked. Just that visual alone made her cringe. As she continued inspecting him, she noticed his shirt collar was drenched from his Jheri curl. His stomach was big and round like a beach ball or a nine-month pregnant woman. Without a doubt, he would have no problem getting a job as a black Santa Claus.

His little dance routine had apparently exhausted him. He was sweating and panting hard. Anabay's mind quickly forgot about black Santa Claus. Instead, she was having a vision of an overweight man on the verge of having an orgasm. Loud as hell, moaning, groaning and not a lot of action. She had read about men like him in a novel when life was good. They love for their women to stroke their egos after sex by telling them how good they were and providing them with play-by-play descriptions of their lovemaking. She wondered, 'What kind of woman would be romantically involved with Willie?' As every woman knows, a man always manages to find himself a woman, no matter what he looks like or has going on for himself. Very often, he will have more than one. It is the woman, on the other hand, who always has difficulty finding a decent man. As far as she was concerned, even if Willie was the last man on earth and even if his dick was made of gold, she would have to pass.

"Mama, is you okay? You seem to be in another world. You going to invite me in or what?" Willie asked, snickering.

Again, he was calling her Mama. Without realizing it, Anabay turned up her nose and frowned at him in disgust. She wasn't his mother and she resented him for addressing her in this manner. It wasn't professional of him, not in the least. His weight and his shortness of breath also concerned her. He looked like he might keel over and die if he picked up one of her heavy boxes. The way her life had been going, Lord knows, she couldn't afford to have his blood on her hands. 'Damn, the curse never ends,' she thought. But, despite all his obvious nonsense, he was standing there at her door ready to work. She had no choice but to let him in.

Brown's Moving and Storage was the cheapest of all the companies she had contacted. As the saying goes, you get what you pay for. She hired him, now she would have to deal with him.

"Oh, I'm sorry. Of course, please come in." Anabay hesitantly stepped aside as he strolled in past her. She couldn't help wondering if she had done the right thing hiring his company. Willie obviously had no class but truthfully, as cheap as he came, paying him was a strain on her pocketbook.

"Thank you, Mama. Excuse me for staring, but I was expecting somebody white. You sounded white on the phone. But you're not white--half-white maybe. So, what are you?"

Anabay hated it when people made comments about a black person sounding white, but she decided to let it go and not respond to Willie and his foolish talk. He stood there gazing at her with sweat pouring down his face and his tongue hanging out of his mouth. Then he licked his lips. Her first thought was, 'Maybe he has a nervous twitch and can't help himself.' She pretended not to notice him staring at her. He reminded her of a hungry country dog about to devour a chicken bone. She felt uneasy, but what could she do? He was already inside and she needed to move.

"I'm Anabay. We spoke on the telephone." She quickly turned away from him and walked into the living room and stood in front of the bay window, her favorite spot in the house. She looked out towards the yard to keep from staring at Willie and noticed the two other men were leaning on the truck, talking and laughing. She guessed they were waiting for him to come back and give them instructions.

Crazy thoughts started flooding into her head like maybe Willie had something else on his mind other than moving her belongings. She positioned herself so she could bang on the window and get the attention of his workers if he tried anything funny. But who was to say, just maybe they were a part of his plan. Realizing it was probably the curse making her have these negative thoughts, Anabay immediately dismissed them and decided to give Willie the benefit of the doubt.

"Let me show you what I need you . . ."

"What a view!" he blurted out, interrupting Anabay and positioning his body right beside hers in the window. "I never knew black folks lived up here in the Cliffs. I thought they just worked up here. Oh man, what you say! My wife would kill to live in a crib like this! If I gave my wife a place like this, she would give up the poontang all the time! I would never have to worry about getting laid! Damn!" he said, grabbing his crotch, snickering and looking out the corner of his eyes for her reaction.

'Oh, my God! Not only is he a Negro without class, he is nasty and raunchy,' Anabay thought, rolling her eyes. 'Maybe he thinks I am some sort of cheap whore.' She was at a loss for words, absolutely speechless. Trying not to be too obvious, she took a few steps away from him, putting distance between them.

"Excuse me for staring at you, but you look familiar. Where do I know you from?" Willie asked, scratching his head, like he was trying to jog his memory.

"This is our first time meeting. We only spoke over the telephone."

"I didn't say we met, I said I seen you before. I'm pretty good at remembering faces, especially pretty faces like yours," he said, pausing, waiting for her response.

She didn't bite.

"I just can't put my finger on it right now, but it'll come to me."

Anabay was uncomfortable. Willie continued staring at her, checking her out from head to foot, like she might be that chicken leg he couldn't wait to sink his teeth into. "God, forgive me for my evil thoughts," she silently prayed. 'Greasy food is the only food this man is used to eating. I'll bet he can tear up some fried chicken or a fried pork chop, or any other greasy food he can get his hands on.'

"I got it! I got it!" he excitedly hollered out. "You that black soap opera mama on One Life to Live or is it All My Chillins? My wife watches you every day!" He giggled.

Willie was getting on her nerves. Anabay wished he would just shut the hell up and do the job he was hired to do. Her patience was wearing thin. "No, I have never been on television," she snapped, turning away and walking in the direction of her dining room. All she could think was, 'What a fool!'

"If you say so. I can tell by the way you answered me, all short and everything, you just don't want me to know who you are, cause you think I'll charge you more money or ask you for your autograph, or a picture, or something."

"Look, I can assure you I have never been on television," Anabay damn-near shouted. "These are the boxes." She pointed to the neatly stacked boxes against the wall labeled Bedroom, Kitchen, Coats, Delbert's toys, and all the rest.

Willie knew he was getting underneath her skin, but he didn't care. He was enjoying himself. "I'm ain't usually wrong," he said, completely ignoring the boxes she had pointed out to him.

"Well, you're wrong this time. I don't know if you heard me, but these are the boxes."

"These are the boxes," he repeated, mimicking her. "What a crib! And you say this is all yours. You did alright for your little ol' self." He was bobbing his head up and down in an approving manner with his lips puckered out.

"Yes, this is my house," Anabay replied in an appeasing tone, hoping he would get the message and begin working.

"And you say you're not a celebrity? You blowing my mind right outta the water!"

"No, I am not!" Anabay snapped, feeling enraged.

"Well, look a here, you got a temper on you, Mama! You don't even know me and listen how you're talking to me. If I was white you wouldn't be talking to me like this, would you? You'd be saying, 'Yes, Mr. Brown. No, Mr. Brown.' Damn shame, the lack of respect a brother got to take these days."

"Maybe if you were white, you wouldn't be asking all these dumb questions."

"Tain't no such thing as a dumb question," Willie snapped back in a raised voice.

Anabay knew she had insulted him.

"Alright, alright!" he said in a gruff voice. "Let's get this job done. We moving your things to Osborne Terrace in Newark. Is that right?"

'What a relief. He's finally ready to work,' Anabay thought to herself, but it was short lived.

"Don't make a damn bit of sense, Mama. You sure you want to give up all this and move to Newark? Ain't no crib in Newark topping this crib. You supposed to move up, not down."

"Stop calling me Mama! My name is Anabay!" She could no longer control the anger and frustration she was feeling inside. Anabay turned to face Willie and looked him dead in his eyes, "Yes, you are absolutely right. There aren't any nice houses in Newark like this one. But it is what it is, so please, just do your job and move my things. You are just too much!"

"Oh, something wrong up in here! You on the verge of tears. I smell a big fat-ass rat. Too late to be crying now, Mama. Let me guess, you one of those high yellow chicks who sold themselves out to a white man. Lord, Lord, Lord, I can spot an old washed out sister every time. I swear I can." Willie was shaking his head from side to side in disbelief. "I'm right, ain't I?"

"What are you talking about?" Anabay could barely speak. She was on the verge of sobbing.

"Come on, you know what I'm talking about. Can't no brother afford to put your ass up in a crib like this, not in this lifetime! No way in hell! I ain't no fool! You either married or you shacked up with a white dude. Who is he? I betcha he's one of those Wall Street caviar-eating fuckers. Excuse my French, but it burns me the hell up!"

"I've had enough! I am sick and tired of your stupid-ass remarks. You're nothing but a motormouth talking just to hear yourself talk. Like an idiot. You don't know diddly squat about me, yet you have the nerve to be standing here making stupid comments. Either do the job I hired you to do or get the hell out of my house!"

"You got a lot of nerve calling me an idiot! I got a news flash for you, Sista, I ain't the one moving away from here. You are! If I had the opportunity to live in a crib like this, I damn sure wouldn't be moving back to the g-h-e-t-t-o." Willie folded his arms across his chest. "And for your information, I could care less what people thinks about me. I speaks my mind and I asks what I wants to."

Anabay was reaching her breaking point with Willie. Ever since he arrived, he had done nothing but add more misery to her life, making her last moments in her home even more unpleasant than they had to be. She was now an emotional wreck, cursing and acting completely out of character. Not meaning to, she blurted out, "I'm not giving in to this foolishness. It's nothing but the Bailey Curse. Damn curse never sleeps. It's never dormant!"

"What you say? You crazy? You a witch or something? Talking about curses and shit," Willie shouted out, walking backwards, holding his hands up in the air. "I surrender. Time to get you moved! Forget everything I said! Sheee it, you crazy as hell!"

Anabay calmed herself down and lowered her voice. "Mr. Brown, I would really appreciate it if you would move my things." She silently prayed that she had not chased him away. To her surprise, he was not frightened, he was still running his big mouth.

"This is the problem with you people. When you get a little money in your pocket, you forgets who you are and where you come from."

"That's not true," she replied, still maintaining her composure.

"Show me around so I can figure out what my men need to load first. You see, Mama, it takes a real professional to load it right and save space, so everything fits on the truck. One job, one trip."

"I'm only moving those boxes stacked against the wall. I have been trying to show them to you ever since you arrived."

"That's it?" Willie asked, with a surprised look on his face. "You won't kidding when you said you didn't have much to move. I can't believe that's it. What about all this expensive furniture I see, like this cherry wood dining room table and chairs.

She ignored him again, "Only the boxes are being moved."

"Ouch! Ouch! I can see from the look on your face, I done hit a nerve. I didn't need my truck or my men," he giggled. "I could have carried these few boxes on my back." He kept chuckling as he moved in closer and nudged her on the arm with his elbow.

Anabay was furious, but she held it in. 'I can't believe this idiot has the nerve to be touching me like I'm somebody he knows. I hired him, he didn't hire me. The no-class, fat, ignorant fucker!'

"Excuse me, now I know something's wrong. What happened to you, Mama? Let me guess, your white husband is divorcing your ass and putting you out. Or maybe, you was just his mistress. Come on, tell Big Daddy what happened to you. I need some information," he said, unbuckling his belt and pulling up his pants and then retightening his belt, showing off dingy, white cotton socks.

"You are getting on my last nerve! Just do the job I hired you to do! Okay?"

"I get mad as hell every time I hear about something like this happening to a sista. One thing about them white dudes, once they're finished with your ass, they'll put you out in a hot minute. I seen it happen plenty of times. They just throw you out like dirty dishwater," he shouted. "Serves y'all asses right, though, for selling out your own race. It's a damn shame, downright sickening. I got three daughters. I tell them all the time, don't get involved with no white dude. Don't do it, Don't do it. Don't do it!"

Willie's rambling was making Anabay's head spin. He had no right coming into her home and speaking to her the way he did. But there was no manager to complain to, about him. He was his own boss.

"Somebody gonna be at the place in Newark when we arrive with your things?"

"Yes, Mr. Otis Jones will be there."

"Damn, that name sounds familiar! Is he your new beau?"

"O Jesus, help me!" Anabay gasped, rolling her eyes.

"Lord can't help you now." Willie let out a sarcastic laugh. "I'm going to have my men start loading your boxes up." He opened the front door and yelled out, "Hey, T-Bone, you and Tank come on in here and start loading this stuff. C'mon. Get a move on!"

After forty minutes or so, he returned to the living room where Anabay was sitting and staring out the window. "Okay, Anabay," he winked, "We got everything loaded. It's been my pleasure and I want to apologize for being a little hard on you. I'm truly sorry for your troubles. Put you trust in the Lord."

The way he said 'put you trust in the Lord' reminded Anabay of a preacher speaking to his congregation. She was actually taken aback because he sounded really sincere. 'Perhaps he does care for me,' she thought.

"Don't worry about tipping. I don't think you can afford it," he said, laughing like a hyena. "C'mon on, fellas, let's move out. One charity case for today is enough. We'll be blessed cause ain't no tip coming our way from this cheap-ass job. I'll be damn lucky if this check don't bounce. I can feel it trying to jump out my pocket already." Willie continued laughing as he patted one of his men on the back.

Anabay was standing in her doorway watching them climb back into their truck when she overheard Willie talking. "You see that woman there? She was used to eating high on the hog. I'll bet you she didn't even recognize her own folks. Now her ride's over and she got the nerve to be moving her black, stank ass back to Newark. Now that's some funny shit." They all were laughing and slapping five to each other.

Anabay just shook her head in disbelief. As if being confused about the curse and her future wasn't devastating enough, now a black man who had no idea about her life had the nerve to be judging her. It wouldn't have been so bad if he was right, but he wasn't. Was her mama right? Had the curse come home to roost, seeking revenge?

Anabay knew it was not possible to believe in a loving God and a curse at the same time. She decided to put one hundred percent of her faith and trust in God. Only he would have the final say about her life. She took one final stroll around the house, wiped her tears away, took a deep breath, locked the door and drove away.

Zenora Knight

Chapter 2

The Legend of the Bailey Curse

Bet (short for Betty), Anabay's mother, had made it a daily ritual to talk to her about the Curse of the Bailey women. Unlike most mothers, Bet never explained the birds and the bees, never talked about men, women and babies, but she made it her mission in life to school her daughter about the big C, The Curse.

Not nearly a day went by that she didn't find a way to make a connection between the simplest of life's events, especially unexplained or unfortunate incidences, to the big C. To Bet, the curse upon the Bailey women was equally important if not more important than the Book of Proverbs. She truly believed what her mother told her, and her mother had only repeated the story that had been handed down throughout generations of Bailey women.

Bet felt it was her duty to educate her daughter about the big C. Anabay hated with a passion listening to those stories over and over again, but out of respect, she just grinned and bore it.

Bet revealed that she too had been a non-believer in the curse until the day she experienced its wrath firsthand.

She said she knew for a fact the Bailey women were cursed, and as Anabay's mother, it was her job to protect her. The big C had a way of turning non-believers into believers and any Bailey woman who did not initially believe in the curse eventually ended up accepting its reality.

The big C was generational, Bet explained and if Anabay listened to her, there was a slim possibility she could avoid it. There were no guarantees, however. She desperately wanted to spare her daughter from the pain and suffering the curse would surely bring, so she purposefully drilled into Anabay's head that she needed to take what she was saying seriously. Bet also felt she had already paid the price for her daughter in terms of the vengeance of the curse.

The secret to avoiding the curse, according to Bet, was to never marry, to live a pure life like a nun and to never have children. If Anabay chose not to follow her advice, she warned, then there was no way she or any other woman born of the Bailey bloodline could ever avoid the curse.

Bet always prefaced her storytelling by saying, "Anabay, I'm only going to tell you what you need to know. There's no need in filling your head with everything that's ever happened to the women in our family." Her next favorite line was, "Things happened that wouldn't have happened if it wasn't for the you-know-what."

She insisted Anabay understand the origin of the Curse of the Bailey Women, which she said started with

Cousin Beulah Ann Bailey, an ancestor who lived well over a century ago. Although no one in the family has ever been able to trace Cousin Beulah Ann Bailey's branch on the family tree, Bet said she definitely existed. Anabay often wanted to challenge her mother about Cousin Beulah Ann's existence, but she knew better--else she would have received a backhanded smack to her mouth.

Cousin Beulah Ann was the daughter of Cousin Jimmy Lee Bailey and Cousin Maybud Crawley Bailey, mountain folks who migrated from the Shenandoah Valley region of Virginia to Fort Mitchell, Virginia, the town where they lived. Fort Mitchell is approximately ninety miles west of Richmond, the state capital.

Cousins Jimmy Lee and Maybud lived and worked as sharecroppers on a farm known as the "Old Place" because it had once been a large slave plantation. The owner was a white farmer known as Tobacco Man. This farm was well over a thousand acres and produced some of the state's finest flue-cured tobacco.

Within two years of moving there, Beulah Ann was born, an amazingly beautiful child, with a fair-skinned complexion, freckles and red hair. Jimmy Lee knew deep down within his heart there was no way in heaven or hell this precious little girl could be his biological child. Both he and Maybud were very dark-skinned people who looked to be overly blessed with a triple dose of pigmentation. He knew the daddy of this baby was none other than Tobacco Man.

Jimmy Lee never confronted Tobacco Man and he never uttered one word to Maybud about the obvious. He didn't blame her because he knew she had no choice and was not a willing participant in the creation of this child. Although everyone gossiped about Beulah Ann being Tobacco Man's daughter, secretly they admired Jimmy Lee for his strength in controlling himself and for not seeking revenge against Tobacco Man. Usually a violation such as this, to a man's wife, was an act well worth dying for.

Back in those days, if you were white, you were always right. If you were colored, you were expected to shut your eyes and saddle your tongue, that is if you wanted to keep on living. That is what Jimmy Lee did. Despite knowing he was not her biological father, Jimmy Lee truly loved and adored Beulah Ann. He practically worshipped the ground she walked on. In Jimmy Lee's eyes, his little girl could do no wrong. He treated her like she was a Goddess of Beauty. As Beulah Ann developed into a teenager, her beauty was something to behold. She was small framed, had a high yellow complexion, prominent cheek bones, thin lips, and a keen nose. Her thick, wavy red hair hung well below her waistline and her hazel-colored eyes changed hues with her moods.

Beulah Ann was aware she didn't look anything like her parents, but she never questioned them and she never suspected Jimmy Lee was not her daddy. She favored him over Maybud because he always made her feel special. She was so close to him, folks said it was a shame she wasn't a boy.

Beulah Ann was a bit of a devil and enjoyed causing friction between her parents. She knew her father would never punish her or allow her mother to severely punish her. Thus, she grew up to be cunning and manipulative, especially towards the opposite sex. When Beulah Ann got mad with her mother, she would often cut-up Maybud's panties and other under-garments.

Jimmy Lee, Maybud and Beulah Ann lived where the other sharecroppers lived--in one of the ten, four-room wood-frame cottages on Tobacco Man's farm. Early one summer morning, when the ground was still covered with morning dew and the sun was rising, Jimmy Lee met his maker in a horrific accident. He was trampled to death by Nelly, an old mule spooked while plowing the tobacco field. Any strange sound would send Nelly into an uncontrollable tizzy. The other sharecroppers and farmhands said it happened so fast, there was nothing they could do to help save Jimmy Lee. They also did not recall hearing any unusual sounds or noises that would have set the mule off. Somehow, Jimmy Lee got caught in between the plow and Nelly's hind legs. The scene was described as one of the bloodiest and most gruesome sights anyone had ever seen. Jimmy Lee's veins erupted like a volcano spurting blood from his body like a rushing river of hot lava down the tobacco field row, as his twisted and mangled body lay motionless underneath the plow.

At the exact moment Jimmy Lee died, Maybud, who was standing in her kitchen shelling black-eyed peas picked from her early summer garden, felt a sharp pain in her stomach as if she had been kicked. She dropped her bowl of peas on the floor and cried out, "Oh, dear God," and ran out towards the tobacco fields, calling out Jimmy Lee's name at the top of her lungs. She could see the other farmhands gathered around in a circle as she desperately tried to reach her husband, but she was held back by the other women who had raced out of their cottages upon hearing all the commotion.

Beulah Ann, who had been asleep, was awakened by all the noise, ran to the front porch in her nightgown and looked on.

On the morning of Jimmy Lee's death, just minutes earlier, he and Maybud had arisen as usual upon hearing the rooster crow at the first sign of dawn. As always, they peeped in on Beulah Ann to make sure she was all right. They went about their morning routines, then sat down to a hearty breakfast of scrambled eggs, fried country ham, fried apples, biscuits and red-eyed gravy made from the stock of the ham grease. Jimmy Lee loved to sop his biscuits in the red-eyed gravy and slurp his hot coffee from a spoon. Every once in a while, he would add some homemade molasses or wild honey. Jimmy Lee loved his breakfast. It was good eating and his private time to spend and talk with his wife before going about his daily work.

On that dreadful morning, both Jimmy Lee and Maybud were unusually quiet, only exchanging a few words, unlike their normal conversations. Maybud asked him if he had heard an owl calling out at midnight, and he told her no. Jimmy Lee had indeed heard the owl, he just didn't want to worry his wife. It was common knowledge that the hoot of an owl at the stroke of midnight meant the angel of death would surely bring death to one's door or to the door of a loved one. They both just went on about their day. Whatever life brought, they would deal with at that time.

Three days later, Beulah Ann saw her father lying in a pine coffin. He was dressed in his Sunday's best, with a small pocket-sized Bible resting on his chest. She was very angry with God for taking her daddy from her and she didn't understand why he had to die. She felt God was somehow punishing her because he knew how much she loved her daddy. In her heavy sorrow, Beulah Ann made a vow to never love another man again in life.

After Jimmy Lee's burial, an eerie sound could be heard coming from the tobacco field where he was killed. This sound grew louder and louder until the sound reached the woodshed, where the wooden planks used to carry his mangled body were being stored. Folks called the eerie sound the death cry. It could be heard from dawn to dusk. The wood planks were eventually burned. This was the only way to stop the sound.

Right after Jimmy Lee's burial, Tobacco Man presented Maybud and Beulah Ann with a piece of paper giving them lifetime rights to live on the farm as the widow and child of a deceased sharecropper. He made up some rule on the spot, which he referred to as "The Golden Rule," that widows and children automatically receive lifetime rights to remain living on the farm and out of respect, the other sharecroppers had to care and provide for them.

None of the other farmers or sharecroppers had ever heard of such a rule and there had been plenty of sharecropper deaths before Jimmy Lee. Their relatives had been forced to move on. Everyone saw through Tobacco Man, he just wanted to keep Beulah Ann close to him. After all, he was her father.

Maybud never got over her husband's death. She also did not take the proper time to mourn because she was so worried about her and Beulah Ann's future. As a result, she was no longer capable of functioning in the world she once knew. Bet told Anabay, back in those days there was no help for colored folks who had nervous breakdowns. They simply did the best they could and folks just called them as crazy.

Two years to the exact date of Jimmy Lee's death, the angel of death struck again, this time claiming the life of Tobacco Man. He supposedly died of natural causes, but many believed Jimmy Lee's spirit snatched Tobacco Man on his anniversary death date for sleeping with his wife. Tobacco Man never admitted Beulah Ann was his daughter; however, on the eve of his death, he summoned her.

The women working in the house overheard him telling Beulah Ann what a special little colored gal she was and that there was something about her he had always liked. He wasn't very specific. Then he told her that he was going to do something out of the ordinary for her, because she was such a smart gal. Beulah Ann did not question him.

In Tobacco Man's will, he left Beulah Ann a sizable nest egg. It was his way of wiping the slate clean before his Judgment Day in the event there was a Heaven or Hell. Miss Martha, Tobacco Man's wife, had always been a quiet and mild-mannered woman who never bothered with her husband's business affairs--that is, until the day his will was read. Miss Martha was so mad she spat bullets upon learning her husband had left money to Beulah Ann, making her one of the richest Negros in the State of Virginia. Rumor had it, Beulah Ann was also richer than most of the white folks in the area. Although Miss Martha did not have any children, she deeply resented having to share her wealth.

Miss Martha knew all along her husband was Beulah Ann's father. She never made a fuss about it because she never suspected he would acknowledge or provide for her--she was a half-breed bastard child, after all. She knew her husband had a fondness for sleeping with colored women. He just loved his chocolate and had to have it. She had always looked the other way.

Miss Martha tried to contest the will, but it was airtight; there was nothing she could do. Her husband's wealth had to be shared. She tried to put Beulah Ann and Maybud off the property, but Beulah Ann was not one who could be run over, even at the tender age of nineteen. Color did not matter to her. Beulah Ann demanded respect from everybody and stood up to Miss Martha. She had no fear of getting lynched or being run out of town.

When she turned twenty-one years old, Beulah Ann purchased a piece of property on the colored side of town and opened the Bailey Café so folks would have someplace to go. Maybud did not like the idea of a café, but deep down she was proud of her daughter. Beulah Ann didn't like being responsible for her mother, but she knew it would have been her daddy's wishes.

The Bailey Cafe was a success from the moment it opened and Beulah Ann became known as a smart and shrewd businesswoman. In fact, she was the only businesswoman in the area. The Bailey Café was open four days a week---Thursdays, Fridays, Saturdays, and Sunday evenings. The menu consisted of fried chicken, smoked barbequed ribs, fish and pork chop dinners with side orders such as rice, collard greens, and mashed potatoes or potato salad. Desserts were normally cobblers and cakes. Although the food was good, folks cared most about the illegal moonshine.

The Bailey Café had a solid red door and was referred to as the Red Door. The house rocked with live music resonating with rhythm and blues sounds and sometimes country and western for the handful of white customers. The aroma of the food and the sound of the squeaky oil-polished pinewood floor planks meant only one thing -- there was a party going on in the house. Beulah Ann was proud the Bailey Cafe was the only place in town where folks didn't see color. The coloreds and whites mingled together.

A few months after the café opened and proved to be successful, Beulah Ann expanded to include an illegal gambling hall that had a separate entrance with a green door. The green door stood for money. Most folks who entered through the green door lost their weekly paychecks to the house. Thus, the Bailey Café became known as the Red Door and the Green Door. Although Beulah Ann was engaging in illegal activities, the Sheriff never bothered her because he knew she was Tobacco Man's daughter.

Beulah Ann was known for running with both the white and the colored folks. It did not matter to her, it was in her blood. She was only interested in pleasing herself and she knew she could have had any man she desired. She didn't care even if the man was married.

If vain was a blood type, it certainly ran through her veins. She was often heard bragging about four things: her beauty, her money, not having the burden of cleaning and cooking for a husband, and not having to care for little snotty-nosed children. She was a great dancer and loved to cut a rug. If one listened to her, she was the greatest dancer south of the Mason Dixon Line.

Her favorite expression was, "I can out dance a bullet blindfolded."

One night after drinking too much of the house illegal moonshine, Beulah Ann let her guard down. She began dancing with Jefferson Styles, the town's wannabe pimp daddy on Friday and Saturday nights and man of the cloth on Sundays. She was feeling so good that she was oblivious to everyone enjoying the side show of her and Jefferson. They were doing what town folks called nasty dancing right there in the middle of the café. Their bodies were intertwined like two snakes mating. They were face to face, toe to toe, and Beulah Ann was nibbling on Jefferson's ear while her hands were rubbing all over his backside. Jefferson was bumping and grinding against her, and his hands were freely roaming and exploring her body. They were both panting and breathing so hard it sounded like two hound dogs in heat. Jefferson became so hot, he let out a mating call that could be heard over the sound of the music all the way down the road.

It was real crowded that night and everybody at the café was so consumed with the show going on, no one noticed when the elf-sized, dark-skinned, nappy-headed woman entered and stood across the dance floor holding an old, rusty, sawed-off shotgun. She was standing there looking directly at her husband practically making love to a woman she despised. The next sound folks heard was the cocking of the shotgun, causing everyone to take their attention off Jefferson and Beulah Ann. Folks could not believe what they were witnessing. The little elf of a woman stood there, like a raging bull looking at a matador waving a red cape.

Folks scattered like roaches and sought cover wherever they could find it--under the wooden round tables or behind the bar. A lot of folks ran out the door.

There stood Cornelia Styles, Jefferson's wife, pointing the old raggedy shotgun directly at Jefferson and Beulah Ann. Everyone knew Cornelia came from a family with a reputation that would make one cringe. They didn't take no shit and were an-eye-for-an-eye kind of folks that no one dared cross, that is, if they valued their life. Cornelia's father was nicknamed Black Jake. He was a big, black-skinned man with red eyes who was proud of his blackness. He was able to trace his lineage directly to Africa. His father was a pure blooded African man from a mean, notorious tribe out of the Congo. These Africans were very militant and difficult to enslave. Jake used to laugh and brag that, although his daddy lived and worked on a plantation, his daddy was never a slave.

Everyone suspected Jake had killed a white mailman after warning him countless times to stop knocking down his mailbox every time he delivered the mail. If he didn't stop, Jake warned, he would take him out of his alcoholic misery. One day, the mailman never completed his route, he just vanished without a trace. No one dared to question Jake about the man's disappearance, not even the sheriff. The local folks believed Jake killed and chopped up the mailman to make slop for his hogs. That year, Jake didn't sell one smoked cured ham to any of the local folks. He only sold his hams to people passing through from out of town and saw his sign, "Smoked Cured Hams for Sale, Secret Recipe."

Fruit don't fall far from the tree, which is why everyone ran for cover when they saw Cornelia. When Jefferson looked up and saw his wife, his face changed from an expression of ecstasy to having one's life flash right before their eyes, like a dead man walking. Everyone knew the party was over.

Jefferson threw Beulah Ann to the floor like she was a hot potato. Cornelia looked directly into Jefferson's eyes while still holding the shotgun and said in her husky Southern drawl, "You ain't nothing but a whoremonger messing around with that tramp." She looked at Beulah Ann and spat out a big chunk of snuff. "Word out is, you can out dance a bullet."

This was the first time Beulah Ann had ever shown fear or cowered to anyone. She sat trembling on the dance floor right where Jefferson had thrown her. She could hardly speak but did manage to say, "Cornelia, please don't. We were just dancing, having a little fun."

"I didn't ask you to speak, you hot-tailed strumpet! I ought to blow your goddamned brains right out of your fucking head," Cornelia shouted, sucking up the snot in her nose.

Sweat beads were popping out of Jefferson's pores. He said shakenly, "Now, Cornelia, Baby, just put the gun down. You knows I loves you, Baby. Me and Miss Beulah Ann just here having a little fun. Just a dance, Baby. Just working off a little steam. That's all, Cornelia." He stuttered, "um, um, work-ing, uh, uh, ing o, off a li-ttle ste-, steam, uh, uh."

Folks never came out from the cover they had secured because Cornelia was still holding on tightly to the shotgun. Cornelia said, "I know you ain't talking to me, making excuses. You call what you doing fun, shaming me and your chillins in public? What kind of man is you anyway, doing the nasty with the town tramp? You both deserve to burn in hell!"

Jefferson continued to beg Cornelia for mercy and to give him a break. "I loves you, Baby, and only you. Let's go home and forget about tonight," he pleaded.

But Cornelia said, "Oh, hell no! I ain't to be played with. I'm going to teach you and Missy here a lesson!"

Folks continued looking on, knowing there was nothing they could do to help Beulah Ann and Jefferson. No one was a match for Cornelia and her shotgun. The room was so quiet -- the only sounds that could be heard were Beulah Ann's and Jefferson's fast breathing and heartbeats.

Cornelia then let out this blood curdling, merciless, "He-he-he, he-he-he, he-he-he," laughter, and pointed her shotgun at her targets. She sat down on a chair and shouted to John Henry, the bartender, to bring her some moon-shine. John Henry was so nervous, he brought her the whole jug, slammed it on the table and scurried back to his cover.

Upon taking a swig of the moonshine and wiping her mouth with her shirtsleeve, Cornelia turned her full attention to Beulah Ann. "You ready to out dance that bullet, Bitch?"

Beulah Ann sat there trembling, whimpering, and shaking her head no.

"I ain't heard you, Bitch," shouted Cornelia. "Cat got your tongue?"

"I said no!" cried Beulah Ann. "Cornelia, please forgive me. This will never happen again. It was a mistake."

"A mistake? A mistake? You know what, Bitch? Your yellow, nasty ass is going to die tonight. Come here, Bitch. C'mon. C'mon." She gestured with her index finger for Beulah Ann to come to her.

Beulah Ann was paralyzed with fear. She sobbed loudly and uncontrollably. Cornelia got up out of her chair with shotgun in tow and grabbed her up by her hair, lifted up her face, and rubbed the old shotgun over her throat. Then Cornelia took the moonshine and poured it on the floor, encircling Beulah Ann in the liquid.

"He-he-he, he-he-he, he-he-he." Cornelia reached in her apron pocket and pulled out an old, greasy, brown paper bag containing a Ball Caning jar that was filled to the rim with a dark, thick, muddy liquid concoction.

With one look at the jar, folks knew it was something evil that was meant to change Beulah Ann's and Jefferson's lives forever. Everyone knew Cornelia's family practiced black magic, but no one ever dreamt Cornelia would go so far as to using it on an infraction such as this. Black magic was serious business and everyone who knew Jefferson, knew he was just being a man. He loved to act like Cat Daddy from time to time, but he always took care of his home and family. Beulah Ann was not the type of woman to be serious with any man. To her, men were just a game.

Cornelia yanked Beulah Ann's head up by her hair and pried her mouth open and said, "Miss Beulah Ann—Oh, forgive me, I meant to say The Miss Beautiful Beulah Ann Bailey, the fairest of them all. The woman all women envy, the woman all the men want, adore, and lust after. Well guess what, Bitch? A Bailey woman will never feel the touch of a good man from this day forward. I curse the blood that runs deep in your veins from this moment until the end of time. I curse you and all the female children born of the Bailey bloodline. Any man that comes unto a Bailey woman will possess evil demons and he will be her downfall, bringing devastation and destruction, poverty, tears of pain, suffering and even death to her or her loved ones."

Then Cornelia opened the jar and poured the nasty concoction consisting of chicken blood, goat urine, chopped up wild boar's penis, and wild herbs all over Beulah Ann, causing her to faint. Folks said the place stunk so bad, it smelled worse than a lion's den.

Cornelia picked up her shotgun and fired off three shots up into the ceiling of the cafe. Pow! "One Shot for the Spirit!" She reloaded her shotgun. Pow! "One Shot for the Flesh!" She reloaded again. Pow! "One Shot to Seal the Curse on the Bailey Women to the end of time."

She turned to Jefferson and said, "Mr. Styles, let's go home."

Jefferson adjusted his clothes, wiped his eyes, stepped right over Beulah Ann and followed his wife home, never uttering a word. He never again strayed outside his marriage or even looked at another woman. He never left home unless Cornelia was with him and, sadly, he never preached in the pulpit again.

Cousin Beulah Ann was never seen again after this night. No one ever knew what happened to her or her mother, Maybud. To this day, the Red Door and the Green Door are still standing on the old Bailey place. Bet warned Anabay never to go near the place else she might disappear too.

Chapter 3

Country Girl

Folks who lived in Fort Mitchell, Virginia, were just plain down-home country folks. They weren't overly concerned with material wealth or keeping up with the Joneses. Most were proud and honest people with deep spiritual beliefs. Overall, they kept life simple. The majority of the men were farmers who tilled the land and raised livestock. The younger generation worked at the local factories and some even worked at a saw mill, owned by a black businessman nicknamed Frog, because of his big, loud mouth.

Mondays through Fridays, everyone worked. On Saturdays, folks got dressed up and traveled to neighboring Chase City, a town with a lot more commerce and activities than Fort Mitchell. There they would buy their groceries and shop in department stores. There was also a drug store, an Alcohol Beverage Control (ABC) store, and a theater where colored folks could watch movies in the segregated balcony section. In the evening, after everyone had taken care of their business, they usually hung out at the local strip mall where there was a laundromat and a pool hall. Across the street, there was a Tastee Freeze that served hot dogs, corn dogs, hamburgers, french fries and other fast food-- and of course, Hershey hand-dipped ice cream.

Sundays were kept holy, and the majority attended Sunday School followed by a long, drawn-out sermon at Old Rocky Mount Baptist Church, a wooden-framed church located on Bible Way Road, with a one-hundred-year history.

In Fort Mitchell, there was a convenience store and a United States Post Office. The railroad tracks served two purposes, to transport cargo and to separate the coloreds from the whites. The schools were in the infancy stages of desegregation when Anabay started school, so she and the other children of color had to be bussed 25 miles each way to the elementary school.

Bet and Anabay lived in a small house behind the Old Rocky Mount Baptist Church. As an only child, Anabay learned early on how to entertain herself. Her favorite things to do were making mud cakes and cutting out paper dolls from magazines. She used to pretend these paper dolls were her real family, complete with a daddy, mama and children. Other times, if music was playing on the television or the radio, she would pretend to be Cousin Beulah Ann dancing at the Red Door surrounded by imaginary customers.

Sometimes she would wander off alone and play on the train tracks or with her white friend, Nessa, who would sneak away from her family and play with her. Nessa's mother would often catch her playing with Anabay and she would switch Nessa's legs all the way back home. Nessa would somehow always find a way to sneak away and play. Anabay was always happy on Sundays because there would be other children to play with on the church grounds.

Summer was the season she loved best. In the evening, nature's orchestra played beautiful symphonies consisting of birds chirping, bullfrogs croaking, the tree frog rib-its, and the crickets singing. During the daytime, she played outside, burning down anthills with wooden kitchen matches and catching butterflies, minnows and tadpoles. At night, she chased and caught lightning bugs, putting them in Ball Canning jars. The universe was hers. She loved the earth's fresh smell after a rain shower and running bare feet through wet grass. Rainbows fascinated her, she imagined finding that illusive pot of gold at the end of the arc of colors.

Anabay loved it when her mother took her to segregated Prince Edward Lake to swim in the muddy water that flowed downstream from the white folks' lake, Prince George Lake. Afterwards, they would stuff their bellies with foot-long chili dogs and lemon custard ice cream. There was a playground with swings, a gigantic sliding board, and a dance hall. Bet said the dance hall was for the fast tail boys and girls.

Anabay cherished most of her childhood memories. She realized growing up in the South molded and shaped her into the person she is now. If it were not for three things, now bad memories, her childhood would have been perfect. The first thing was constantly hearing about the family curse, the second was being told the true story about her conception, and the third was anything associated with her step-daddy, Finch. She wished these experiences had never happened and she often asked God why these things had afflicted her.

At an early age, Anabay fantasized about moving away from Fort Mitchell. She had big dreams, an unbounded imagination and she desired life at a faster pace than the ordinary folks she knew. One day when she was twelve years old, she shocked her mama, who was in the middle of her storytelling. Anabay blurted out that she did not believe and never would believe in the Curse of the Bailey Women. After hearing her daughter's declaration, Bet decided it was time to take her storytelling to the next level. She shared her own personal experience with the curse, which involved Anabay's daddy.

Bet told Anabay, although she was her little bastard child, she still adored and loved her as much as any woman who had conceived her baby out of love. She compared Anabay to Cousin Beulah Ann, saying that they both were very beautiful and special, and that they had more in common than she cared to think about. "Maybud and I both had unwanted pregnancies, but we loved y'all just the same," Bet said to Anabay.

According to Bet, these were the circumstances. She was seventeen years old and it was Christmas Eve. It was a harsh day, downright bone-chilling cold, with snow, ice and blistery winds. One couldn't see but a few feet in front of you. She and her three younger sisters were happy because they had gone out the day before and chopped down their Christmas tree and had decorated it with popcorn garlands and pine cones gathered during the fall.

Late that afternoon, Bet's mama, Anabay's Grandma Fannie, put Bet in charge of the house and her sisters because she was leaving to go to Chase City to look for their daddy, who was married to someone else. Bet said her mama was caught up in a love triangle. When Anabay asked who the man was (because she wanted to know who her grandfather was), she was shocked when Bet answered, "Cooch Thomas." Cooch was a.k.a. Frog, that big, old, obnoxious, loud-mouthed man who owned the sawmills.

Bet explained that Frog's wife Lizzy and her mama had once been best friends. Frog had been dating both of them on the sly and ended up getting both of them pregnant at the same time. He had to make a choice, so he choose Lizzy to be his wife. Fannie was devastated because she loved Frog and she believed he loved her equally. Fannie had no doubt in her mind, the family curse was responsible for Frog choosing Lizzy over her, despite it being common knowledge that Lizzy's family had a little money and a lot of land. Her family gave Frog his start in the sawmilling business.

As far as Fannie was concerned, Frog was her husband. She refused to entertain the thought of another man and felt her unconditional love would eventually persuade him to leave his family for her. After seventeen years, she ended up with three babies and was still this man's mistress, depending on him for monetary stipends and small rations of his time.

But this year, according to Bet, her mama was livid. It was Christmas Eve and Frog hadn't been around since Thanksgiving. By now, he usually would have given her some money so she could at least buy her girls a little something for Christmas. He knew Fannie didn't have much money and that she constantly worried about keeping food on the table and clothes on her girls' backs.

Frog had a ritual. He always stopped by on Christmas Eve and presented each girl with a brown paper bag containing a navel orange, a red delicious apple, a candy cane, some hard candy and a few nuts. Sometimes he would throw in a nickel or a quarter. Bet said her daddy really hadn't been doing anything special for them because she knew for a fact, he had been swiping these gift bags from the church. He just added a ribbon to dress the bags up. When Anabay wanted to know what all this had to do with her daddy, Bet told her to hold on, she was getting to that part.

Fannie, who was known to be hot-headed, had been sipping moonshine all day before she finally left home. She was tired of Frog's shit and she intended to find him in town, hopefully with his ugly-ass wife (Fannie's favorite description of Lizzy) and give both of them a piece of her mind. She wanted a lot of people around so she could make a big scene and embarrass them. The nerve of him treating his set of children by her like this!

Each year, Fannie would swear she never wanted to see Frog again in life, but usually within a week into the New Year, she would be back seeing him and acting like nothing ever happened.

Bet recalled one incident that truly hurt and angered her mama to the point of cutting Frog out of her life for good. They had met on the Drakes Branch Road for a little tryst when Lizzy's car drove by. Frog panicked and insisted that Fannie get into his car trunk. In the meantime, Lizzy had turned her car around and had driven back to speak with her husband. They talked for a few minutes and then they drove off together in Lizzy's car, leaving Fannie to bake in the hot car trunk for over an hour. Fannie was so angry and hurt that she slapped the shit out of Frog when he returned and refused to see him for over two months.

Returning to her earlier story, Bet said after her mama left for Chase City, she and her sisters looked out the window for a sign of their daddy. They knew the weather was bad, but they still expected him to show, since he had never missed a Christmas Eve. They saw a figure approaching their house and they became excited, but as the man got closer they realized it was not their daddy but a man named Q, the town drunk. According to Bet, every town has one or two drunks— harmless, childlike critters who are addicted to alcohol and engage in the simplest of activities. Q loved children and he would often give them treats.

Q had seen Fannie in Chase City and figured he had time to score what he had been secretly desiring. It was not unusual to see him walking down the road right before sunset, especially on Saturdays. He would change his clothes without a wash-up and would go into town to see who he could see.

After visiting town, Q always walked home, unless he became too drunk or did something silly to get himself locked up, like peeing behind a tree on Main Street. He always stayed in jail until he sobered up, which was usually the next day or sometimes Monday morning. If he stayed until Monday, the local sheriff would drive him to the sawmill and collect Q's bail from Frog, who always paid because Q was one of his best workers.

Bet and her sisters saw Q making his way onto their front porch door, but they knew they could not open the door. They were disappointed, however, because Q always brought treats for them. Q frantically knocked on the door. Bet said she shouted out that she could not open the door because Mama wasn't home. She reminded Q of the rule -- if Mama's not home, nobody is allowed in. Q told Bet he had seen Fannie in Chase City and she had asked him to stop by and sit with them because she was running late. Bet didn't believe him, because her mama had always told her to never open the door, not even for God.

Initially, Bet refused to open the door. This made Q very angry, but he persisted, which scared them. They didn't know what to do or think. They had never seen him act out this way. Bet said they panicked. They ran away from the sight of him, from inside the house. They were running from room to room, closing all the curtains and pulling window shades down. Q was running around the outside of the house faster than they could secure the windows. He was peeping in, banging on the windows, and rattling the doors to the house and yelling, "Bet, let me in. Bet, let me in."

Then Q started yelling, "Open up the door, you little pickaninnies! I got treats! I got penny lemon cookies, B B Bats, Kits, Sugar Babies, Hot Balls, Squirrel Nuts, and Chip Tatoes. Old Q even got your favorite, Pepsi Cola, and the peanuts are already floating in the bottle." Bet's sisters got excited hearing about all those goodies and begged her to open the door, but she refused. Bet knew if she opened the door and her mama found out, she would have to prepare a switch for her own whipping.

Then Bet begin to think, 'Maybe Mama did ask Q to stop by with the treats and stay with us until she gets home. If I don't let him in, I will be in even bigger trouble.' She rationalized that there had to be a reason why Q was being so persistent to come in. It now made sense, Mama asked him to. Besides, she was tired of hearing her sisters begging and crying for the treats.

Bet opened the door and Q walked in. He immediately called her a "little plaited-head silly goose." He handed the soda bottle and the bag with the treats to her sisters and told them to go into the bedroom, to close the door and not to come out until he called them. Next, he pulled out a pocket switchblade knife and had his way with her. Bet said she will never forget the pain he inflicted upon her or the stench of his rotten teeth which smelt like unrefrigerated, three-day-old cooked cabbage. After he finished, Q told Bet she was clean, untouched like Jesus's mama, the Virgin Mary.

Fannie never made it back home or learned what happened to her daughter. Folks said she pitched a fit in town when she found Frog and, afterwards, she stopped by the ABC store and purchased a fifth of gin to drink on her way home. She was so drunk, she fell in a ditch and froze to death. Her body was discovered on Christmas morning. Bet said from that point on, the curse was validated for her.

Frog wanted nothing to do with his children by Fannie. A few weeks after her mama's death, Bet said she and her sisters were in Chase City and saw Frog walking down the street. Her younger sisters ran up to him yelling, "Daddy, Daddy, Daddy!" Frog completely ignored them, spat on the sidewalk and kept on walking. Bet said she hated her father because he is a very cruel man and forbade Anabay to ever tell anyone he was her grandfather.

Fannie's daughters were split up and taken in by various relatives. Bet was shipped off to live with her Uncle Percy in Raleigh, North Carolina. There, she was able to hide her pregnancy from the local folks and give birth to Anabay. Sadly, Bet was unable to have any

more children because of the damage to her body. Q
went to jail and eventually died there.

Bet did not use one ounce of discretion when she told
Anabay about her daddy. Eventually, realizing how
painful it was for her young daughter, she apologized to
Anabay, despite feeling she needed to know the truth.

After learning about her daddy, Anabay wished her
mother had made up a story—something along the lines
that her daddy was a sawmill man who died an
honorable death hauling pulpwood. Thinking back, she
guessed her mama just wanted to punish her for
refusing to believe in the family curse.

Watching her mama and her sister Kitty, Bet's baby
sister, Anabay realized they were troubled women.
Both of them naturally blamed their troubles on the
curse and they both loved men. They believed a no-
count, lazy-ass man with nothing to offer but his body
parts to warm them at night was better than standing
alone with no man at all. She often heard them saying,
"A piece of man is better than no man at all." As Anabay
grew older and wiser, she often wondered where their
dignity was. Observing them made her more
determined than ever to leave Fort Mitchell and have a
different life.

Then there was Finch, her stepdaddy, who Anabay felt
ruined a portion of her childhood. She was five years
old when he came into her life. It was on a warm
October day and she and Bet were in the front yard
raking leaves when they saw a man walking up the road

with a knapsack strapped to his back, using a tobacco stick as a cane. He had an unsteady limp and dragged his left leg.

Upon seeing them, Finch stopped and asked for a dipper of cold water from the well. He told them he was on his way to Farmville, Virginia, and was walking because he was down on his luck. Anabay watched her mother's eyes light up like a Christmas tree.

After she gave him the water, Bet invited him to stay for supper. "Surely you could use a hot, home-cooked meal. Why don't you stay for supper?"

"The pleasure is all mine," he replied.

Well, this invitation turned into Finch becoming Anabay's stepdaddy. He told everyone that he had been shot in the leg while serving in the Vietnam War.

Anabay never wanted to eat from the same fork or spoon Finch ate from because he was so dark. His complexion was black as coal, the blackest person she had ever seen in her life. She believed he was even darker than her ancestors, Cousins Jimmy Lee and Maybud Bailey. He frightened her. She just knew some of his dark skin would rub off on her.

Whenever she looked at Finch, she saw only his big pearly white teeth and the whites of his eyes. At first, he was nice, but it didn't take long for his true colors to emerge, defining who he really was, a mean-spirited man. He started mistreating them.

Bet, of course, accepted his treatment because she believed she was under the spell of the Bailey Curse. In her heart of hearts, she believed she would never find a good man so, what the hell, any man would do. It was better than being alone, Anabay often heard her say.

Finch didn't work. He piddled around occasionally doing odd jobs for folks but mostly he just sat around drinking Jack Daniels. The more he drank, the nastier and meaner he became. He used to make Anabay sit on his lap. If he was in a good mood, he would give her a nickel.

Anabay remembered feeling what she thought was a long black snake moving in his pants, pressing against her bottom. She used to wonder how he could keep a snake in his pants and how did it breathe and eat. Every time she sat on his lap, she made sure her body was as stiff as a board because she didn't want to be bitten by his snake and die. Anabay figured out later, her mama knew what Finch was doing but never said anything to him because she was afraid he would leave her.

Aunt Kitty, a short, chubby, light-skinned woman with little squinty eyes, had a nervous breakdown and returned to Fort Mitchell to live with them. She believed she was fighting a sex demon, her soon-to-be ex-husband, a midget nicknamed Little Man, who performed as an acrobat clown with the traveling fair. In her crazed imagination, Kitty believed her husband could turn into Popobawa, a large, bat-like creature with one eye and a very large penis. Even after she moved out on him, she continued to believe he could turn into a bird, fly down the chimney and have sex with her. She used to wrap layers of rags and clothing around her private parts at night and rub peppermint oil all over her body to keep him away.

Anabay overheard her aunt telling Bet that she just couldn't take living with her husband anymore because he was a real-life sex demon in the flesh. She referred to him as being a very aggressive, deranged shape-shifter who stalked her and other female fair workers at night. She was at the end of her emotional rope and blamed him for her mental illness. Aunt Kitty believed the family curse was responsible for her ending up with Little Man as her husband.

Prior to her aunt moving in with them, Anabay over-heard Bet encouraging her sister to hang in there with Little Man. "Most women would love to have a man with such a strong appetite for sex. At least you won't be sleeping alone. Having a man is better than not having a man at all. Soon, your body will adjust and everything will be just fine. Kitty, sex is like food. All of us women need it."

Two weeks after Kitty moved in, things drastically changed in their house. Anabay remembered waking up and hearing her mama crying hysterically. She thought somebody had died, but soon learned Finch had packed his bags and left town in the middle of the night. Bet was beside herself with grief.

Anabay learned later on that Finch had been embezzling money from an old couple in Chase City, who had hired him to do some repair work on their home. He had apparently snooped around and found blank checks. Before anyone was the wiser, Finch had forged the couple's names and cashed twenty-five hundred dollars' worth of checks. She overheard Bet telling Kitty how Finch had packed up and left in the middle of the night. Otherwise, the couple's son was coming to kill him.

Anabay never understood how a woman so beautiful, as her mama, could have been with a man like Finch. Bet was petite, had a reddish skin tone and long, thick brown hair. Her big hazel colored eyes, though, were her most attractive feature. She and Finch were certainly Beauty and the Beast. Looking back, Anabay came to the conclusion that Bet hated being alone and was willing to accept a man, even one like Finch, at any cost.

Boy, was Anabay happy to learn Finch had moved on. It elated her to know she would never have to look at his blackness again or feel that old black snake poking at her butt. She wished he had left a long time ago. Anabay made up her mind that someday she too, would leave and she started imagining life beyond what Fort Mitchell could offer her.

A year later the County Fair returned to town and Kitty decided to reunite with Little Man. Anabay, who always eavesdropped on grown folks' conversations, heard her aunt say, "What the hell, he won't leave me alone anyway, so I just as well go on and be with him." One week later, when it was time for the fair to move on, she packed up and left with her husband. The truth was, she was more miserable without him.

Now that Finch and Kitty were out of her life, Bet decided it was time to start attending church every Sunday, instead of on occasional Sundays. Finch had allowed them to go to church only when he felt like it. Anabay hadn't minded this about him, since she was never a big fan of going to church anyway, except to play with the other children.

The preacher at Old Rocky Mount Baptist Church was Pastor Paul Wiggins. He was long-winded as he screamed and hollered in the pulpit, playing on the folks' emotions and pocketbooks. His favorite expression was "Ain't that right, Church!" He was a short man who reminded Anabay of a squirrel because his fat cheeks poked out from his face, as if he was storing acorns. He always wore black polyester suits with red suspenders to hold up pants that were at least two sizes too big.

Every Sunday after church, Pastor Wiggins would fill his belly at a member of the congregation's supper table, smacking his big greasy lips and licking his fat fingers as he ate everything in sight. It wasn't long before he started coming over to their house. On these occasions, Bet always prepared extra special meals. She would serve fried chicken, fried salted herrings, potato salad, string beans, fried corn and homemade yeast rolls. For dessert, she would serve a fruit cobbler with homemade vanilla ice cream.

Anabay noticed whenever there was homemade ice cream, Pastor Wiggins always stayed longer and Bet would change her bed linens shortly thereafter. Then for the for rest of the week, Bet seemed to be extra happy. Anabay never forget one particular Sunday evening after he left. She asked Bet why she always locked her out of the house when Pastor Wiggins was there. Bet slapped her dead in the mouth and shouted that she had crossed the line and, as she put it, stepped out of school. Back in those days, adults were quick to tell children they had stepped out of school when they inquired about something that was considered strictly adult business.

When Pastor Wiggins was over, Anabay would usually walk down to the Meheran River and throw rocks, and have dream sessions about what her life was going to be like when she grew up and left home. It always seemed like it took forever for him to leave. But right after-wards, Bet would call her to the house to eat. She remembered the food being cold but delicious. Of course, all the best pieces of fried chicken had been eaten. Nonetheless, Anabay got to partake in the special dinner prepared for the man of the cloth and she enjoyed every bite. Bet never worried on Sundays about cooking too much food, since it was the voracious Pastor who was coming to supper.

Every morning at seven thirty sharp, Anabay would watch the Greyhound bus pass by and would dream of getting on that bus, never to return. The destination didn't matter. She just knew one day she was going to purchase a one-way ticket and never look back. She couldn't wait to become of age so she could leave and be on her own. Her mama's words were always in her head, 'For most, life is like playing cards, you never know what hand you will be dealt. But in your case, Anabay, the Curse of the Bailey Women is yours to bear.'

Anabay's body started changing around age thirteen and she started looking giggly-eyed at the local boys. One Sunday morning, she saw Claudale Jones, a light-skinned, gray-eyed, curly-haired boy sitting in church with his mother and four little brothers. They all were very cute, but he was her age and he stood out from the rest of them. Just one look at him and Anabay knew she loved him. The church clerk introduced his family to the congregation. They had just moved to Fort Mitchell from the area of Virginia known as Tidewater. After that Sunday, Anabay never fussed about going to church, but she wasn't going for the singing or to praise God. Her only purpose was to look at Claudale Jones.

It wasn't long before they started playing together after Church. Soon after that, he would walk to her house and play with her every day after he finished his chores. They became best friends. It didn't matter that he was a boy because she was more tomboy than girly girl. Anabay loved him. Claudale had been assuming the role of the man of his family since his father's death, when he was ten years old.

Anabay would always take him to her favorite spot on the riverbank and share her dreams about someday leaving Fort Mitchell. When she asked him what he wanted to do when he grew up, he always replied, "I reckon I'll put me up a doublewide trailer next to Mama's house and help her out on the farm."

Anabay told him she was going to purchase a one-way Greyhound bus ticket and never look back. He would say, "Girl, you dreaming."

She would reply, "You watch and see."

She eventually persuaded him to leave with her. She wanted to leave home when they both turned eighteen but he convinced her to wait. Claudale said they needed to have money in their pockets when the time came to leave. He also wanted to make sure his mother and brothers would be all right without him.

Zenora Knight

Chapter 4

A Dream Comes True

Friday, January 29th, 1988 finally arrived. This was the day Anabay and Claudale had been looking forward to since graduating from high school five years earlier. They were starting their lives together by moving away from home to Newark, New Jersey. They both had been working factory jobs and saving their money. Anabay toiled on the assembly line as a candy sorter at the Russell Stover factory in Clarksville, Virginia, and Claudale was a general laborer making pallets at the Box Factory in Chase City.

The weather was frigid, "colder than a witch's tit," as the old folks used to say. Anabay paced nervously back and forth on her front porch watching and waiting for Claudale to come walking up the road. She kept looking down at her new, gold-tone Timex watch on her wrist, a birthday gift from Bet, but there still was no sign of him. She was doing her best not to panic, but the Greyhound bus was scheduled to come over the hill in exactly twenty minutes and it rarely ran late.

Anabay was deeply in love with Claudale and wanted nothing more than to spend her life with him--but that life had to be away from Fort Mitchell. She refused to settle for small-town existence. She knew he was struggling with leaving his mother and four younger brothers behind because they depended on him. Anabay understood how important Claudale's family was to him. She prayed for him to find the courage and strength to leave.

Suddenly she spotted him walking towards her, wearing his green army fatigue bomber jacket and his favorite Just Fishing baseball cap. He was carrying a small brown weathered suitcase and from where Anabay stood, she could see the vapor from his breath as he approached. When he finally reached her, icicles had formed from his nostrils, sticking to the top of his mustache. She threw her arms around his neck, kissed his cheek and whispered in his ear, "I love you."

Anabay hadn't been certain Claudale would leave his family, so she told him how proud she was of him. She truly admired him for being such a responsible person. In her eyes, it meant he was a family man and he would be a wonderful husband and father someday. Not only was Claudale handsome, he was hardworking, intelligent, patient and had a good sense of humor. Anabay felt truly blessed that he loved her enough to move away with her.

"Thank you, Jesus!" Anabay shouted.

"What's that for?" he asked.

"I am just thanking God for you."

Her mother didn't seem at all surprised to see Claudale. Bet sat in her Amish oak rocking chair in front of the wood-burning stove, rocking back and forth, looking out the window, waiting for the Greyhound bus to come and take her only child away.

Anabay kept pinching herself to make sure this moment was real and not some dream she would wake up from. She and Claudale stood on the porch cuddled up together to fight the cold. Although she felt excited and happy, her heart ached for her mother. Anabay couldn't help peeping through the window at Bet rocking back and forth in the same chair she used to rock in while reading bedtime stories and telling her all about the Bailey Curse.

Finally, they saw the bus approaching. Anabay desperately wanted to run inside and give her mother one last hug but there was no time. Besides, Bet had locked the door. She had made it perfectly clear to her daughter, that if she left home today, there would be no coming back. Anabay grabbed one final look at Bet, who had stopped rocking and was standing up with a blank stare on her face, shaking her head no, letting Anabay know she was making a big mistake.

With seconds to spare, they gathered up their suitcases and crossed over the road. Claudale flagged the bus down and they boarded, paying cash for their fares. The bus was practically empty so they selected seats in the middle.

"You sure you're ready for this?" Claudale asked, squeezing Anabay's hand. Tears streamed down her face. "It's not too late. We can change our minds. I saw the look on your mama's face."

"No! It will be fine. We have to do this. We can't look back." Anabay wiped her eyes dry and managed a smile.

Richmond was the first official stop on their journey. There, they changed buses northbound for New Jersey. Anabay was feeling hungry as the bus approached the Washington D.C. Bus Station three hours later. She turned to Claudale, who had been resting his head comfortably on her shoulder. "Claudale, are you hungry?"

"Yeah, a little bit. Where are we?"

"D.C."

"When the bus stops, I'll hop off and get us something to eat. I'm sure they got to have some vending machines. I'll grab some Nabs or something. Which one you want, cheese or peanut butter?"

"That's not going to be necessary. I made us some sandwiches with the leftover chicken from last night's supper and I have a few pieces of lemon sour cream pound cake."

"Your mama's fried chicken! G-I-R-L! Now, that's what I'm talking about! Your mama can flat out put a hurting on some fried chicken! Anabay, I love you. You think of everything."

"Wait, there's more."

"What you talking about?"

"I packed a few bananas and have a thermos of sweet tea." Anabay was pleased that Claudale was happy with her idea of packing food. She reached down and handed him the chicken sandwiches she had wrapped so neatly in wax paper. "Let's eat."

Claudale had made arrangements for them to stay with his Uncle Otis and his wife, Aunt Lillie Mae, who lived in Newark. Lillie Mae also happened to be Anabay's great-aunt (Grandma Fannie's sister), but she had never met the lady and Bet rarely talked about her. She and Claudale both found it ironic that Claudale's great-uncle ended up marrying Anabay's great-aunt.

Otis and Lillie Mae Jones owned and operated a boarding house. From what Claudale told Anabay, they were quite successful and also very nice people. He and his brothers had spent a couple of summers with them in Newark when they were younger.

Anabay was bewildered why her mother didn't have a relationship with her aunt. Claudale deduced that Lillie Mae was probably estranged from her relatives down south because she had refused to allow the so-called family curse to hold her back in life like the other women in her family. After high school, she left Virginia with the love of her life, Otis Jones, and never looked back. Claudale warned Anabay not to mention any foolishness about a curse to Aunt Lillie Mae because it might make her uncomfortable or angry and jeopardize their living arrangements.

It all sounded good to Anabay. She was just happy to be with the man she loved and happy her aunt shared her sentiments about the family curse.

"Honey, I am so excited!" Anabay exclaimed as she stroked her hand across Claudale's cheek. He peered down lovingly at her with his gray eyes. The way he looked at her sometimes sent an electrifying, passionate charge of love throughout her body. He was definitely a handsome, drop-dead gorgeous man. Back home, he was known as one of those fine, light-skinned men with good hair and light eyes--a man who could produce pretty babies. There were only a handful of men like these in Fort Mitchell and Anabay definitely felt lucky and proud that one of them belonged to her.

"You know, Anabay, I'm happy you talked me into leaving. You are absolutely right--there is no future for us back home. Now we have an opportunity to make something of our lives," Claudale reflected. He sweetly kissed her hand.

"Claudale, you left chicken grease on my hand!" Anabay laughed, wiping her hand on his shirt sleeve.

"Girl, you already know where I would put this chicken if we were not on this bus!"

"Stop it, you're being a nasty boy!" She covered her face with her hands, giggling.

"I know. You love it, don't you?"

She laid her head on his shoulder. "Claudale, I'm glad we left home, too. I just wish we had a little more money between us. Do you think they will charge us much?"

"No, Anabay, they won't. They understand. They left home many years ago just like us."

"Claudale, are you sure they have space for us?"

"Anabay, why are you so worried? They are expecting us. We are family. If they didn't have room, they would have said so. You need not worry about a thing."

"I hope so. I guess I'm still haunted about some of the things Mama said."

"Baby, get this through your head. As long as I have breath in my body, I'm going to protect and take care of you. You will never have to worry. This is my promise to you and please never forget it." He then lifted her head off his shoulder and passionately kissed her.

Claudale had an aura about himself that made her feel safe. Listening to him vowing to take care and provide for her made Anabay feel like she already had achieved a successful life.

Hours later, the bus driver finally announced, "Newark, New Jersey. Next, New York City, The Big Apple."

"Hallelujah! Praise God! Anabay's eyes filled with tears of joy upon hearing the driver's words. She was like a kid in a candy store when they exited the bus. "Honey, this is so amazing. Newark is more than I ever imagined! It's eight thirty in the morning and look at all these people! I've never seen so many people in my life in one place! They're stirring around like little ants. So many cars and tall buildings and listen to all the noise!" Anabay interlocked her arm tightly into Claudale's, and they walked through this foreign land so as not to get separated.

"I know, Baby, it's a lot, but we'll get used to it. It's been a few years since I was last here, so let me ask this guy at the newsstand if we are walking in the right direction to Osborne Terrace."

An old Asian man with cold-whipped wrinkled red skin nodded his head yes, never making eye contact with them. He just kept on selling newspapers.

"Thank you, Sir," Claudale said to the old man.

Anabay could tell Claudale was proud he knew the way. He stuck his chest out a little more, straightened up his shoulders, grabbed her hand and they continued walking. They both were too excited to notice how cold it was.

"Claudale, I've heard that people who live in the North are unfriendly. That seems to be the case with the old man at the newsstand."

"Anabay, I don't think that's the case with all northerners. He was just busy selling papers, that's all."

"You're probably right. Claudale, stop for a moment!"

"What's wrong? You tired?"

"No, I just wanted to look at that beautiful canary polka dot dress in the window with the matching shoes and pocketbook. How gorgeous! You would never see this back home."

"You want to go in and see how much it costs? Perhaps we have enough money."

"Don't be silly! I want us to save our money so we can get our very own place as soon as possible."

They continued walking, taking in the sights. Finally, they reached the house on Osborne Terrace, a large three-story white and black Victorian house that sat on a corner lot.

"Uncle Otis and Aunt Lillie Mae sure live in a big house. Looks like we could get lost in there. Claudale, I feel so nervous. What if they don't like me?"

"Stop it, Anabay! Why wouldn't they like you? You don't have one scared bone in your body. Why do you think we're here? This was your dream. It sure wasn't mine, so don't you let me down now, Baby. They are regular people. It will be fine. Let's ring the bell." Claudale was a little taken aback. He had never seen her so unsure of herself before.

Ding dong. Ding dong.

"That's enough." She jerked his hand away from the doorbell.

"Who's there?" A women's voice was heard through the intercom.

"We are looking for Aunt Lillie Mae and Uncle Otis Jones," Claudale playfully replied.

"Is that you, Claudale?" the voice responded.

"Yes, Ma'am, we are here."

"Oh, Child, it's your Aunt Lillie Mae. I'll be right there."

"Lord, Lord, Lord! Look at you, Child! You all grown up!"

Aunt Lillie Mae then turned her attention to Anabay, looking her up and down. "I didn't think your mama was really going to allow you to leave. Otis! Otis! Come on. The children are here."

A tall, thin, high-yellow man with a toothpick hanging out of his mouth and wearing suspenders with khaki pants came down the stairs. "Well, well, well, good to see you, Boy. And who is this pretty little spring chicken clenching onto your arm so tight?"

"Aunt Lillie Mae and Uncle Otis, this is Anabay."

"Honey, we know who you are," said Lillie Mae. "You are my niece. We finally meet and never mind my husband. Once a flirt, always a flirt. Y'all come on in."

They walked into the huge house. The front door was a grand entrance to a foyer with two large rooms on both sides. Each room contained detailed crown molding, large doors and high gloss hardwood floors. Anabay was impressed. It looked rich, as if made for royalty. She felt very uncomfortable. Here she was, face to face, with an aunt she didn't know and who looked nothing like the other women in her family. She was more curious than ever as to why there hadn't been any contact between her mother and Aunt Lillie Mae.

"Anabay, who would ever have thought you'd be married to my husband's nephew. Let me show you y'all's room upstairs. Y'all got to be tired after that long exhausting bus ride. I know, I've ridden that bus plenty of times."

Anabay wondered to herself where her aunt had ridden the bus, because it certainly hadn't been to Fort Mitchell. Perhaps she was just making small talk. They followed Aunt Lillie Mae up the arched staircase.

"After y'all freshen up, we'll talk in the parlor and have some of my coconut pie and tea. Here we are. I chose this room for y'all because it's nice and airy. It allows for good energy to flow for a young couple just starting out. I saw the look on y'all's face when I mentioned marriage, so I'm inclined to ask--are y'all married?'

It was apparent Aunt Lille Mae never lost her southern drawl. Anabay felt too embarrassed to answer the question so she looked at Claudale, waiting for him to respond, since he knew her better than she did.

 "Not yet, Aunt Lillie Mae, but we're working on it. I hope it's not a problem," Claudale answered.

"Well, it's none of our business," she replied in a friendly tone. "But I'll just say this, the key to a successful life is doing what's right."

"Yes, Ma'am," replied Claudale.

"Well, one room was requested and that's what we prepared. We're running a rooming house here, so we don't ask too many unnecessary personal questions."

Uncle Otis yelled from the bottom of the stairs, "Lillie Mae, why don't you come on downstairs and give those kids a few minutes to themselves. I know you're up there smothering them to death."

Aunt Lillie Mae walked back to the top of the stairs and yelled down, "Otis Jones, let me handle this. You will have your time. I'm just getting them settled in, so why don't you go in the kitchen and turn the tea kettle on and cut my pie. Okay, Sweetie?"

"All right, I guess I can do that. Ain't got no choice," he mumbled under his breath, walking away.

It looked to Anabay like Aunt Lillie Mae knew her way around her husband. She was just the opposite of him. She was a dark-skinned, thick, curvaceous woman who wore her long, black hair in an upswept bun. Her personality was genuinely warm and inviting. Hospitality was her passion.

"There are fresh towels and linens on the chair and the bathroom is down the hall to the right. It ain't much but y'all are certainly welcome. I'd better check on Otis. I don't like a man messing around my kitchen too long."

They both said thank you to Aunt Lillie Mae and gave her a hug. She quickly made her way down the stairs.

"Claudale, I hope they don't have a problem with us not being married," Anabay whispered.

"Anabay, I wish you would relax. We just got here. The house is beautiful, isn't it?"

She knew he was trying to make her relax by changing the subject. "Yes, it is. It sure is big. How many rooms do you think they have?"

"I used to know, but I forgot. Maybe fifteen."

"I love the way the staircase balcony overlooks the foyer."

"Yeah, it's nice," he said, smiling.

Claudale and Anabay rested for a few minutes before starting down the stairs. Uncle Otis was at the bottom of the staircase waiting for them. Aunt Lillie Mae was seated in the parlor.

"Come on in and sit down. Have some of your aunt's coconut pie. It's the best pie you'll ever taste in your life. I'll tell you, if we weren't sitting as pretty as we are, we would find a way to market these pies. They would make us a mint," Uncle Otis said, winking at his wife.

"Oh, don't listen to your uncle. He says that just to keep me baking them for him. Sometimes I take orders from local churches for programs and funerals, nothing too big. I just don't have the time to bake like I want to and run this house at the same time. It's a lot of work."

"I know it's a lot of work. Lillie Mae keeps asking for help and when I offer to get her some help, she turns it down. She knows she don't want nobody scurrying around in her house." Uncle Otis paused for a few seconds. "Your aunt and I are going to give you kids a break. First two months, no charge. After that, $100 a week and that includes clean sheets and towels. Now, if you want three meals, which would be our three-hots-and-a-cot, then it will cost you a little extra," he said, not cracking a smile. Claudale had already warned Anabay about his uncle's dry sense of humor. "What do you think, Lillie Mae? With a couple of extra chores around here, you think we can afford to feed them?"

Lillie Mae laughed. Only she understood her husband's sense of humor.

Claudale glanced at Anabay with a smirk on his face. "That will not be a problem. We appreciate everything that you are willing to do for us and of course, we want to pay our way. Hopefully, we'll be able to save enough money and get our own place in a short while."

Again, Anabay was proud of Claudale for taking charge and speaking up to Aunt Lillie Mae and Uncle Otis, letting them know he was the man in charge of them as a couple.

"Yes, we are very grateful. Thank you both very much," Anabay said sheepishly, feeling the need to join the conversation.

"Claudale, I got you a job down at the shipyard where I used to work. You'll be loading and unloading ships. The pay is damn good. You start next Monday. The boss there is a fair man. If you work hard, you can be promoted to a foreman in a few years."

Claudale's face lit up. He sprang to his feet and shook his uncle's hand vigorously. "Thank you, Uncle Otis! I will make you proud! You won't be sorry, not one day, that you got me this job. Thank you. Thank you again."

Aunt Lillie Mae had a sly look on her face. "Now as for you, Young Lady, I spoke to the laundry service that does our linens and you can start working there whenever you're ready. It's just a little something to hold you over until you find a better job. Never be too proud to start somewhere."

"Oh, I'm definitely not too proud. I am very grateful. Thank you so much, Aunt Lillie Mae." Anabay didn't know what was on her aunt's mind, but she had plans of her own. She had every intention of going to school, getting herself an education, and finding herself a good job.

Uncle Otis and Aunt Lillie Mae's son, Aaron, came running down the stairs, yelling "Moms and Pops, see you later. I won't be back in time for dinner."

"Hold on, Aaron. Take a second and come in here and greet your cousins," Aunt Lillie Mae yelled out to him.

Aaron backtracked into the parlor. He was tall and slender and had a golden-brown complexion with dimples. He was wearing black slacks, a white collared shirt and a black cardigan sweater. Aaron appeared to be in his twenties and was quite handsome.

"My man, Cousin Claudale! It's been a long time," Aaron said, embracing Claudale with a man hug. He turned to Anabay with an extended hand. "I'm Aaron and you must be Cousin Anabay. Moms told me you guys were moving in. Welcome! Welcome! Welcome! So, how was your trip?"

"The trip was fine," they both said at the same time.

Aaron began checking the time on his watch. Wherever he was going, it sure seemed urgent. It was obvious he wasn't interested in a meet-and-greet session. He appeared not to have heard a word they said. "I'm sorry I can't stay and get more acquainted. I have an important business meeting in New York City. I'm working on something B-I-G. Trust me, I'm getting ready to blow up! Won't nobody have to work around here no more." He kissed his mother on the cheek-- "Love you, Moms" --and dashed off.

With a proud look on her face, Aunt Lillie Mae turned to Anabay and said, "Aaron is our only child."

"Yeah, I often wonder where we went wrong," Uncle Otis interjected.

"Otis, please don't start! The kids don't want to hear that kind of talk. Aaron is doing just fine. Like I always tell you, Otis, you are too hard on him."

Looking annoyed, Uncle Otis snapped back, "Lillie Mae, I pray that you are right. That boy is confused. He don't like to work at nothing. A hard day's work would do him good instead of chasing around some unrealistic pipe dream he's conjured up."

"Enough, Otis!" Aunt Lillie Mae said in a stern voice.

Anabay and Claudale looked at each other because they both knew things weren't going well. Aunt Lillie Mae had a look on her face that let Uncle Otis know he was in the doghouse for airing their family's dirty laundry in front of guests. Aaron was their only child and she protected him like a mother bear protects her cub.

Suddenly, the atmosphere had changed from warm and welcoming to combative and tense.

"This pie sure is delicious," Claudale said awkwardly.

Zenora Knight

Chapter 5

Good News

Anabay and Claudale quickly settled into their new living quarters in Newark and received more love and support than they ever imagined from Aunt Lillie Mae and Uncle Otis. Exactly one year to the date of their arrival, they got married. Aunt Lillie Mae and Uncle Otis put together a small informal reception for them, inviting only a few friends and extended family members to share in their union. Aunt Lillie Mae cooked and baked for days for the occasion. She truly loved cooking and entertaining. Everybody was family to her and having people in her home, eating her food and enjoying themselves, brought so much joy to her.

Life in general was wonderful. Everything was going well--far beyond what they had planned or could have perceived. Claudale was working long hours at the shipyard and Anabay had a new job working in a diner while attending culinary classes full time at the local community college. Within three years, they had saved enough money to move into their own apartment, four blocks away from Aunt Lillie Mae and Uncle Otis. The apartment was spacious and convenient to both of their jobs. Anabay thanked God every day for giving them the courage and the good sense to move away from home. The curse had become a distant memory.

The sun was rising and Anabay, who hadn't slept all night, was filled with excitement because it was their moving day and she had a surprise for Claudale that would make things even more perfect for them. He was still asleep, so she sat up in the bed and started shaking his shoulders back and forth. "Good morning! Time to rise and shine!" He brushed her off and continued sleeping like a baby.

She leaned over and kissed him on the lips. Still, he didn't react. 'I know what to do,' Anabay thought. She used her tongue to trace his jawbone to the back of his ears before flickering her tongue in and out of his ears. Then she gently nibbled and kissed his earlobes while blowing warm morning breath into his ears. This little technique always drove him crazy. She could feel his body coming to life.

Of course, he responded by grabbing her hand and guiding it down towards his groin. Not only was Claudale handsome, he was blessed with a big penis that didn't require much to arouse. Gripping and massaging his rock-hard dick, Anabay knew he was ready. He turned over and began kissing her nipples until they stood up at full attention and her vagina throbbed. Moving slowly downward and kissing her belly button and the inside of her thighs, he eventually began to dine, making her want him even more. They made hot, passionate love until they both were drenched in sweat and their insides were filled with each other. Afterwards, they lay there, skin to skin, catching their breath, while staring into each other's eyes.

Anabay felt so reassured by the love she saw in Claudale's eyes and she felt truly blessed to have him as her husband. He made her feel safe, happy and on top of the world without any regrets. As he stroked her cheek with his index finger, he said he knew leaving home hadn't been easy for either of them, but they had done it. As long as she was happy, he was thrilled. He told Anabay he truly loved her more than he could find the words to express and that she should never forget it.

Anabay was captivated, entranced by his loving words. She reciprocated by telling him how much she loved him and how proud she was that he was her husband. "I have a wonderful surprise for you, but it has to wait until we're in our new apartment."

"What is it, Anabay?" Claudale asked excitedly.

He always acted like a child on Christmas morning whenever a gift or surprise was involved. Anabay could tell from the look on his face, he could hardly wait.

He started guessing. "A Lazy Boy recliner?" Claudale had always wanted a recliner to rock back in and put his feet up after a hard day's work.

"I'm not telling," Anabay teased, throwing her arms around his neck.

He continued to beg her to reveal his surprise. "I know you bought me that chair. Right?'

When she didn't answer, he playfully put her in a scissor lock and tickled her until she begged for mercy, but Anabay kept true to her word and didn't reveal the surprise.

The aroma of fried ham, apples, yeast rolls and coffee wafting all the way upstairs let them know Aunt Lillie Mae had prepared a special farewell breakfast for them. They quickly showered, got dressed and walked downstairs, only to find her sitting at the table with a long face, sipping a cup of coffee.

"Good morning, Aunt Lillie Mae," they greeted her.

"Aunt Lille Mae, we're going to miss you and Uncle Otis so much," Anabay said, patting her on the shoulder.

"I'm going to miss y'all too, especially you, Anabay. Having you here with us gave me a connection to my family back home. I've been so distant from them." Aunt Lillie Mae was on the verge of tears.

Anabay was floored by her words--she felt a big lump in her throat. This was the first time she ever heard her aunt acknowledge her relatives, her blood, back home. There were so many questions she wanted to ask, but Claudale made her promise to never initiate a conversation about family with Aunt Lillie Mae. Besides, he was standing there giving her a look to let her know 'do not go there.'

Quickly changing the subject, Chaudale asked, "Where is Uncle Otis?"

"Claudale, didn't he mention to you that he had to take his car to the shop today?"

 "No, he didn't say anything to me. I would have gone with him had he said something. Wonder why he didn't say something? That's not like him."

"Otis is not good at saying goodbye. He'll be alright though -- y'all come by in a few days." Aunt Lillie Mae pulled out a tissue from her apron pocket and blotted her eyes.

Moving was quite emotional for Anabay and Claudale, too. Aunt Lillie Mae and Uncle Otis had made them feel so welcomed and comfortable in their home, and it was wonderful for them, being around their family. Nonetheless, they were determined to stay true to their goal, a place of their own. They sat down and ate a breakfast fit for kings and queens.

"We are going to miss having y'all around. It's hard to believe three years went by so fast," reflected Aunt Lillie Mae.

"Sure did," replied Claudale, tightly squeezing Anabay's hand. "Anabay and I will be back so often you'll still have to charge us rent."

"That's sweet, but it's not going to be the same. Y'all better get moving. The door is always open here. Take that basket on the counter. I packed lunch, dinner and two of my pies. With all y'all got going on today, there won't be no time for cooking."

"Thank you, Aunt Lillie Mae, you shouldn't have. You're too kind. I can't wait to start cooking delicious meals for my handsome husband," Anabay said, smiling lovingly at Claudale.

 "Oh, I bet you will, Dear. He is a blessed man. I pray that he continues to appreciate you."

"Aunt Lillie Mae, you don't have to worry about that— I'm made from the same stock as Uncle Otis," Claudale proclaimed, grinning broadly.

 "I hear you." Aunt Lillie Mae had a doubtful look on her face.

Lots of hugs and kisses were exchanged. They waved goodbye to Aunt Lillie Mae, who stood on the front porch until they were out of sight.

*****

Anabay and Claudale stood hand and hand in front of their new dwelling.

"Well, here we are, Baby Cakes, our very own place!" He was smiling from ear to ear. "Wait a minute."

"What's wrong?" Anabay was clearly puzzled.

With a serious look on his face, he said, "It's you and me now, Baby."

"And."

"Well, I'm really stuck with you now!" He playfully scooped his wife up in his arms, lifted her up off her feet and spun her around before carrying her across the threshold.

"Claudale! Claudale! I'm getting dizzy! You're crazy," Anabay squealed.

"You love it!"

"You're so spontaneous--I never know what you are going to come up with next. But don't you worry, I'm going to make our home comfortable for you. A man's home is his castle. I love you, Mr. Claudale Jones."

"I love you more, Mrs. Anabay Bailey Jones." He laid her down on their new brown, green and red floral-colored sofa delivered from the Lazy Boy furniture store, a present from Aunt Lillie Mae and Uncle Otis. This was their wedding gift to them, living room furniture.

They were starting Chapter Two in their lives, being on their own as husband and wife. Chapter One was leaving Fort Mitchell. They both were so excited being in their very own apartment and inhaling the aroma of fresh paint and new furniture.

"OK, we're home now. Where's my surprise? Should I close my eyes?" Claudale asked, looking around the apartment for some clue. "I don't see a recliner. So, where is it? I want to know."

"Yes, you have been patiently waiting. Claudale, sit down beside me."

"OK, I'm sitting."

"Claudale, do you know how blessed we are?" Anabay decided to have some fun with her husband and watch the excitement build up in him.

"Yeah, woman, I do. Now, where is my surprise? Stop playing."

"I know you know we have been blessed but, Claudale, do you really have any idea how good God has been to us?" She wanted to string him along a little bit longer. "God has been blessing us when we didn't even know he was blessing us. God is good!"

"Okay, I see what you're doing. I'm just going to sit and wait until you finish." Although the suspense was killing Claudale, he was trying his best to act cool. He sat back on the sofa, calmly turned on the television and started flicking the channels.

"Claudale!"

"Yes . . . Anabay," he mumbled, not taking his eyes off the television.

"I just want you to understand. We were blessed to have left home, to have stayed with Uncle Otis and Aunt Lillie Mae, to have found employment and to have saved our money and found an apartment we can afford. Most importantly, we are blessed to have our health."

"Stop teasing me! What and where is my surprise?"

"The surprise I have for you is greater than anything you could ever purchase, more precious than gold and it is a part of you and me."

"What's that? Your mama or my mama coming to visit?"

"No, silly."

"You ready to know what the surprise is?"

"I've been ready."

"OK." Anabay grabbed his hands and placed them on her stomach. "Good news. We're pregnant! We are having a baby! Isn't that wonderful?"

Claudale's demeanor changed instantly. He jumped up from the sofa to his feet like a raging bull who was being branded with a hot iron while having a red cape waved in front of his face. Frightened and shocked by his reaction, Anabay jumped to her feet. His nostrils were flared and he was snorting as he pushed past her and started ranting, not making any sense.

"Anabay, what in the hell have you done? What the fuck! I don't want any babies! Are you crazy? How in the hell did you let this fucking shit happen?" He yelled at the top of his lungs, then he threw his body to the floor, pounding the hardwood floor with his clenched fists over and over, breaking the skin until his knuckles bled. "Damn, woman, you messed up," he cried out

"Stop it, Claudale! Stop it! Have you lost your mind?" Anabay protested. This was the first time she had ever seen any violence in him. Prior to this moment, she would have sworn he wouldn't have hurt a flea. Claudale had always acted like he loved children and had always been so good with his younger siblings. She just assumed he wanted kids of his own. They had never discussed having children.

Anabay realized men have many different reactions when they initially learn they are going to become fathers, so she decided to remain calm and to help him process this information. He was genuinely upset and she didn't want to push him over the edge, so she remained calm and tried to calm him down. She knew that it was important to address him by his name and to speak to him in a softer tone than he was speaking to her.

Inhaling and exhaling a couple of deep breaths and counting to ten, Anabay pushed past her fear and confronted him, hoping to bring him back to reality. "Claudale! Honey, couples get married, they have children, they raise their children, they become a family, you do understand? It's a natural thing."

Claudale just looked right through her as if she wasn't there. He hadn't heard a word she said.

Anabay yelled out, "Claudale!" No response came from him, so she yelled his name again, "Claudale! What is the problem?" He still did not answer. It was like he was in a trance. He turned his back, grabbed the doorknob, then stopped. At least he wasn't yelling and acting in a violent manner.

When he turned around, she no longer recognized him. His face was that of a mean, dark, fiery demon revealing itself for the first time. This was not the face of the man she had fallen in love with and married. Shocked, yet relieved that he had pounded the floor instead of her, Anabay realized her life and her baby's life would have been over at this very moment. Immediately, she thought about her mother's incessant warnings about the curse on the women in their family.

Anabay was now in a panic. She tried not to show any fear but her heart was beating very fast and her hands were trembling. 'Who is this man?' No longer could she remain calm, "Claudale, please settle down. I know this comes as a surprise to you, and I know we weren't planning on having a baby right now, but it's going to be alright. You're scaring me. Everything's going to be all right, Baby, I promise you. Life is going to be good. Now, please calm down! Just settle down, Baby!"

Claudale did calm down. It was like the demon disappeared. His voice was measured, but stern and cold. "No, Anabay," wiping the tears from his eyes, "You don't understand. I don't want any children, I never have. My mama had too many kids and because of that, I never wanted children of my own."

Anabay reached out to touch him, but he pulled away from her.

He continued to speak. "You see, I made myself a promise that I would never bring a child into this world that would have to depend on me. I don't want the responsibility of children. I've seen it too many times-- the cute little innocent bastards come into the world and suck the life out of you. They are nothing but little demon blood suckers."

"No, Claudale, you're wrong. Children are gifts from God."

"Children are not gifts, woman! You have it all wrong! They are curses straight out of hell! How could you do this to us? Life was going to be beautiful! Now it's over!"

Anabay felt a warm sensation running up her legs as she began to get angry with him. She could barely contain herself as she shouted out, "Over! Over! How can you say this, Claudale? I didn't do anything to us! I thought you would have welcomed the news. Children are blessings, not curses."

"Who have you told, Anabay?" he yelled.

"Why are you shouting at me? Stop it."

"Who have you told?" He grabbed her arms and pulled her in closer to him until their bodies met. "Who?"

"Let go of me. You're hurting me?"

He continued demanding, "Who?"

"No one. I wanted you to be the first to know. It's bad luck to share the news prior to your first trimester."

"Good, because we're not going to keep it!"

"What are you saying, Claudale?"

"We're not keeping it. We're going to get rid of it."

"Claudale, have you lost your mind? I am not going to do that!"

"Listen, Anabay. I don't want any children, not even one fucking baby. Do you understand me? Now you need to make up your mind, it's either me or your baby!"

"My baby? So it's my baby now, not our baby? We are married," she shouted.

"Bitch, you heard me. Me or your baby? It's that simple." Claudale grabbed his keys and headed for the door.

"So, I'm a bitch now? Claudale, where are you going?"

"Look, woman, don't ask me any questions. I am no longer obligated to you or that thing you're carrying in your belly!"

"Claudale, we are married." Anabay cried.

"Not for long. I'm only married to you on paper. You lost your rights to me once you got yourself knocked up." He left, slamming the door behind him.

Zenora Knight

Chapter 6

Who is this Man?

Folks who are spiritually strong would say, turn your situation over to God. Anabay's mother would say, it's the curse, live with it. Anabay refused to believe in the big C so she had no other choice but to let go and let God.

Several months passed, and Anabay was still in shock over her husband's reaction to her pregnancy. The majority of men, at least normal men, would be proud, jumping for joy at having fathered a child. No, not her Claudale. The day she told him she was pregnant was still very raw and fresh in her mind, like it happened yesterday. She had not planned on getting pregnant and although they had never discussed having children, as far as she was concerned, that conversation wasn't necessary. It's such a natural thing to fall in love, get married and have babies.

Her husband was no longer the loving, caring, gentle man she had fallen in love with and married. That side of him had vanished like a thief in the night. A mean-spirited man was now dwelling inside him, controlling his every thought and move, leaving her to wonder if the family curse was responsible for this upheaval in their lives. Claudale was now spending all his time gambling and drinking. He was rumored to be running around with Cookie, a bartender who worked at the Kitty Kat Lounge. He rarely came home from work, that is, if he even went to work. Sometimes, she didn't see him for days at a time.

Anabay took her wedding vows seriously from day one. She now found herself praying continuously, asking God to give her husband the wisdom and the courage to be the man he was born to be. She asked God to give her the patience and the understanding to be the best wife possible and at the end of her prayers, she asked God to forgive her for not kneeling because she was too pregnant. It seemed like her prayers were not being answered, but she kept on praying, refusing to accept the situation the way it was.

It was late September, and the days were getting darker earlier. Anabay turned the television to the six o'clock news and walked over to the window and peered out, hoping to see Claudale walking up the street from work. He would normally come home around this time when things were good between them. Clearly, it was wishful thinking, there was no sign of him.

As usual, she was in for another long and lonely night, so she decided to take a shower and go to bed early, as if that would make a difference. She adjusted the shower water temperature as hot as she could stand it before stepping in. Lathering her body all over with a new bar of Lux soap, she stood directly under the showerhead for about thirty-five minutes, allowing the water to hit every inch of her body. The bathroom was so fogged up from the steam, she could barely see as she reached for her white oversized bath towel, part of a his-and-hers set, a wedding gift.

After drying off, Anabay went into the bedroom and started rubbing herself down with cocoa butter to help prevent stretch marks. She couldn't help thinking, 'This is the kind of thing a husband should be doing, rubbing his pregnant wife down.' But not her husband, he was nowhere to be found. She just wanted to curl up in bed and forget about everything. She pulled the covers back and crawled into her bed, burying her head into her pillow and taking in the aroma of Downy fabric softener on her freshly washed linens. It was one of the few smells she could tolerate. She tossed and turned before grabbing another pillow and stuffing it between her legs, keeping her knees from touching. She was finding it damn near impossible to find a comfortable position in bed because the mattress was too soft.

Claudale had insisted that they purchase their mattress from Montgomery Ward and he only wanted this particular mattress because his mother had the same one. Ever since they moved away from home, Anabay noticed that he had started speaking very highly of his mother as if she were a role model for all women. He wanted everything done like his mama did it. Although there was a better-quality mattress at Sears Roebuck for the same price, Anabay hadn't made a fuss about it because she wanted him to be happy. After all, she was the one who had convinced him to leave home with her and he was her knight in shining armor.

Unable to fall into a restful sleep and in between dozing off, Anabay noticed the time on the nightstand clock: 12 a.m. – 2 a.m. – 3 a.m. - 4:45 a.m. and finally, 6 a.m. She awakened to daylight creeping in through her bedroom blinds. 'Just maybe he came home in between my dozing off,' she thought to herself. Instinctively, she reached over to feel for him, only to be greeted by cold sheets. She lay there staring up at the ceiling, wondering, 'Where is he? Is he laying between Cookie's legs, resting after making love to her all night long while I lay here alone with a belly full of baby?'

Her imagination was running helter-skelter when she heard him unlocking the door around six thirty. What a welcome sound! As bad as she wanted to confront and question him about his whereabouts, she decided not to, because what mattered most, he remembered his way home. It was also Sunday morning and Claudale coming home was a miracle in itself. It was what she had been praying for. Most weekends he was gone who knows where.

Anabay decided to stay in bed, pretend to be asleep and wait for him to come back to the bedroom. Ten minutes passed and he still hadn't peeped in, so she called out to him, "Claudale! Claudale!" She knew he had to have heard her, but she wasn't at all surprised when he didn't answer. He was obviously still angry about the baby. She was determined to keep the faith that everything was going to be all right.

Anabay believed once their baby was born, the old Claudale would snap back completely with his daddy instincts intact. She believed he would automatically fall in love with his child and life would return to normal for them. She was doing her very best to maintain a positive attitude and not worry.

She heard him moving around in the kitchen, opening and closing the refrigerator and rattling pots and pans. He was getting ready to cook breakfast. She continued lying there patiently, hoping he would at least come into the bedroom and speak to her. Although she was hungry, the smell of bacon frying and the aroma of coffee were making her nauseous. Anabay thought to herself, 'It sure would be nice if he made enough food for me.'

It was obvious by now, he wasn't coming into the bedroom so Anabay slipped her bathrobe on and walked into the kitchen. Claudale was standing in front of the stove, pouring his cheese eggs into the cast iron fry pan, a wedding gift from his mother. He was so proud of that fry pan. He told Anabay it was the only gift he could remember his mama giving him since he was ten years old.

"Good morning, Honey," she greeted him, reaching for a hug.

"Get off me," he said, jerking away.

He reeked so badly of alcohol and cigarettes, the smell was hard for her to stomach. She had never known him to smoke cigarettes, but occasionally, he would drink a shot of Jack Daniels. This morning, he smelled like he had drunk the whole bottle. His hair was uncombed and full of little white lint balls, and his clothes were dirty and wrinkled. His shirttail was hanging out the back of his pants and he had even missed a couple of belt loops. He looked disheveled, like he had been sleeping in a gutter.

"Claudale, you look a mess and smell bad! You have been drinking!"

"No shit," he said, slightly turning his head, giving her a quick glance.

"Why don't you sit down and let me scramble your eggs? I'll fix your plate." Anabay reached for the spatula he was holding.

"Gone!" he said, jerking the spatula away. "I don't need your help. You have done enough!"

She ignored him. "OK, that's fine. Did you make enough food for me and your baby? You know I'm eating for two. We're hungry," she said, cracking a smile and rubbing her stomach, hoping to relieve some of the tension between them.

"Hell no! Make your own."

"OK," Anabay paused. "Claudale, I hope you change your attitude because our baby will be here soon. We haven't even picked out a name or done any shopping. We haven't made any preparations at all."

He continued plating his food and placed the fry pan in the sink. "I won't be here," he said, sitting down at the table, slurping his coffee out of his favorite black "Virginia is for Lovers" cup. "Name it what you want! You, Uncle Otis and Aunt Lillie Mae should name the baby and go shopping since the three of you are so damn happy," he said, never looking up.

It was true. Uncle Otis and Aunt Lillie Mae were ecstatic about the baby despite being disappointed in Claudale's behavior and attitude. Aunt Lillie Mae said the way Claudale was acting made it hard for her to believe he and Otis were blood-related. She always reminded Anabay to keep the faith, to believe in God because he was a miracle worker and to ask him to deliver Claudale from his sins. Everything is going to be all right, she kept reminding her niece. Anabay wanted badly to ask her aunt if she thought the family curse had anything to do with Claudale's behavior, but she kept her promise not to breathe one word about the Big C.

Uncle Otis hadn't said much, but Anabay knew through Aunt Lillie Mae that he wasn't leaving this situation entirely up to God. Instead, he had been trying to talk some sense into his nephew. According to Aunt Lillie Mae, her husband was about two minutes from knocking some sense into Claudale's head if he didn't straighten up his act. She even revealed that Otis had been talking about driving Claudale back to Virginia and giving him a good old-fashioned whipping in a woodshed.

From the expression on Claudale's face, Anabay knew he wasn't talking just to hear himself talk. He was dead serious. He had a plan. "OK . . . where are you going to be?" she asked, fearing his answer.

"Back home to Mama. She told me you were not the woman for me. Home wasn't good enough for you. She said you always thought you were better than everybody else, with those big, foolish ideas of yours. I should have listened to her. Blood's always thicker than water," he said with a stone-cold look on his face.

His words pierced her heart, sapping all her energy. Her heart was in her stomach and her body was trembling. She couldn't believe what he just said to her. Anabay swallowed hard. "What are you talking about?" She looked into Claudale's eyes. Those beautiful eyes that once comforted her and made her feel safe now frightened her. "You can't do that, Claudale!"

"Woman, please, consider it done," he snapped back and sucked his teeth.

'Some things are better left unsaid,' Anabay was thinking to herself. Feeling betrayed and abandoned, she could no longer listen to or sit in his presence. She was convinced her husband had truly lost his mind. "You just can't do that to me! I love you," she shouted as she stormed out of the kitchen and headed to the shower.

Church service was in two hours and she definitely was going to church. She was desperately in need of prayer.

Matter of fact, the way she was feeling, she needed the entire congregation to pray for her.

Zenora Knight

Chapter 7

The Power of Prayer

Anabay arrived at church just as Sunday School was ending and the church was packed because it was communion Sunday. Brother Glover Davis, who was ushering, went out of his way to find a seat for her on the first floor of the sanctuary. Anabay was grateful to him because she certainly didn't have the energy to walk up the stairs to the balcony.

After the choir finished singing the opening hymn, Pastor Owen Tisdale III made his grand entrance as usual from the rear of the church, marching in a slow dramatized strut. He sang in his astounding tenor voice "Lord, do it. Lord, do it for me right now." Pastor was a handsome man in his late forties. He was tall with a lean muscular build and a thick black mustache. Effortlessly, his voice could climb from tenor to a high C, then plunge to a deep baritone. Pastor knew he could sing and he always used his incredible vocal range to stir up the emotions of the congregation, especially the women, who were often seen fanning themselves and twitching around in their seats.

Once he reached the pulpit, he grabbed the microphone and shouted, "I figured I better blow my note now. Ain't God a good God!"

There was a joke among the women parishioners that Pastor had a panty-dropping voice. Anabay even overheard Aunt Lillie Mae, of all people, confessing that if Pastor sang a solo to her in private she would have to temporarily forget about Uncle Otis and do the unthinkable.

Anabay's flagging spirit was uplifted by the sermon, more so than any other Sunday she could remember. She felt like it was being preached just for her. She was probably one of the few women in attendance who cared more about the message than Pastor's singing voice. Her husband remained the only man she had ever desired.

Pastor preached from Psalm 127:3, "Behold children are a heritage from the Lord, the fruit of the womb, a reward," and Proverbs 15:20, "A wise son maketh a glad father, but a foolish man despises his mother." Anabay wished Claudale could have heard this encouraging sermon. When Altar Call was announced, she did her best to get up out of her seat and make it down the aisle, but she was blocked by the Pastor's harem. Pastor's harem was a secret nickname Anabay had given to a group of church women who always managed to jump in front of everybody else just to get close to Pastor Tisdale.

After the service, Pastor Tisdale stood in his usual place, the church vestibule leading to the Sanctuary and Fellowship Hall, because he wanted to greet as many church members and visitors as possible. "Good afternoon, Mrs. Jones. How are you doing this fine Sunday afternoon?" He grabbed Anabay's hand, interlocking her hand between both of his sweaty palms.

"I'm doing OK, Pastor," she replied, trying not to sound forlorn. She noticed the gold diamond rings he wore on each finger.

"Just OK? The Lord has blessed you to see another fine day and you're doing just OK?" he asked with a wide grin on his face. Pastor always appeared happy and he was passionate about inspiring others. "Where is your husband on this beautiful Sunday?"

"He was home when I left."

"I see. Sister Lillie Mae came to see me and shared with me about your temporary marital problems. She was hoping I could speak to you and your husband about the situation and give some good old spiritual guidance. Do you think he will come to see me?"

"Pastor, I don't even know my husband anymore. He is not the man I married."

"Hm, oh really. Well, don't be so dismayed. There is nothing God can't fix," he replied, while continuing to hold and pat her hand. "Would you be in agreement for me to stop by your home?"

"I would like that, but I never know when he's going to be home."

"I tell you what. You said he's home today, right?" Pastor looked as if a light bulb had been turned on in his head.

"He was when I left but there's no guarantee he's still home."

"Well, then, there is only one way to find out and there is no better time than today. Let's go into the Fellowship Hall, grab a bite to eat and we'll be on our way. Are you driving?"

"No."

"Well then, it will be my pleasure to drive you home."

Anabay didn't see Pastor again until after he had finished eating and greeting all the people. When he finally made his way over to the table where she was seated, she noticed a few of the women shooting dirty looks her way.

Pastor looked real handsome that day. He was dressed in an expensive, tailor-made, Italian wool, navy blue suit with a white shirt and a blue and white paisley print silk necktie with a matching pocket square, and black alligator shoes.

"Shall we be on our way, Sister Jones?"

"Yes."

Anabay felt all the evil looks and daggers thrown her way as she and Pastor made their way from the Fellowship Hall.

Pastor opened the passenger door and waited for her to get into his black shiny Cadillac sedan with personalized license plates, "Rev TIS III." The showy car was parked in his designated parking space directly in front of the church.

'Wow, what a gentleman! I imagine being a preacher's wife comes with a lot of first-class perks,' Anabay thought to herself as she settled into the front seat of the car. 'I've never been in such an expensive car. These leather seats are more comfortable than any chair I have at home.'

"Very nice car, Pastor!"

"Why, thank you, Sister Jones. A fine ride such as this should be referred to as an automobile."

"Oh, I see." Anabay felt silly, but she recognized her pastor's arrogance. "I know your wife must enjoy riding in this automobile."

"Well, if she does, it is only in spirit," he replied, laughing and looking into his rearview mirror before pulling out into traffic.

"What you mean, Pastor?"

"Well, Sister Jones, that's self-explanatory. Sister Tisdale's earthly body is deceased, but spiritually she walks beside the Lord."

"I'm so sorry, Pastor, I didn't know." 'Well, that explains why those fat ass women are in your face every Sunday,' Anabay thought to herself.

"Don't be sorry. Heaven is the ultimate place we are all striving for." He laughed. "I have been a widower for quite some time."

"You must get lonely."

"There's no time to get lonely when doing the Lord's work."

"This automobile is so fine! You don't feel a bump or a pothole. It's like riding on air," Anabay said, making small talk.

"Yes, that's luxury for you," he smiled as he turned on her block. "Aw, Sister Jones, I'm blessed to find parking right in front of your building." Pastor exited his vehicle, walked around and opened the door for Anabay.

Before entering her apartment building, Anabay overheard him talking to young boy standing outside. "Young man, I'll pay you a buck fifty to keep an eye on my fine ride. Make sure nobody touches it or even looks at it too hard. If they do, just whistle and I'll come running."

Claudale was stretched out on the sofa. He never heard them walk in.

Anabay shook him. "Claudale, get up. We have company."

"Damn it, woman, leave me alone!"

"Get up, Claudale! Reverend Tisdale is here!"

"What da?" Startled out of his sleep, Claudale jumped up from the sofa, causing him to be momentarily unsteady on his feet. "Hey, Reverend Tisdale," he said, then he quickly shifted his focus on Anabay, not giving Pastor a chance to respond. "Anabay! You siccing the Rev on me now? The Preacher! Are you serious?" he yelled.

"Brother Jones, calm down. There is no need for all of this uproar," Pastor Tisdale quickly interjected.

"No disrespect, Rev, but my wife brought you here in my home for what?"

"Brother Jones, I asked to come here and have a word with you."

"Pastor, growing up, my mama always taught me to never disrespect a preacher man. I know this is no social call and I don't appreciate my wife bringing you here, surprising me. But I'm going to follow my raising and hear what you got to say." Claudale plopped back down on the sofa.

"Well, then . . . Sister Jones, why don't you give us some time alone to talk?" asked Pastor.

Zenora Knight

Chapter 8

Just a Hiccup

"What a great paint job! I love it, Claudale!" Anabay was so happy and excited as she entered the small bedroom they were turning into a nursery. Claudale had spent the entire day painting while she sewed yellow and blue teddy bear curtains for the windows.

"Thank you. I wasn't too sure about this yellow color at first, but I like it now. It makes the room look airy and bright," he said, stepping back to admire his handiwork.

"I told you so. Maybe you should listen to your wife more often."

"I hope you know, sooner or later, we're going to have to change this color to blue, for our son," he winked, patting her on the belly.

"I can't wait to sit in here and rock our baby while reading nursery rhymes!" Anabay exclaimed.

"He's not going to be interested in nursery rhymes. I'm going to teach him how to hold a football from the minute he pops out," Claudale joked. "Matter of fact, I'm going to bring a football straight to the hospital."

"Oh really?"

"Yes, really. I'm going to pull the football out, right in the delivery room."

"I know you want a son, but it could be a girl."

"Yes, it could be, but the odds are, it's going to be a boy. My family produces boys, not girls. I have four brothers, remember? All jokes aside, it doesn't matter, so long as our baby is healthy and has his daddy's good looks," Claudale laughed while rubbing Anabay's stomach and pulling her in closer to him.

"Whatever! A baby boy or a baby girl can have their daddy's looks as long as they have their mommy's brain," Anabay said playfully, as she pulled away to answer the telephone.

"Oh, you're real funny, Anabay," he said, smiling at her as she exited the room.

Anabay didn't know what Pastor Tisdale did or what he said to her husband, but whatever transpired, it had worked a miracle on Claudale. He was back to his old self, the man she knew and loved. Happy days were here again. Claudale never revealed to her what the two of them discussed, and neither had Pastor.

They were equally excited about the arrival of their baby. It was three weeks before her due date and they had been spending every waking moment preparing and planning. Everything was pretty much done except a final decision on the baby's name.

When she returned to the nursery, Claudale was sitting in the middle of the floor, exhausted. He had been working from the time he got up and it was now late afternoon. "Who was on the phone?" he asked.

"Aunt Lillie Mae and Uncle Otis are on their way over here."

"I thought they left early this morning for the Poconos."

"I thought so too, but Aunt Lillie Mae said Uncle Otis couldn't get himself together, so they're leaving now. They want to stop by and see us."

"I know what this is all about," he said, sighing and knitting his eyebrows.

Anabay felt bad for her husband. Guilt and pain were written all over his face. She knew he deeply regretted how he had behaved upon learning of her pregnancy, causing everyone to lose faith in him. Although he was back to his old self, Aunt Lillie Mae and Uncle Otis were not completely comfortable leaving her under his watchful eye as they headed out of town to celebrate their anniversary.

"Uncle Otis doesn't trust me to take care of you and our baby. That's why they are coming over here," Claudale said.

"It's OK, Honey. They're just being overprotective, like old folks do sometimes--overbearing mother hens." Anabay knew Claudale was right but she was not about to make him feel any worse than he already felt. He was back at home with her, and that's all she cared about.

"Anabay, I know I caused all of this, but I'm still embarrassed--and I'm hurt no one trusts me. You probably don't trust me, either."

"I trust you. I'm your biggest fan. Just let them come over and see how well we're doing now. Let them have their say. They'll see, there's nothing to worry about and be on their way. That's all."

"All right. That's fine. I sure hope Uncle Otis don't come out of his mouth wrong to me because I'm a man and this is my house. I don't want to have to drop his old ass."

"Claudale! Don't say that." Anabay knew he was serious.

*****

Uncle Otis and Aunt Lillie Mae finally arrived. After engaging in some small talk, they handed Anabay a piece of paper with their contact information, and departed.

"See, Claudale, their visit wasn't that bad," Anabay commented, as they prepared for bed.

"Yeah, it was. Didn't you notice how he was looking at me, like he was sizing me up or something? Out of respect, though, I didn't say anything. I just let it go. Guess I deserved it for acting like a fool. Monday, on my way home from work, I'll stop by Montgomery Ward and pick up the crib," he said, quickly changing the subject.

"Not Sears?" Anabay knew the answer before she asked.

"Hell, no! You know I don't buy nothing from Sears."

"How well I know," she said, under her breath. Claudale and his mother blamed Sears Roebuck for his father losing his spark in life. He said his daddy devoted most of his life working for Sears Roebuck and then one day out of the blue, he was fired without any explanation. His daddy became very depressed, gave up on life, and eventually died, leaving his mama a widow with a house full of children.

*****

Claudale came home after work on Monday with the crib and a bunch of fresh flowers, purchased from the corner newsstand

"For you, Babycakes," he said, greeting Anabay with a kiss and handing the flowers to her.

"I love it, Honey!" she exclaimed, throwing her arms around him, giving him a peck on his lips. "Claudale, I'm so happy you're back to being yourself. I love you."

"I'm sorry about everything I put you through. I just had a relationship hiccup, I guess."

Claudale worked for hours putting the crib together and Anabay was happy--the happiest she had ever been in her life.

Chapter 9

A Friend Indeed

Claudale leaned over the bed and gave Anabay a quick goodbye kiss before grabbing his jacket and rushing out the door to the barbershop. He always left home early on Saturday mornings to get his hair cut, simply because he wanted to be the first in the chair. He never liked sitting around socializing and he hated it when the panhandlers and hustlers came into the barbershop, begging and trying to sell their hot merchandise. It distracted the barber, who took forever to cut his hair. He promised Anabay he would return by noon to take her to lunch and to see an early evening movie.

Anabay had a few hours to spare before he was due back so she continued lying in bed, staring up at the ceiling and thanking God for being so good to her. She was looking forward to spending the day with her husband. They had talked about how they wouldn't be able to be as free and spontaneous with their lives when the baby arrived. They had agreed to do as many adult things together as possible, before their lives changed forever.

Suddenly, Anabay had a burst of energy. She was feeling like she could run a marathon--the complete opposite of how she had been feeling. During the past several months, she had no energy whatsoever and was constantly dealing with swollen feet and backaches, all side effects of pregnancy. Now feeling pumped up, she practically leapt out of bed. She had a strong desire to clean, so she begin dusting and mopping, and changed the bed linens. 'Claudale is my king and he deserves to come home to a clean house,' she thought.

Anabay was feeling proud. She had cleaned their apartment from top to bottom and her energy level had not subsided. She decided to get dressed for their afternoon outing. Suddenly, she felt a tinkle of warm water streaming down between her legs.

'Oh, my goodness, bad timing!' was all she could think. Anabay knew there was no need to get excited, she wasn't due for another two weeks. Besides, she wasn't having any contractions. 'It's probably a false alarm triggered by all the housework,' she figured.

After she changed her damp underwear and finished dressing, she lay on the sofa to wait for Claudale. As a precaution, she was going to have him take her to the emergency room. She only hoped the wait in the E.R. would not be too long.

Anabay was awakened two hours later by stomach cramping, similar to menstrual cramps, but much stronger. 'No way is this a false alarm,' she thought to herself. 'I am in labor. Where is Claudale?' Thinking maybe he had returned but hadn't awakened her, she got up from the sofa and looked for him in their bedroom and in the kitchen, but he wasn't there. He was definitely late. Now, she was getting nervous.

She reached for the telephone to call for an ambulance, and to her surprise, there was no dial tone. Claudale had promised to pay the bill on his way from work yesterday. He knew it was the last day to pay before their service would be interrupted. It had never crossed her mind to ask him if he had taken care of the bill. The notion of the curse entered her mind. She hadn't given the curse a second thought since Pastor had visited and given Claudale an apparent strong talk that seemed to have set him straight.

Anabay was starting to shake and hyperventilate. Her legs felt wobbly. She made her way back to the sofa and sat down. She didn't know what she was going to do. "Let me think, let me think," she said aloud.

The barbershop was three blocks away. She knew Claudale wasn't still there--he never hung out there. Anabay sensed that he wasn't coming back any time soon. She could feel it in her bones. She worried, 'I should have never let my guard down--things were going too good to be true.' She knew firsthand what he was capable of. With her contractions getting stronger and closer in sequence, she knew she had to do something.

Aunt Lillie Mae and Uncle Otis were not expected back until tomorrow and she didn't have a telephone to call them with, anyway. Besides, they were too far away to help her. 'What am I going to do?' "Damn you,

Claudale!" she whimpered. There was no time to wonder about his whereabouts, she knew their baby was getting very close to making his or her grand entrance into the world. She had to get to the hospital. Then it dawned on her, 'The woman next door! She seems nice enough in passing. She's probably home. Today is Saturday, after all.'

Anabay had no choice. "Lord, please let this woman be home," she prayed in desperation. She swallowed her pride, walked as best she could across the hall and rang her doorbell.

She heard movement coming from inside the apartment and finally the door swung open. 'Thank you, Lord!" Anabay silently gasped. Through her pain, she could not help noticing how beautiful the woman looked. Matter of fact, just about every woman she saw these days looked stunning. Her neighbor was light-skinned, had a pixie haircut and looked to be medium height. Her lips were freshly painted with red lipstick as if she was expecting guests. Her skintight black pants showed off her curves.

Anabay took a deep breath. "I'm so sorry to bother you. I'm your neighbor from across the hall, apartment 2C. Do you have a telephone?"

"Of course, I have a telephone," her neighbor replied.

"Would you mind calling an ambulance for me?" Anabay asked, wincing in pain. "I'm in labor and my husband isn't home."

"Oh, shit!" the woman responded, looking terrified, as if she had been ambushed. She quickly gathered herself, and guided Anabay into her apartment, gently pulling on her arm. "Please, come in and have a seat on the sofa. Oh, hell, make yourself comfortable. Put your feet up. My name is Septi."

Septi definitely appeared nervous. "Damn! Let me pull myself together. There's no time for small talk." She scrambled for the telephone, accidentally dropping the receiver on the floor. "Fuck!" she blurted out, picking up the receiver. "I told you to put your feet up." Septi lifted Anabay's feet up, practically throwing her back onto the sofa.

"I'm calling now." Septi gave the address to the 911 operator. "Hold on a minute," she said, turning to Anabay, "What's your name?"

"Anabay Bailey Jones."

After the call ended, Septi slammed the receiver down. "I can't believe this shit is happening! Can I get you something? A towel? Water? What can I do? They are on their way."

"I'm OK. Oh, Jesus, I am in pain!" Anabay cried out, feeling faster and stronger contractions. She tried to sit up.

"Damn it! I told you to take it easy and to keep your feet up." Again, Septi rushed over and placed Anabay's feet back up on her black leather sofa.

"Your sofa is too beautiful!" Anabay moaned.

"Don't be silly. You're having a baby, for God's sake."

Between contractions Anabay's mind cleared a little. "I'm so sorry for imposing on you like this."

"Don't be ridiculous. Just be glad I was home. So, you are the wife to the man I see coming in and out next door?"

"Yes. Claudale. He's my husband and he's about to miss the birth of our baby." Anabay moaned again with a contraction. "He left this morning to get a haircut. I have no idea where he is. He should have been back by now," Anabay cried out again, gasping for breath.

"I pass by him all the time in the hallway. He's a bit arrogant, isn't he? He's probably with that bitch I see him with down at the bar. Oops! I'm sorry. I shouldn't have said that."

Anabay was not prepared for what Septi had just revealed. It confirmed what she already suspected. Her heart dropped. She wasn't sure if Septi just wasn't thinking when she blurted out about Claudale or if she said it intentionally and was apologizing to be polite. After that bombshell, Anabay didn't know what was coming first--a heart attack or her baby. She was in too much pain to question Septi about what she knew.

"Anyway, there's no time to think about him. You've got a baby to deliver!" Septi quickly changed the subject, trying her best to make light of things. "Where is the fucking ambulance? It's taking forever!" She walked over to the window and pulled back her curtains, hoping to glimpse an ambulance approaching.

Anabay moaned. "This is the worst pain I've ever experienced in my life. Maybe my husband was right."

"What?" Septi turned to Anabay with a puzzled look on her face. "Your husband was right about what?"

"He said babies are demons."

Septi was confused. "What the hell! Why would he say such a ridiculous thing?"

"After I told him I was pregnant, he said he didn't want any children. He changed for the worst. But after he met with our preacher, he changed his mind and was happy about us being pregnant." Anabay caught herself, 'Why am I telling this stranger my life story?' It was too late now and she was in too much pain to care. Besides, none of this would have happened if Claudale had come home.

"Wow! That's crazy. I don't know what I would do if I had a husband and he said some fucking shit like that to me! I probably would cut his dick off. He wouldn't have to worry. There would be no more babies--at least not from him."

"Well, Septi, that's the story."

"Your husband sounds like a real idiot. It's obvious he doesn't want to be married or be a father, because a child is a blessing from God."

Anabay inhaled and exhaled.

"That's exactly what I tried to get him to see at first, but it took our minister to help him to see it. How can babies be so sweet and cause so much pain?" Anabay cried out.

"It's called 'labor' for a reason," Septi chuckled, helping Anabay to find a more comfortable position.

The pain Anabay felt was unbearable, nothing like she had expected or imagined. "Lord of mercy, just take me now," she moaned.

"Hang in there. The ambulance should be here in a minute. It's a good thing this is your first baby because the first one usually takes a little longer to arrive. Try your best to take it easy, OK."

"I'm trying," Anabay gasped.

Septi knew she didn't like Claudale the minute she laid eyes on him, but talking to his wife just confirmed everything for her. 'There's no way I'm going to be friends with them as a couple,' she thought. 'That man is a real asshole!'

"I've never had a baby, but I know you are supposed to do some inhaling and exhaling. Come on, let's try it together. Inhale slowly through your nose and then exhale thought your mouth. How did that feel?"

"It didn't help!" Anabay moaned.

"Sorry." Septi continued talking, trying to help her relax. "Anabay, you have a unique name. I like it."

"Thanks." Anabay felt her most recent contraction start to subside. "Septi, your name is unusual too."

"I am named after my Italian father."

"You're Italian?"

"Half and half," Septi giggled. "Italian and black, but I go by black," she said, smiling as if she was informing Anabay of something that wasn't obvious.

"That's interesting." This was all Anabay could manage to say, bracing herself for another contraction.

"Yeah, it wasn't easy growing up as far as the interracial part goes. My parents moved to Italy a few years ago after my father retired." Septi never missed an opportunity to share her heritage with anyone.

Anabay sensed that deep down, her neighbor was proud to be the product of an interracial couple. Before she could respond, they heard sirens approaching.

"You hear that?" Septi jumped up and ran over to the window. "They're finally here. If I were in your place, I would have lost my fucking mind by now. Let me get the door."

Anabay could hear the relief in her voice.

Within a few minutes, a male and female paramedic rolled a stretcher into the apartment.

By now Anabay's contractions were coming closer and stronger. They were not letting up.

"Try to relax. Slowly inhale though your nose and exhale through your mouth," the female paramedic instructed, as they helped her off the sofa onto the stretcher.

In the midst of her pain, Anabay thought of Claudale. 'Here I am, going to the hospital to give birth to our child without him, and he's probably with that woman Septi was talking about. This is not the way things are supposed to be.' Anabay tried to chase away thoughts about the curse on the women in her family.

"Septi, please let Claudale know that I have gone to the hospital." Anabay wheezed, barely able to speak through her pain.

"He doesn't deserve to know shit!" Septi blurted out in front of the paramedics.

Anabay said nothing.

"Would you like for me to go with you to the hospital?" Septi asked.

"You would go with me?"

"Sure, I would. You shouldn't have to go alone, Girl! You need a friend."

Anabay felt a wave of gratitude to her neighbor. It was as if she had known her all her life.

Chapter 10

Bundle of Joy

Septi rubbed Anabay's shoulder as the paramedics rolled her out of their apartment building into the back of the waiting ambulance.

"Hang in there, Anabay," she kept repeating.

After the paramedics secured Anabay in the back of the ambulance, the driver turned on the siren and drove straight to Newark Beth Israel Hospital. Upon arrival, she was immediately rushed into the Delivery Room. Everything was happening so fast, there was no time for Anabay to think about her husband. She was grateful to her neighbor for being by her side. Septi stepped right into Claudale's role, holding her hand, wiping her face and comforting her.

"Push! You can do this," Septi said, mimicking the nurse and the doctor.

"No! I can't do this! It hurts! Oh, my God!" Anabay cried out.

"I can see the baby's crown! Mrs. Jones, I need you to give me a big push. Come on Mommy, you can do this!

"Anabay, you heard what the doctor said! Girl, you better push that baby out! You can to this, Anabay!

Brace yourself---breathe deeply and then push like hell!" Septi was really into the birthing experience.

The doctor and the nurse laughed, telling Septi that she had missed her calling. They both agreed that she was an excellent birthing coach.

"Hell, no! I'm not cut out for this shit!" Septi blurted out.

Anabay felt like her insides were being used as a punching bag by a heavyweight boxer, while the outside of her body was being pummeled with a heavy-duty linked chain, simultaneously. The pain was a million times worse than any monthly cramping she had ever experienced.

"I can't do this! I will never have another baby!" she cried out before giving it one big push, this time bringing her child into the world. She was overcome with joy, hearing her baby crying for the first time.

"It's a boy. Good job, Mommy!" Dr. Olu Obi, the Nigerian doctor, announced with his thick accent. He looked at Septi, "Do you want to cut the umbilical cord?"

"Anabay, do you want me to do it?"

"Yes, please, Septi." Anabay wished Claudale was here to share this special moment with her, but the reality was, he wasn't there and she was surrounded by strangers.

"Babyboy Jones!" Dr. Obi said as he held the baby in the palms of his hands and lifted him high up in the air like he was doing some kind of Kunta Kinte ritual. "You are born to do great things," he said before handing him off to the nurse.

"8 pounds, 8 ounces--a healthy baby boy! He's a real cutie," the nurse said, placing the baby in his mother's arms.

Anabay's eyes filled with tears of joy as she held her baby. "Oh my God, he is so beautiful and innocent," she cried. "He is a bundle of joy."

"Yes, he is definitely beautiful, and so sweet," Septi said, joyfully watching Anabay ooh and ah over her son.

"Thank you, Septi. I don't know what I would have done without you."

"You're welcome, Anabay. You're a real trooper. I never knew birthing a child was so amazing. Thank you for allowing me to be a part of your experience."

"Do you hear yourself thanking me? Septi, you are a very special person. You took the time to help someone you just met. I truly appreciate all you have done for me. I mean it, from the bottom of my heart."

"Don't be silly. A sister has to help another sister out in a time of need," Septi smiled and then she started ranting about men. "One thing I've learned--you can't depend on most men for anything and I don't care if they're your husband or your boyfriend! They are all unreliable," she said, with a look on her face like she hated men.

Anabay's happy moment was being spoiled by Septi's ranting but she wasn't about to say anything to her, because she had helped her out in a big way. Anabay didn't want to appear ungrateful.

"Septi, I need another favor."

"What is it? Just ask."

"Please go home and see if Claudale is there and let him know I'm in the hospital with our son."

"I am not doing that. I thought I made myself clear." Septi frowned and rolled her eyes.

Anabay could tell Septi was serious, but she needed her to do this for her. "Why not?" she pleaded.

"He doesn't deserve to know," Septi snapped, raising her voice.

"Septi, it's not about what you think of him right now. He is my husband and the father of my child. He does have the right to know, regardless of how you feel about him."

"Sure, he has the right to know. I also have the right to say what I will do and what I won't do."

Anabay was completely puzzled how this woman could switch from being so helpful to being so stubborn. "Why are you being so hard on him? You don't even know him?"

"Listen Anabay, I want to be your friend, but between you and me, right now I need to keep my distance from that man of yours. If I see his ass, I will have a few not-so-nice choice words for him. I have no tolerance for a man who mistreats a woman, period! As a matter of fact, I'm surprised you want him to come running to your bedside. Look at the shit he's put you through. I feel sorry for your ass!"

Anabay turned away and faced the wall. She didn't want to talk to her or look at her any longer.

"So, what's your son's name?" Septi asked, breaking the silence and acting like she hadn't just insulted Anabay.

"I don't know," Anabay answered abruptly.

"Are you upset with me?" Septi asked, clearly knowing the answer before asking the question.

"That's why I need my husband here--to help select a name."

"That's crazy! You mean to tell me you two haven't even picked out a name? You guys knew you were having a baby. What kind of shit is that?" Septi chuckled.

Anabay had never heard a woman curse as freely as Septi.

Zenora Knight

Chapter 11

Bitter Sweet

T he next morning, Anabay woke up expecting to find her husband sitting by her bedside. Why hadn't she heard from him? She was really disappointed and dumbfounded. She knew, despite Septi's threat not to tell him that she had given birth, her newfound friend couldn't possibly be that cold. After all, this woman had gone out of her way to help her. Anabay convinced herself--Claudale knew and he was on his way to the hospital to see her and their son.

*****

Septi marched into Anabay's hospital room around eleven o'clock, not looking like her usual spunky self. Something was definitely bothering her.

"How is the new mommy feeling today?" she asked, placing a vase of fresh cut flowers on the hospital tray table. Then she walked over to the window and opened the blinds, letting the sunlight flow in. "You're lucky to be in the bed next to the window," she commented, smiling at Anabay. Septi could tell by the look of disappointment on her new friend's face, she wasn't happy to see her. It was apparent, she was hoping for her husband.

"I feel pretty good. Just wondering why Claudale hasn't come here," Anabay responded in a low, strained voice.

"Do you like the flowers? I bought a present for your son. It's just an outfit for him to wear home." Septi handed Anabay a baby blue shopping bag.

"Thank you. You shouldn't have--you have already done too much. I don't know how we'll ever be able to pay you back." Anabay politely forced a smile.

"Who's we?"

"Claudale and myself, of course." Anabay was taken aback by her question. She was miffed that Septi sill wasn't acknowledging her husband.

Now, she had her answer. Septi hadn't reached out to Claudale and told him about the birth of their son. Anabay found it hard to believe how this woman could be so insensitive by not putting aside her personal feelings for something as important as this. She wanted Septi to leave.

"Well, I'm not looking for you to pay me back. That's what friends are for." Septi cleared her throat.

"You didn't tell Claudale, did you? That explains why he isn't here."

Septi shifted her body toward the window and looked out.

Anabay was feeling annoyed. "Septi, why didn't you let Claudale know I gave birth? You know my home phone is disconnected and I can't call him."

"Anabay, I just want to be a friend to you and your son, that's it." Septi had every intention of telling Claudale that his wife had given birth, had he come home last night. She was here today just to be a much-needed friend.

Septi sighed and hung her head. "Well, you're going to need a friend, especially in the days ahead of you."

"What are you saying?" Anabay didn't like the way Septi was acting. She figured this woman was either just plain crazy or something was wrong and she just wasn't saying.

"Your husband. . . "

"What about my husband?" Just tell me the truth! Did you see him moving out last night?" Anabay was really worried now, more so than ever. Before Pastor Tisdale's intervention, Claudale had threatened to leave her and move back home.

Septi hesitated. She was having a difficult time finding the words to tell Anabay what she knew. A part of her wished she hadn't opened her door for this woman, but she didn't believe in mere coincidences. The universe sent Anabay to her door so she could help her. 'After all,' Septi thought, 'I do have a Master's Degree in Social Work.'

"Just tell me," Anabay demanded.

"I don't know how to tell you this, other than just to say it. Last night when I got back home, the police were knocking on your door."

"The police! Is Claudale in jail? He promised me--he would stay out of trouble." Anabay looked confused.

 "Anabay, police don't come to your door to notify family of an arrest."

 "What are you saying?"

Septi could see the frustration on her friend's face. Just as she was about to speak, a middle-aged, stone-faced, black man wearing a gray suit walked into the room.

"Good morning," he said, glancing at Septi and giving her a familiar look, like he knew her.

"Who are you?" Anabay asked, disappointed that this was the second person coming to visit her who was not her husband.

 "My name is Detective Tucker with the Newark Police Department." He flashed his badge. "Are you Mrs. Jones?"

"Yes, I'm Mrs. Jones."

"I am so sorry to inform you that your husband was murdered last night. He was the victim of a tragic, senseless crime and I promise you, I'm going to do everything in my power to catch the person responsible

for his death." He sounded like a programed robot.
Then he reached out for her hand.

Anabay quickly jerked her hand back. "Don't touch me!
Get out! Get out! Claudale is not dead and you know it!
Get out!" she yelled before blacking out.

A few hours later, Anabay awakened to see Uncle Otis
and Aunt Lillie Mae by her bedside. Her aunt was
holding her hand and wiping her forehead with a wet
towel and humming, "God Will Take Care of You," an old
gospel song. She immediately stopped humming when
Anabay opened her eyes.

"I'm so sorry, Baby," Aunt Lillie Mae tearfully cried out.
Then she crawled into Anabay's bed and wrapped her
arms around her grand-niece, consoling her.
"Everything's going to be all right. Let it all out. Go
ahead and cry," she said repeatedly. "Tell the Lord all
about your troubles."

"It was my stubbornness--my damn stubbornness
caused all of this. Now, Claudale is dead because of me,
because of me!" Anabay cried.

Uncle Otis was sitting at the foot of Anabay's bed with
his head buried in his hands. "We shouldn't have gone
away on our trip. I knew he was struggling, but I
thought he was going to pull through. I sure hope they
catch that creep that did this to him. He needs to rot in
Hell!"

After a couple hours more of crying and asking "Why?"
Anabay composed herself enough to listen to her aunt

and uncle's advice. She knew she had to find the strength to go on without her husband. Her number one priority had to now be her baby boy.

They explained that Claudale had been stabbed the previous night after he got into a dispute with some man over a dollar, while gambling. They assured her-- Claudale loved her very much and he would always be with her in the spirit.

Their words were comforting to Anabay, but they didn't make her feel any better. She felt nothing but anger and deep sorrow. She was beginning to believe that she, too, was another victim of the family curse.

"What happened, exactly?" Anabay cried out, wanting to hear the story again. She secretly hoped this was all a mistake or a bad dream.

After hearing the tragic details again, she felt light-headed and lifeless. "Oh, dear God, tell me it's not so," she cried hysterically.

Uncle Otis and Aunt Lillie Mae agreed to make the final arrangements for Claudale. Before leaving, they assured her they would be back tomorrow.

*****

The next morning Septi walked into Anabay's hospital room and found her curled up in bed, in the dark, looking miserable. "Good morning, my little mommy. How are you doing this morning?" She turned the lights on and opened the window blinds.

"Not well," Anabay sobbed.

"You need to sit up. It'll make you feel better. You haven't even touched your breakfast. You need to eat to keep your strength up," Septi said, clearly trying to lighten up the atmosphere.

"I don't feel like sitting up or eating right now." Anabay could barely lift her head off her pillow.

"Have you seen your son this morning?"

"No."

"Come on, Anabay! Life is for the living, not the dead. You need to snap out of your funk. I'm going to ask the nurse to bring him in to you?"

"No, not now," Anabay snapped.

"OK, have it your way."

"My baby is fine. They said they're going to bring him in here soon."

"So, has anyone else been here to see you?"

"Yeah, my aunt and uncle. They told me everything. It's hard to believe people can be so mean. My husband's life was snatched away from him over a one-dollar bill. Four quarters." Anabay wept.

"Yes, people can be evil. It's an unfortunate thing," Septi agreed. She could tell from Anabay's red and swollen eyes that she had been crying a lot. "Did they tell you that they pronounced him dead downstairs in the emergency room?"

"No, Septi, they spared me those details." Anabay wiped her tear-filled eyes.

"Well, Girl, I got that information from the police! Just think about it. While you were here upstairs, your husband was downstairs fighting for his life. That's some wicked shit! I'm sure if they had known, they would have rolled you downstairs to see him before he took his final breath. They said he fought for his life like a champ!"

"Septi, you are unbelievable," Anabay whimpered, shaking her head.

"There's more. The police said he probably would have lived had he not been so hotheaded and chased the man who stabbed him. This caused him to lose a massive amount of blood."

Anabay was beside herself with grief. She cried out, "Why are you telling me all of this?"

"Because you need to know the truth. You will never know now if he would have stepped up and been a father to his child."

"Enough! Enough, I can't take anymore!" Anabay wailed.

A heavy-set Jamaican nurse, who was attending to Anabay's roommate, pulled back the curtains. She looked annoyed. "Excuse me," she said in a thick Jamaican accent, shaking and pointing her finger at

Septi. "You, Young Lady, you got loose lips and you speak with an untamed tongue. You are very inappropriate. What is your intention? To make this lady sick? And you call yourself her friend!"

"Give me a fucking break, Lady!" Septi snapped at the nurse. "She's only had a baby, not a fucking heart transplant. She has every right to know the details of her husband's death."

"I beg your pardon?" The nurse took a step forward.

"You heard what I said," Septi continued snaring at the nurse.

"Miss, I'm going to have to ask you to leave or I'm going to call security. You are upsetting the patient. This is a hospital. People need peace and quiet to get well. This woman been through enough!"

"Go on and call Security. I don't give a damn. They're probably just as incompetent as you and the rest of the staff in this shithole! I was leaving anyway. You aren't worth my time." Septi walked towards the door.

"You need to help her look after her baby instead of torturing her," the nurse fired back.

"The hell with you, Lady!" Septi hissed. "Do your fucking job and mind your goddamned business. Anabay, I'd better leave before I go off on this bitch." Septi stormed out of the room.

Three days later, Anabay and Delbert Claudale Jones were discharged from the hospital. They moved in with Uncle Otis and Aunt Lillie Mae.

Uncle Otis shipped Claudale's body back home to Virginia for a proper burial.

 Anabay felt a lot of guilt over her husband's death, but she believed in life after death. As she mourned, she kept reminding herself, 'There will be joy in the morning.'

Chapter 12

New Gig

After a brief stay with Aunt Lillie Mae and Uncle Otis, Anabay and her son moved back to her apartment. Two years later, she accepted a job as a bookkeeper at the Brunswick Correctional Facility. The salary was good and the benefits were excellent. The only thing she hated about working there was the sound of the big steel gates slamming shut and locking her inside. It was a sound she never got used to.

Those nearest and dearest to her were not happy about her working at the prison--but a job was a job, money was money, and she had to do what she had to do to survive, now that she was a single parent. Although she loved waitressing and interacting with the public, the income simply was not enough to sustain her and Delbert. After reimbursing Uncle Otis for Claudale's funeral, she placed the balance of his life insurance proceeds in a savings account.

Anabay did her best to adapt to her new work environment, except for the sound of the gates. The only difference between civilians who worked in the prison system and the inmates was, at the end of the day, the civilians went home. The realization that one could potentially be at the mercy of inmates, because they certainly outnumbered the few people who worked there, concerned her. Every day, she prayed to God for protection.

She gave up attending classes at the Culinary Institute because she didn't have the time, between working full time and taking care of Delbert. These days, she needed to take things nice and slow, one day at a time. Very often, she would give herself pep talks: "Sink or swim. I can do this. I have to do this alone. Help me, Jesus."

Aunt Lillie Mae and Uncle Otis kept Delbert while she worked. This was a big relief to her, knowing her baby boy was being well taken care of.

Living next door to Septi had both advantages and disadvantages. It was nice having Septi around to talk to. On the other hand, Septi was hard to take sometimes, with her bossy ways and stream of opinions. Anabay will never forget how Septi reacted when she told her about her new job at Brunswick Correctional Facility.

"A job in a prison! Anabay, have you lost your mind?"

 "Look, Septi, here we go again. You are not the boss of me. You think you know everything. A job is a job. "

"Anabay, I don't think I know everything. But as your friend, I don't like the idea of you working in a prison. You can't be that desperate!" Septi's hands were on her hips and she was glaring at her with those big eyes of hers.

 "It has nothing to do with being desperate. . . "

"If it's not about desperation, then what the hell is it about? Will you please tell me, because I must be missing something?"

"Let me see. Oh, I know what it is. A paycheck!"

"Anabay, I'm just concerned about you. You are so naive!"

"I'm a grown woman. I can handle myself."

"I know all of that," Septi replied, "but it has nothing to do with what I'm trying to say. It's just that you're working around all those low-life, scum-of-the-earth jailbirds. It's a dangerous place to work. As a single mother, you need to think about your son."

"You're partly right. But working there is not that bad."

"Oh really! Since when? Those prisoners can riot at any time and you could die. Those motherfuckers don't give a damn about anyone."

"There might be a good man or two in there. You know, with a little rehabilitation and the love of a good woman, a man can be turned around," Anabay said looking and sounding serious, even though she was just baiting Septi.

"Now I know you done lost your damn mind! Are you sick?"

"I'm only kidding." Anabay burst out laughing so hardm she almost cried. It felt so good to her, getting the best of Septi.

"That's not funny."

"Well, don't worry about me. I have everything under control. Besides, no man will ever take Claudale's place in my heart or my bed."

"I certainly hope you are in control of yourself because I know what I am talking about."

"Are you speaking from experience?"

"Change the subject."

"I'm sorry. I didn't mean to hit a nerve." Anabay could see that she was getting under her friend's skin and she was enjoying every minute of it.

Working in a prison was not Anabay's dream job, but it definitely was an unusual experience. Nonetheless, she was determined to give it her best shot. The worst part of the job was seeing all those men, young and old, in the system. 'No wonder there's not enough men around--they're all locked up,' she thought.

Prison was like a city behind walls. Some inmates just stood around while others were busy scrambling from place to place. The correctional officers were essentially patrolling policemen.

Anabay never allowed herself to get distracted by the inmates whistling and calling out to her, making her feel like a juicy hamburger with legs. Instead, she focused on her work. Whenever she walked across the prison yard, she always heard the same old lines, "Hey, Miss Tang, you sure looking good, girl. I wish I could go past these gates with you at five." She would simply smile politely because being pleasant might just one day save her life.

Anabay would never forget the day she met Kandy. She found it hard to believe someone so handsome and charming could end up in a correctional institution. He didn't look like the typical inmate, he didn't walk or talk like an inmate and he certainly didn't smell like an inmate. But he was indeed a prisoner, Inmate #555252. Kandy stood about 6'2", had a deep brown complexion, broad muscular shoulders, and nice thick lips. His beautiful smile lit up the room every time he flashed it. He was an inmate trustee who worked in the bookkeeping office, primarily on prisoner cash accounts.

Kandy always carried himself like he was somebody. Anabay had a gut feeling about him; surely, he had to have been successful at some point in his life. She wondered what he did to cause himself to be locked up. Every morning, he would wait for her to arrive and escort her across the courtyard to the business office. Of course, this didn't stop the other inmates from whistling and catcalling out to her.

"Hey, Miss Ana. How are you doing today? I must say, you look lovely as usual." Kandy would repeat this greeting to her everyday like a parrot. He never called her by her full name, just Miss Ana. There was something about the way he said Miss Ana that made her feel a twinge of discomfort.

"I'm doing well, Kandy. What about yourself?"

"I'm doing wonderful now that you're here."

She didn't want to be rude, since he appeared to be such a nice man who'd probably had a bad break in life. So she ignored his little pickup lines--but she still yearned to know his story. Sometimes, she would notice him staring at her and she definitely received the vibe that he liked her a lot.

"It's been a long day, Miss Ana. You have a good evening."

"You too, Kandy."

Anabay straightened up her desk, grabbed her purse and rushed out of the office to catch the #25 Express bus. She needed to pick up Delbert before six o'clock because Aunt Lillie Mae had choir rehearsal this evening. A car certainly would have made life easier for her, but there was no way she could afford one right now.

*****

"Delbert! Mommy's here!"

Delbert was always happy to see his mommy, even though he never lacked for love and attention from his aunt and uncle. Anabay was ever so grateful to Aunt Lillie Mae for potty training him. This had been a big help to her.

"Hi, Mommy," Delbert said excitedly, as he ran into her outreached arms.

"How's my big boy?"

"Fine. Mommy, can we go to the toy store on the way home?"

"Not today, Delbert. You have enough toys."

"Please! Mommy, please!"

"Delbert, what did we talk about the last time you asked for a toy?"

"You said I can't buy a toy every day."

"And why, Delbert?"

"Because money don't grow on trees," he answered, with his head hanging down, sulking.

"That's right. I'm glad you remem ....."

"Money is on trees, Mommy. You just can't reach it."

"Pardon me, Delbert Jones."

"Just playing, Mommy."

Delbert was three years old, and Anabay recognized there was a void in his life by not having a father.

Although she was doing her very best, she still felt guilty about not being able to provide a two-parent home for her son.

*****

'What an exhausting day this turned out to be,' Anabay thought to herself. Sleep was not coming easy tonight. She tossed and turned all night, while burying her face deep within her pillow trying to block out the sound of those big steel doors slamming shut and locking her inside the prison.

Chapter 13

Cell Block D

"Yo, Kandy, you sleep, man?" asked Juice, Kandy's next-door neighbor in Cell Block D.

"Naw, Juice, what's up?"

"Can we talk with mirrors?"

"Hell no! I don't want to see your crusty black ass. Say what you got to say."

"So, what's happening with you and that pussy I see you with all the time."

"Why, Juice? You jealous?"

"Naw, man. I just know when you up to something."

"You wrong this time, Bro."

"What's up then? I see the two of you walking across the yard talking all the time."

"We work together, Fool."

"Talk to me," Juice insisted.

"Well, to tell you the truth, she's a prissy, stuck-up bitch. I don't think she's been fucked in years. She's going to explode when I stick my dick in her pussy. I just know it," said Kandy.

"Man, how many women you going to destroy?" Juice asked.

"You don't know what the hell you're talking about. This one is a keeper."

"I never heard you talk about a split like this before."

"Man, did you forget that I'm about to be paroled?"

"You one slick mother! What about your wife and kids?" asked Juice.

"What's it to you? You don't give a damn about my wife and kids. You just concerned about your own ass."

Juice was a five foot, eight inch, deep chocolate, overweight gay man who loved being incarcerated. He hated the responsibility of providing for himself--and besides, prison provided him with all the play he could handle and more.

"You dumping your wife?" Juice asked.

"Hell no! Maybe at first. She'll wait for me like she always does."

"That's some rough shit, Dude!"

"Who the hell are you to judge me? You're the one who is always looking for somebody to stick their dick up your big ugly ass." Kandy let out a rasping chuckle.

"Say what you want about me, at least I don't go around hurting people like you do!"

"I always end up back home with Justine, but there's nothing like the smell of a new pussy. It's like that new car smell--makes you want to ride it all the time. Once that new smell is gone and it's banged up, it's just another old pussy. You can take it or leave it."

"You are disgusting! Bet'cha you wouldn't want some dude to treat your mama or daughter like that, would you, Man?" Juice sounded unusually serious.

"Stop preaching to me with your fat ass. We're not talking about my mama or my daughter and stop asking me so many goddamn questions. I got to play it cool until the time is right, then I'll bang it. You know how the game works."

"Whatever you say, Man."

"Look, Juice, the bottom line is you're just worried I might cut your fat ass off. And I just might do that unless you chill your ass out."

"I know how to remain cool. It's just that I have needs too. "

Kandy sucked his teeth, "Carry your bitch ass off to sleep! I got a lot of thinking to do."

"Do you want to meet me in the shower in the morning?" Juice was only half-teasing. "Officer Diggs is in charge of the cell block in the morning and you know how he rolls. Hope I see you."

'Juice is one fucking, needy, pathetic queen,' Kandy thought to himself, before drifting off to sleep with Anabay on his mind.

Chapter 14

Caught Off Guard

Delbert barreled into Anabay's bedroom, shouting at the top of his lungs, "Mommy, wake up! Wake up! It's time to go to Aunt Lillie Mae's house! I'm her helper today!"

"Morning, Sweetie Pie. You're up mighty bright and early," Anabay managed to utter, sounding sleepy. 'The alarm clock hasn't even gone off yet,' she thought to herself.

"Mommy, I am helping Aunt Lillie Mae today!"

"Helping Aunt Lillie Mae--aren't you special! Climb into bed with mommy for a few minutes."

"No, Mommy, we have to hurry!" Delbert was anxiously tugging on her comforter.

Anabay observed that her son was looking more and more like his father. She couldn't help thinking how much Claudale would have loved his little boy.

"Get up, Mommy! Get up!"

"What are you helping Aunt Lillie Mae do?"

"Bake coconut pies!"

"Oh, that's really nice. How many pies are you baking?"

"Aunt Lillie Mae said lots of pies! More pies than I have fingers!"

"Well, we better get you ready then. That's a lot of baking."

"I know, Mommy. When I am bigger, I won't need Aunt Lillie Mae. I can bake them all by myself. Right, Mommy?"

"Yes, Baby, you'll be able to bake them all by yourself with your very own little hands."

"Mommy, you're so silly!" Delbert giggled.

"Why?"

"Because my hands will be big hands when I am bigger!"

"You are so smart! Last one in the bathroom is a rotten egg!"

"OK, me first!" Delbert took off running down the hallway, laughing all the way.

* * * * *

Anabay was free to concentrate on her job after dropping Delbert off. She was looking forward to interacting with Kandy at work. She had to admit, she was very much attracted to him. He excited her and frightened her at the same time.

Walking into the prison and hearing those doors slam shut and lock made her jump every time. Although she had been working at the prison for a while, it was a sound she could not get used to.

Kandy was waiting for her on the other side of the gates dressed in a freshly pressed blue denim shirt and starched blue denim jeans, the standard inmate uniform.

"Hey, Miss Ana, how are you doing today? I must say, you are looking lovely as always."

"Good morning, Kandy."

"Should we head straight to work or should we stop by the diner for coffee first?"

"That's funny, Kandy, I don't see a diner."

"I know, Miss Ana. I'm just using my imagination about what life will be like for us on the outside," he winked.

"Wait a minute, Kandy. What are you talking about? What do you mean?"

Kandy remained silent. He stared straight ahead, avoiding all eye contact with her. When they arrived at the business office, he stood back like a gentleman and allowed her to unlock the door and walk in first.

Anabay immediately turned on the lights and looked around to make sure everything was in order before sitting down at her desk. She wondered, 'Us on the outside! What in the world is he talking about?'

"Kandy, I'm disturbed by what you just said, about 'Us on the outside.' I need to say something to you."

"I figured you would. I have something to say too, but ladies first."

"OK, I'll go first. I hope you understand what I'm about to say. It appears I've made a big mistake befriending you and permitting you to call me by my first name. It goes against the rules and regulations of the prison."

"Oh, I see!" he sighed.

"When I was hired, this is one of the first things they stressed during orientation--do not get personal with the inmates. It's considered a breach of security."

"I thought I was more than just an inmate to you." Kandy rolled his eyes and folded his arms across his chest.

Anabay was completely floored. She wondered to herself, 'Why he would say such a thing. Have I missed something?' "Well, Kandy, you are an inmate and my job is very important to me. I have a little boy at home who depends on me. I can't afford to lose my job."

"Miss Ana, I know all about your son and your life. Your little boy also needs a father."

"Excuse me?"

"Look, I'm sure you're a great mom, but face it, you will never fill the shoes of a father."

"Listen, Kandy, you're out of place. How do you know so much about me anyway? I never shared my personal life with you."

"No, you haven't. In here, we can find out anything we want to know. I've listened to you. Now, you need to hear me out."

"But I wasn't finished."

Kandy had a furious look in his eyes. He stood up and placed his hands on her desk and leaned forward, staring directly into her eyes.

Anabay felt unsafe for the first time since working with Kandy. He was in prison, after all, and she didn't know why. He could have murdered his wife or he could be a serial killer. She prayed silently to God for protection.

"Don't say another word. I know where you're coming from. Now, listen to me, woman. I can't help what happened to me but, trust me, I am not your typical inmate. I am a man who is doing time! This place does not define me. When I walk out of here, I will be the same man that walked in here. You better believe me, I'm one hell of a man!"

"That's great, Kandy, but what does this have to do with me."

"Miss Ana, we both damn well know you have feelings for me. Why deny it?"

'Oh, my God! Maybe he sensed I haven't had sex in a long time. I hope I haven't been that obvious. Damn! It's the Curse,' Anabay thought to herself. "Yes Kandy, I do have feelings for you--but as a person, not as my man."

"That's a crock of bullshit!" he snapped back.

"Look, Kandy, I don't want to offend you, but I need my job."

"Forget about this damn job. Jobs come and go. We are talking about us. When you have a chance at love, you better grab it."

"Us! What do you mean us and love?" Anabay was caught off guard and completely perplexed by what he was saying.

"Just stop it, Miss Ana! You're a grown-ass woman! Act like it!"

"You have no right to speak to me like this!" Anabay began feeling for the panic button underneath her desk.

"As your future man, I have all the right in the world. Put aside where we are right now and don't press that button. Don't do it," said Kandy, in a calm voice.

Anabay quickly put her hand back on top of her desk. She didn't want to set him off. "Kandy, I would be lying if I didn't admit that I like you and that I find you attractive. I happen to think that you are a wonderful person but what I feel doesn't change the facts----"

"What facts? That I am an inmate that you happen to be in love with?"

"This conversation is over, Kandy! Over right now!" Anabay mustered up enough nerve to speak firmly.

"Look at you--so cute, raising your voice. Miss Ana, I can tell that you are a sophisticated woman, but you cannot hide your thirst for love. Your desire for me is all over your face. Being in here does not make me less of a man. Matter of fact, it makes me more of a man for surviving this shit. I'll be out of here soon. Don't miss an opportunity to accept love because you can't see beyond what's in front of your eyes."

Anabay couldn't believe he was being so insistent. "Excuse me!" she responded.

"You need to understand this--being here in this prison, doesn't make me desperate for a woman. Don't fool yourself, even in here, more pussy is being thrown in my face than you can ever imagine. I choose you. I am a damn good man and I am offering to take care of you, to comfort you, to make love to you, and to be there for you in every way possible. I promise you this, you won't find another man out there who's willing to shower you with love and affection, like me. Miss Ana, I know I can give you the life you deserve when I get out of here."

Anabay was feeling weak and vulnerable, like her knees were caving in from underneath, but she managed to stand up. She put on her serious face, looked him square in his eyes and said, "Right now, Kandy, you are making me real uncomfortable."

"The truth always hurts."

"You are twisting my words up, Kandy!"

"I don't think so. What's it going to be, Miss Ana? A real woman would be true to herself. You are a real woman, aren't you?"

He moved in closer to her, staring directly into her eyes. She could smell his spearmint breath. He grabbed her hands and placed them around his neck, before wrapping his muscular arms around her.

"Miss Ana, when was the last time a real man hugged you and squeezed you real tight like this? Oh, you smell so good, Baby. Just trust me. I'm going to make you happy. Everything's going to be all right. Just give this man permission, Miss Ana, to love you," he whispered.

Anabay stood there speechless and paralyzed, melting in his arms. She could feel his dick pressing against her pelvis and she didn't resist when he planted his lips on her lips. His warm tongue tasted so good and sweet to her as it moved deeper and deeper into her throat. Without realizing it, she had surrendered and was kissing him back, passionately. Their two tongues were intertwining like two snakes mating.

Suddenly, she snapped back to her senses and jerked away from him. "Kandy, this can never happen again!" Anabay was upset with herself for allowing an inmate to cross the line with her and put her job in jeopardy. If they had been caught kissing, she would have been fired on the spot, no questions asked. He, on the other hand, would have been hailed a hero and received high fives from the other inmates.

"Why did you pull away, Baby? You just going to leave me hanging like this?" asked Kandy with outstretched arms, looking down at his crotch.

"Kandy, I'm going to tell you one last time--there is no us, nor will there ever be an us! Leave me the hell alone!"

Zenora Knight

Chapter 15

The Dreamer

Anabay was a nervous wreck after her encounter with Kandy. Her mind was racing out of control. 'Maybe someone saw us kissing ... What if there was a hidden camera in the office ... I'm going to lose my job, 'and on and on.' To make matters worse, Kandy was walking around with a smug look of satisfaction on his face, letting her know he had played her like a fiddle. She couldn't take the tension anymore, so she pretended to be sick and left work early.

Her first stop was Aunt Lillie Mae's to pick up Delbert, but they were out delivering pies. When Aaron volunteered to bring Delbert home, she was more than grateful to him. She couldn't wait to get home and jump in her bed.

Anabay was unlocking her apartment door when she heard a familiar voice. "Good God, not today," she mumbled to herself. 'I'm not in the mood for her two cents today.'

"Anabay, are you OK?" asked Septi.

"Yes, Septi, I'm fine. Why do you ask?"

"I called your job and they said you left early."

"I'm fine. I'm just tired, that's all."

"Tired from what?"

"Why were you calling me? You know I'm not supposed to accept personal calls, unless it's important. Did you forget? I work in a prison."

"Relax. I just called to see how your day was going in lock-up," Septi answered, sarcastically.

"My day was hectic. I'm going to lay down and get some rest now."

"You should have listened to me. I told you working in that prison was not the job for you."

"I'm fine. The job is fine. See you later, Septi."

"Where is Delbert?"

"Aaron is bringing him home."

"That loser! I wouldn't let him within ten feet of my child."

"Septi, must you always be so negative?"

"Call me whatever you want, but I can sure spot a loser when I see one."

"See you later, Septi. I'm going to take a nap before Delbert arrives."

"Suit yourself."

Septi returned to her apartment and sat by the window, waiting for Delbert and Aaron. As soon as she spotted them, she went and stood in front of her door.

"Hi, Delbert. Are you OK?"

"I'm OK, Aunt Septi. You saw me coming down the street?"

"I sure did. I couldn't wait to kiss those cute cheeks of yours." Septi hugged Delbert and smothered his face with kisses. He giggled.

"Good evening to you, too. You're looking beautiful as always." Aaron had a big grin on his face, showing all thirty-two pearly whites.

"Hello, Aaron," Septi had a cheesy smile on her face.

"Damn, you said Hello Aaron, like it killed you or something." Aaron was sounding dramatic.

"Well, what can I say?" Septi shrugged her shoulders.

"You didn't have to come out of your apartment. Nobody was coming to see you anyway," Aaron responded, trying to get under her skin.

"I'm just looking out for Delbert."

"He doesn't need you to look out for him. He's with me. Hello! He is my cousin, my blood. We are related. Did you forget?"

"No, I didn't forget--that's the problem. What's in the bag?"

"Look at you! You didn't halfway speak to me, now you're being all nosy. If you really must know, I brought two bottles of champagne to celebrate with Anabay. My multi-million-dollar clothing line is about to be launched."

"Oh, really," Septi was skeptical.

"Yes, really. I met an agent who knows Magic Johnson and he showed him my sports jerseys. Magic loved them! The NBA will be wearing my jerseys next season! The contract is being written as we speak. I'm in the money, Girlfriend!"

"That's wonderful, Aaron!" Septi had a wide smile on her face.

"Listen to you--changing your tune already! Money talks, don't it?" Then, Aaron mocked her, "That's wonderful Aaron," switching into a high-pitched girly voice.

"I could care less about you or your deal," Septi said, curtly.

Aaron turned his attention to Delbert. "Let's see if your mommy's home. Knock on your door, Delbert."

"OK, Cousin Aaron."

"Mommy, I'm home."

"Hi, Delbert. Did you have fun today?" Anabay asked, embracing him.

"Yes, Mommy. We baked lots of pies and Cousin Aaron bought me pizza and soda."

"That was nice. Did you thank Cousin Aaron?"

"Yes, Mommy. Can I watch cartoons now?"

"Just for a little while. Then you have to get ready for bed. Septi, what are you doing here?"

"I wanted to see my favorite little boy."

"Delbert, say goodnight to Cousin Aaron and Aunt Septi."

"Goodnight, Cousin Aaron and Aunt Septi," Delbert yelled, running off to watch cartoons.

"Aaron, thank you for bringing Delbert home."

"No problem. The little guy needs a man to take up time with him," Aaron replied.

"I know, Aaron. I really appreciate all that you do for my baby."

"Give me a break!" Septi interjected, rolling her eyes.

"Septi, would you please mind your own business? Delbert does need a man in his life and Aaron is perfect."

Aaron held up the two bottles of champagne. "It's time to celebrate!"

Anabay was curious. "What are we celebrating?"

"I am signing a multi-million-dollar deal with the NBA. They love my jerseys. Anabay, did you hear what I said? They loved my jerseys! This is the deal I've been working on! I'm going to be rich!" Aaron was dancing around in circles. "They loved my jerseys, I'm going to be rich!"

"Congratulations, Aaron. That's great! Have you shared the news with your parents?" asked Anabay.

"They were the first to know, but you know how Pops is. Septi, you down for celebrating with us? I'm ready to pop the cork on these babies and toast to my success."

"I'm sorry, Aaron, but I don't feel well tonight. I wish you all the success in the world and I promise, I'll celebrate with you another time," Anabay interjected.

"That's too bad, Anabay," Septi laughed. "I'm going to make an exception and have a toast with Aaron, even though I don't like his ass."

"I'll bet you'll love me when those dollars start pouring in. I can see you now, rolling on the ground making angels, saying, I can't believe it. Better be nice to me, Girl, if you want me to remember you when I blow up." Aaron was jovial and happy, dancing and prancing around, laughing, and hugging both Septi and Anabay.

"Well, you and Septi go right on ahead and celebrate. I'm going to have to pass tonight. Aaron, please know, I always have your best interest at heart."

"Damn, it's not going to be the same without you, Anabay," he said. "All right, we'll catch you later."

Aaron and Septi left for Septi's apartment.

*****

"Come in, Aaron, and don't even think I like you because of your contract," Septi joked.

"Look, I just want to celebrate my big break, that's all, nothing else. Unfortunately, it's got to be with you," he joked. "I brought some plastic champagne glasses in case you don't have glasses."

"What do I look like, a Bama? Of course, I have champagne glasses? Let me get them."

"Here's to me!" Aaron exclaimed.

"Yes, here's to you. Much success. What kind of champagne is this? I've never heard of this brand. I hope it's not some old headache champagne!"

"Woman, shut the fuck up and drink the damn champagne. You talk too much," he said playfully.

Septi started dancing and singing, "Aaron's in the money! Aaron's in the m-o-n-e-y! Aaron's in the money! Aaron is the m-o-n-e-y! So Aaron, when is this big deal expected to take place?"

"The contract should be signed, sealed and delivered to me within the next couple of weeks. Magic's lawyers are in the process of drawing it up."

"So, it's Magic now? What happened to Mr. Magic Johnson?"

"Well, you know, partners don't call each other mister," he said, grinning.

"Oh really?"

"That's right. I'm brilliant, Baby. My contact told me Magic was blown away by the quality of my designs and fabrics. He's away on business this week, but my man assured me Magic wants to meet with me and seal the deal as soon as he returns."

"I know your parents must be very proud of you."

"I hope so. Want some more champagne?"

"Aaron, you did bring two bottles, right?"

"Yeah, I sure did."

"Well, I'm going to drink until it's all gone," Septi laughed. "Bring on the bubbly." She lay back on her sofa. "Tell me about your parents. I saw the expression on your face when I mentioned them."

"My parents are from the old school. They don't know how to think outside the box. They would rather see me working a nine to five j-o-b, with a regular paycheck."

"Really!"

"Yeah, they don't understand. They won't even lend me the seed money that I need to get started."

"Seed money?"

"I don't feel like talking about that right now. This is supposed to be a celebration."

"Come on, I want to hear about it," Septi said, continuing to press the issue.

"I need to have fifteen sample jerseys made for the meeting with Magic and his people and I asked my parents for the money--of course, they said no."

"That's ridiculous! What's wrong with them? I find that surprising. Anabay said your parents were smart people."

"Some people are just penny foolish, if you know what I mean. If they put the money up for me, they would get their money back three times over. All they do is save, save, save. I guess it's better for me in the end, cause, when they die, their money is going be all mine anyway."

"If Magic likes your jerseys so much, perhaps he'll put the money up for the samples."

"Girl, you don't understand. It doesn't work like that. Let's forget about all this for now. I don't want to talk about it anymore. We're celebrating. I'll work the details out later."

"What do you mean?" she asked.

"When I meet with Magic, I have to look professional. I have to present him with a business plan and samples."

"Yes, you should. But will you be ready?"

"Do you have any idea how many business plans Magic looks at in a month? He is a businessman. I got to represent."

"Isn't there anybody you can borrow the money from?"

"Like who?" Aaron asked.

"I don't know? Surely you must know someone."

"Girl, you dreaming. People ain't got no money to lend nobody."

"I have an idea who you could ask."

"Who?"

"Ask your mother in private for the money."

"Ask Moms? Are you kidding? She does nothing without my pop's approval. She is really old school. You wouldn't happen to have it, would you?"

"Wait a minute, Aaron! You are going too far now!" Septi shot back.

"Look, I'm serious, Septi. You appear to be a smart woman. We can draw up a repayment agreement and I'll sign it. I will pay you back with interest."

"How much money are you talking about?"

"Twenty-five hundred dollars."

"That's a lot of money, Aaron."

"That's peanuts compared to the money I'm going to be making."

"You mean you don't have any money saved up?"

"No, Baby, I don't. Not right now."

But you're a grown-ass man!"

"No kidding! I'm an entrepreneur and my returns are about to kick in. Let's drink up."

Aaron and Septi were feeling really good and relaxed. They both lay back on the sofa in slumber positions.

"It's getting late, Aaron. You need to go," Septi said, abruptly.

"Why? I haven't finished my champagne."

"Well, drink up then and go," Septi demanded.

"Why are you rushing me out? Is it because I asked you for the money?"

"No, it's not the money."

"So, what is it then? All of sudden, another personality is kicking in!" Aaron had an idea from the look in Septi's eyes what she was thinking. He was ready.

"To be honest with you, champagne makes me horny," she replied.

"Me, too. Champagne always makes my dick hard. Look at it, trying to get out." Aaron rubbed his hand between his crotch and slid back on the sofa, moaning, as his eyes rolled back into his head. He unzipped his pants, allowing his dick to emerge like a king cobra getting ready to strike.

"Aaron, please! Put your shit back in your pants! I don't want to look at it," Septi tried to sound disgusted.

"Damn, Girl, you can't let this good dick go to waste. Ain't nobody got to know," he continued moaning.

"Aaron, you are really pressing your luck. You know the way to the door."

*****

The next morning, Septi rolled over in bed, with a serious hangover, "Damn! It's morning," she said, opening her eyes.

"How was it?" asked Aaron.

"Are you talking to me?"

"No, I was talking to my dick. I always ask my dick every morning, how was your night. Of course, woman, I'm talking to you."

"Look, Aaron, I have a serious headache."

"Want me to help you forget about your headache?"

Septi could see his dick growing through the sheets. "Hell no! Don't touch me! The champagne has worn off, OK. I want you to get the fuck out!"

"I certainly hope you're not going to take back the check you wrote me last night."

"No, but if you don't hurry up and get your ass up out of my bed, I might do that. I can't believe this shit. I slept with your ass and I don't even like you." Septi was feeling disgusted with herself. 'How could I have slept with him, I barely know his name. Damn.'

"It wasn't about liking me. Once you laid your eyes on my big hard dick, it was over. You couldn't resist," Aaron laughed, poking his chest out.

"Whatever, Aaron. Please leave now."

"I'm leaving. Is it all right to cash your check today?"

"I don't write rubber checks."

"That's not what I'm implying. A lot of people postdate checks."

"You have the check. Now, for the last time, get the fuck out of my bed and out of my apartment. I want to pretend this never happened!"

"No problem, Baby, I'm leaving. It's not going to be easy for you to forget about me. I laid one powerful pipe on your ass last night. You were moaning and groaning all over the place. I know my shit felt good to your ass-- probably the best dick you've ever had. I guarantee you this--you're going to have wet dreams about my dick. It's lethal, Baby. Septi, before I go, on a serious note, how was the sex?" he laughed.

"I'm trying real hard not to remember last night and if you don't leave, I am going to take my check back! As far as I'm concerned, what happened last night did not happen. Do you understand?"

"Don't worry. I don't kiss and tell. When your withdrawals get to be too much for you, here's my card. Call me." Aaron had a big grin on his face.

"Goodbye, Aaron!" Septi pushed Aaron out of her door and slammed it shut. She thought to herself, 'Damn, what the hell was I thinking? Every time I drink champagne, I get hot and horny, and this time I went overboard. Stupid me! I even lent the fool money! Shit, I'm nothing but a tramp! I hope I just didn't pay twenty-five hundred dollars for some dick because it certainly wasn't worth it.'

Chapter 16

Dangerous Flirtations

Anabay tossed and turned all night long thinking about her situation with Kandy. She prayed no one had seen them kissing. The thought of losing her job scared her to death. She also needed to address a bigger issue--Kandy was under the impression that she was in love with him. This completely baffled her. 'Where in the world had he gotten an idea like this?' Other than one moment of weakness, she had always made sure to keep it strictly professional with him. Truth be told, she enjoyed every bit of attention he showered on her, but she had never entertained any notion about being romantically involved with him.

She woke up at five thirty in the morning, feeling exhausted. She had not slept well at all. Whenever she closed her eyes, Kandy's face would be there, staring back at her. She could still taste his warm, sweet tongue and feel the hardness in his pants. Several times during the night, she drifted off to sleep only to be suddenly awakened out of erotic dreams drenched in sweat and with her heart beating fast.

Anabay lay in bed for a while thinking about Kandy and everything that transpired yesterday. She resolved that she was going to set the record straight with him today.

She was going to make it clear to him--I am not in love with you. We are not a couple and we will never be a couple.

She arrived at Brunswick at her normal time. For the first time, Kandy was not standing on the other side of those steel gates smiling and waiting to escort her to the business office. She was disappointed he wasn't there, yet at the same time, she was relieved he was nowhere in sight.

 He was already sitting at his desk, appearing to be deep in concentration, when she entered the office. "Good morning, Kandy."

"Good morning, Mrs. Jones," he answered, not bothering to look up and make eye contact. The tension in the office was very thick.

"Kandy, we need to talk. I don't want there to be any misunderstandings between us."

"I have nothing to say to you until you confess you have feelings for me."

"Come on, Kandy! Be serious!"

"I'm being serious. If I were on the outside of these gates, you would be thrilled to have a man like me. You would be so excited right about now, you would be calling all your girlfriends and telling them all about us."

"Please understand this--there is no us! You and I are only coworkers. Yes, I do think you are an attractive man but that does not mean I want you to be my man.

Somewhere along the line, you have misinterpreted our relationship."

He laid his pen down and stood up. "I haven't misinterpreted a goddamn thing! What about yesterday? I guess I just imagined us kissing. Why do you have a problem owning your feelings and desires for me? We both know you enjoyed me kissing you. I could tell by the way you were sucking on my tongue and by your body language. You didn't even want to leave my arms, did you? I hate game playing!"

"Kandy, you need to face reality. You are an inmate. There is no way I'm going to get involved with you and jeopardize my job."

"I'll be a free man soon."

"What did you do anyway to end up in prison?"

"It's about time you asked me that question instead of judging me, without knowing all the facts."

"So, what did you do?'

"Not a damn thing."

Anabay sat down at her desk and focused her attention on what he was about to reveal, "I'm listening," she said.

"I worked as a financial planner for County Bank, and money came up missing in a few client accounts. Being black, of course, I was blamed. I just know I was set up by my damn boss, but there wasn't any way for me to prove it. He was clever enough to make sure all the evidence pointed to me."

"How much money was involved?"

"Over half a million dollars."

Anabay was shocked by the large amount of money. "Are you serious?" she asked.

"I'm dead serious. Whoever set me up opened offshore accounts in my name. I lost everything--my freedom, my reputation and all my investments."

"Why didn't you get an attorney and fight back?"

"Miss Ana, all my assets were frozen and confiscated by the Feds, even my condo in Fort Lee. I didn't have any money. I had to use the services of a public defender and you know they don't care anything about you. I didn't stand a chance."

"What about friends and family? Wasn't there anybody who could have helped you?"

"I had no one to turn to. A few years ago, my parents were in a horrific automobile crash. My father was killed instantly and my mother's injuries were so severe, she's been confined to a nursing home ever since. I'm kind of glad my dad wasn't around to see what happened to me. I was his pride and joy. It would have killed him to see me go to prison."

"What about brothers or sisters?"

"I'm an only child. The only other relatives I have are a few cousins. They were in no position to help themselves, much less me."

"So how much time did you get?"

"I took a plea deal. Five years, straight time with no early parole. I was looking at fifteen to twenty if it went to trial."

"Kandy, I'm so sorry."

"I'll be all right. I'm an educated man. I graduated from Harvard University with a BS in Business Management and Accounting. Miss Ana, I know when I get out of here I'll be able to get back on my feet in no time."

"Will you still be able to work in your field?"

"Yeah, I can. As part of the plea deal, I'm able to keep my licenses and my case has been sealed."

"Thank you for sharing your story with me."

Kandy smiled as he walked over behind Anabay's chair and massaged her shoulders and lightly kissed her neck. "You're a special woman. Give me a chance. I won't disappoint you."

Upon hearing Kandy's fanciful story, Anabay's heart was open to the possibility of accepting him into her life. She was no longer in denial about her feelings for him. 'Perhaps God sent him to me,' she rationalized. 'Why else did I end up working at Brunswick? There are no coincidences, as they say.' She was still plagued with feelings of guilt about having feelings for a man other than Claudale. She also knew the people closest to her would never accept Kandy if they knew about his past. If their relationship ever went to the next level, she would have to keep his past a secret—a skeleton buried deep in a closet. Kandy was all she could think about as she floated around on cloud nine.

* * * * *

A few months into her romance with Kandy, Anabay arrived at work one morning to find a message in her mailbox from Warden Thompson requesting her to report to his office immediately. Pure panic set in. Her heart began beating so fast she thought it was going to jump out of her chest. Anabay just knew she was going to be fired because of her relationship with Kandy. Her mind was bombarded with uncontrollable thoughts--
'Oh, my God, what if Kandy was wrong about there being no hidden cameras in the accounting office? All of the evidence will be there staring back at me in black and white! The family curse has come back to bite me for being so stupid and getting involved with an inmate!'

After about ten minutes, she composed herself enough to leave her office. Everything around her appeared to pass in slow motion as she walked up the stairs and down the long corridors to the warden's office.

"How can I help you?" asked a round faced, old lady, who reminded Anabay of Aunt Bea on the Andy Griffith Show.

"Good morning. I am Anabay Bailey Jones. Warden Thompson requested to see me this morning." Anabay was so petrified, she could hardly spit out her words.

"Warden Thompson is in Cell Block D. He will be back in about twenty minutes," the woman responded in a cold, dismissive tone, before returning her full attention to the papers on her desk.

Anabay remained standing in front of her desk. "Excuse me. Should I wait?"

"No, you can go to your post. I will call you when he's ready to see you."

"Thank you." Anabay was now even more panic-stricken. 'Why is the warden in Kandy's cell house?' This confirmed her worst fear. 'The warden is probably questioning him right now about his relationship with me.' There was no doubt left in her mind, 'I'm going to be fired today.' Anabay's thoughts fled back for a split-second to Aunt Bea. 'Fat Face had a lot of nerve, telling me to report back to my post. Who does she think she is? I work in an office just like she does.'

The telephone was ringing when Anabay opened her office door.

"Good morning. Business Office."

"The warden will see you now," said Aunt Bea.

"Thank you. I'll be right there." 'What will be, will be,' Anabay thought to herself, closing the door.

Warden Thompson was standing by Aunt Bea's desk reading his telephone messages. "Mrs. Jones, you can go directly into my office and have a seat. I'll be right in." His tone seemed pleasant enough.

Warden Thompson was an attractive, tall, muscular man with piercing steel gray eyes and light brown hair. He reminded Anabay of Pierce Brosnan, the "Remington Steele" guy.

"Mrs. Jones, thank you for responding so promptly," he said, shutting his office door.

"You're welcome, Warden Thompson," Anabay said, biting down on the inside of her bottom lip.

"You have worked for some time here in our facility alongside one of our inmates, Keith Jackson."

"Yes, Sir, I have," Anabay replied. She tried her best to look cool even though she was melting down on the inside. 'Lord help me,' she prayed. 'Now I know for sure, they know everything about me and Kandy. This job is history.'

"Has he mentioned anything to you out of the ordinary or have you noticed anything unusual about him lately?"

"No, Sir, nothing that I can think of, at the moment. He has always kept it strictly professional with me."

"I see," the warden replied, with a doubtful look on his face.

His body language told Anabay he didn't believe her. She wondered if she was digging a deep hole for herself. 'Can I be arrested for fraternizing with an inmate?'

Warden Thompson sat behind his big desk staring at her. The silence in the room crept in, making Anabay even more nervous and causing her to feel like she was being interrogated. The stillness was so overwhelming, she decided to break the silence by nervously asking, "Warden Thompson, is something wrong?" She held her breath for the answer.

"Yes, there is definitely something wrong," he replied.

Anabay's heart stopped beating at this point. 'This is it,' she thought. 'I should just confess and be done with it. I just hope it does not become a scandal in the newspapers. I will have brought shame into the lives of those closest to me--Aunt Lillie Mae, Uncle Otis, Septi, Delbert and all the folks back home. Everyone will be so disappointed in me. How will I live with myself?' The guilt had already set in and it was eating her alive.

"Warden Thompson. . . " she sheepishly began.

"I don't know if you've heard yet, but Cell Block D is on lockdown," he said, interrupting her.

"No, Sir, I didn't hear about it. What happened?" She now had a slight hope that this possibly wasn't about her and Kandy, but she wasn't sure.

"One of our veteran officers was stabbed very early this morning."

"That's horrible! Is he going to be all right?"

"Yes, he's going to make it. However, I must say he had it coming."

"Excuse me?" Anabay was shocked the warden had made such a remark and that he had the nerve to make it in front of her.

"Oh, nothing," Warden Thompson said, dismissively.

"Warden Thompson, I don't understand. What does all of this have to do with me?"

"Well, the incident is under investigation and, since you have been working with Inmate Jackson, I need to know from you if he has ever said anything or acted in any way that might implicate him in this matter."

"Are you saying Inmate Jackson was involved in the stabbing?" Anabay was desperately hoping he wasn't involved.

"Mrs. Jones, every inmate housed in Cell Block D is involved with the stabling. Until we know which inmate or inmates are directly responsible for what took place, they are all guilty."

"I just know Inmate Jackson wouldn't be involved in stabbing anyone." Anabay wondered if she was saying too much.

The warden looked puzzled. "And why is that, Mrs. Jones?"

"I just don't think so. He's not that type of person."

Warden Thompson abruptly stood up from behind his desk, "Mrs. Jones, I thank you for your input. I'm going to have to send you home until further notice."

"I don't understand."

"Oh, I'm sorry. I thought you understood how it works. The prison is now in complete lockdown. No civilians are allowed in here until Internal Affairs has completed their investigation."

"Really!" Anabay responded with surprise. She learned about this policy in training but she never expected it to affect her. "How long can I expect to be out of work?"

"We will call you back when the matter is resolved. No need to worry—you'll be kept on payroll until further notice. I'll have an officer escort you back to your office to clear your desk and walk you off the premises."

"Thank you, Sir." Anabay felt like the weight of the world had been lifted off her.

* * * * *

Four weeks passed and Anabay had not heard one word from the prison. Every day, she would search the newspapers for articles about the stabbing but found nothing. She was curious about what had happened and wondered if Kandy was somehow involved. He was, after all, an inmate in Cell Block D. She couldn't always say that she had been the best judge of character. Just look at the man she married. She never even realized he didn't want children. Anabay was in deep thought and jumped at the sound of her telephone ringing.

"Hello," she said, picking up the receiver.

"Hi, Anabay."

"Hi, Septi. It's not like you to call so early in the morning. Is everything OK?"

"I'm good. I'm just passing some time. I'm waiting for my next client to come in for recertification. I was just wondering if you've heard anything from your job."

"Not yet. It's funny that you ask that question because I was just thinking about work when you called. I have to admit, receiving a paycheck without having to work for it can become quite addictive."

"Now you're beginning to sound like these professional welfare mamas having babies and collecting welfare checks," Septi laughed, teasingly.

"Girl, please! I miss working. But, this time off has been a blessing because now I can spend more time with Delbert.   Believe me, he is a handful."

"Well, I hope the prison is being on the up and up with you. Something doesn't sound right. It's been weeks and you haven't heard anything at all, right?"

"Yep. I'm not going to worry. I'm just going to enjoy this precious time with my son."

There was a pause in the conversation.

Then Septi asked, "Speaking of Delbert and your Aunt Lillie Mae, have you heard from Aaron?"

"The last I heard, he was in the Bahamas."

"The Bahamas! Is he meeting with Magic Johnson?" Septi asked excitedly.

"Magic Johnson?" Anabay laughed "Don't tell me you believed that line. Aaron is there chasing after some Bahama mama he met."

"You've got to be kidding me!" Septi was shocked.

"Septi, remember when he brought Delbert home and pulled out champagne, talking about celebrating? Well, he left a few days after that."

"Are you serious? When is he coming back?" Septi felt betrayed and used.

"He will probably be back when the woman gets tired of him and buys him a ticket home. That's what I heard his father say."

"Is he still on schedule to launch his clothing line? He said he was meeting soon with Magic Johnson to market his NBA jerseys."

"Come on, Septi! You didn't really believe that, did you?"

"I sure did. He sounded so sincere."

"According to Uncle Otis, Aaron is a dreamer and a pathological liar. He's all talk and no action. He talks about a clothing line but he hasn't produced a thing. That's why his parents won't give him any money."

"I didn't know that about him. He sure talked a good game," Septi replied, feeling like a sucker inside. "Damn, he is a real creep."

"What did you say?"

"Nothing important. Talk to you later, Girl. My appointment is here." Septi hung up the telephone in disbelief, wondering how she could have been so stupid and gullible to have fallen for Aaron's lies.

Chapter 17

Not Hungry for Food

Another two months passed, and Anabay still had not heard one word from her job. She was trying hard not to panic. She hadn't heard from Kandy either--but she was not unhappy about this.

Anabay came to the realization that she was caught up in a fantasy with Kandy and that he was probably only playing her anyway. Men like him are masters at sensing a woman's vulnerabilities and when two people work close together like they did, it's easy to cross the lines. 'Whatever was I thinking? How could I have been so stupid, messing around with him the way I did?' She constantly asked herself these questions. She feared her involvement with him may have cost her the job at Brunswick, but she thanked God for bringing her back to her good senses.

Anabay arrived at Aunt Lillie Mae's house early to drop Delbert off so he could spend the day with her and Uncle Otis. She never thought she could feel this way, but OMG, she was really looking forward to some alone time.

"Hey, Baby, I have missed you so much!" Aunt Lillie Mae said, embracing Delbert and smothering him with kisses.

"Hi, Aunt Lillie Mae. Can I watch cartoons?" Delbert asked, in between giggles.

"Anabay, Child, how you doing? Y'all come on in. Just hang your coats in the closet. Delbert, your Uncle Otis is sitting in the back in his favorite chair. Go on back there and ask him to turn on cartoons for you."

Delbert took off running. "Uncle Otis, Uncle Otis!"

"Aunt Lillie Mae, I really appreciate you letting Delbert come over here today. He has really missed the two of you. He asks about y'all all the time."

"Honey, no need to thank us. We love having him around. Believe me, that boy brings a lot of joy to me and Otis."

"Excuse me, Aunt Lillie Mae, is that garlic I smell?" In the foyer where they were standing, the pungent odor was overwhelming.

"Yeah, it is. You do know what day this is, don't you?" The inflection in her voice suggested that Anabay should be aware of whatever day it was.

"It's Friday."

"Anabay, it's Friday the 13th, the day of bad luck. I always sprinkle salt across the entrances to the house, then I chop up a little fresh garlic and place some in the corners in each room."

"What's that supposed to do?"

"It keeps any bad luck or darkness from entering into your home, Child."

"Wherever did you get that idea from?" Anabay asked, trying hard not to show how foolish she thought her aunt was being. She was shocked, learning that her aunt, a devoted Christian woman and pillar in her community, was also a superstitious woman who practiced pagan rituals.

"I learned about this growing up down South," she replied. "Ask your mama. She'll tell you all about it."

"I don't remember her ever doing anything like this on a Friday the 13th," Anabay replied. "Does Uncle Otis believe in this, too?"

"Otis only believes what's in front of his face. Listen to me, Anabay, be very careful today," warned Aunt Lillie Mae.

"I try my best to be careful every day, Aunt Lillie Mae, but thanks for the advice," Anabay said, hugging her goodbye. "I'll call you later and let you know what time I can pick Delbert up."

When Anabay got outside, she burst out laughing. In her mind, she kept picturing how serious her aunt looked, warning her to be careful on Friday the 13th. 'I'll bet she has never shared this belief with Pastor Tisdale or any other church member,' Anabay thought to herself. 'All that old southern superstition is just another manifestation of the family curse.'

By now, it was ten o'clock and Anabay was dying for a cup of coffee so she popped into the deli on the corner by her apartment building. The line was long, so she placed her order and leafed through a magazine to pass the time. Suddenly, someone lifted her hair up and blew hot breath on her neck. She jumped, yelled out loud and turned around to confront her invader, only to find Kandy standing there laughing and flashing his big bright smile. Anabay couldn't help laughing and smiling back at him. He embraced her in his strong arms and planted a kiss on her cheek.

"Kandy! Oh God! It's you. I can't believe it! You're out!" Anabay exclaimed.

"Yep, I'm free as a bird. You didn't believe me when I told you I'd be out soon, did you?" he asked with his eyebrows raised and his index finger resting on her nose.

He was dressed in black from head to toe -- black sweater, black slacks and shiny black shoes. This was Anabay's first time seeing him in street clothes. Without a doubt, he was definitely a good-looking man.

"I believed you, I um, um—" she stumbled.

"Come here, Girl, and give me some more love," he said, pulling her into him and hugging her again.

"How in the world did you ever find me? Do you live in this neighborhood?" Anabay was curious to know the answer.

"I looked you up in the phone book. I was on my way to your apartment building when I saw you walking in here."

"Do you want a cup of coffee?"

"No thanks. Just looking at you is all the caffeine I need," he answered.

She ignored his comment and paid for her coffee. "Kandy, let's sit down over here and talk."

"I prefer to talk in private in your apartment. I'm a tall guy. I know you don't want me to be all crunched up in those itty-bitty chairs, do you? Don't worry, I'm not going to eat you up. Not right away, anyway," he said, winking his eye.

"Kandy, I'm going to be honest with you. I'm nervous about you coming up to my apartment. My place is a mess. I was planning on cleaning it up this afternoon." Of course, Anabay was lying. She just didn't feel comfortable being alone with him. The man had just been released from prison and after five years, she knew sex was going to be at the top of his to-do list.

"Come on, Miss Ana, you know me better than that. I don't care what your place looks like. I just want to sit and talk and catch up on things. That's all."

"Okay, I guess we can talk for a little while but I don't have much time. I have to pick my son up in an hour." Again, she lied.

They walked down the block, up the stairs and entered her apartment.

"Very nice place you have here, Miss Ana."

Anabay led him into her living room. "Make yourself comfortable, Kandy. I'll be back in a minute. I want to change out of these clothes into something a little more comfortable."

"Damn, Miss Ana, you're full of surprises! You don't pussyfoot around, do you?" he yelled back. "Let me know when you're ready for me to come in there."

He was making her nervous, so she hurried up and changed into an old washed-out navy blue sweat suit. When she returned to the living room, Kandy was in the process of taking his shoes off. A disappointed look blanketed his face when he looked up and saw her walking towards him fully dressed. Anabay pretended not to notice and sat down on the sofa, making sure to keep ample space between their bodies.

"So, Kandy, what's going on at the prison? I have been sitting home for three months waiting for them to call me back to work."

"Haven't you heard? They're investigating you."

"Investigating me! For what?" Anabay was deeply concerned. Kandy just validated what she suspected all along.

"For fraternizing with an inmate. You knew it was prohibited, didn't you?" His voice had a real serious tone to it.

"Oh my God, they found out about us! I just knew it! What am I going to do now? This is going to be on my permanent employment record. I'll never be able to find another job. This is so embarrassing. I feel sick! Oh my God, it..."

Kandy burst out laughing. "I'm just kidding with you. No need to have a panic attack."

"Don't play with me like that! You almost made me have heart failure! I've been so worried, thinking that they found out about us." She had to laugh at herself. "I must say, you really got me good. Warden Thompson told me someone in your cell block stabbed an officer. You weren't involved, were you?"

"Do you really think I would be sitting here right now if I was stupid enough to get involved in a prison stabbing? Please, give me more credit than that." The look on his face let Anabay know, she should have known better than to ask him a question like this.

"Why do you think they haven't called me back?"

"I really don't know. I heard the prison is being audited by the feds and that they are planning on letting a lot of folks go. Shoot, after the lockdown, I never went back to the business office either."

"I guess I have no other choice but to wait it out," Anabay sighed.

"That's all you can do. As long as you're being paid, don't worry about it. Besides, I don't want you back there working anyway. Now let's change the subject to us. Come closer and let me hold you in my arms and give you a hug. I have really missed you."

"Kandy, we already hugged at the deli."

He sucked his teeth and moved his body closer to her. "Come here, woman." He put his arms around her and began kissing her.

Anabay tried to resist him, but his tongue tasted so delicious, she lost the fight. She hugged him back and they kissed, and they kissed, and they kissed again and again. Her body had betrayed her mind, and her will power had flown out the window. His hands were roaming all over her body and he was trying to unhook her bra. She knew she had to stop him.

"Hold up, Kandy! We're moving too fast," she said, trying to catch her breath.

"Ah, Baby, please don't stop. You feel so damn good. I've wanted you for so long. I've tasted your sweetness in my dreams. Make it a reality for me, Baby, please. Ah, Baby, Baby," he moaned, holding her tightly in his arms as he whispered, "I just want to make mad passionate love to you right here, right now."

Anabay's body craved his touch. Deep down, she wanted him to take her but internal panic set in. 'What have I done? This man is fresh out of jail and is now here ready to resume and consummate a relationship with me. I did this to myself. I should never have fooled around and flirted with him while he was in prison. It was unprofessional of me. I'm scared to death. At least I had a safety net at the prison. Here alone with him I have no protection. He might think I'm a teaser and get violent with me. Why didn't I stop myself from kissing him back? What am I going to do? Think, Anabay, think.' She pulled back from him.

"Kandy, we really don't know each other very well. You need to know and understand something about me. I prefer to take things slow, especially when it comes to an intimate relationship."

"Miss Ana, what is my favorite flavor of ice cream?"

"I have no idea."

"It's butter pecan. Is that intimate enough for you? Now scoot your booty back over here so I can flip you and eat you like a pancake."

"Stop being silly, Kandy."

"I am being serious. You want me to be serious? How about this? Take off your panties and sit down on this sofa right in front of me. I'll show you how serious I am."

"I will not!" Anabay fired back, despite the fact her pussy was wet with excitement. "I know it's hard for you since . . . "

"Damn right, it is hard. You want to feel it?" he asked.

"You didn't let me finish. I was trying to say that, since you haven't had sex in years, it might be hard for you to control yourself."

"I apologize if I'm coming on too strong for you. Don't worry, I never have and never will force you or any other woman to do anything they don't want to. It's just that I have been waiting an eternity for you. I guess I can wait a little longer. You are definitely worth it," he said, before leaning over and kissing her on her forehead. "Now, give me a tour of our bedroom."

"Our bedroom? What are you talking about?"

"I'm moving in here with you and your son."

"What!"

"Got cha!" he said, laughing. "Seriously, let me see the rest of your apartment. These apartments are nice and spacious. I will be moving in here real soon, though," he said, looking dead into her eyes.

Anabay wanted him to leave after showing him the rest of her apartment. "Kandy, I have to leave now and pick Delbert up."

"I'll go with you."

"That's not a good idea. Remember what I said, I like to take things slowly." She emphasized the word 'slowly.'

"Miss Ana, I really don't feel like being alone. Today is my birthday and I don't have anyone to celebrate it with me. Mama is in a nursing home and, after five years, I don't know how to contact any of my cousins or old friends."

"Oh, my God, happy birthday, Kandy! Why didn't you tell me?" she said, embracing him. He sounded so sad and so sincere, he melted her heart. "You know what? I'm going to cook dinner for you tonight and I'll celebrate your birthday with you. How does that sound?"

"That sounds great, Miss Ana. I'm really touched that you're willing to do this for me. What about your little boy?"

"Delbert can stay over at my uncle and aunt's house. Kandy, I want you to promise me one thing--that you will leave after dinner."

"I promise. Why don't I just stay here until tonight then?"

"I have a lot of running around to do--to prepare for tonight. Come back at six thirty."

"Whatever you say. Thank you so much. See you at six thirty."

Kandy left, reflecting on Anabay's behavior. 'I'm going to tap that ass tonight and it ain't even my birthday.'

*****

Anabay glanced up at the clock on her kitchen wall. It was 6 o'clock, and the birthday dinner she had prepared for Kandy was ready. She made a slow-cooked pot roast with carrots and potatoes, collard greens, macaroni and cheese and old-fashioned cornbread. Of course, she baked him a birthday cake from scratch and bought his favorite flavor of ice cream, butter pecan.

She was deep in thought, second guessing herself for offering to celebrate Kandy's birthday with him. It hadn't dawned on her until this very minute that she had probably set herself up for an intimate encounter with him. She wondered if her subliminal mind had overridden her rational thinking mind because, deep down inside herself, she really wanted to have sex with him. There was no denying it, a part of her really liked him and found him attractive--and the other part of her screamed, 'Stop, danger ahead.' He could be so macho and overbearing at times, the complete opposite of her beloved Claudale.

Anabay showered and thumbed through her closet for over twenty minutes, looking for something stylish and comfortable to wear. She knew Kandy would come on strong and use every technique he knew to undress her. She finally slipped into a burnt orange and white polyester crewneck maxi drawstring dress. She hoped this outfit would serve her purpose.

Kandy rang her doorbell precisely at six thirty. When she opened the door, he was standing there holding a single red rose.

"For the love of my life," he said, presenting the rose to her and planting a quick kiss on her lips.

She noticed he was still wearing the same clothes from earlier--all black.

"My, my, my, my, Miss Ana! You look invitingly delicious. I could bite you! Woof, woof!" Kandy barked, snared and clamped down on his teeth like a dog.

"Everything's ready. Just lay your jacket on the chair in the living room, wash your hands and come on into the dining room," she said, completely dismissing his playful stunt.

"It smells real good in here, just like my mama's Sunday dinner," Kandy commented before going into the bathroom to wash his hands.

Kandy ate like it was his last meal. It gave Anabay joy to see him savoring her food.

"Miss Ana! Miss Ana! Baby, you sure enough can burn! I haven't had a home-cooked meal like this since before my mother became ill. Thank you so much for dinner. Everything was delicious, simply scrumptious. What a perfect evening!"

"Thank you, Kandy. I'm glad you enjoyed it. I wanted to make a special meal for you tonight. You've been through so much."

Kandy reached over and held her hand. "I'm counting on you making this evening even more special for me."

The way he was staring at her made Anabay nervous. She gently reclaimed her hand and hopped up from the table. "It's birthday cake time. I have your favorite, butter pecan ice cream. Do you want some? "

"Of course, I want some," he replied, emphasizing the word "some." "Why else would I be here?" he mumbled under his breath, audible enough for her to hear him. He really wanted to say, 'Fuck the dessert, I want some pussy.'

Anabay pretended she hadn't heard what he said and started clearing the dinner dishes from the table.

"Why don't you take it easy, Baby? Just relax a moment. Dessert can wait. Right now, I just want to chill out. Why don't we lay down on your bed and just hold each other for a while?"

"Kandy, I guess you didn't hear a word I said earlier."

"I heard you loud and clear. Look, I am a man. I've spent five years of my life in a goddamn prison for a crime I didn't commit. Don't you think it's only natural for me to want some loving right now. I can't lie -- my collar is real tight. I understand how you feel and, like I said before, I'm not going to force you to do anything you don't want to do. I know you don't want to have sex, but can you at least give me some affection. Is that too much to ask? All I'm asking you to do is to lay down with me. Just let me hold you and feel you. I really need this, Baby. OK?"

"I'll see. Let me just finish clearing up these dishes," Anabay said nervously.

The doorbell rang. 'Perfect timing,' Anabay thought to herself.

"Damn, somebody's at your door. Let's be quiet. Maybe they'll go away."

"It's nobody but Septi, my neighbor. Remember? I told you about her."

"Is she the nosy woman who's always in your business?"

"Yep, that's her. I might as well open the door now, otherwise, she'll keep coming back," Anabay said as she scurried to the door. She didn't let on, but she was happy about the interruption.

"Not so fast. Come back over here. Let me spank that booty of yours."

"Please, Kandy, not now."

"Just kidding. Let her in. I'm looking forward to meeting the broad."

Anabay opened the door and Septi marched in as usual.

"Girl," Septi announced, "I had one rough-ass day! Damn, something sure smells good up in here! What did you cook?"

"Septi, go into the dining room. I want you to meet someone."

"I'm sorry, Anabay, I didn't know you had company."

Kandy was already standing, waiting to greet Septi.

"Hello, I'm Septi, Anabay's friend and neighbor," she said, surveying him from head to foot with her big eyes. Septi was salivating at the sight of the fine specimen of a man standing there before her.

Kandy extended his hand. "Hello, Septi. My name is...."

Anabay butted in before he introduced himself. "Septi, I'd like for you to meet Officer Jackson. He is a correctional officer at the prison."

"Nice to meet you, Septi."

"Likewise," she said, extending her hand. "What is your first name?"

"Keith." Kandy was sizing Septi up, too. He could tell by the way she was dressed, in skin-tight pants and a low-cut blouse, that she was the type of woman who owned her sexuality.

"Anabay never mentioned she had such a handsome co-worker."

"Why, thank you. It's an honor for me to be in the company of two of Newark's finest women. You two are about the finest women I have ever laid my eyes on!" Kandy said, smiling from ear to ear.

"Flattery will get you everywhere," Septi blushed. "I didn't mean to interrupt your evening. I should leave." It was obvious she didn't want to go.

Anabay didn't want her to leave either because she didn't want to lie down with Kandy. "Septi, you're not interrupting us. There is plenty of food left. Sit down. Let me fix you a plate."

"Are you guys sure? I feel really bad for busting in on your evening."

"Miss Septi, sit down and eat some dinner. The food is delicious. I was just getting ready to leave anyway," Kandy said, winking at her.

"Are you two sure I'm not interrupting?"

"Yes, we're sure," Anabay insisted.

"So, Mr. Jackson, may I call you Keith?"

"Of course, you can."

"Did you come over to give Anabay an update on her job?"

"No, I came by to check up on her. We've become good friends after working together. Well, ladies, I wish I could stay longer but I need to go home and get some rest because I'm on the early morning shift." Kandy grabbed Septi's hand and planted a hand kiss, "Miss, Septi, it's been a pleasure. I hope to see you around."

"The pleasure is all mine," she replied, smiling.

Anabay walked Kandy to the door. He kissed her on the lips and then he grabbed her hand and rubbed his index finger in the palm of her hand. Anabay hated that. It was such a common, nasty thing for a man to do. Men who do this think they are communicating some top-notch secret. Little do they know, it is a complete turn-off for most women. 'I hope he didn't rub Septi's palm too,' she thought to herself.

"Bye, Baby," he whispered to her. "I'll call you later."

Kandy was pissed that Septi had interrupted his evening with Anabay, but then he realized it was for the best. He was thinking to himself, 'Anabay likes to play silly little girl games. I really don't have the patience to deal with her whining ass tonight. I need to get laid. I'm gonna find myself some pussy from somewhere.'

Anabay walked back into the dining room where Septi was waiting to bombard her with questions about Keith. "Well, aren't you the sneaky one? You never told me about your correctional officer friend."

"Septi, there is nothing to tell."

"You've got to be kidding me! What do you mean, nothing to tell? He is a handsome man! No wonder you cooked dinner for him. I would cook for his ass, too, with those big ol' pussy lips of his," Septi chuckled.

"Trust me, Septi, I have no interest in Keith."

"You're crazy then! A man with lips like his can tear a pussy up! I know what I'm talking about!" Septi said excitedly.

"You're being ridiculous."

"Come on Anabay, I know you got to be attracted to him. Not only is he fine as hell, but he appears to be a gentleman."

"Yeah, he is a nice guy, but I really don't know that much about him."

"Well, you knew enough about him to invite him into your home and cook for him."

"Septi, I'm really tired and I just want to go to bed. Let me pack you up some leftovers," Anabay said, hoping she would get the hint and leave.

"Can I help you wash dishes?"

"No, I've got everything under control," Anabay said, handing to her the doggy bag she had prepared.

"Thanks for the food. I really appreciate it and I'm sorry again for interrupting your date," Septi said, teasingly.

"Septi, good night." Her nosiness got on Anabay's nerves. On this night, however, she was glad for her intrusion because it got rid of Kandy.

*****

The telephone rang.

"Hello?"

"Who loves you, Baby?"

"Who is this?" Anabay asked.

"It's me! Nobody else better be calling my woman this time of night," Kandy responded.

"Why did you leave so abruptly?"

"I did that so you could get rid of your friend. Is the coast clear?"

"Yeah, she's gone home," Anabay answered.

"She lives two doors down from you, right?"

"Yeah, across the hall."

"I found her to be a bit overbearing, but I can see she feels very close to you. I'll bet, not one day goes by that she doesn't check in on you."

"You got that right. She can be so annoying at times."

"Enough talk about her. Put on something sexy and sheer for me. I'll be over in a few minutes."

"Kandy, I really…. Damn it," Anabay cursed to herself, realizing he had hung up the phone on her.

Chapter 18

Secrets

"Y**ou are quite the man! I must admit, I really admire your confidence," she said, while looking into her lover's eyes and running her fingers through his chest hairs.

"Why, thank you. You are quite a woman yourself," Kandy reciprocated.

"I was pleasantly surprised when you knocked on my door. How did you learn to be so bold?" she asked, feeling mesmerized by him.

"What do you mean? I don't know why you would be so surprised. You knew I wanted you."

"We barely even know each other, yet you had the audacity to knock on my door in the middle of the night."

"Well, I liked what I saw. You're pretty bold yourself, Girl, sleeping with me. I was a perfect stranger."

"What can I say? Sometimes I like to take a chance and live life dangerously, you know, on the edge," she said, smiling. "I must say, I hit the jackpot with you."

As they turned to face each other, she slithered down to his lower body cavity and began lightly pulling and running her red fingernails through his pubic hair and massaging his dick until it grew hard and ready. "You got it going on! I've never experienced a man as hot as you. You exploded like you haven't had sex in years," she exclaimed.

"I don't mean to boast, but I always perform like that." Kandy was smiling.

"You wore my ass out last night!"

"You know what, you are a very special woman. Most ladies would never admit that."

"Well, it's the truth."

"You're one hot mama yourself. I could have fried me some bacon and eggs between those thighs of yours."

Kandy pulled Septi up, laid her flat on her back and whispered, "Such a pretty lady," as he nibbled on her tiny tea cup breasts.

She wondered if he had figured out that her breasts were the gateway to her sexuality. Stimulating her breasts made her wide open to anything from cartwheels to roller skating around the house naked.

Kandy stabbed his hard dick deep into Septi's vagina. "Damn, woman, this is some good ass pussy! Damn good pussy! Shit!" His eyes rolled back into his head as he moved his hips up and down as fast as he could, not missing a stroke. "Mmmm . . . mmmm," he moaned.

Her body easily accommodated his enlarged, erect penis. Septi was in a state of pure ecstasy, moaning and groaning, and shouting out uncontrollably. "Yes, Keith! Oooh aahhh, oooh aahhh! Yes, Keith. Fuck me harder, Big Daddy! It's your pussy! Tear it up! Fuck me harder! Oh yes! Fuck me! Fuck me!"

Her nasty talk really excited Kandy. He began banging her vaginal walls forcibly, causing her head to knock up against her wooden headboard.

Septi was oblivious to the head knocking since all her engorged nerve endings were below her waist. When she was on the verge of orgasm, Kandy deliberately pulled out of her. He scooted down in the bed, parted her legs and inserted his tongue in her pussy.

Septi momentarily thought she had died and gone to heaven. "Oh yes, Oh yes! So damn good! Shit! Stop it— I can't take it anymore. Please Baby, Stop!" The pleasure he was inflicting on her was so intense, she began crying and begging him to stop. She tried to free herself by closing her legs but his large hands clamped down on her thighs, preventing her from doing so.

She begged for mercy.

Kandy then flipped her on top of him and plunged his dick back in her pussy. It only took a few seconds for Septi to experience the mother of all orgasms. The experience was so surreal, she lost complete control of her body. Upon regaining her bearings, she felt happy and satisfied, but also confused and disoriented. Silently, she wondered if what she experienced was an orgasm or was it body convulsions.

He held her tight in his large muscular arms until her breathing normalized. "You OK, Baby?"

"Wow," was the only word Septi could manage to utter. When she eventually opened her eyes, she noticed that Kandy had a look on his face like he was the master of the universe. He continued cradling her in his arms until they both fell back to sleep.

Septi woke up first an hour later with a throbbing vagina. She was beyond elated to be lying next to such a fine specimen of a man as Keith Jackson. He met all the criteria she wanted in a mate: he was tall, good looking, physically fit with broad shoulders, had all his teeth, had a job and boasted a big dick to boot. She thought to herself, 'The universe has finally come through for me. I have hit the jackpot and it's better than winning the lottery.' She raised up on her elbow and was in the process of leaning over to plant a kiss on his cheek when he woke up.

"Hey," Kandy said sleepily.

"We overslept. Don't you have to go to work?" Septi asked.

"Naw, baby. Today's my day off."

"But you said last night at Anabay's that you needed to leave early to get ready for work today." Septi replied, sounding confused.

"I know what I said. I made up an excuse to leave so I could get with you. Once I saw that cute ass of yours, I wanted you bad. I couldn't help myself. What about you? You got things to do today?"

"I had an appointment to get my hair done, but I left a message canceling it last night, after you came over."

"You're a naughty girl! How did you know we would end up in bed doing it all night long?"

"I didn't. I only knew what I wanted to happen," Septi said, giggling.

"Well, in that case, you ready for some more of this?" Kandy said as he massaged his penis.

"Keith, I am fucked out and I know you must be too. Right now, I need to take a shower and drink some coffee." Septi turned and started climbing out of the bed.

"Well, I need for you to do a little something for me. Big Daddy's not finished yet."

Septi turned around to face him but her eyes immediately narrowed in on the big hard penis he was cupping in his hands. She thought to herself, 'This motherfucker is unreal! I can't believe this shit! Now I have to give him some head on an empty stomach.' She reluctantly crawled down in the bed and started sucking his member.

After taking a shower together, they sat in the kitchen drinking coffee and talking.

"Keith, do you have any romantic interests in Anabay?" Septi inquired.

"No, she's not my type. She's just a really sweet lady who happens to be raising a little boy all by herself. I was getting with her to see if I could be a mentor or role model to the kid. Black boys who don't have fathers or any other positive male role models in their lives have it hard in life."

"You are absolutely right," Septi agreed. "Not only are you the bomb in bed but you're a man with good values and character. Delbert is my heart. Anabay would be a fool not to allow you to be a part of his life."

"Time will tell, but for the moment, we need to keep our relationship under lock and key. I know how I feel about Anabay, but I think she may be a little sweet on me. She needs to be handled with kid gloves, if you know what I mean."

"I agree. She's my best friend. I don't want to do anything to spoil our relationship. So, Keith, where do we go from here?"

"I like to take it real slow with the women I get involved with," he answered.

"Women? Women? You mean to tell me you deal with more than one woman at a time!"

"Calm down, Baby, of course not. I've been at this relationship game for a long time and I like to take it slow and really get to know any woman I get involved with. You don't have to worry about a thing. I've gotten a good taste of your sweet ass and I'm not about to let you go." Kandy wasn't caught off guard in the least by the conversation. He knew good dick was always followed by a line of questioning, chicks trying to claim ownership rights. 'It never fails,' he giggled to himself.

Septi couldn't help blushing all over herself. It flashed in her mind, 'He just might be my Mister Right.'

"I'm hungry. You got anything to eat in here other than coffee," he asked.

"Not really. I didn't get around to going to the market this week."

"Well, let me school you right now. If you want me to be your man, you need to rise up and be a woman. Real women properly feed their men. You want to keep riding Big Daddy, then you need to feed me. Men need protein to keep their dicks strong. Understand?"

Septi was taken aback. 'He sure is arrogant and demanding,' she thought. "Tell you what, let me run down to the deli and buy us some breakfast sandwiches."

"You do that and bring me two of them and something sweet to eat, like some cookies or a devil dog," he said, playfully smacking her behind as she passed him on her way out of the kitchen.

Septi was so full of joy, she practically skipped to and from the deli. She was about to insert her key into her apartment door when she glanced down the hall at Anabay's apartment and thought to herself, 'This is going to be a hard secret to keep.'

Chapter 19

An Idea Is Born

'I wonder what happened to Kandy last night? He said he was coming back,' thought Anabay, waking up.

She was dreading it, but she knew she needed to have a serious conversation with him and make it clear to him, there is 'no us.' He was being way too aggressive and it was turning her off. The nerve of him, looking up her address and heading over to her apartment without calling or being invited. She wasn't comfortable about getting involved with him so soon after his release from prison. Besides, right now, she wanted to focus all her attention on Delbert. Anabay was determined to set the record straight with Kandy.

'That's it, enough thinking about him,' she decided. 'I need to get down to the Post Office before twelve o'clock. It was three weeks before Christmas and Anabay was taking Delbert to see the Christmas Lights at the Bronx Zoo this Saturday evening. She had a lot to do today, so she hurried up and got dressed and made a mad dash to the Post Office.

The line at the Post Office was almost out the door. Feeling slightly annoyed, Anabay thought to herself, 'This Post Office is a joke. All these postal employees are walking around like zombies and only one window is open. It's Christmas season. This is ridiculous!'

Finally, after she stood in line for over forty minutes, an old gray-haired postal worker asked, "Miss, may I see some identification?" The man looked to be in his seventies. "You can sign here," he said, handing the certified letter to her.

"Thank you, Sir." Anabay felt sorry for the old man. She hoped she wouldn't still be working when she got to be his age. That was one good thing about the Post Office, they never fire people. She decided to wait and open the letter when she got to Aunt Lillie Mae's house.

The back door was unlocked, so she felt free to walk in. Uncle Otis was sitting at the kitchen table in front of his place setting. Anabay admired the way her aunt always preset her husband's place setting for every meal. She thought, 'I love the way Aunt Lillie Mae takes care of Uncle Otis. If Claudale were alive, I would do the same for him.' There wasn't any doubt in her mind, Lillie Mae and Otis truly loved each other.

"Hey, Anabay, you out and about early."

"It's afternoon, Uncle Otis. I'm here to pick Delbert up. We're going to see the Christmas lights at the Bronx Zoo tonight."

"That's mighty nice. Y'all going by train?"

"Yes."

"He's still sleeping. Do you need some money?"

"No, I'm OK, but thanks for asking. Delbert sure is sleeping late."

"He stayed up late playing with Aaron."

"When did Aaron get back?"

"Last night. I was hoping he stayed wherever the hell he went," vented Uncle Otis.

"Uncle Otis, you know you don't mean that."

"I do mean it. That boy needs to grow the hell up and get a job and start being responsible for himself. He depends on us for every little thing. It don't make a damn bit of sense."

"Where's Aunt Lillie Mae?" asked Anabay.

"She went to the A&P to buy some coconut and butter."

"I know what that means."

"Yep, she got another big order for a Christmas party at the Community Center."

"That's good. Baking pies keeps her busy."

"I know, but she's getting tired--although she'll never admit it. I can see it, though. That's why I want Aaron to make something out of his life before we leave this earth."

"Stop talking like that, Uncle Otis."

"I'm speaking the truth. Nobody is born to live forever. We're all living on borrowed time and getting older by the day. The thought of leaving that boy our savings and our houses is quite disturbing. You want to wake Delbert up now or let him sleep?"

"He can sleep a little longer. He's got a big night ahead of him."

"I'm about to eat lunch. Want to join me?"

"Sure, I would love to but first I have to open this letter from my job," replied Anabay, as she sat down across from Uncle Otis and tore open the envelope.

"Bones a little stiff," he commented, standing up and walking over to the stove. "Let's see what Lillie Mae prepared. Oh yeah, roasted chicken with stuffing, baked macaroni and cheese, and some good old cabbage," he said, lifting the lids off the pots.

"That sounds more like dinner," giggled Anabay.

"One thing about my wife--she always makes sure that I eat a balanced meal. My Lillie Mae is a damn good woman."

"I don't know why I opened this. My employment has been terminated." Anabay looked sad and was visibly shaken.

"What?"

"The letter states that due to the privatizing of the prison, my position has been eliminated. A severance check for ten thousand dollars is enclosed."

"Ten thousand dollars is a nice piece of change, considering you haven't worked there that long,"

"I know. I'm just surprised and, believe me, I'm not complaining. It does seem like a lot of money, but it won't last very long without any other income coming in."

"To tell you the truth, Anabay, we've always worried about you working at the prison. It just don't seem like a job for a lady. There must be some other kind of work you can do."

"It paid the bills, Uncle Otis." Anabay's face was scrunched and she was on the verge of tears. She was truly worried about Delbert's and her own future. She couldn't help but wonder if the family curse was toying with her.

Uncle Otis felt sorry for her. He could sense the pain she was in so he decided to share with her an idea he had been thinking about.

"I've been thinking about this for a long time. Maybe you and Lillie Mae can go into business together. You've been to culinary school and like to cook, and her baking business has really been expanding. Right now, she's getting more orders for cakes and pies than she can keep up with. Why not use your skills and go into business for yourself, doing something you really enjoy doing? You two can open up a restaurant."

"A restaurant--are you serious?" she asked, feeling excited and surprised at the thought of co-owning a business. "That sounds wonderful, Uncle Otis!"

Otis saw the strong interest in her eyes. He knew she loved the idea and would give it her all. "I'm dead serious. Working for yourself is the only way to make some real money in this world."

"I know I didn't just hear my father say that," Aaron smirked, walking into the kitchen wearing an Oscar De La Renta silk robe and matching pajama pants. He rubbed the sleep out of his eyes. "Hey, Anabay. I must be dreaming because I know I didn't just hear my father admit the only way to make some real money is to work for yourself."

"Hi, Aaron. You sure have a nice tan! Where have you been?" asked Anabay.

"I just got back from taking myself a little MT," Aaron answered.

"What is MT?" asked Anabay.

"MT stands for Me Time. I was feeling burnt out so I went to the Bahamas and just relaxed and recharged my body. I tanned in the sun, went skinny-dipping, and met a lot of pretty women. Man, those women in the Bahamas sure love me. They didn't want me to leave."

"I wish they had kept your black ass there," interjected Uncle Otis.

"Leave it to Pops to make me feel unwelcome in my own home."

"You got it all wrong, Boy. This here is your mama's and my house. You don't have a dime in it."

"You know what, Pops, I'm going to ignore what you just said. Besides, you only talk to me like this when Mom's not around. What's this I'm hearing about you owning your own business, Anabay?"

"We were talking about expanding your mother's baking business," said Uncle Otis.

"Is Moms in on this?"

"No, not yet and I don't want you to say anything until after I present the idea to her," said Uncle Otis.

"Pay me twenty dollars," teased Aaron, holding out his hand.

"Boy, if you don't carry your sorry-ass behind out of here and look for a job, I'll hog whip you beyond recognition," Uncle Otis said with a look of disgust on his face.

"See you later, Anabay," laughed Aaron.

"Oh, Aaron, I almost forgot. Septi has been asking about you."

"I'm sure she has." Aaron exited the kitchen, shaking his head and smiling.

"Anabay, what was that about?" Uncle Otis was puzzled.

"I am not sure, your guess is as good as mine," she replied.

"I didn't know Aaron knew your friend Septi."

"They met."

"Are you sure they just met once?"

Anabay didn't understand why Uncle Otis was being so inquisitive. Did he dislike his son that much? By the look on his face she could tell he was serious. He wanted answers.

"Did anything happen between the two of them?" Uncle Otis continued bombarding her with questions.

"Like what, Uncle Otis?" Anabay was beginning to think maybe Aunt Lillie Mae was right -- that he was too hard on Aaron.

"You know what I mean. Are they attracted to each other?"

Anabay laughed. "Oh no, that would be too funny. Septi and Aaron cannot stand each other. You don't know my friend Septi, she's not easy to get along with."

"Whatever it's about, promise me that you will tell your friend to stay far away from Aaron. He is bad news. I don't care if he is my son. Given the chance, I'll warn any woman that comes within ten feet of that boy."

"Aaron doesn't appear to be that bad of a person."

"Trust me, you have not been around him long enough to know the real Aaron. Anabay, promise me you'll tell her to stay clear of him, and, if you see them getting familiar with each other, please let me know."

"Uncle Otis! I will do no such thing--spying on my friend and my cousin like that!" Uncle Otis was not making any sense to Anabay. She was beginning to feel--maybe he does have some deep-rooted negative obsession to sabotage his own son. 'Could this too be a part of the family curse?' she wondered.

Uncle Otis knew Anabay was not comfortable with their conversation, so he changed the subject. "What do you think about my idea of going into business with your aunt?"

"I love the idea and I am definitely interested." Anabay was relieved he got off the subject of Septi and Aaron.

"Well, just think about it. It makes perfect sense. You love to cook and Lillie Mae loves to bake. Why not combine your skills together and open a restaurant? As I said before, owning your own business is the only way to secure your financial independence. And besides, I'll be able to rest in peace, knowing you and Delbert are secure."

"Uncle Otis, stop it! Why do you insist on talking like this?"

"Because everybody's got to die. People never like to talk about death and that's why they're never prepared when the time comes."

"Do you think Aunt Lillie Mae will like the idea?"

"You kidding me? She's going to love it. It's always been her dream to own a restaurant. Timing is everything. Besides, she worries just as much as I do about you and Delbert. This will be perfect."

"You're probably right," Anabay commented.

"I know I'm right. The best thing you can do for yourself and for your son is to become your own boss so you can become self-sufficient. This way, you don't have to depend on nobody."

"It sounds wonderful. I don't have a job right now, that's for sure," she remarked.

"Anabay, sometimes things happen for a reason. Leave everything to me. I'll talk to Lillie Mae and get back to you."

"Thank you, Uncle Otis. You and Aunt Lillie Mae are such a blessing in my life."

"We're family, Baby Girl, and family takes care of one another."

"Uncle Otis, do you believe in the Bailey family curse?"

Uncle Otis laughed. "I've forgotten all about the curse on the Bailey women. It's been such a long time since I've heard anyone mention that stupid mess. Don't tell me you believe that old tale."

"When I was growing up, that's all my mama talked about, each and every day without fail. I can honestly say, I do not believe in the curse. But, I will admit, sometimes strange things happen that make the curse seem like a possibility."

"Well, you need to keep those thoughts out of your head and start making smart decisions and concentrate on designing your life--make your own luck. If you continue to believe in that old foolishness, it will only hold you back."

"You're right. Thank you so much, Uncle Otis." Anabay kissed him on the check and went to wake up Delbert.

Zenora Knight

Chapter 20

Mr. Manipulator

D ing dong, Ding dong.

Anabay wasn't surprised at all when she opened the door and saw Kandy standing there. He was dressed in a Nike blue velour sweat suit and with a black leather jacket draped over his shoulder.

"Hello, Miss Ana," he said, flashing his beautiful smile.

"Hi, Kandy. What happened to you last night? You said you were coming back."

"I know. I was so tired -- I laid down for a quick nap and the next thing I knew, it was morning."

"You should have called me before coming by. This is not a good time. I'm leaving shortly. I'm taking Delbert to see the Christmas lights at the Bronx Zoo this evening."

"Wow, what a beautiful thing to do with your son, Miss Ana! I always knew you were a great mom. Where is the little guy? I would love to meet him."

Anabay paused. "Kandy, please don't take this the wrong way -- I'm not comfortable with you meeting him yet." She went on with emphasis, "We're not in a relationship and I don't want Delbert exposed to a lot of different men. Right now, the only men in his life are his Uncle Otis and Cousin Aaron."

Kandy stared blankly at her for a few seconds and responded, "Wow, it's like that, huh. I thought we were beyond that."

"Well, we aren't beyond that! Look, Kandy, we barely know each other, other than the little time we spent working together at Brunswick. Like I told you before, I do like you a lot, but you're moving way too fast for me."

"Miss Ana, it's not my intention to impose myself on you and I do apologize if I'm being too aggressive. It's just that I've been through a lot these past five years and I'm anxious to jump-start my life.   I'm counting on you and your son playing a big role in my future. Just let me come in and meet him. Please. You can introduce me as Uncle Keith and I promise you, I won't stay long."

Anabay reluctantly stepped aside and allowed Kandy to enter her apartment. He followed her into the living room where Delbert was stretched out on the floor playing with Legos and watching cartoons.

"Delbert, baby, come here. I want you to meet my friend. His name is Uncle Keith."

Delbert glanced up at Kandy, then ran over to his mother and grabbed her leg, trying to hide his face from him. Delbert was the type of kid who was shy, that is, until he warmed up.

Kandy bent down and started playing peek-a-boo with the little boy, who was still holding onto his mommy's leg. Anabay was pleasantly surprised when Delbert immediately warmed up to Kandy and appeared to be having the time of his life as evidenced by his loud giggling. She watched approvingly as Kandy swooped Delbert up in his arms, threw him up in the air and caught him. It made her happy, knowing her son was interacting with an intelligent and patient man.

Anabay was truly overwhelmed. Her baby had taken to Kandy like the proverbial fish to water. She stepped out of the room briefly to answer the telephone and when she returned, she found them both lying on the floor, laughing, talking and playing with the Legos. Feeling like a third wheel, she excused herself and began getting ready for the evening's event.

"Sorry to interrupt the party, guys," Anabay yelled out. "Delbert, Mommy needs to dress you now. We need to be on the five o'clock Path train."

"No, Mommy, I don't want to go. I want to stay here and play with Uncle Keith," cried Delbert.

"Delbert Jones, you heard what I said. We're going to the Bronx Zoo to see the Christmas lights. Don't give me any backtalk. Now get up and put the Legos back in your toy box."

"No, I don't want to go," screamed Delbert. He ran over to Kandy and started crying on his shoulder.

"Hey, Little Guy. You heard your mommy. Now, be a big boy and put your toys away. It's time for you to get dressed."

"No, I don't want to go the old zoo. I hate the zoo and all the stupid old animals. I want to play with Uncle Keith," screamed Delbert, who by now was in the middle of a full-blown temper tantrum, kicking his feet and banging his fists into the floor. He reminded Anabay so much of Claudale, the day when she announced her pregnancy.

She was on the verge of losing her patience and was about to yank Delbert up, when Kandy intervened, "Miss Ana, let me handle the situation. Obviously, your son needs a father figure. Just go in the other room and give us a few minutes alone. I want to have a little talk with him, that's all."

Anabay wasn't sure if she should leave her son with him, but she did.

When she returned to the living room, Delbert was back to his happy self and was putting the Legos away in his toy box. 'Wow,' she thought, 'Maybe Kandy was right about my little boy needing a father figure.' She also noticed Delbert didn't complain when she dressed him, like he normally did.

"It's time to go. Delbert, say good-bye to Uncle Keith," instructed Anabay, grabbing her pocketbook.

"'Mommy, Uncle Keith's coming with us," Delbert said excitedly. He ran over and grabbed Kandy's hand.

"What?"

"Yes, Uncle Keith's coming too," Kandy arrogantly said, with a Cheshire cat smirk on his face.

Anabay was furious. Not only had this man insinuated himself into her life, but he had the balls to have manipulated himself into her son's life as well. Delbert was happy and ready to go, so she decided to bite her tongue for the moment. She grabbed her coat and purse, locked the door, and the three of them left for the train station.

Anabay figured Kandy didn't have any money so she paid for their fares. Her anger towards him quickly vanished once the show began. The Christmas lights were absolutely spectacular and they enjoyed the show immensely, especially Delbert.

"Miss Ana, you got twenty dollars on you?" Kandy whispered in her ear.

"Yes, I do," she replied, confused.

"Let me hold it. I want to buy Delbert some cotton candy."

"Kandy, I'll take care of all expenses."

"Miss Ana, you don't understand. It's important for your son to see me, the man, pay the expenses, not you, the woman."

She slipped twenty dollars into his hand.

After the show, Delbert feel asleep and Kandy carried him all the way back home in his arms so Anabay was glad he had come with them.

They arrived back home around eleven thirty. Anabay immediately undressed Delbert and put him in bed. She was on her way back to the living room to have that talk with Kandy when she noticed that the bathroom door was open, but the lights were not on. As she got closer, she saw the silhouette of Kandy's body standing up at the toilet with his manhood hanging out, peeing.

For a split second, a red flag popped up in her mind. What kind of man comes into a lady's home and pees freely like this? She knew the answer, either a married man or a man who is used to living with a woman.

Kandy walked back into the living room and put his jacket on. "Miss Ana, I'm leaving now. Thank you for a truly enjoyable evening. I really like Delbert. He's a great kid. I'm looking forward to spending a lot of time with the both of you."

Anabay tried not to show it, but she was disappointed that he was leaving. "It was a nice evening, Kandy. I'm glad you had a good time."

Kandy embraced her and kissed her on her cheek. "See you later, Baby."

Kandy walked down the street smiling and laughing to himself. He was thinking, 'I know I shocked the shit out of her ass tonight. She thought I was going to hang around, begging her for a piece of ass. Now, she'll think twice about playing games with me. Anyway, I don't have anything left for her tonight. Septi wore my ass out!'

Zenora Knight

Chapter 21

Player, Player

Kandy awakened at 5:30 a.m. sharp, a habit ingrained in him from prison, and slowly eased out of bed. He didn't want to disturb Anabay. He thought to himself while getting dressed, 'Damn, let me get the fuck out of here before her ass wakes up. I'm bored out of my mind screwing this little southern belle. Everything's got to be traditional and clean, man on top, woman on bottom, that's the extent of her skills. She's so fixated on her own perfect little world that she doesn't even know how to step out of the norm and get downright nasty with her man. She's nice but, man, is she naïve and boring as hell in bed.'

His penis was getting hard as he shifted his thoughts to Septl. 'That Septl, on the other hand, that woman knows how to bring it. The only problem with her ass--she's too damn smart for her own good.'

He was real quiet, moving around the bedroom. After dressing, he tiptoed out and grabbed his jacket from the front hallway closet and left the apartment, locking the door behind him. He walked swiftly across the hall to Septi's apartment and rang her doorbell.

The doorbell startled Septi out of a deep sleep. Her heart began beating fast with anticipation because she knew it was nobody but Keith at her door. Ever since they hooked up, horniness and feelings of being unsatisfied were a distant memory. They had been having sex at least three times a week for months, and she was more than happy to have him as her very own private sex machine.

Septi reached over and grabbed the clock on her nightstand and saw that it was six o'clock in the morning. 'Damn, he's here early! I hope this Negro isn't taking me for fucking granted. I'm glad he's here, though, but I can't show it. I'm going to put on a serious face and play hardball with his ass. I'll show him I'm no plaything.'

"It's mighty early, isn't it?" Septi asked, yawning and trying her best to sound annoyed.

"Is it a problem?" Kandy asked.

"Of course not. It's just that you haven't been around for a few days."

"I've been busy working. A man can't live off sex alone." Kandy smiled and lightly patted her right breast.

Septi knocked his hand away. "Some people get paid for sex."

"Then you should pay me. I'll accept your money. I got some really good dick for sale," he laughed.

"Don't flatter yourself. There's a whole lot of dick floating around out there. I don't need to pay you or any other any man for it," she snapped back.

"That's funny. I don't see any dicks knocking down your door, banging to get in."

"You're fooling yourself if you think you know everything about me." Her temperature was rising.

"Girl, you're so hungry to get laid, I know nobody else is banging that pussy," he chuckled.

"Maybe I have a big appetite for sex." Septi rolled her eyes.

"You sure do. That's why we're sexually compatible. Woman, stop acting like you're not happy to see me and cook me some breakfast. I just got off from pulling a double and I'm starving," he said, playfully slapping her on her ass.

"How come I never see you in your uniform?"

"I always change into my street clothes before I leave work."

"Why? I always see correctional officers out in the streets dressed in their uniforms."

"They're stupid. When you wear your uniform in public, you set yourself up as a target," Kandy responded.

"Target for what? You're not a cop."

"Don't have to be no cop. There are a lot of criminals and folks out there who don't like correctional officers. They blame us for keeping their family members locked up and some of them even try to get revenge. You also got to remember, there are ex-inmates on the streets I could run into."

"That sounds crazy and farfetched to me."

"Crazy as it sounds, it's a fact of life. Me, I'm from the old school. I know how to survive. I've been doing this job for a long time. Let's change the subject. I'm not here to have a conversation about my uniform."

"I was just curious, that's all."

"Fix me some breakfast and I'll give you something to be curious about," Kandy said, pulling Septi in closer to him.

She put her arms around his neck and they began kissing. "Is feeding your stomach and having sex the only two things you ever think about?" she asked, giggling.

"Yep! Those two things are very important to a man. You know that."

"Well, I don't cook for any man," Septi declared as she turned and walked away.

"I'm not just any man. I'm your Big Daddy and don't you ever forget it," he said, smacking her ass again. "I'll be in the bedroom waiting for my breakfast."

Septi followed him into the bedroom. "OK, I'll order some food."

"Woman, you crazy! You better learn how to cook and save yourself some money. Anyway, do what you have to do cause I'm hungry."

"Is that supposed to be my problem?"

"Listen to me, Septi. You're a beautiful, intelligent woman but if you don't learn to relax and treat a brother right, you're going to have a hard time keeping a man. You're always going to find yourself alone."

"For your information, not every woman wants or needs a man."

"Since when?" he asked, raising his eyebrows.

"I don't know what kind of women you're used to dealing with, but I am my own woman. I only need a man for one thing, and to tell you the truth, I really don't need a man for that," Septi said.

"You'd better calm your ass down and start acting like a woman instead of a hard bitch. If you did that, you wouldn't have to continue settling for drive-by dick. You need to take some lessons from your friend Anabay. She's a good old-fashioned Southern woman," Kandy teased.

His words pierced Septi, making her steaming mad. "You got to be kidding me! If Anabay is such a good woman, why isn't your ass with her instead of here, with me? Get the fuck out of here and go on over to her place for some of that good old warm Southern hospitality," she shouted.

"Septi, chill out! You're always flying off the handle and missing the point. I'm only telling you the truth. If you want a man in your life, you need to step up your game," he shouted back at her.

"Well, I resent you comparing me to Anabay," Septi sulked. "Are you sure you don't have a romantic interest in her?"

Kandy knew he had Septi just where he wanted her. He sucked his teeth, "Woman, stop running your mouth and get me some breakfast. I need my strength so I can wear your pussy out. That is what you want, right?"

After Kandy grubbed down his breakfast of bacon, sunny side-up eggs, grits, hash browns, gravy and biscuits, it was business as usual.

"The food was all right for takeout, but home cooked is better. You need to learn to cook," he insisted.

"I guess like Anabay?" said Septi, with a sarcastic undertone.

He ignored her. "Come over here woman and take off those PJ's. Let Daddy see that ass of yours!"

Septi complied.

"Damn, Baby! Your ass looks good! Let's take a shower together. Umm, Umm, Umm. I'm getting hard as a mother. How about giving Daddy some showerhead?"

Septi stepped into the shower, feeling her nipples harden at the thought of her and Keith pleasuring each other.

"Damn, girl, go deep," Kandy moaned out. "Think of yourself as sucking on a black licorice stick."

Listening to Kandy's cries of passion delighted Septi. It was confirmation that she was pleasing the man she was entangled with at the moment. She felt electrified as the water trickled down their bodies.

They moved from the shower to the bed like two wet seals in heat, and Kandy gently crawled on top of her using his well-mastered sexual skills. He was more than capable of satisfying any woman.

Feeling his damp body pressing up against hers and hearing and feeling the rhythm of his hips made Septi's eyes roll back into her head and her toes crack. Everything was right with the world, at this moment anyway.

After they finished, she noticed him getting drowsy, so she shook him. "Keith, don't fall asleep! Get up! I've got to go to work. If I keep messing around with you, I won't have a job."

"Well, then, you better carry your crazy ass on to work cause I'm not looking for no dependents." He was energy-zapped.

"Very funny."

"What time is it anyway?" he asked.

"It's ten past eight."

"By the way, when was the last time you saw Anabay?" Kandy was smirking. He knew Anabay was Septi's Achilles heel and he wanted to rub it in.

"I haven't seen her in a while. She gets home late, now that she's working with her relatives on the restaurant they plan on opening. Why are you asking about her?"

"No reason," he answered, sounding nonchalant.

"You know what, Keith--I feel offended that you're asking me about her--right after you've finished screwing my ass," Septi blurted out, trying to hold her anger in check.

"I thought you were such a tough girl. You only need a man for one thing, right? You just a titty!" Kandy bent over and kissed Septi on her forehead. "Let me wash up and get out of here so you can get ready for work."

Septi felt a lot better knowing he was only teasing her.

He dressed and she escorted him to the door. "When will I see you again?"

"I don't know. It depends on my work schedule. I'll be in touch." He kissed her good-bye.

Septi closed the door and was walking back to her bedroom when she heard voices. "Oh shit, I hope he didn't run into Anabay! She'll know he was coming out of here. Oh, shit!" She looked through the peephole.

Not seeing anyone, she gently opened her door and had the shock of her life. She saw Keith opening the door to Anabay's apartment with a key.

Zenora Knight

Chapter 22

Man of the House

'Son of a bitch! How dare he leave my bed and run straight over to Anabay's,' a confused and fuming Septi thought to herself. 'It's eight fifteen in the fucking morning! What business could he possibly have with her this early and why in the hell does he have a key to her apartment? It wouldn't surprise me if he's banging her ass too. Fucking men! They're all alike. They will fuck anything moving, even a snake. I'm going to get to the bottom of this shit.'

Septi showered and dressed for work in black spandex pants and a black turtleneck sweater. 'I'm going over there right now and make sure Keith's ass is not there doing something he has no business doing. He is about to get the biggest shock of his life. He has no idea who he's messing with. I will blow his game at a drop of a dime."

Septi rang the doorbell and knocked on Anabay's door and waited, but no one came to the door. She thought to herself, 'That's strange--they're not answering the door. I can hear the TV so I know they're home. Besides, I just saw Keith go inside there. Anabay and Delbert always open the door for me. Now I know something is up.'

She knocked harder on the door, shouting out, "Anabay, I know you're in there. Open the door." Still, no one came to the door. Septi began frantically ringing the doorbell and banging on the door like someone was chasing her. Finally, she gave up and regained her composure. 'What the hell am I doing? I can't go around acting like this. I must be losing my goddamned mind. I'd better carry my black ass on to work.'

Behind closed doors, Kandy was stretched out on the sofa sipping a glass of orange juice and watching Eyewitness News. "Miss Ana, why didn't you open the door for your friend? I know you heard her yelling and knocking." He had a sly smile on his face.

"I heard her. I just didn't know how to explain to her why you would be sitting here in my living room this early in the morning," Anabay answered.

"It's none of her business why I'm here. She's not your mama. You don't have to explain diddly squat to that woman."

"I know that. I didn't feel like dealing with her this morning. Wonder why she was carrying on like that anyway? What do you think?"

"She probably thinks we've got something going on."

"Don't be silly! Why would you say that?"

"Because she's one nosy-ass woman. I'm sure she's been snooping around and monitoring my comings and goings from your place and has put two and two together."

"Well, I'd rather she find out about us later than sooner. Good thing Delbert was engrossed in his cartoons-- otherwise he would have opened the door for her. You left real early this morning. Where did you go? You couldn't have been out interviewing."

"I woke up early, so I grabbed a cup of coffee from the deli and took a long walk to clear my head. I'm really nervous about the interview I have this afternoon with Fidelity Securities. Finding a job has been a lot harder than I thought it would be. It's so degrading having to explain over and over again why I did time in prison. It's so unfair. The black guy gets the time while the big shot white guys only get a slap on the wrist."

"Kandy, keep thinking positively. Just be honest and upfront when you go on interviews. Tell them how someone framed you at your old job and how you had to do time even though you were innocent. If you do this and keep grinding the pavement, sooner or later, a company will give you a chance."

"That's exactly what I've been doing, Miss Ana, but you know how white folks are. Whenever I disclose that I've served time, the atmosphere in the room changes immediately. They don't even give me a chance to explain. They cut the interview short and say the same thing every single time, "We will get back to you.""

"You have to keep on believing in yourself. I certainly believe in you. You're going to land on your feet, you'll see," assured Anabay, gathering up her belongings to leave. "Delbert and I will be home late tonight."

"That's cool. How's everything going with the restaurant anyway?" Kandy asked.

"Everything's on schedule. Our grand opening should be soon. It's a dream come true for me, so you keep the faith. Your dreams will come true too."

"I sure hope so. It would be wonderful to land a good job again."

"Delbert, time to go. Did you remember to drink your orange juice?"

Not yet, Mommy," Delbert yelled, running into the kitchen. "Mommy, I don't see the juice."

At that moment, Anabay spotted the empty glass on the floor by Kandy. "Kandy, don't tell me you drank his orange juice!"

"Shit, yeah. How was I supposed to know it was his?"

"Come on, you knew it was his. You know I make him fresh orange juice every morning. I didn't make you any because you had already left."

"What's the big deal about some juice?" Kandy was clearly annoyed.

"You know how much he loves the juice I make for him."

Kandy rolled his eyes and sucked his teeth. "Just buy his little ass some juice from the deli. Juice is juice. He won't know the difference."

"That's not the point, Kandy! He does know the difference. I have been squeezing his juice for him ever since he can remember."

"Give me a freaking break!" Kandy said under his breath.

"Delbert, let's go," Anabay commanded, clearly pissed.

"Mommy, where is my orange juice?" Delbert asked, walking into the living room from the kitchen.

"Baby, Mommy forgot to make you juice this morning."

Delbert started crying, "Mommy, you never forget! I want my juice, Mommy, I want it! I want it now, Mommy!"

"Delbert, we'll stop by the store and I'll buy you some juice on the way to Aunt Lillie Mae's house."

"No, Mommy, I want to drink my juice now!" Delbert dropped to the floor and began screaming and banging his fists into the floor and kicking his feet in a temper tantrum.

"Delbert, come on, baby. Mommy is so sorry. I promise, I'll buy you some juice from the store."

"What the hell! If this ain't some bullshit right! You better get your little ass up off that floor before I come over there and give you something to cry about for real!" Kandy shouted at Delbert.

"Kandy, stop it! Don't talk to him like that! He's my son!" Anabay shouted.

"Look, woman, you need to step aside. I'll be damned if I'm going to let you make a sissy out of this boy before my very own eyes. Get up, Delbert," Kandy ordered.

Delbert jumped to his feet and ran behind Anabay. "Mommy! Mommy, help me."

Kandy grabbed Delbert by the arm and said in a stern voice, "Stop your crying right now, you hear me! Your mommy said she's going to buy you some juice from the store. You understand that, don't you?

Delbert whimpered, "Yes."

"Now look at me, Boy. Until you're able to pay some bills up in here, you have no say in this house. You got that, Boy?"

Delbert whispered, "Yes."

"Now put on your jacket and be on your way." Kandy sat back down on the sofa and picked up the remote control.

"Kandy, what you have just done is completely unacceptable to me! I discipline my son, not you!" Anabay was mad as a hornet, zipping up Delbert's jacket.

"Well, perhaps I don't have any further business here if you feel the need to confront me in front of your son."

"Perhaps you don't," she snapped at him.

"I guess you want me to leave then. I was only trying to help Delbert. Do you want him growing up in a home without a male to give him proper guidance?"

"I cannot allow you to talk to my son like you did. Yes, you should leave. Have your things out of here by the time I get back home tonight. Leave my key on the table."

"Whatever you say. You know what? You are one dumb bitch!" Kandy was very angry.

"Goodbye, Kandy. Delbert, let's go. I'll buy some oranges and make juice for you when we get to Aunt Lillie Mae's."

Anabay left, slamming the door behind her. She was shaken to her core. Over and over in her mind, she kept saying, 'I can't believe he called me a bitch.'

This was the first time she and Kandy had ever argued. She thought to herself, 'I was really into him and I thought he was into me and Delbert too. Good thing he revealed himself before I got in too deep with him. There is no way I'm ever going to allow him or any other man to abuse my son. Claudale is gone and Delbert is the product of our love. He is everything to me. I'll miss Kandy, but Delbert will always come first with me.'

Kandy was agitated about what had transpired between him and Anabay. He was ranting inside, 'Damn, I'm glad her ass is gone out of here. Now, I have the crib all to myself to think. Shit, the stuff I have to lie about and put up with! Goddamn women! You can't live with them and you damn sure can't live without their asses. All they think about is having a perfect little world to brag about to their family and girlfriends. Fuck that shit. It's not about them and their fucking asses. It's about what a brother needs. If she thinks for one minute I'm going to allow that little brat ass son of hers to come between us, she'd better think again. It ain't happening, captain. I'm not going nowhere. She hasn't figured it out yet, but she's my meal ticket.'

He became even angrier thinking about Septi trying to bang Anabay's door down. 'She probably saw me coming in here with her nosy ass. That's the problem with bitches like her, once a brother lays some good pipe on their asses, they think they own you. Well, I don't give a damn if she did see me coming in here. It's none of her goddamn business and I'm going to let her know that, the next time I see her ass. She's crazier than a mother! She's got more balls than any bitch I've ever fucked before. If she crosses me, she'll find herself floating in the Hudson River.'

Kandy kept on with his internal tirade. 'Anabay's got a lot of nerve too. There is only one man under any roof where I rest my head, whether it's temporary or permanent, and that one man is me. She should know this about me already and if she doesn't, she's going to find out soon. Let me take a shower and cool my ass down. I think I'll walk on over to the old neighborhood and pay my Missus a visit. I need to stroke her big ass anyway, just in case things fall apart here. I'll spend the night with her and make her feel special. This will give Miss Southern fried, prissy-ass Anabay some time to think about how she reacted this morning. I need to hurry--I damn sure don't want to be around when that bitch across the hall comes home from work.'

Kandy dressed and headed for the door, but then he thought, 'Let me leave a note 'cause I'm not about to leave my key.'

He wrote, "Dear Miss Ana, so sorry about what went down this morning. Guess the job interview had me all wound up. My cousin Freddy called and his wife is in the hospital. He asked me to babysit his kids so I'll be spending the night at his house."

Kandy reread the note and began laughing so hard, out loud, that one would have thought someone was there laughing with him. He was thinking to himself, 'Ain't no bitch ever caught my ass in a lie. I know how to out-think them and stay one step ahead of them.'

Kandy walked down the street with the mid-March sun beaming down on his face and the wind beating against his cheeks. "Damn, it's nippy out here," he mumbled out loud. "It's true what they say, a black man can't stand no cold weather. It's like mixing oil and vinegar."

Zenora Knight

Chapter 23

Daddy's Home

After a ninety-minute walk, Kandy arrived at the intersection of Clinton Avenue and Bergen Street, his old neighborhood. He was eager to see what changes had taken place during his absence.

He paused on the corner for a minute or so, soaking in the sights and sounds of this familiar place. 'Nothing's changed much. Yep, there's the liquor store, Field's Chicken Shack, the pizzeria, the Jamaican bakery and that nasty-ass Chinese restaurant.' It was almost four o'clock and the streets were full of people, young and old. Music (rap and rhythm and blues) was blaring from boom boxes and from the souped-up vehicles of young wanna-be gangstas.

'This place is in my rearview mirror now--I'm miles ahead of these folks,' Kandy thought to himself, before turning right on Clinton. He was halfway up the block when he felt a tap on his back and the sound of a familiar voice, "Yo, Dude! My main man, Keith Jackson--Kandy, the Fucking Kid."

Kandy turned around, and there stood one of his old running partners, Billy Barnes, a.k.a. Big Blue on the streets. The two men slapped each other five and embraced.

"Man, I thought it was about goddamned time they let your ass out of the big house. Been a lot of changes on the street since you been gone. What halfway house they got you staying at anyway?" asked Big Blue.

"The one in South Orange. But you know me--I comes and goes as I pleases. Nothing or nobody gonna put constraints on my ass. I set the tone first day there with that punk ass dude running the place."

"You talking smack. How'd you set some tone at a half-way house?" laughed Big Blue.

"Just hold my jacket."

Kandy took off his black leather jacket, rolled up his sleeves and flexed his muscles.

Big Blue's eyes almost bulged out of his eye sockets. "Damn Dude, what the hell they been feeding your ass in the big house? Must have been a lot of spinach cause your arms look just like Popeye's!"

The two men slapped each other high five again and they both laughed so hard, tears were in their eyes.

"I'm heading to the Lollipop Lounge over on Spruce Street. Why don't you come on and go with me?" asked Big Blue.

"I don't remember no Lollipop Lounge on Spruce. Is it new?"

"You remember the Kitty Kat Lounge, don't you?

"Yeah."

"Well, that place went out of business and was replaced by the Lollipop Lounge. That's where us old heads hang out now. If you come with me, you're going to see a lot of your homies and, guess what, your girl Cookie is still the bartender. I bet you remember her!" said Big Blue, winking at the mention of Cookie's name.

"I can spare a little time. Let's go." Kandy was secretly thinking, 'Damn, I can't believe Big Blue let himself go like this. The brother needs some serious dental work and some Tic Tacs, too.'

Kandy was treated like a rock star at the Lollipop Lounge, receiving much love and respect from everyone there. His friends and acquaintances embraced him and treated him to food, drinks, and blunts while hanging on to his every word about prison escapades. They shared with him what was currently going on in the streets, who the major players were, who was in jail and who had died. Big Blue egged Kandy to flex his muscles again, and everyone was in awe of his physique, especially the women. Several ladies slipped their phone numbers to him. 'The kid still got it--women trying to hit me up,' he thought.

He was having such a good time socializing, he lost track of the time. "Damn, it's close to nine o'clock. I'd better carry my ass on home and deal with the Missus," he said to his friends. As he was preparing to leave, he purposely stood still for a moment so he could take a mental snapshot of his surroundings. He had felt right at home and had truly enjoyed the smoky, lively atmosphere. After embracing all, he said, "See ya!" and departed.

Kandy was feeling mellow and in full swagger, walking the four blocks to his house. Gangs of teenagers were hanging out on every street corner, but he didn't feel intimidated because he knew how to carry himself, with confidence. After all, he used to be 'The Man' on these streets. 'If one of these young punks step to me, they're going to learn something,' he thought.

He could see that the house was in a state of serious deterioration when he stepped up on the porch. 'Justine should be ashamed of herself. She's letting this house go to hell,' he thought, shaking his head and knocking on the front door.

"Who is it?" Kathy, his oldest daughter, yelled.

"It's me, your Daddy," he answered.

"Daddy's home, Daddy's home!" Kathy screamed, unlocking the three locks on the front door. She jumped into her daddy's arms and planted kisses all over his face.

The next sound heard was the stampede of eight running feet followed by eight arms reaching out to touch and embrace their daddy from his four other children, Kash, Kenny, Kareem, and Kimberly.

Kandy hugged and embraced each of them. "Where's your mother?"

"Mommy, Mommy, Daddy's home!" the kids were shouting out in unison.

Justine, Kandy's wife of fifteen years, walked into the living room, holding a dishcloth in her hand. She was wearing a purple, polyester housecoat and sneakers on her feet. Her face bore a definite look of disgust.

"You just going to stand there or are you going to come and give your husband a hug and kiss?" Kandy asked, with his arms opened and a wide grin on his face. Secretly, he was shocked by his wife's appearance, so he tried to play it off. 'Looks like she's put on another twenty to thirty pounds. Good God, she's a piece of meat all right!' he thought to himself.

Justine had been his high school sweetheart. Back in the day, they were the "it" couple, the Ken and Barbie of the hood. Justine stood at five feet, six inches, had a beautiful deep-brown complexion, long, thick black hair and big brown eyes. In high school, she had been a straight A student, a cheerleader, and voted the female most likely to succeed by her classmates. College had been a consideration, but she opted instead to get a job and to marry Kandy after he made it clear he was not about to wait around for her to finish school. When they got married, Justine was a size ten. Now, she was a size twenty-four.

He walked over to Justine and embraced her in a big bearhug. "Come here, woman, and give me some love."

Justine melted in his arms, although she tried hard not to show it. His arms felt so inviting, her body surrendered to his touch and she couldn't help smiling from ear to ear. She always had a problem when it came to her husband, she could never stay angry with him for long periods of time. He was just too charming and too damn good looking. Although he had major faults, he belonged to only her on paper. Nobody could take that away from her. "So, you finally made it home," she said, sarcastically.

"Woman, what are you talking about? I was just released. You know I couldn't leave the halfway house right away."

"Save it, Keith. You were released months ago. I'm nobody's fool. I also know you've been down at the bar eating, drinking and getting high." Justine turned and walked away. This was her way of letting him know she was pissed off.

Kandy sucked his teeth, waved his hand at her and continued playing, laughing and talking with their children.

Justine returned to the living room around eleven o'clock. "Bedtime, everybody. I don't want to hear no backtalk, you hear me? Y'all won't be able to get your little asses up in the morning."

The kids reluctantly said their goodnights and went to bed.

Kandy had the munchies, so he barreled into the kitchen and started rummaging through the refrigerator for something to eat. "Nothing in here but dairy products, milk, eggs, butter and cheese," he mumbled. He closed the refrigerator door and opened up the cabinets. "Nothing in here either but some bread, peanut butter, jelly and cereal. Hey, Justine, I'm hungry."

Justine entered the kitchen looking combative with her hands on her hips. "So, where you been, Keith? At one of your bitches' house? What happened? Did she get tired of your sorry ass and kick you out or did the bitch finally realize you're nothing but a con? I know one or the other had to have happened--that's the only reason your ass came crawling back here tonight."

"I'm not in the mood for your nagging tonight, Justine. I'm starving. Fix me something to eat."

"I'm not fixing you a goddamn thing! You should have eaten at your bitch's house before she threw you out."

"I'm telling you, woman, for the last time --- I've been staying in a halfway house. They wouldn't let me out on my own until today."

"And I guess they wouldn't let you make a phone call, either," Justine said, not letting up.

"I didn't want to contact you until I could come and visit with you and the kids. I can only stay the night, but in three more months, I'll be completely free to live back at home."

"And my dead mother is sitting in the living room as we speak. You are a bald-faced liar and you need to cut the crap!" Justine felt frustrated by her husband's lies. She thought, 'When is he ever going to stop lying? He should know, I know all his tricks after all these years. It's the same old shit, nothing new.'

"Woman, stop trying to push my buttons. I'm telling you the God's honest truth."

Justine moved in closer, raising her voice. "I know when you're lying. You can't bullshit me. I've known you far too long. Matter of fact, I know you better than you know yourself." She hated it when he lied to her. She had already verified his release date and she knew he was somewhere, conning somebody. She was all too familiar with his routine and she knew, sooner or later, he would show up on her doorstep.

Kandy was getting hot under the collar. He could feel his blood pressure rising. He felt like saying, 'The way you look, Bitch, you should be grateful I've even stepped one foot in this motherfucker,' but he restrained himself. Instead, he said, "Look, Justine, stop the bitching and fronting like you're not happy to see me. I have every right to be here. You're my wife and these are my kids. I came here as soon as I could. Why is there no food around here?"

"Because those five growing kids of ours eat up everything in sight. But you wouldn't know that— you've been eating your three-square meals for free in prison. It's hard having to do everything around here by myself--cook, clean, wash, feed and clothe them. I should have listened to my mama. She told me I would have a hard life if I married you. The handwriting was on the wall, I just couldn't see it."

"Damn it, woman! Stop running your mouth! You don't know when to quit!" He was furious.

Justine sensed she was skating on thin ice, so she immediately backed down. "I'll make you some grilled cheese sandwiches." Her mind flashed back to the day Kandy got so angry, he almost strangled her. When his temper became unleashed, he could turn like a ferocious pit bull and God have mercy on whoever his anger is directed towards.

Kandy wolfed down the sandwiches. "I can't believe how much the kids have grown, especially Kash. That boy looks like he's grown over a foot since the last time I saw him."

"Keith, it's time for my recertification. I'm going to need you to go with me down to the Welfare Department. That way I can add you back to my grant and get more money and food stamps."

"Justine, I'm not going with you down to no fucking Welfare, begging for their measly handouts."

"Excuse me! How in the hell do you think we survived while you were locked up? You certainly weren't able to send us any money," she snapped back.

"Look, Woman, things are about to change around here. My parole officer is working on getting me a job as a counselor in a group home for boys. I'll have to spend most of my nights away from home, but the pay is good. I'll be able to support you and the kids. Forget about welfare."

"And just when are you supposed to get this job?" asked Justine, with a strong hint of skepticism in her voice.

"I should be working by the beginning of June."

"I'll believe it when I see it," she replied. "We've managed to do OK but, like I said, it has been hard on me. I'm tired of being both the mother and the father to our kids. Kash likes to run the streets all the time and Kathy is already boy crazy at ten years old. Just last week, Kareem got suspended from school for three days for punching a kid in the eye. It's exhausting raising these kids by myself, but you wouldn't have any idea about it, would you?"

Kandy was thinking to himself, 'You're tired all the time because your ass is too goddamn big.' "Look, Baby, I'm sorry I haven't been here for you and the kids. I promise you this, though--this time I'm home for good. I've made a vow to myself never to do anything in life to get locked up for again. When this parole period is over, I swear to you, I'm coming home and I'm going to be the husband and the father you and the kids deserve."

"Keith, I can only hope and pray that you're speaking the truth and that you're serious about changing your life this time," Justine said, looking serious. Her heart was palpitating because she had been waiting a very long time to hear these words out of her husband's mouth. With every fiber of her being, she wanted to believe him, but in her gut, she knew he was conning her.

"Come over here, Baby, and sit by me. You're treating me like I'm a stranger instead of your husband. What you got on under that housecoat? I'm hungry again and it's not for some sandwiches," Kandy said, flashing a sexy smile and winking at her.

Justine's heart started beating fast and her knees felt weak, like they were giving way under the weight of her body. Her husband truly rocked her world. He never failed to arouse her sexually. But at the same time, she felt an overwhelming sense of dread because she was ashamed of her body. "Keith, I'm too tired tonight. Besides, I need to straighten up around here."

"Tired? Who have you been giving my stuff to?" he asked, knowing full well Justine was faithful to him.

"You know the answer to that," she said, playfully elbowing him.

"I'll help you and then we can take a shower together." He knew Justine was self-conscious about her body and this was his way of teasing her.

"I don't need any help. Go on to sleep and get out of my way." Justine was trying to look and sound agitated.

"As you wish. but don't keep me waiting long," smirked Kandy, slapping her behind.

Justine liked the way he said, "Don't keep me waiting long." It had been years since she last had sex, and she could feel her vagina contracting at the thought of her husband giving her some. She hurried up and finished her household tasks.

In the meantime, Kandy had taken a shower and was lying on the bed with a towel around his waist, watching television. Justine was blown away by his chiseled body when she entered the bedroom. She snatched up her nightgown, ran into the bathroom, and started hyperventilating. All kinds of crazy thoughts came flooding into her mind. 'I'm not good enough for him, I'm too fat to turn him on, he's going to be disgusted by my body, and on and on.' After thirty minutes of self-deprecating thoughts, she showered thoroughly, making sure her private parts were clean before putting on her 5X nightgown. When she came back to the bedroom, he was sound asleep. Justine was disappointed and relieved at the same time. She turned off the television and quietly climbed into bed.

Kandy was awakened by the vibration of her body settling into bed. He turned towards her and started feeling her breasts through her nightgown. "Why are you wearing clothes to bed? Sit up, let me take them off. I want your nipples in my mouth."

Just his words alone made Justine's body hot and ready. She took a deep breath. "Keith, can I be honest with you? I've gained some more weight and I'm scared you might be turned off by my body."

"Justine, how many times I got to tell you. I love you. I will always desire you. It don't matter to me if you're fat or thin. You are my wife and my best friend. We've been together all our lives and I will always want you. Besides, you know I like a woman with some meat on her bones. Come on, let's take this shit off you now."

Kandy was a master of foreplay. He kissed Justine hard and long while his hands massaged her breasts. He slid down in the bed and started sucking on her nipples, alternating between the right and the left breast and with his right hand, he parted her legs and started fishing for her clit. "Tell me you saved this good pussy for me," he whispered, trying to sound eager.

In ecstasy and in between moans, Justine replied, barely audible, "You know I ain't been with no other man."

"Bingo! Umm, I got the little man in the boat," he whispered. He started kissing her clitoris while Justine lay back, biting her lips with her eyes closed. Her lower body was responding and moving in rhythm with Kandy's tongue. He kept applying the pressure until she had an orgasm. By this time, Justine was moaning and breathing so hard, he knew it was time for the grand finale. He inserted his dick into her and began humping.

Kandy was excited, chanting, "Who's your daddy? I can't hear you? Whose pussy is this? Say it loud! Say it louder!" When she didn't answer him back fast enough, he playfully slapped her thighs.

Justine was moaning and crying out, "Keith, I missed you so much! Bang it up! Fuck me, Daddy. It's all yours!"

Their voices plus the sounds of the mattress and the box spring squeaking from the weight of Justine's body and Kandy's hard thrusting were so loud, it sounded like a locomotive traveling at full speed down a train track.

"Daddy, stop it! You're hurting Mommy." Kareem, their youngest son came bursting into their bedroom.

Kandy looked at him, not missing a stroke. "Daddy's not hurting Mommy. Now get your little narrow ass back to bed! I'll explain everything to you in the morning."

"But you are, Daddy. Why are you on top of her?" Kareem cried.

A panting and out-of-breath Justine yelled out, "Do what your Daddy told you and close the goddamned door behind you."

Kandy and Justine finished what they had started. 'Good God Almighty! It's a good thing that I have a good back. She can't say now, I don't know what exhaustion is,' Kandy thought to himself, drifting off to sleep.

Justine fell asleep with a big wide smile on her face. She slept like a baby. When she woke up in the morning, her smile quickly evaporated when she realized Kandy was long gone and he didn't even say goodbye.

Chapter 24

Cat Fight

Septi kicked her shoes off the minute she walked through her door. 'Damn, there's no place like home.' She was flipping through television channels with her remote control when she heard loud voices outside her apartment.

'What's all the commotion in the hallway?' she wondered. She sprang up from her sofa to the door, pressing against the peephole. 'What the fuck? That's Anabay! Who's she talking to? Is that Keith? Yep, that's his ass all right. Motherfucker! I know damn well they had to have heard me banging on the door yesterday.' "I'm going to confront their asses right now," she declared, out loud. She swung her door open and placed her hands on her hips. "Hi, guys. Is everything OK? I heard some noise and thought I'd check it out."

"Hi, Septi. Everything's fine. We're just talking. You remember Keith, don't you?"

Kandy stood there, holding up the wall with a sly grin on his face. "Nice to see you again. I'm sorry, how do you pronounce your name again--is it Setti or Septi?"

"You know goddamn well what my name is, you low-life scumbag!" Septi couldn't control her anger and feelings of pure hatred towards him because the truth was staring back at her, square in the face. This man had been using her as his side piece. His romantic interests lay with Anabay and it was obvious --- they were involved with each other. His body language, the look in his eyes, and his pretending not to know her name said it all.

"Septi! What is wrong with you? Why are you being so rude to Keith?" Anabay was floored by Septi's attitude and the way she spoke to Kandy.

"It's OK, Miss Ana. I'm not offended by your neighbor's rudeness. Obviously, she is a miserable woman on the inside."

Septi had a defensive air about her as she stood in her doorway, rolling her eyes back and forth at Kandy, with her arms folded across her chest."

"Anabay, please tell me you're not involved with this dirt bag. You can do a whole lot better than his ass."

"Septi, you are out of line! First of all, Keith is my friend and, secondly, I choose for myself who I get involved with. You need to stay out of my business with your nosy self! What is this all about?"

"Girl, you are so fucking naïve, it's a goddamn shame. Let me enlighten you about Prince Charming here. He's nothing but an old player. He ..... "

"Miss Ana, your friend is jealous over our relationship. Come on, let's go inside and let her cool down," Kandy interjected, nervously tugging on Anabay's arm.

"You know what, Septi? I am sick and tired of you meddling in my business! My God, I can't even enter and exit my own apartment without you staring me in the face and putting me through the third degree. You need to stop it."

"I'm looking out for you. You should be grateful," Septi shouted.

Kandy was still tugging on Anabay's arm to go inside her apartment. "No, Keith, I'm not going inside! Septi needs to be put in her place! I'm going to deal with her right here, right now!" Anabay shifted her attention back to Septi. "Septi, for your information, Keith and I are in a serious relationship. We are living together and we are planning on getting married and moving far away from you. How do you like those apples?"

"Married! Now I know you've lost your damn mind? You don't even know this dude!"

"Dude? My fiancé's name is Keith! Who do you think you are? You're always criticizing and passing judgment on everybody you meet! The last time I checked, I was a grown woman! I make my own decisions! I certainly don't need your permission or approval to fall in love!" Anabay was so upset, tears began streaming from her eyes.

"Anabay, you are moving too fast! Slow it the hell down! Believe me, you have no idea what your man has been doing behind your back."

"Why don't you educate me, then? You seem to know my boyfriend better than I do," Anabay sobbed.

By now, a couple of neighbors had opened their doors to observe, making Kandy feel even more uncomfortable.

"Enough of this bullshit! This is ridiculous!" Kandy shouted out angrily. He was literally freaking out on the inside because he could see from the hateful look in Septi's eyes, she had no compunction whatsoever about exposing his infidelity. He turned to Anabay, "Baby, don't lower yourself like this. This is not you, shouting back and forth in the hallway with this crazy woman. Come on, let's go inside and leave her to her madness."

Septi was enjoying watching him squirm. "Go on inside, Mr. Jackson! Slither inside like the spineless creepy crawler you are! Where are your balls now, Big Man? If you were a real man, you would tell your fiancée the truth about your extracurricular activities!"

"I don't know what the hell you're talking about," Kandy shouted at Septi. Although he appeared to be cool on the outside, he was actually melting down on the inside. He wished he could get his hands on her and shut her up permanently.

"Oh, yes you do. I'll bet you a hundred dollars you haven't forgotten about the...."

Kandy turned to Anabay, "I'm not going to stand here and take this chick's crap anymore." He turned to face Septi and shouted out, "Enough of your harassment!

You know what? I'm going to call the police on your ass right now!"

"Please do! Please call the police," Septi teased.

"No! No! No!" shouted Anabay. "Do me a favor, Keith, go inside. Please. I can handle this."

"I'm not leaving you alone with this jealous, deranged woman. Why, she's crazier than a bed bug! I don't trust her." He turned to Septi, "You'd better be damn glad you're a woman, because otherwise I--"

"Or what! What you gonna do, Big Man?"

"Just go inside now, Keith," Anabay demanded.

"If you insist. But if you need me, I'm right on the other side of this door."

"That's right, run on inside. You punk-ass whore-dog motherfucker!" screamed Septi.

"Bitch," he mumbled under his breath.

Kandy stood with his ears pressed up against the other side of the door listening, with his stomach in knots and his fists clenched. He was mad as hell with himself for not being in control of the catfight about to unfold between the two women on the other side of the door. He was furious with Septi and, in his mind, he was calling her every name he could think of. Oh, how he wished he had kept his dick in his pants. 'That bitch is no joke,' he thought to himself. 'I'll get street and fuck her yellow ass up if she keeps messing with me. The nerve of that dirty bitch, trying her best to humiliate me in front of Anabay. She's one vindictive whore! She's just itching to spill the beans about me. Now, all my plans are going to be ruined. God damnit! Fuck!'

"Anabay, I thought we were best friends. I don't even know you!" Septi shouted..

Anabay took a deep breath, knowing the time had come for her to put her friend in her place once and for all. She thought back to the night when they first met and how Septi had made those painful, piercing remarks about Claudale not being there for the birth of their son and how insensitive Septi had been when Claudale died. She was fed up to her eyeballs with Septi's intrusive behavior and with all the snide and negative comments Septi continuously made about the people Anabay cared about.

Anabay forced herself to calm down and she lowered her voice before speaking. "Septi, I want you to understand this. You are my best friend and I love you dearly, but you need to stay in your lane. I am sick and tired of your nosiness and your insensitivity. You had no right to attack Keith the way you did and yell out all those obscenities about him. He is my man and if you can't accept him, then perhaps you can't accept me and Delbert either. I'm--"

"So now you are putting Delbert in the middle of this!" Septi interrupted. "How dare you bring Delbert into this? I'm the one who had to cut his umbilical cord when his low-life father was nowhere to be found."

"I'm not going to waste any more of my time going back and forth with you, Septi. Have a good night."

Septi stood there, shaking her head. "There's no hope for you, Anabay. You're going to deserve everything that's coming your way for being so stupid!" She turned and slammed the door behind her.

"Good night!" Anabay responded, slamming her door.

"My little Miss Ana, you're full of surprises! Girl, you got a lot of fire in you. I like a woman who stands up for her man." Kandy was beaming from ear to ear. He draped his arms around Anabay and pulled her in closer to him. "I am so proud of you. I just want to hold you tight and never let go. My girl!" On the inside, he was thinking, 'Damn, that was a close call.'

"It's not about you, Kandy. Septi needed to be put in her place," Anabay said, slightly jerking away from him.

"Oh yeah? It's about me all right and it's serious. One minute you're kicking me out, then in the next minute, I find out we're engaged and are going to get married. Damn, Baby, you sure are good. You move fast. I just love it! Oh, I just love it!" he laughed.

"Look, Kandy, it's not funny. You know good and well I only said those things to shut her mouth up. She got on my last nerve today and I just couldn't hold it in any longer. Septi always has to put everybody down and she never has anything good to say about anyone."

"You were good, Baby. Come here and give me a hug." Kandy continued laughing and embracing Anabay. "Damn, Baby, you sure feel good. Please tell me everything is all right between the two of us."

"No, everything is not all right between the two of us. I am still very angry with you for disciplining Delbert yesterday. He is my son and I am the one who does the disciplining, not you. You had no right to speak to him in that rough manner, like you did. I am very protective of him and I'm not ready to share parenting him with you or anybody else, for that matter. You and I have come to a crossroad and I think we need to slow it down and rethink our relationship."

"Come on, Miss Ana, we've been through this already. Being overprotective of your son is only going to hinder him from growing up and becoming a real man. I'll admit, I was tough on the little guy, and for that I apologize. But it irks me when I see all you women babying your sons to death. Little boys need two things --- discipline and a strong male figure in their life. I thank God every day for my father. He was my role model and my best friend."

"Look, I know what you're saying is true. It's just that I'm not prepared emotionally right now to share raising Delbert with anyone. His father and I were very much in love and Delbert is the product of our love. Unfortunately, Claudale was taken away from us too soon."

"So Delbert's got to pay the price for that?" Kandy interrupted.

"No, that's not what I'm saying. I was saying Claudale died without ever laying an eye on Delbert. I know I'm overprotective but I can't help it. Delbert is and will always be the most important person in my life."

"No argument from me. Delbert should be the most important person to you. I just want to be a part of both of your lives." Kandy's voice started breaking up and his eyes teared up. "I have always wanted a son and I'm sorry if I overstepped my boundary, but I love that little guy. I love him."

"I believe you care about Delbert and I really appreciate you for it, but I'm not comfortable with you disciplining him. We are still getting to know each other. Let's change the subject. I made it clear to you yesterday morning that you should move out and leave my keys on the table. Why did you walk up on me in the grocery store? Were you following me?"

"I don't have to follow you. I know your habits. I wanted to see you and apologize to you for the ugly things I said. It's been bothering me."

"I accept your apology, but that doesn't mean we're going to pick up where we left off. Like I said, we need to slow it down because the bottom line is, I'm not going to let you or anyone else mistreat my son.

"I never mistreated the boy. I was tough on him because I don't want to see him growing up to be a sissy boy," Kandy declared.

"Delbert's my baby! There is nothing wrong with me showering him with love and affection and I'm going to do so until the day I die. There is a right way and a wrong way to discipline children and speaking harshly to them is definitely the wrong way. And do me another favor, Kandy--please stop using the words 'sissy boy' when referring to my son. I don't like it."

"You'll never hear those words out my mouth again and I apologize again, to the both of you, for my behavior. You two are my family now. I love you guys and I'll do whatever it takes to make the both of you happy. I promise not to interfere in your parenting of Delbert. Please give me a second chance, Miss Ana. I love you so much and I don't want to lose you. Please, say it's not over between the two of us."

"Kandy, just relax, OK?"

"I can't relax. I'm the underdog in this relationship."

"What does that mean?"

"Look at you--you're about to own your own business and I can't even land a job. How do you think that makes me feel?"

"I don't know, Kandy. I just assumed you were happy for me."

"Don't get me wrong--I am very happy for you. It's just that your success makes me feel inferior to you. I did my time and I still can't catch a break. I fear you won't need or want me around once your business is up and running. I guess I'm not used to having such a strong, successful woman in my life."

"That's really touching, Kandy, but you shouldn't feel like that. I know you've been having a hard time trying to get back on your feet and I have no doubt you will."

"I know you're right, but sometimes it can be downright discouraging. I've been on so many interviews and haven't gotten one damn offer yet."

"Give it some time."

"I have. It's been a few months already. Sometimes I get the feeling somebody has blackballed me. This type of thing is common in the securities industry. My criminal record was supposed to have been sealed--but who knows, maybe people remember and are still talking."

"You think so?"

"I sure do. I've seen it happen to other people before."

"Well, don't give up. Everything is going to be all right."

"Thanks for your vote of confidence. Having your support keeps me motivated. Just knowing that I'm a part of your and Delbert's life has given my life a new meaning. A family of my own is all I've ever wanted."

"That's nice, Kandy."

"Miss Ana, I don't think you understand. I have always wanted a family and I have always dreamed about having a son to run and play with and to teach him about the facts of life and manhood. I have really fallen in love with you and Delbert and I want so much for the two of you to love me back. I want to get to know your aunt and uncle too. Is that ever going to happen?"

"As I said before, we need to slow things down. You will be introduced to them when the time is right."

"You're not ashamed of me, are you?"

"Don't be silly. That reminds me, Delbert and I are going to stay over my aunt and uncle's house tonight. I only came home to pack our overnight bags."

"What about me? You just going to up and leave me like this?"

"You weren't supposed to be here, remember? Uncle Otis and I have an appointment with the contractors for the restaurant at seven o'clock in the morning. It's better for us to sleep over there. This way, I won't have to wake Delbert up so early in the morning."

Kandy grabbed Anabay's hands and stared into her eyes. "Tell me you still want me and that nothing has changed between us--except we're slowing it down."

"Nothing has changed, Kandy, and of course, I want you in my life." Anabay surprised herself, when these words came pouring out of her mouth. There were two dueling Anabays inside of her. The emotional, needy Anabay had won the battle, overruling the thinking, rational, mother-hen Anabay, who had every intention of ending this relationship. Kandy had touched her heart in a big way with his candid talk and especially when he revealed his vulnerabilities to her. "You're going to be fine. There's plenty of food in the refrigerator."

"Can we fuck before you leave?"

"Since when did you start referring to our lovemaking as fucking?"

"Relax, Baby, you're too stiff," Kandy said, laughing and pulling her in closer to him. "I was talking about a quickie. It would be good for both of us to release some tension. What do you say?"

"I have too much on my mind to think about sex right now. I need to pack." Anabay pulled away from him.

"All right, Babe, whatever you say." Kandy realized he needed to chill out and play it cool if he wanted to hang on to Anabay. He had big plans after all, for spending all that money she would soon be making in her restaurant. One more mistake with her could end up costing him everything. He was sitting on the sofa pretending to be relaxing when she walked from the bedroom, carrying a big overnight bag.

"I'm leaving now. See you tomorrow evening."

Kandy jumped up and embraced her. "Bye, Baby. I'll be here waiting for you with bated breath. Are you sure we can't squeeze in a quickie?"

"Kandy!"

"Just teasing! Your reaction was priceless," he laughed. "See you tomorrow."

Kandy couldn't relax. Septi was deep in his head. He kept reflecting on how she had taunted him and tried to expose him. She was his worst nightmare--a dick-crazed scorned woman. He knew from experience that there would be no reasoning with a woman like her and that she wouldn't stop until she got her revenge. 'Septi thinks she's is a sophisticated woman but in reality, she's nothing but a backstabbing hooker,' he thought to himself.

He was pacing back and forth from the kitchen to the living room, trying to figure out how to deal with her. There was no way he was going to allow Septi to blow up his spot. 'I guess I'll just have to confront her ass head-on. There's no other way,' he decided. He walked down the hall and rang her doorbell.

Septi walked to the door and looked through her peephole, and saw him standing there. "What the hell do you want?" she shouted.

"Open the door. We need to talk," Kandy demanded.

"We have nothing to talk about."

"Like hell we don't! Now open the door before I'm forced to kick it in!"

Septi cracked her door and blocked the doorway with her body to prevent him from entering. Kandy shoved right on in anyway, almost knocking her down.

"Excuse me. I didn't invite you in. How dare you just push past me in my own home." Septi was fighting mad. She felt like kicking him in his balls. "What the fuck do you want?"

"Look, Septi, I am here to make peace with you. I never meant to hurt you. I'm sorry you had to find out about me and Anabay like this." Feeling desperate, he knew he had to somehow calm her down, otherwise, she would eventually ruin everything for him.

"You know what, Keith, you're nothing but a low-down dirty dog. You rang my doorbell at six o'clock in the morning, fucked me for two hours and then you marched your funky ass back down the hall to Anabay's apartment, pretending to be her devoted fiancé. You've been fucking me for months! You are full of shit! I hate men like you!"

"Look, you and I had some good times. We both enjoyed each other. Besides, you always acted like you didn't want or need a man. Why don't you admit it--you were just using me for your own sexual pleasure. I was nothing more than a human dildo to you and now you've got the nerve to be mad with me because I hooked up with your friend."

"You are unreal! It's unbelievable how you twist things up to take the responsibility off yourself. I wonder if Anabay would see things your way?"

"I wonder if she would still consider you to be her best friend if she knew you had spread your legs wide open and invited her man in every chance you got?" Kandy shouted at Septi. "I know what she would think. She would think you're nothing but a dirty, back-stabbing bitch."

"Get the hell out! I don't want to hear another word out of your fucking mouth," Septi shouted back.

"I'm leaving, but let me be clear. You better keep your mouth shut. I'm not playing. You open your mouth about us to Anabay and you'll see a side of me that you will regret," Kandy threatened.

"I don't give two cents about your threats. You, on the other hand, better be scared of me because I will tell her everything if you ever threaten me again. Got that? Now get the fuck out of my apartment!"

Kandy started walking towards the door, then he turned around. "You know what, Septi? I'm going to miss that coochy of yours. You sure know how to work it, Girl. Like a pro! Are you sure you've never worked on the streets?" he chuckled.

"Get out! Get out!" Septi yelled, slamming her door behind him. Then, she slid down on her floor and cried like a baby. She had developed emotional feelings for him, and reality was a bitter pill to swallow. Keith

Jackson was nothing but a dog and the way he spoke to her tonight proved he had no respect at all for her or women in general. Septi knew she was caught between a rock and a hard place because she didn't want to lose Anabay's friendship. For the moment, she had no other choice but to keep her mouth shut.

Kandy's heart was racing as he walked back into Anabay's apartment. He was mad as hell that his threats didn't seem to faze Septi. "I hate that bitch," he shouted out, pounding his fists into the wall. He knew it was in his best interest to have left her apartment when he did, otherwise, he probably would have done something he would have regretted. "I should have fucked her while I was over there. That's probably the only thing that can calm down a horny bitch like her," he laughed to himself.

Zenora Knight

Chapter 25

Go Fly Away

Septi was an emotional wreck after the confrontation with Anabay and Keith. Feeling betrayed by both of them, she was angry and hurt. As far as she was concerned, Anabay was nothing but a sneaky, man-lover who had stabbed her in the back. Anabay was supposed to be her best friend, yet she never uttered one word about being involved with Keith. What kind of best friend does something like that? If Anabay had mentioned that she had a romantic interest in Keith, then she, Septi, would never have slept with him. To make matters worse, when she tried to tell Anabay the truth about her two-timing dog of a boyfriend, not only did she defend her man, she cut Septi off at the knees in front of the bastard.

As far as Keith was concerned, there were no words to describe the hatred she felt towards this man. She delighted herself, thinking nasty and violent thoughts about him, like shooting him in both of his kneecaps or taking a nutcracker and squeezing his balls to smithereens. Every time she saw him, she wanted to slap the silly smirk off his face. Septi hadn't felt so used up for sex like this since she was a teenager. She was angry with herself for freely giving her body to him the way she did, even though the sex was some of the best she ever had.

Her anger waned after a few weeks and she started missing Anabay and the close relationship they once shared. Although both were pleasant whenever they bumped into each other, things were not the same between the two former best friends. An undeniable, uncomfortable chill permeated the air.

Septi made sure to keep a low profile as she continued monitoring their comings and goings from afar. From what she observed, all parties involved, including Delbert, seemed quite happy. She finally admitted to herself, she was envious of their relationship and that she had wanted more from Keith than just to be his sex partner. He had taken advantage of her because she came across as an easy woman who was only interested in getting laid.

'Perhaps I jumped the gun,' she thought. 'Maybe he does love and care for Anabay.' Septi was on a new mission to think only positive thoughts about her best friend and her man, despite having serious doubts about Keith's ability to be a loyal and committed man. She knew from experience; cheating men are like leopards--they don't change their spots.

She was settling back into her loveseat when her doorbell rang. "Damn, what now?" she mumbled. She opened her door and to her surprise, Anabay was standing there. "Come in," Septi offered.

"Hi, Septi. I'm glad you opened your door for me," Anabay said, smiling.

"Why wouldn't I open the door for you? You're my best friend. Come in. Can I offer you anything?"

"No, I'm all right. I'm very tired, though."

"You do look tired. What's going on?" asked Septi.

"I want to break the ice and apologize to you for being so abrupt with you. I hope we can go back to being best friends like we used to be. I really miss you."

"Anabay, I'm the one who should be apologizing to you. You are a grown woman and if you chose Keith to be your man, even though I don't understand why, it does not give me the right to disrespect your choice or your relationship."

"Please tell me what you have against him. Has he ever done anything to you?"

Septi took a deep breath and decided it was best to hold her tongue. "I just don't like him." She didn't have the heart to tell her friend the truth about her boyfriend-- that he had been screwing both of them at the same time. It angered her every time she thought about how foolish and horny she had been.

"Is that all you have to say? You just don't like him! I know you're more mature than that."

"Well, what can I say? It's the God's honest truth. That's how I feel."

"You really should get to know Keith. He's a good man and he makes me happy."

"Anabay, am I hearing you correctly? He makes you happy?"

"Yes, he makes me very happy. I haven't felt this happy since Claudale was alive."

"What the devil is wrong with you, Anabay? You haven't been involved with any other man since Claudale died, except him. There's plenty of nice men out there. Don't settle for the first one that comes your way."

"There you go again, trying to run my life and tell me what to do."

"I'm speaking the truth, whether you like it or not. What do you see in him anyway? And how much do you really know about him?" Septi asked, raising her eyebrows.

"I know that he is a genuinely kind, caring and thoughtful man and that he loves me and my son very much."

"Give me a fucking break!" Septi sucked her teeth and rolled her eyes.

"Look, Septi!"

"No, Anabay, you look. I am sorry but I don't like that man. There are things about him that you don't know."

"There you go again. If you know something about Keith that I should know, spit it out. Go ahead, I'm listening."

"I don't have anything else to say. I just have some strong negative feelings about him. I'm going to say one more thing and then for the sake of our friendship, I'm not going to say another word about your man. My gut is telling me that he is a good-for-nothing loser and that he's going to ruin your life."

"Septi, you know what? The devil is always busy and I'm afraid he is working through you. Like you just said, for the sake of our friendship, I'm going to pretend I didn't hear those words you just spoke."

"I don't want our friendship to end either, especially over a man the likes of him. Let's make a pact -- don't mention his name to me and I won't say anything about him to you."

"Yes, let's do that," Anabay agreed.

"Well, I can see your mind is made up about Keith. Never again will I try to convince you that he is no good. You'll have to figure it out for yourself. I'm not going to be that friend that said I told you so. You have my word."

"Thank you. Now, let's change the subject."

"Anabay, I'm glad we had this conversation."

"Me too."

"So, how is Delbert?"

"Delbert is fine. He's spending the night with Aunt Lillie Mae and Uncle Otis. We have been working really hard these days, trying to get everything ready for our grand opening."

"That's wonderful. I'm so proud of you. By the way, what's your restaurant going to be called?"

"The name is SisBros' Southern Cuisine," Anabay answered proudly.

"SisBros'. That's an interesting name. How did you come up with that?"

'It's a combination of sisters and brothers. Aaron suggested the name."

Septi rolled her eyes at the mention of Aaron's name. "It's certainly a creative name. I like it. Are you sure you're up to the task of running a restaurant?"

"To be honest, I'm scared and excited at the same time. Thank God, Aunt Lillie Mae and Uncle Otis are partnering with me, otherwise, I wouldn't be in a position to open a restaurant. They are so wonderful to me. Do you know they're footing most of the costs? I had to practically force them to accept money from me to pay for some of the expenses."

"Wow, they are indeed good to you!"

"All I know is, I'm going to give the restaurant all I've got and I'm going to keep the faith that it will be successful."

"Anabay, I have no doubt, Sisbros' Southern Cuisine is going to be a huge success. When is the grand opening going to be?"

"It's going to be in three weeks."

"Fantastic! Can I do anything to help you prepare for it?"

"Can you hand out some flyers at your job?"

"Sure, I'd love to."

"That's wonderful, Septi. I'll drop the flyers off to you in the morning on my way out. Remember, keep the date available on your calendar."

Anabay could tell Septi had reservations about attending, by the expression on her face. "Please tell me you're coming?"

"Well," Septi hesitated before answering. "I don't know if it's a good idea for me to come."

"What do you mean? Of course, you're coming. I can't do this without you by my side."

"I don't know. I need to think about it."

"There's nothing to think about. You're my best friend. You have to be there. Besides, I'm not taking no for an answer."

"OK, Anabay. I'll see what I can do."

"Now that every thing's all settled, I'm going home, straight to my bed. I'll drop the flyers off in the morning."

Anabay got up and walked towards the door.

"Anabay."

"Yes, Septi."

"Never mind. Have a good night." Septi wanted badly to tell her about Keith being a cheater, but she just couldn't bring herself to do so.

*****

The next morning Septi hopped out of bed, sticking her feet into her slippers, when she heard her doorbell ringing.

"I'm coming, Anabay."

She opened the door and rolled her eyes at the sight of Kandy standing there dressed in a short, white terry cloth bathrobe with matching slippers, waving the flyers at her.

"What are you doing here?" she hissed.

"Good morning. My wife asked me to drop these flyers off to you so you can do some advertising for our business."

Without acknowledging him, Septi reached up and tried to snatch the flyers out of his hand.

Kandy intercepted her hand and held the stack of flyers high in the air. "You know I'm smarter than that. Invite a brother in for some coffee."

"Nope!" Septi reached for the flyers again, but he quickly put the flyers behind his back. She tried to close her door, but he blocked it with his foot.

"Not so fast," he said, marching past her into her apartment.

"Look, I promised Anabay that I would be nice to you, but I don't like you. Now put the damn flyers down and get the fuck out of my apartment. You are not welcome here."

Kandy ignored her and sat down on her sofa. "Come on now, you don't have to be so hostile. Let's make peace for the sake of your friend."

"You may have cast a magical spell on Anabay, but it won't work on me. You and I will never--and I mean never--be friends! You got that?"

"It's not magic, Baby, it's all about the loving. All it takes is good loving. You experienced it for yourself, didn't you?" He leaned back and began massaging his crotch.

"You're disgusting! I want you out of my house now!"

Kandy flicked his tongue. "Why don't you let me service you while I'm here. Go take a shower. I feel like going downtown on you right now, but first you need to clean up the streets," he laughed, continuing to stroke himself.

Septi was feeling sexually aroused. Memories of his head buried deep between her thighs and his big juicy pussy lips kissing and sucking on her as if there was no tomorrow, flashed in her mind. Oh, how she used to beg for his mercy. In this very moment, she wanted very badly to have sex with him. She also knew if she displayed any sign of weakness, her body would betray her and she would end up back in the sack with him. She straightened herself up. "I want you to leave!" she demanded.

"Like hell you want me to leave! You know damn well you want me. That's why you freaked out when you found out about me and Anabay."

"Keith, you obviously come from another planet! Is that the reason you have a problem understanding the English language? Understand this -- I hate your ass with everything I got! Now get the hell out before I change my mind and tell Anabay everything you did with me behind her back!"

He walked up to Septi. "Be careful who you threaten."

Septi was seeing red. She wanted him out of her house. 'How dare he threaten me!' she thought, moving away from him and opening the door for him to leave.

On his way out, Kandy purposely brushed up against her body so she could feel his erection and whispered in her ear, "I was just testing you anyway. This dick belongs to Anabay."

"Asshole!" Septi shouted out, slamming her door shut.

Chapter 26

The Grand Opening

Tonight was the big night, the grand opening of SisBros' Southern Cuisine. Anabay wanted everything to be perfect from the décor to the music to the food to the door prizes and even down to herself.

She looked absolutely radiant walking up to the podium in a black, silk Tamotsu evening gown accented with a diamond solitaire choker and matching diamond stud earrings. Her shoulder length hair was bouncing as she walked in her Ralph Lauren black patent leather, three-inch open toe pumps. Her only regret this evening was--Claudale was not alive to be a part of her accomplishment. After all, it was what they both had wanted--a better life.

'Lord, all things are possible through you. Please give me the strength to speak in front of all these people,' Anabay silently prayed to herself, standing at the podium, surveying all the eyeballs staring back at her. This was her first public speech, so quite naturally, she was a nervous wreck despite looking cool on the outside.

"Good evening, ladies and gentlemen. My heart is overflowing with joy as I stand here before you to welcome you to SisBros' Southern Cuisine. I can't thank each and every one of you enough for taking the time out to come and celebrate our grand opening with us. We have worked very hard to make this night possible." Tears began to fill her eyes. "What a blessing!" Everyone stood up and clapped. "Tonight, didn't come without many challenges, but we made it. Hallelujah! God is good and without his guidance and his blessings, this night would not have been possible."

The people responded with enthusiastic clapping.

It was a full house, and everyone in attendance felt very special as they sat around the dining room tables adorned with white tablecloths and centerpieces of white and pink potted fresh orchids. The atmosphere was perfect.

"First and foremost, I would like to introduce a very special lady, a pillar in our community. She shared my dream of one day owning a southern style restaurant. Without her hard work and sacrifices, I wouldn't be standing here tonight. She is also one of the best cooks and bakers I have ever met. Without further ado, I would like to introduce my aunt and dear friend, Lillie Mae Jones."

Aunt Lillie Mae stood up, turned around so everyone could see her black sequined pantsuit, and waved. The crowd of people rose to their feet and applauded wildly.

Anabay was feeling more comfortable as she continued to speak. "I would like to introduce another very important person who prefers to remain behind the scenes. He is truly our backbone, the person who had the skills and the knowledge to put everything in motion and here we stand tonight. Many of you know this man and, like his wife, he is also a pillar in our community. He will literally take the shirt off his back and give it to you if you need it. He is very near and dear to my heart. Uncle Otis, please stand up."

Everyone jumped to their feet again, giving Uncle Otis a warm round of applause. Uncle Otis stood up and bowed. "Thank you, thank you," he repeated until the applause simmered down.

Anabay continued speaking. "Everyone knows the saying, behind every good man there is a good woman. Well, Uncle Otis and Aunt Lillie Mae have proven that statement to be a fact. It smells good in here and I know everyone is ready to eat. I know I am," she chuckled. "However, I need a couple more minutes of your time to introduce two other very important people in my life. Come up here, Delbert, my handsome son. I love you dearly."

Delbert ran up to his mother and grabbed her hand. He was dressed in white pants and a white shirt with a red bow tie. The crowd clapped again. Whispers could be heard, "That boy sure is cute."

"And the second person I would like to introduce to you is someone who has helped me to understand that when tragedies strike in life, you pick yourself up, brush yourself off, and keep on moving." Anabay's voice started quivering and her eyes were tearing up. "This person has been there for me through it all."

Septi stood up and walked towards the front of the room in order to be closer when Anabay announced her name. 'What a surprise, I was not expecting any recognition at all,' she was thinking. 'How sweet of Anabay to pay tribute to our friendship. No wonder she made sure I came tonight.'

Anabay looked out into the audience. "Keith, would you join Delbert and me up here?"

Kandy had a huge grin on his face and was flashing all thirty-two pearly whites as he strolled up to the podium dressed in a Ralph Lauren black tuxedo and black alligator shoes. He grabbed the microphone from Anabay. "I just want to share with everybody here what I know to be true -- this woman is truly amazing and she and her son mean the world to me. She thinks she is the blessed one but, believe me, I am the blessed one for being a part of their lives." Kandy picked Delbert up and put his arms around Anabay, "This woman is a diamond and this little man is a star."

Again, everyone in the room jumped to their feet and applauded and whistled, except for Uncle Otis and Aunt Lillie Mae. They were taken aback by Anabay's big revelation since they had no idea she was romantically involved with anyone. They tried their best not to reveal how shocked they really were.

Anabay took control of the microphone again. "Well, I think I've said just about everything I needed to say. For your entertainment tonight, the gospel group, the Lunenburg Travelers, will be performing in about forty-five minutes. All of the food tonight will be served buffet-style and we can eat right after the food is blessed. Pastor Tisdale, would you please do us the honor of blessing the food?"

Pastor Tisdale walked up to the podium. "God is truly good. Let's bow our heads in prayer. Heavenly Father, we thank you for allowing us to assemble here tonight in this fine eating establishment. Lord knows, we as a people don't often get to break bread in a place owned by one of our own. I bless this food and I pray that you will bestow your blessings on this restaurant and on Sisters Lillie Mae and Anabay Jones, and on Brother Otis Jones. May they be successful and may they be rewarded with prosperity for all of their faithfulness and hard work. In Jesus's name, I pray. Amen. Good God Almighty, that food smells good enough to eat," Pastor joked, making a beeline to the buffet.

Kandy grabbed the microphone. "Let's celebrate! Eat, drink and enjoy!" he proclaimed. Anabay was standing by his side with a look of pride on her face.

Septi had no choice but to bow her head while the minister prayed, but she was absolutely dumbfounded and speechless. Her eyes were teary, her heart was heavy and she was feeling light-headed, like she was about to faint. She couldn't believe what had just happened. Anabay, her best friend, had caused her to make an ass out of herself. 'How could Anabay do this to me. She just met that fool and he's nothing but a fucking dog. I'm the one who's been there for her since day one. I'm the one who helped her ass when she knocked on my door begging for help because that no-good husband of hers, Claudale, was nowhere to be found.' Septi was mortified. She knew everyone saw her rise to accept an honor that wasn't meant for her.

Her shock quickly turned into anger. 'I'm not taking this shit from that man-loving bitch!' She started walking towards Anabay and Kandy, who were busy walking hand in hand, greeting and mingling with the customers.

Septi was blinded by rage as she continued making her way towards the happy couple. 'They think they're hot shit, especially that fucker, Keith. I can't stand his arrogant ass. I'm going to give both of them a piece of my mind.' Suddenly, she felt a pair of arms wrapping around her waist, pulling her back, and stopping her dead in her tracks. When she looked down, the first thing she noticed was a gold and diamond Rolex watch and large hands with manicured nails cupped slightly below her breasts.

Feeling a wet tongue entering her ear and the smell of Juicy Fruit breath, she heard a voice whispering, "Pull yourself together. You're being very obvious."

For a moment, she thought, 'Hey, this might be my lucky night,' until she turned around and realized it was

Aaron. "What the fuck are you doing?" Septi demanded, swiftly pulling away from his grip.

"I am keeping you from making a complete ass out of yourself."

"What are you talking about? Get away from me, you loser. You got a lot of nerve approaching me after you ripped me off. I shouldn't be surprised at all by Anabay's actions. After all, you and she are from the same family."

"Look, I don't know what you're talking about, but everybody here tonight saw you stand up because you thought Anabay was going to introduce you as being that special friend," Aaron said.

"I didn't stand up for that reason," Septi insisted.

"Cut the bull crap. You were obvious. Listen, you had every right in the world to think she was referring to you. Who is that dude with her, anyway?"

"Why do you care?"

"Who is he?" Aaron persisted.

"He's bad news."

"I believe I'm detecting some jealousy here," Aaron replied, teasingly.

"You don't detect shit," Septi yelled. "I am not jealous, trust me."

"Lower your voice. Whoever he is, he is sure making Anabay happy. I don't think I've ever seen her glow like this. Damn, she didn't even look this happy when Claudale was alive."

"That's because she is a dumb, country-ass bitch who doesn't know her ass from her elbow," said Septi, fuming.

"Damn, girl, you raw!" laughed Aaron.

"Damn right, I am. Now leave me the fuck alone. I got business to take care of." Septi took two steps away from Aaron in the direction of Anabay and Kandy.

"Don't do it. Leave them alone. You're going to make a spectacle of yourself and hate yourself in the morning." He quickly grabbed her arm and pulled her back to him.

"Take your motherfucking hands off me!" Septi jerked away from Aaron's grip. She was fighting mad.

"Don't do it, Septi!" Aaron pleaded.

"No country bumpkin and her ghetto-ass man are going to make a fool out of me."

"Why you calling him ghetto? He doesn't act ghetto and he sure don't look ghetto. Matter of fact, the brother looks damn good."

"What the fuck would your sorry ass know?"

"Now, I'm a sorry ass? Septi, listen to me. You need to forget about them. Why don't you and I cut out of here? It's obvious you can't exercise any self-control and I really don't care to be here anyway. You need to calm down. Let me take you to dinner."

"Look, Aaron, where do you get off approaching me about anything? You ripped my ass off and took a trip to the Bahamas with my hard-earned cash. Now, you've got the balls to stand here like you're some high-minded individual trying to save my dignity. You'd better leave me the fuck alone before I go off on your ass!"

"Come on, Girl, let it rest. I'll explain everything, but not here and not now."

"I don't want to talk to you. The only words I want to hear coming from your lips are, 'Here's your money.' Now excuse me. I have to go." Septi pulled away from him, making a quick dash to the front door.

For the first time in his life, Kandy was feeling like an important man, although deep within, he knew he hadn't done anything but impose himself into Anabay's life. This evening had been a major breakthrough for him though, Anabay introducing him as her man to the public.

Septi was his only problem now. She was definitely a scorned woman and he knew from experience how vicious a scorned woman could be. He had been observing her all evening and he saw Aaron stopping her from approaching him and Anabay. Kandy thanked his lucky stars because he could tell by the angry look on her face, Septi wanted a confrontation. He had fucked a lot of chicks in his life, but she was by far the one chick he was sorry he ever gave any dick to. She was dangerous. He could feel it in his bones.

Kandy excused himself from Anabay and made his way to Septi. "Leaving so soon?" he asked gloatingly, placing his body in front of the door, blocking her from leaving.

"Excuse me. I'm leaving," Septi said, looking at him, dead in his eyes.

"Don't think for one moment I haven't been watching you," Kandy replied.

"You're in my way," Septi said, in a raised voice.

"Everyone's here to celebrate. What's your big rush?" he asked, smirking.

"This must be the night for low-down, dirty, grimy motherfuckers to come out. Why don't you crawl back under that rock you crawled out from? Now get the fuck out of my face before I raise my voice louder and cause a big scene." Septi was livid.

"Oh yeah, I dare you. Go for it." He leaned over and whispered into her ear, "No need to be mad just because I won't fuck you anymore."

Septi stood there visibly shaken. She was debating in her mind if she should kick the bastard in his balls or go off on his ass and make a big scene.

"Hey, Septi, you ready to go?" Aaron yelled out, walking towards her.

"Yes, I have never been so ready to get out of here."

Kandy turned to Aaron with his hand extended. "I don't believe we've met. My name is Keith Jackson. I am Anabay's man."

"Look, Man, I don't care who you are. Now excuse us." Aaron grabbed Septi's hand and tucked it in his arms like they were a couple, and they casually walked out the door.

"Hey, Septi, see you later," Kandy yelled out.

"He makes me want to puke," Septi said to Aaron, rolling her eyes.

"Forget him. He's a punk. I already know it."

"You're right, Aaron. Thank you."

"No problem, Septi. You helped me in a big way when I needed help, so why wouldn't I return the favor?"

"I appreciate you helping me tonight, but I'm still not excusing you for my money."

"You are more than welcome, but I really would like to know what's up between you and that Keith fellow."

"Nothing is up between us. I just can't stand his ass, that's all."

"Come on, you are talking to me--Aaron. I've been around long enough to know better."

"Just worry about paying me back my money before I take your ass to small claims court," Septi snapped.

"Let me set the record straight. I did not rip you off. Yes, I did use some of the money to fly to the Bahamas for a business meeting with Magic Johnson. When I borrowed the money from you, I had no idea my contact was going to arrange for us to meet in the Bahamas. You need to understand this -- when an investor is willing to meet with you, it is always on their terms."

"Whatever. I still don't believe you."

"I'm speaking the truth and, believe me or not, the meeting was a success."

"But Anabay said......"

"Look, I don't give a damn what Anabay told you. All her information comes from my father, who has no faith in me because I refuse to work a traditional nine to five job like he did. He doesn't understand--I want to write my own paycheck. Instead of working for the man, I want to be the man. Just look at this event tonight. Isn't it obvious my folks have no faith in me at all? Anabay is only a niece yet she's the one they've set up in business. How do you think that makes me feel? They won't even give me one copper penny for my dream."

"Aaron, I will admit, that is a tough situation. I would be mad as hell if my parents did some shit like that to me."

"I only came out tonight to support Anabay. She has never done anything to me. When everything's said and done, I'm going to show my parents that I have succeeded without their help. Septi, don't worry. I'm going to pay you back your money and then some for trusting and believing in me."

"I really want to believe you, Aaron."

"And if you act right, maybe I'll make you my wife," he teased.

"You're really pushing your luck now," Septi giggled.

"No, really. I think you are a lovely lady and I have a lot of respect for you even though you gave it up to me on our first date."

"First of all, it was not a date. Secondly, it was the champagne," Septi laughed, then playfully punched Aaron on the arm.

"Ouch! Now you want to hurt me. I hope you don't go around drinking champagne with strangers," he joked.

"You asshole! You know we both just got caught up in the moment."

"Yeah, I know. It was a damn good moment, too. Do you want to get something to eat?" he asked. "I know a cozy little place where we can grab a bite."

"No thanks. I just want to go home."

"Well, let me drive you there, then. I'll feel better knowing you arrived safe at home."

"Thank you. Aaron. I can honestly say I would like that."

"Got any champagne?" he joked.

"Hell no! That's not funny. No champagne tonight."

Aaron was secretly hoping to score with Septi this evening.

Chapter 27

Reality Bites

Ding dong! Ding dong! Ding dong! Someone was urgently ringing her doorbell.

Anabay yelled out, "Who's there?" She opened the door, purposefully looking straight ahead, instead of looking down. "I don't see anybody out here, maybe the wind was ringing my doorbell."

"Mommy, it's me!" Delbert giggled.

"That's strange. I hear my baby's voice, but I don't see him. Where are you, Delbert?"

He started jumping up and down, waving his hands in the air. "Mommy, Mommy, look down! Mommy, Mommy, I'm here!"

"There you are! Anabay looked down with a big smile on her face. She grabbed her son up in her arms and planted kisses all over his face. He laughed and hugged her back. This was a game the two of them had been playing since moving into their new home on Pine Cliff Way. Delbert was fascinated with the doorbell and he rang it every chance he got.

Everything had happened so fast in Anabay's life since her husband's death. First, there was Kandy, the new man in her life; second, owning a restaurant; and third, purchasing this house in Englewood Cliffs. Regardless of how tired or overwhelmed she was feeling, she knelt down every night and thanked God for all the blessings he had bestowed in her life. She certainly didn't want God to think she was taking Him for granted.

The 4,000-square-foot ranch-style house located on Pine Cliff Way in Englewood Cliffs, New Jersey was an absolute dream. Anabay loved everything about her home, especially the large windows that wrapped around the living room exposing breathtaking views of the Hudson River and the Manhattan skyline. The grounds were gorgeous, with a sprawling backyard for Delbert to play in. What a blessing! The people back home wouldn't believe her if she told them that she could stand in her living room and see the Hudson River and Manhattan. The mighty Hudson River would make the Meherrin River in Virginia look like a stream and the New York City skyline was something folks only saw pictures of in books.

Uncle Otis and Aunt Lillie Mae sold the property to her at a price well below market value. They had purchased the house years ago, intending to use it as a second residence but they ended up renting it out instead. This house, in particular, was a bone of contention in their marriage because Lillie Mae felt Aaron, by birthright as their only child, should inherit everything they owned. Otis, on the other hand, felt Aaron would squander everything they had worked so hard for and he was on a mission to make sure his son didn't get that opportunity. As far as he was concerned, the only thing Aaron deserved to inherit from him was his last name. To keep the peace, they agreed to sell Pine Cliff Way and to bequeath their home in Newark to Aaron. Otis told Lillie Mae, "Newark is more of Aaron's element."

From the moment Anabay laid eyes on the house, it felt like 'home, sweet home,' but for the life of her, she just couldn't understand why her aunt and uncle would want to sell this fine, beautiful house rather than to live out their lives here. And what about Aaron? Surely, he would love to live in a house like this. She knew it was wrong to question God's will and blessings in her life, so she quickly cast these thoughts aside. Despite feeling elated and on top of the world, thoughts of the family curse often crept back into her consciousness. 'Perhaps the Bailey Curse somehow got reversed and is now pouring out blessings, instead of mishaps that bring pain and suffering,' Anabay found herself thinking.

Business was booming at SisBros' Southern Cuisine. After receiving great reviews in both the New York and New Jersey newspapers, customers poured into the restaurant in droves. It was not uncommon to see lines around the block and the waiting time for a table was often in excess of an hour, especially on weekends. Anabay, Aunt Lillie Mae and Uncle Otis were ecstatic over how well the business was doing--they wished they had leased a larger facility to accommodate more customers.

Anabay's dream was for SisBros' to become a world-famous restaurant like Sylvia's in Harlem and then, to franchise the business. By no means was she interested in challenging Sylvia Woods for her title, "The Queen of Soul Food." Anabay just wanted to be successful and to make a name for herself. She had read up on Sylvia Woods's life and was astounded by how much the two of them had in common. They both were born and grew up in the South. They both married their childhood sweethearts, and they both moved to the North with dreams of a better life. The thing that really blew Anabay's mind was learning that they both had received big breaks upon starting out in their respective careers. Sylvia's break came when a former employer recognized her talent and sold their restaurant business to her. Anabay's break came from Uncle Otis and Aunt Lillie, who saw the potential in her and helped set her up in the business. Their lives were so parallel, it was downright scary.

After reading Sylvia Woods' story, Anabay admired her even more. She took Delbert to Sylvia's restaurant one evening for dinner, hoping to catch a glimpse of the Queen of Soul Food, but no such luck. After dining there, she was more determined than ever to make her dreams come true. She felt deep sorrow that her beloved Claudale was not alive to share in her success, as Sylvia Woods' husband was doing.

Anabay considered herself to be a hard worker, but she had no idea just how hard it really was to own and operate a restaurant. Nonetheless, she had made a vow to herself during the planning phase, "With God's help, if the doors to SisBros' Southern Cuisine opens, I'm going to put it on the map," and this is exactly what she intended do.

The working hours at the restaurant were long and grueling, leaving her very little time to spend with Delbert. He was too young for kindergarten, so Uncle Otis cared for him during the day while she and Aunt Lillie Mae toiled in the restaurant. It comforted Anabay, knowing that in Uncle Otis, her son had a real man for a role model. Besides, Delbert loved him to death.

Her daily routine consisted of dropping Delbert off with Uncle Otis by seven o'clock in the morning and picking him up around ten o'clock at night. Many nights, he slept over there because she felt guilty about waking him up. She cherished the little time she had with her son, making sure to give him extra kisses and to tuck him in bed every chance she got.

Kandy was the only distraction in Anabay's life right now. They had been living together for over a year and he was still unsettled and unemployed. Sometimes, he acted like he had two personalities. One Kandy was sweet, considerate and caring. The other Kandy was sullen, moody and selfish. He even ran hot and cold with Delbert, in addition to spending her money up like crazy every chance he got. He had left her feeling disappointed more times than she cared to admit. Inwardly, she questioned if they could make a life together. She loved him, but deep within, she knew she was not in love with him.

Reality was starting to set in for Anabay. No longer could she ignore the truth about Kandy--he had just forced himself into her life. Truth be told, she knew very little about Keith Jackson a.k.a. Kandy other than what he shared with her. In hindsight, she should have looked deeper into his background before getting involved with him. She regretted not standing her ground when he announced he was moving in with her---he never officially asked. Now, she had many doubts and questions about him, like, 'Why hasn't he been able to find a job? What does he do all day when he's not out interviewing?'

A man who doesn't work--well, that was a foreign concept to Anabay. She was raised in Virginia and back home, men worked, period. Kandy said he had a few offers but he had to decline them because the salaries were insulting to a man with his credentials. Whenever the subject of job search came up in conversation, he would immediately become very defensive.

Then there was the matter of money. His extravagant tastes produced frequent, annoying requests for funds. The last time she handed him some cash, she almost blurted out, 'Dude, where is your pride?' Knowing that he was a well-educated man who had a bad break in life, she tried her best to be supportive of him.

She had wanted to buy him an inexpensive suit from Syms Department Store on Route 17 for the SisBros' grand opening, but he claimed the suits there didn't fit him. She ended up paying nine hundred for his tuxedo and shoes from Saks Fifth Avenue. She also spent several hundred dollars on clothing for him--upgrading his wardrobe for job interviews. Every week without fail, he was hitting her up for at least one to two hundred dollars, supposedly for transportation and pocket change.

Anabay observed the look in Kandy's eyes when they first toured the house at Pine Cliff Way and his eyes spoke volumes. They were saying, "I have arrived." One would have thought he was buying the house, not her. He was making comments, "The first thing we're going to do is upgrade this kitchen. This is the perfect spot for a swimming pool." He declared the small room next to the living room to be his office. Anabay thought to herself, 'An office for what? You don't have a job.' She was really taken aback when Suzy Chung, a decorator with Drexel Heritage Furniture Store, mentioned he had called and requested office furniture catalogs. Anabay made it clear to Suzy, she was not going to pay for any furniture that she didn't personally order.

Anabay hadn't the time to sort out her relationship with Kandy, but she was sure about one thing--Delbert was and always would be her priority. His happiness and welfare were everything to her. She missed Septi a lot, too. She would have loved to invite her over to see the house, but she knew her best friend and the man in her life couldn't stand each other.

Kandy was beginning to feel uneasy too. Ever since Sisbros' opened, he sensed a change in their relationship. Anabay was devoting all of her time and energy to work, leaving very little time for him. He also sensed something else was up with her. He couldn't quite figure it out. She appeared distant and he couldn't easily charm her like he used to when he first got out of prison. He knew she was running out of patience with his phantom job searches. When she was at home, one hundred percent of her attention was devoted to that spoiled-ass brat son of hers, in Kandy's view.

He knew if he wanted to remain in Anabay's life, he would have to come up with a whole new master plan or get her pregnant. Every night when she returned home from work, he desperately tried to shower her with love and affection by massaging her feet and shoulders and waiting on her every need. This was the price he was willing to pay to remain in her good graces. He was living the high life now and he intended to continue sharing in the fruits of her labor. His biggest worry was that bitch, Septi. He hated her and he was going to make sure she stayed out of Anabay's life.

*****

The time was ten thirty, when Anabay looked down at her watch. In one hour, the lunchtime crowd would come stampeding through the doors. She had been on her feet since six thirty and she was exhausted.

She and Aunt Lillie Mae decided it would be wise to hire an additional person to help out in the kitchen. Without the help, they feared the kitchen staff would burn out quickly. Anabay was thinking about a food prep person, someone who could assist with a variety of tasks. Anabay sat at her desk thumbing through the stack of resumes requested from the Culinary Institute, but the sounds of pots and pans and the aroma of food cooking made it difficult for her to concentrate.

She leaned back, closed her eyes and thought about how far she had come. She was now in a position to hire and fire people. 'What an accomplishment for a country girl who left home with nothing but a suitcase and some fried chicken sandwiches in a greasy brown bag,' she laughed to herself. Never in a million years did she imagine she would one day be an entrepreneur.

"How long have you been standing there?" she asked, opening her eyes.

"Long enough to be in awe of your beauty."

"What a nice thing to say, Aaron."

"I mean it. You are a very attractive woman."

"Thank you. I know you're looking for your mother. I believe she's in the storage room."

"I already saw her. I'm here to see you now."

"OK." Anabay was puzzled. She couldn't imagine what he wanted to see her about.

"I'm just going to be straight and maybe you will say it's none of my business, but . . . "

"What is it, Aaron? I don't have a lot of time. I have to help out with lunch."

"Why did you hurt Septi's feeling the night of the grand opening?"

"What are you talking about? How did I hurt Septi's feelings?"

"Maybe you didn't realize it, but you most certainly did."

"If I did, it's a surprise to me. Please tell me how I hurt Septi's feelings. I only saw her briefly before everything started and then I didn't see her the rest of the night."

"If you didn't see her the rest of the night, didn't you find that to be odd?" asked Aaron.

"I never gave it any thought--so much was going on that night. I just figured we missed each other and we would catch up later."

"Well, have you spoken to her since?"

"No, I haven't, now that you mention it. I just haven't had the time. This place consumes all my waking hours and energy. Ask your mother, if you don't believe me. Tell me what I did to offend Septi." Anabay didn't have the foggiest idea about what he was talking about. In her mind, she hadn't done anything to Septi.

"You introduced your man as your best friend, the person who has been there for you since day one. That was a slap in Septi's face."

"It never dawned on me that she would have been offended by that. I never meant to hurt her. I was just stroking Keith, that's all. I wanted to make him feel special, as the man in my life. I will call her and apologize. She knows she's my best friend." Anabay wondered why this was just now coming up, months after the grand opening.

"I would appreciate that. I know it would mean a lot to her." Aaron was thinking, 'Septi was right--Anabay is naïve.'

"Consider it done. Aaron, have you ever thought about working here?"

"You have got to be joking, right?" He had the feeling his father had put Anabay up to asking him about working in the restaurant.

"No, I'm serious. We need to hire another person and since you aren't working, this would be a good opportunity for you to earn some money."

"Don't insult me like this," Aaron snapped back. "I have my own things going on and I'm not about to work in some hot-ass kitchen, getting all greasy and smelling like fried pork chop sandwiches. Pops put you up to asking me, didn't he?"

"No, I just thought about it as we were talking."

"Anabay, do me a favor. Leave all that job stuff alone and just call your girl," Aaron said as he got up to leave.

"Who's in here making time with my woman?" Kandy said, opening the door without knocking.

"I can't believe this!" Anabay threw her hands up in frustration. "How do you guys think I'm supposed to get any work done around here if I keep getting interrupted?"

"Am I disturbing something in here?" Kandy asked, looking directly at Aaron.

"Yes, you are. I have work to do. This is a place of business, not a social club." Anabay spoke abruptly, raising her voice in frustration.

"I just stopped by to see the love of my life. Why is he here?" asked Kandy, looking directly at Aaron.

"Anabay, I'll talk to you later," Aaron said, shaking his head and closing the door behind him. Aaron had been reserving his feelings about Keith, not wanting to pass judgment on him based on how Septi felt about him. But after this encounter, he knew immediately he didn't like the brother.

"Kandy, did you have to be so rude?"

"I ain't got no time for that chump."

"That's not nice. You don't even know him."

"I know all I need to know about him. Anyway, I stopped by because I miss you. You left so early this morning, I didn't get a chance to get me a piece."

"Look, I have a lot of work to do before we open for lunch. Why are you really here?"

"Is that any kind of way to greet me?"

"I'm sorry, but I am extremely busy today. I have a lot to do before lunchtime."

Kandy leaned across Anabay's desk and kissed her on her cheek. "I came by to see you because I miss you. Just seeing you and touching you helps me get through my day."

"Good! Now that you have seen me, you can leave."

"I know, Baby, but the last few nights, you've been knocked out, dead to the world."

"Kandy, do you think this work is easy?"

"No, Baby, I know you have been working really hard and I understand. But, I have needs too. So rather than wait for you to come home all tired, I thought I would come to see you. I need you to take care of me."

"Take care of you! What are you talking about?" Anabay asked, rolling her eyes.

"You know what I mean," he pouted, pointing down to his crotch.

"You've got to be kidding me!"

"No, actually I'm not. I need my dick sucked, Baby. It's hard as a rock. It's so damn hard it hurts."

"Are you crazy? In the middle of the day? Right here? In my office?"

Kandy walked over to the door and locked it. "Come on, Baby," he said. He pulled his pants down and plopped his naked butt on her desk, right on top of the resumes she had been reviewing.

"Kandy, please!"

"Come on, Baby. Just touch it. You know you want it. It will rejuvenate you. Think of it as a booster shot of energy."

Anabay complied, but she didn't like it one bit. She just wanted to get him the hell out of her office.

"Thank you, Baby. That didn't take too long."

"No, it didn't, but this can never happen again. It's crazy."

"It's not crazy to keep the flame burning. Why don't you admit it--you enjoyed it just as much as I did"

"It was different, but......"

"But what?" he asked, smiling.

"I don't know how to put it."

"Well, since you don't know how to say what you're thinking, it's probably something you shouldn't be saying," he said, pulling up his pants. "I will just say this -- dealing with a man named Kandy, you have to expect moments like this. There is a reason I'm called Kandy."

"And what is that reason?"

"I was nicknamed Kandy because of my romantic spirit. I have always been sweet and smooth with the ladies. As a matter of fact, not to be bragging, it's amazing how

many women still walk up to me and offer me pussy."
He laughed, proudly sticking his chest out.

"I don't find that funny."

"Well, it's the truth. You don't have a thing to worry
about, though--I don't cat around anymore. Those days
are long gone for me. I have enough wisdom to be a
one-woman man. I just like a little spontaneous sex
every now and then. That's one of the secrets to a long,
happy life with me."

"I see," Anabay said, feeling annoyed with the
conversation. "Spontaneous sex doesn't pay the bills
around here. Now, please go."

"You know you enjoyed it," Kandy laughed, brushing
Anabay's hair away from her face. "Do you want me to
do you?"

"Kandy, I really have to get back to work."

"Oh, let's not forget about lunch," he laughed. "I bet
your lunch crowd would skip lunch if they knew what
just happened in here. Anabay Jones giving blow jobs in
the work place."

"That's not funny," snapped Anabay.

"You're a nasty girl," he continued, laughing.

"Kandy, please leave. You're getting on my last nerve."

"Just kidding, Baby. Anyway, you're my nasty girl, and I
love you. Before I go, I need you to pay me for that
booster shot I just gave you."

"You're full of jokes, aren't you?"

"Yes, I am, but I also need some money. Why are you looking at resumes?"

"We have to hire additional kitchen help."

"Don't you think you are moving a little too fast? How are you ever going to turn a profit if you spend the money as fast as you make it?"

Anabay could feel her blood starting to boil. Who was he to tell her what to do? He, who had nothing, as far as she was concerned. "Excuse me?"

"Don't take it the wrong way. I am just saying from a financial advisor point of view, you shouldn't spend the money as fast as you make it. You need to take it easy. This business is new--therefore, everybody is flopping in here to eat. Have you given any thought to what happens when the novelty wears off?"

"Excuse me, Kandy, the only one spending my money as fast as I make it is you. How many times have you been here this month with your hand out?" Anabay was mad as hell.

"Now that's a low blow. How do you think I'm supposed to find a job without any money in my pocket? I have an idea. Since you're looking to hire another person, why don't you hire me to be the manager here. I have a financial background and the skills to run the business side of the restaurant and you can do what you do best--

cook. If you did that, you wouldn't have to work so hard and you would have more time to spend with Delbert."

Anabay immediately nixed Kandy's offer. There was no way she was ever going to allow him to get a foothold in her business and put her relationship with her aunt and uncle in jeopardy. His arrogance, which she once found attractive, was really getting under her skin now. "Kandy, did you not hear me? The restaurant needs kitchen help, not a manager." 'Let me get this fool out of here,' Anabay thought to herself. She walked over to her safe, opened it and handed him three hundred dollars.

"Thanks, Baby." Kandy leaned over and kissed Anabay. "See you later." Kandy walked down the street to the bus stop, thinking to himself, 'I'm going to give Justine a hundred and fifty dollars. This should keep her big ass off me for a while. Fucking women!'

Zenora Knight

Chapter 28

The Unveiling

"**I** hate this motherfucking place! It smells!" Kandy said to Justine, turning up his nose.

Justine was full of anxiety because she knew how impatient her husband could be when he didn't want to do something and he definitely didn't want to come down to the Welfare Office with her. She had insisted, however, that he accompany her this time because she was sick and tired of having to take the full responsibility of caring for their family. Besides, she needed to be recertified, and he needed to be added to her grant to increase her benefits.

Kandy, Justine and their five step-laddered children sat in the waiting area. Whenever Daddy was around, the children behaved themselves because they knew he didn't play. He would get on their asses in a hot minute.

"We've been here twenty minutes and her fucking ass hasn't come out yet," Kandy said, exasperated.

"Just relax, Keith. Our caseworker won't keep us waiting long. She never does and, please, don't talk like this in front of our children! We've come here plenty of times before and we always manage to do whatever we have to do," pleaded Justine.

"How many times do I have to tell you, woman! Don't correct me in front of the kids," Kandy snapped.

* * * * *

Septi was sitting at her desk thumbing through file folders, waiting for her appointment when the telephone rang. "Good afternoon, Department of Social Services."

"Hi, Septi. It's me."

"Hey, Anabay, what a surprise! I haven't heard from you in while. What's going on?"

"Aaron stopped by to see me today."

"So, what does that have to do with me?" Septi asked.

"Well, he told me that I hurt your feelings the night of the grand opening, when I introduced Keith as the special friend in my life, instead of you."

"That's interesting. Sounds to me like Aaron needs to mind his business." Hearing Aaron cared enough to go to Anabay on her behalf made Septi feel good, but she wasn't about to admit anything.

"Anyway, Septi, I want to apologize to you. It was never my intention to hurt you. I just wanted Kan...Keith to feel like a part of us."

'Only a stupid man-lover would sacrifice true friendship for a man! How dumb is that shit?' Septi thought, as she sat in silence listening to her.

"Septi, are you there?"

"Yeah, I'm listening." Septi wished Aaron had kept his big mouth shut after hearing Anabay's lame excuse for hurting her.

"Will you forgive me? I really miss you."

"I'm not sure what Aaron's talking about, but we're good. I miss you, too. How is the restaurant going and how is the new house?"

"Everything is good. The restaurant is a lot of work and we're still unpacking and decorating the house."

"I'm so happy for you, Girl, and I wish you all the luck in the world. Before I forget, how's my favorite little boy?"

"Delbert's fine. He asked me the other night if we could stop by and see you, but it was too late. He was so disappointed when I told him we would have to see you another time."

"Oh, that's so sweet. I miss him, too. Anabay, I would love to talk longer, but I need to review some paperwork before my next client arrives."

"Of course, how rude of me. I forgot, you're working."

"Girl, please! I would rather talk to you any day, but duty calls. Bye."

Septi walked out to the reception area to call her next client. What a shock! 'It can't be. Am I seeing correctly?' she questioned herself. 'The man sitting with that fat-ass woman and all those kids resembles

Keith Jackson a lot. Wait a goddamn minute, that is Keith Jackson! I would recognize his ass anywhere, considering I have seen him butt naked.'

Septi walked back into the reception desk, looked at the sign-in sheet and saw the name Justine Jackson. "Oh really," she said aloud. 'They have the same last name so they are definitely related. She's too young to be his mother, but she could be his sister. I will have to see about this. Ah ha, she's here to see Denise James. I'm going to find out the lowdown on this broad."

"Hey, Denise. Got a minute?"

"What's going on, Septi?" Denise was sitting at her desk buried in paperwork.

"The woman waiting in the lobby, Justine Jackson--is she your client?"

"Yeah, she's my client. She's here for her recertification. What about her?"

"She looks to be a bit impatient," Septi commented.

"She's early, but she's going to have to wait. I saw her out there. Believe me, it's not her who's impatient--it's that crazy-ass husband of hers."

"Are you referring to the man with her in the lobby?"

"Who else--Keith Jackson. He just got released from prison and she probably pressured him into coming here with her so he could be added to her grant."

"Prison?" Septi's face turned white and her jaw dropped. She was appalled. "Prison! Are you kidding me?" she asked Denise again.

"Yes, prison. What's wrong with you? You look a little pale."

"Nothing is wrong with me. He just looks like someone I used to know."

"Who, an old boyfriend?" Denise asked sarcastically.

"No, don't be silly."

"Child, count your blessings that you don't know him, because that dude is bad news. He's been in and out of prison most of his life and every time he gets out, he knocks Justine up and then he goes back in. It is crazy! He is real street too! They call him Kandy on the streets. I hate it when he comes here with Justine because he is one rude, mean, arrogant son of a bitch."

"I can't believe this shit! Are you serious?"

"Why are you so surprised? You know the story with a lot of our clients. I don't like many of them but I do happen to like Justine. She is a sweetheart and it's sad she allowed that man to ruin her life. I don't know why she continues to put up with his trifling ass. You seem to be awfully interested in the Jacksons. Septi, do you have something to share with me?"

"I'll talk to you later. I have to take my appointment."

"Oh, OK," Denise said, sounding puzzled.

'Goddamn it! I can't believe this shit! First, I get ripped off by Aaron's ass but that's nothing compared to sleeping with a damn jailbird,' Septi thought to herself, her emotions raging with anger. 'Anabay must have gotten involved with his sorry ass while working at the prison, but I'll guarantee, she doesn't know about his wife and kids. I really can't believe this shit! His ass just got out of prison and he's got the nerve to be pretending to be a correctional officer. And Anabay, sweet Anabay of all people, is going along with this shit. She's got to be real desperate for a man. Now everything's making sense--why I never saw his ass in a uniform and oh, that swagger of his! I couldn't figure it out, but now everything's making sense. He has that same little bop in his walk like inmates have. I feel so stupid, used and dirty! I could kill that motherfucker! I'm going to conduct my own investigation and get to the bottom of this shit! Fuck! Fuck! Fuck!'

* * * * *

Septi deliberately stayed late at work and waited for her coworkers to leave before charging into Denise's office. She began rummaging through all the files on her desk.

"Bingo! Justine Jackson!" She took the file back to her desk and began reading and taking notes. All personal information was there--Social Security numbers, dates of births, children's names, home address, home telephone number and even Justine and Keith's marriage certificate. As she was jotting down their home address, it dawned on her that they lived in the heart of the ghetto. She continued examining the papers and finally her eyes landed on Keith Jackson's rap sheet. "Oh, my God! What a long rap sheet! How did he ever get out of jail?" she blurted out unintentionally. She sat there in disbelief as she read his history -- armed robbery, attempted manslaughter, embezzlement, forgery, child endangerment, possession of an illegal substance with the intent to distribute, domestic violence, and on and on.

Septi thought to herself, 'I know Anabay doesn't know all this shit about her handsome Keith Jackson, or maybe she does. Some women will settle for anything just to have a man. His damn rap sheet is downright scary. No woman in her right mind would get involved with this fool.'

Setting down the thick file, Septi was so furious she could barely contain her thoughts. 'I got news for you, Mr. Keith Jackson a.k.a. Kandy--I am not afraid of your black ass! You have met your match, you goddamn, motherfucking jailbird. You have fucked with the wrong sister this time. You have no idea what a problem you've created by fucking with me. Just wait until I see your lowlife ass again. Boy, do I have a surprise for you!'

It took about thirty minutes for Septi to calm herself down. She returned the file to Denise's office and her thinking became clearer. 'I need go home and digest this shit. Keith Jackson is no joke. He's a dangerous character. I need to really think this situation through.

I swear to God, I don't know when, where or how, but I'm going to blow his shit up if it's the last thing I do.'

 Septi grabbed her purse and left.

Chapter 29

The Time is Right

Septi understood all too well how and why Anabay had fallen in love with Kandy. Not only was he handsome, sexy, and charming, but he had an attractive arrogance about him. He carried himself like he was the cat's meow with his big, beautiful infectious smile. He also had a way of looking at you with those dark eyes of his--it was enough to make a woman melt inside. Yes, Mr. Jackson was definitely a head-turner and any woman who didn't know the truth about him would feel proud as hell to walk down the street on his arm.

She knew Anabay was too deep in love to see the bigger picture about her man--that he was nothing but an old jailbird player. Septi reflected on the first time she met him at Anabay's apartment. He definitely had the look of a man hungry for sex. Septi surmised that she must have reciprocated the look back to him. This explained why she had not been totally surprised or taken aback when he rang her doorbell in the middle of the night. Now angry with herself for having given herself to him, Septi was on a mission to expose Kandy for the pure dog he was. After all, if one sleeps with a dog, one surely will get fleas.

Septi had been struggling with the decision to expose Kandy ever since she saw him with his family at the Welfare Office. Would she be doing it for all the right reasons? Would she lose Anabay's friendship forever? In the final analysis, she could not continue to call Anabay her best friend and stand idly by and watch this man run his game on her and Delbert. The decision was clear and final, she would have to intervene, no matter the consequences. At least she would have done what she could do.

The time was right to expose Kandy, and Septi vowed to make it happen today. She was sick and tired of being a bad boy magnet and she prayed her actions today would somehow purge her soul from attracting these types of men to her in the future.

After weighing all her options, she decided exposing Kandy to his wife Justine would be a slam dunk. Septi imagined with pleasure the ensuing carnage this would cause--Justine going off on his ass and putting him out, Justine confronting Anabay about their marriage and his kids. 'Yes,' thought Septi, 'This is the best way to bring this bastard down. When I finish with Mr. Keith Jackson, he won't know what hit him. I'll chew him up and spit him out like I've done many times before with trifling ass men. Anabay will be hurt at first, but after she absorbs all the facts, she'll be grateful to know the truth about the liar, the cheat, the snake-in-the-grass he really is.'

Although she was committed to her plan, Septi still had an ounce of doubt. Did she hate Kandy more for dumping her after sleeping with her, cutting her off from some real good sex, and bruising her ego? Or, did she only hate him for using Anabay? Either way, the man had to be stopped. He was a married career criminal, well below the standards of any decent, self-respecting woman.

*****

Septi was deep in thought as she boarded Bus #22, thinking about the day she saw the Jackson family at her job and how she had snuck and read their confidential file. What she did was strictly prohibited, but she just had to know the truth about Keith and Justine Jackson. Anyway, reading their file was better than asking Denise too many questions because she might have become suspicious or even figured out that she had some romantic link to Kandy. Septi had never given anyone anything to gossip about and she wasn't about to start now.

She exited the bus and crossed the street to Elm Place. Feeling extremely nervous, a thousand thoughts raced through her mind. Halfway up the block, she spotted the house. The number 39 was hanging off a bent sign in front of the dwelling. Her heart felt like it was going to beat out of her body as she walked closer, gasping for air. There wasn't any doubt, this was the right house. It was the only unkempt house on the block. The front porch was missing floor planks, the screen door was ripped, the front window was taped up with gray vinyl duct tape and white sheets were hanging in the windows, serving as curtains. Trash was strewn about the yard—in all, it was a terrible sight. Septi was not surprised at all to see the condition of the house, considering how much time Kandy spent either in prison or womanizing. Justine appeared to be too lazy to care.

She was trembling as she stuck her hand through the ripped screen and banged the door knocker. Her nerves were so bad she couldn't recall what she had planned on saying to Justine and panic really set in when it dawned on her--Kandy might be home. She could feel her heart racing. The palms of her hands were sweating and her mouth felt dry, but there was no turning back now. She prayed to her higher self for the courage and strength to complete her mission.

The door swung open and there stood a girl who appeared to be about ten years old with a short, matted, kinky afro, wearing a Phat Farm pink sweat suit.

 "Yeah?" the girl answered, smacking bubble gum and blowing bubbles almost twice the size of her narrow, ashy, chocolate face.

Septi thought, 'Another child without any home training.' "Hello. Is your mother home?"

"No, she said she ain't here."

Septi thought, 'Poor thing, she can't speak proper English.' "What did you say?"

"I said she said she ain't home," replied the girl, impatiently.

"I thought I heard you say your mother said she wasn't home."

"Yeah, so what?" she replied, rolling her eyes, with her hands on her hip.

Septi felt relief momentarily upon hearing Justine wasn't home, but that moment was short lived and replaced with being pissed off after it dawned on her what the little girl had said to her--the thought of Justine hiding behind her daughter instead of coming to the door like a grown woman. Now, she was more determined than ever to meet and confront Justine, and it was obvious Kandy was not at home. This left her feeling comfortable and even more empowered to move forward with her plan. She had come too far to walk away now. There was no way this clueless little girl was going to stand in her way. Septi was on a mission. Her best friend's future was at stake.

The little girl and Septi stood there staring in a standoff.

"Ouch! Damn it! A loud thump and a wailing scream was heard coming from the back of the house, as if someone or something had fallen.

"Ma! Ma, are you all right?" The girl took off running towards the back of the house.

Septi followed behind her and was immediately hit with the smell of cat urine and the sight of a dirty litter box in the foyer. She almost puked. It reminded her of the days when she first started her job, making unannounced visits to her clients' homes.

The little girl opened the door to a bedroom and there Septi recognized Justine, who was stretched out on the floor. No doubt about it, it was the same woman she saw Kandy with at her job."

"Are you OK?" Septi asked.

"Who the fuck is you?" asked a clearly disoriented Justine.

"My name is Septi. I apologize for walking into your home, but you sounded like you might need some help."

"Damn it, Girl, can't you do anything right? I told you to say I won't home," Justine said, scolding her daughter.

"I said what you told me," the girl snapped back.

"Well, if you did, why in the hell is this strange woman standing here in my fucking bedroom?" Justine yelled back.

"I'm here to see you about a personal matter," Septi interrupted.

"Well, if that's the case, you should be still waiting at the fucking front door! How the hell you just going to walk your ass up in my house and into my bedroom, of all places? Nobody invited you in!"

"You are absolutely right. I'm sorry." Septi extended her hand to help Justine up off the floor.

"I'm fine," Justine said, frowning at the sight of Septi's hand. I slipped over this shoe box on the floor. I'm going be sore in the morning," she said, rubbing her hips and brushing off her donkey butt, while struggling to get up.

Septi looked closer at Justine and was shocked by her size. She surmised that she weighed at least three hundred pounds. 'Damn,' Septi thought, 'Now, that's an ass and a half!'

"You from R.A.C?" Justine asked.

"No. What is R.A.C?"

"You never heard of Rent A Center? You black, ain't you? Everybody and their mama who's black done heard of Rent A Center."

"Well, I'm black and, no, I'm not familiar with Rent A Center." Septi was lying. She was indeed familiar with Rent A Center--in fact, she had an account there, but she was not about to reveal that to Justine.

'I don't know what kind of black person you are,' Justine was thinking to herself. 'You're a skinny one--need some meat on your bones.' Justine looked straight at Septi, "I told my daughter to answer the door and say I won't home cause I figured you was from R.A.C. I didn't pay my bill this month and believe me, they don't mind coming and taking your shit right out your house."

"Well, you can relax. I am not from Rent A Center."

"What the hell you want then? It better be damn important!"

"I can assure you, It very important. Can we speak in private away from your daughter?"

Justine knew exactly what Septi wanted. She had been through this many times. She decided to play the game. "Let's go into the living room. I am not used to strange women in my bedroom. My bedroom is private between me and my husband, if you know what I mean. Jesus, it's a good thing these walls can't talk!" Justine smirked.

Septi knew exactly what Justine was referring to. The last thing she wanted to be reminded of was having sex with Kandy. She hated to admit it, but his dick was one of the best she'd ever had. Septi exhaled, not wanting to make eye contact with Justine. Instead, she focused on the crayon-marked walls and soiled carpet that smelled moldy and dusty. There was a large pile of clothes strewn on the loveseat, and toys and shoes were all over the floor. The inside of the house made the outside look great.

Septi knew Justine had inherited the house from her mother, after reading her file. 'It's a damn shame the way some folks treat their property,' Septi thought. The house had such potential. She began to feel a twinge of anger towards Justine and Kandy because they didn't appreciate their home. She, on the other hand, had been working hard every day and saving her money to buy a house, but could not yet afford one.

"Have a seat," Justine said, moving the clothes to the other side of the sofa.

"I'm fine standing. I won't be long." The thought of sitting on such a soiled sofa made Septi's skin crawl.

"Well, hope you don't mind, I need to sit down," said an out-of-breath Justine.

"No, please, it's fine. I apologize again for coming unannounced, but I didn't know what else to do."

"Do about what?"

"I need to speak to you about your husband."

"What about him? Is you his Parole Officer?"

"No, I'm not."

"What you want then?" Justine really wanted to say to Septi, 'Cut the crap. You been dumped by my husband, get over it,' but she decided to let Septi have her say. She had vowed to herself that when the next scorned woman showed up at her door, she would slam the door in her face after shouting out, "Get over it, Bitch. I know all about it."

"Well, I don't know any other way of saying it other than just to say it. Your husband is having an affair with my best friend."

Justine thought to herself, 'This is a first. This woman wants to blame it on another woman.' "Girl, please, you came to my house to tell me that?" Justine laughed in her husky voice. "You've got to be kidding me! I almost broke my hip for this bullshit." Justine laughed so hard her stomach hurt.

Septi couldn't believe it. She was thinking, 'This woman is stupid. No self-respect at all.' Septi was puzzled. "That's your response? You laugh? You find what I said funny? I don't understand."

"He a man, ain't he?" Justine continued laughing so hard, she almost peed on herself. "That was a good laugh! I haven't laughed like this in a long time! Oh God, my stomach hurts," she could hardly speak, from laughing.

"I'm confused. What are you saying, Justine? Don't you care? Are you saying you're OK with your husband having an affair because he's a man?" Septi asked, bewildered.

"Let's not get it twisted. Of course, I care, but what can I do about it? I've learned to live with it. He's been cheating on me since the first day I met him." Justine broke down, laughing again.

"I don't think you understand. He's not just messing around -- he is in a serious relationship. I can't believe you have no clue. Stop laughing, damn it!"

"I'm sorry, I couldn't help it. I'm tickled. It's one of the best laughs I've had in a long time! I needed that!" Justine tried to put on a straight face. "Why do you care about what my husband is doing? You sure it ain't you that's involved with him?" she asked, smirking. "Listen to me, if it's not your friend or you, it will be some other woman."

"Maybe you don't care, but I care because he is using my friend and I don't want to see her hurt. Besides, I hate to see a man cheat on his wife and use other women for what he can get." Septi was upset, she didn't understand Justine and women like her. They gave their husbands permission to cheat and disrespect women.

"Well, Honey, you don't love men then, because all of them cheat and most of them are users and besides, your friend is a grown-ass woman. I'm sure she knows exactly what she's doing and can take care of herself."

"Of course, she can take care of herself, but that's not the point. You know yourself, your husband can be charming. I guess she's blinded by dick. We've all been there."

"No shit! What do you expect me to do about it? People are responsible for their own actions." Justine knew there had to be more to the story than Septi was revealing, otherwise, why would she be standing here in her home. 'He's probably screwing both of them at the same time – he certainly done close friends before,' she thought to herself.

"You're his wife. You can let him know what you found out and you can demand that he stop seeing her," Septi said, raising her voice.

Now that Justine was able to control herself, she leaned back on her sofa. "Girl, please! A woman is powerless when it comes to a cheating man. Don't you know that? A man is going to do what a man wants to do. You think you're the only woman who has ever showed up at my door singing that same old song?"

"If that's the case, why is it still happening? You could have put a stop to this shit the first time it happened," Septi cried out in frustration.

"We been married for years and I've never been able to stop him. So, unless you know of some magical way to stop my husband from cheating, let me know. Otherwise, you're wasting my time. Wife or no wife, a man is going to do whatever he wants to do."

"I hate to tell you this--you're pretty sad. Your reaction is not that of a normal wife who finds out her husband is cheating on her," Septi said, sulking.

"I don't give a damn what you think about me. Keith is my husband and we've been married a long time. He's never going to change and he's not going to leave me for no other woman, neither. Only place he going to leave me for is prison."

"I don't understand how you can continue to be married to a man like him. Why didn't you give him an ultimatum when you found out the first time he was cheating on you? Things might be different for you now," Septi said, in a surrendering tone.

Septi struck a nerve with Justine, pissing her off. 'How dare this bitch walk up in my house and tell me how to handle my husband,' Justine thought. 'I know how to handle my business.'

"Look, Missy, I'm not listening to any more of your bullshit. Who the hell are you to pass judgment on me? My children love having their daddy around, for whatever time he's around, and I'm not going to take that away from them. So, I deal with it. They adore their daddy. He's not all bad. On Saturday, we're going as a family to the community Easter egg hunt and then we'll all go to his mother's house and spend the night, and then we'll all go to church with her on Sunday. You want me to take away the few good times they have with their father? I don't think so. Now, I want you to get your skinny ass out of my house!

"I am not asking you to take anything away from your children. But for God's sake, make him respect you and them," Septi pleaded.

"Believe me, I ain't nobody's fool. I gets mine's. You need to go now and get yourself some. Good luck to you. Oh, excuse me, I meant to say good luck to your friend." Justine giggled and winked her eye.

Septi didn't understand how any woman could be so nonchalant upon finding out that her husband was cheating on her. If she was married and a woman showed up at her door and told her that her husband was cheating on her, she would have turned into a stark raving mad black woman. She would have shot the messenger for bringing the news, killed her husband for his infidelity and then his girlfriend for getting a piece of her man.

She hurriedly walked out of Justine's house. 'What a complete fucking waste of time this was. I don't believe this shit,' she thought. 'I have no other choice but to tell Anabay the truth myself. I'll see her next Sunday on Easter. I'll tell her then.'

Chapter 30

May the Truth be Told

Lillie Mae and Aaron returned home from Easter Sunrise Service. It was a tradition with them to attend church together every Easter Sunday. Aaron was his mother's pride and joy, and Lillie Mae basked in glory, as the church folks bombarded her with compliments about Aaron and made a big fuss over how handsome he was. Of course, the single church sisters all wanted to know if he was married or had a girlfriend. Showing her son off on Easter Sunday morning gave Lillie Mae more joy than listening to the pastor's sermon.

Otis never attended Easter Sunrise Service. His excuse was, he wanted to give up his seat to sinners who only attended church on Easter so they could repent and feel good about themselves the rest of the year. Truth told, he didn't like getting up early. He opted instead to remain at home and to assist in the preparations for the brunch he and Lillie Mae hosted every Easter, at noon. Pastor Tisdale and other church members would be attending along with extended family and friends. Otis's job was straightening up the house, vacuuming and dusting, and going to the florist to get fresh flowers--so that when his wife returned home, all she had to do was start cooking.

"Aaron, it sure was a wonderful service! Pastor Tisdale sure knows how to preach the truth," said an exuberant Lillie Mae.

"I enjoyed the service too, Moms, but you know more than anything, I love escorting you to church on Easter," Aaron said, turning and giving his mother a peck on her cheek. "You know you were the best-dressed woman in the church, don't you? You always knock it out the ballpark."

"Don't be silly," Lillie Mae said, smiling from ear to ear.

"Moms, you had to have noticed the way all the women were cutting their eyes at you. I overheard them whispering about your suit and your hat."

"Aaron, stop playing. You know that didn't happen."

"Oh, yes it did. I swear it did."

"Aaron! You know better than to swear. You just left church," said a frowning Lillie Mae, in a scolding tone. She knew her son was telling the truth -- she just didn't want to let on to him. Lillie Mae was indeed the best-dressed woman at church and that is what she had always set out to do. Once again, she did not disappoint. All eyes were on her. Every year, right after New Year's Day, she would start searching every catalog she could get her hands on for the perfect outfit. It had to be the most expensive and prettiest Easter suit, the biggest and fanciest hat decorated with flowers, ribbons, bows, feathers, or fruit, and matching purse and shoes-- anything that made her stand out from the rest of the women. Sunrise Service was a silent, unspoken fashion show and it was her goal to be the star of the affair.

Aaron and Lillie Mae walked into the kitchen, looking for Otis.

"I guess Otis is still out. I hope he won't be too late. Are you excited about the brunch?" Lillie Mae asked Aaron.

"Moms, where's this question coming from? You've never asked me that before. What's this all about?" Aaron knew exactly what his mother was hinting at. He was very excited, but he dared not show it. He was going to keep cool.

"Aaron, this is the first time you have ever invited anyone to our home since your best friend, Michael."

"I know. I will always miss Mike."

"We all miss Mike. He was such a nice young man. But, God needed him more," said Lillie Mae, rubbing Aaron's back.

"I know, Moms, but it just wasn't fair." Aaron stared straight ahead, choking up.

"Aaron, always remember --- we can't question God's will. He and only He knows best. Now, you still haven't answered my question," Lillie Mae said in an upbeat voice, trying to lighten the atmosphere.

"What question?" Aaron was deep in thought, reflecting on the death of his best friend Michael, who was killed in a tragic car accident the day before his graduation from high school. He was thinking about how he had gotten into the car with Michael and then got out because he heard a voice telling him to exit. He also knew his mother would have been very upset if she ever found out he was riding in a car with the King brothers, who were always looking to race somebody. That day the brothers were racing each other. The youngest brother driving the car Michael was riding in lost control of his vehicle and crashed into an electric pole, killing only Michael. Although it had been years since Michael's death, whenever Aaron thought about the accident, he relived it as if it had just happened. He still harbored guilt for not telling his friend to get out of the car and to take the city bus home like they always did.

"Are you excited about Septi coming to brunch?" asked Lillie Mae.

"I'm happy she accepted my invite. I think she'll enjoy herself. I like her a lot."

Lillie Mae turned to Aaron and gave him a big smile, stroking his cheek, "Well, I think she is a nice girl. I am happy for you."

"Moms, you know what's so funny? We didn't like each other when we initially met."

"I didn't like your daddy either when I first met him. Love has a way of happening."

"Hold up, Moms. I didn't mention anything about the possibility of love."

"I know you didn't, but I have a feeling." Lillie Mae was smiling.

"Have you mentioned anything about Septi to Pops yet?"

"I casually mentioned that you were seeing Anabay's friend, Septi."

"Why did you have to go and do that? I know he had something negative to say."

"You know your daddy. He didn't say much."

"I really don't understand him sometimes."

"Aaron, your daddy loves you very much. He just wants you to be successful."

"I know that but being successful is not about working a nine to five job down at the shipyard. It was good for him but it's not what I want for myself."

"I know, Baby. Everything's going to be all right, you'll see," assured Lillie Mae.

"We'll see how he acts when she comes to brunch. We both know he'll find something negative to say."

"What can he say? He is going to love Septi. What's not to love about her? She's a very attractive, hard-working girl and she is Anabay's best friend. And, you know how he feels about her."

"I know. You would think Anabay is his child, instead of me. Enough about Pops--I'm not going to let him spoil my day. Life is looking good for me and I'm going to enjoy myself. I never imagined myself getting serious with someone."

"Aaron, we can't control the time we fall in love--it just happens when you least expect it. I'm happy for you. And, don't you worry about your father. He'll fall in line and he'll be happy for you too. Besides, I would love to have some grandchildren running around here so I can spoil them before I get too old."

"Hold on, Moms, you're really getting ahead of yourself," laughed Aaron.

"No, I'm not!" Lillie Mae said, smiling.

"Moms, you're making me nervous. I'm going upstairs to change my clothes."

"Me, too. I've got a lot to do before the guests start arriving." Lille Mae walked into her bedroom. "Otis, what are you doing here? You should have left by now to pick up the flowers. Everybody will be here soon."

"I know," Otis replied, sounding somber.

"What's wrong? Don't you feel well?"

"I'm fine. I just don't like it," he said, turning up his nose in disgust.

"You don't like what?" Lillie Mae was clearly confused.

"About what you told me a couple days ago."

"What did I tell you?" asked Lillie Mae.

"About Aaron seeing Anabay's friend, Septi."

"You've got to be kidding me. What's wrong with that?" Lillie Mae was annoyed. Her husband didn't care for anything their son did.

"I just don't think it's a good idea."

"Otis, what is your problem? You're not happy about anything Aaron does. I would think you'd be happy. Remember when you thought he was gay. That bothered you--why, I don't know. Now he has an interest in a woman and you are upset about that. What's going on with you?"

"I'm not happy about him being involved with that gal. I'd rather he be gay."

"Otis, you are not making any sense. What do you have against Septi?"

"Nothing's wrong with her. It's Aaron."

"OK, Otis, I heard enough! Aaron is our son. He is a grown man and he can damn well have a relationship with whomever he chooses to get involved with. As long as he's happy, you should be happy for him."

Whenever Lillie Mae became upset with Otis, she used his name a lot. She was sick and tired of his attitude towards his own son. "Otis, you're not making any sense. Why do you hate Aaron? He's your son."

"I don't hate the boy. He just . . . oh, never mind." Otis was raising his voice because he didn't want to continue the conversation. He had his reasons and that was the end of the conversation. Period. There was nothing Lillie Mae could say to make him change his mind.

"Otis, lower your voice. Aaron will hear you. What is your problem? You're just a controlling, grumpy old man! Just because he didn't want to work down at that old shipyard, you've been on his case ever since. He is entitled to live his life any way he sees fit. He ain't got to follow in your footsteps."

"That's ridiculous. That boy shouldn't be seeing anyone until he gets himself together as a man."

"Answer this then, Otis Jones -- did you have yourself together before you looked at me?"

"Not the same."

"Otis, I've had enough of your foolish talk. You've spent your whole life down at that old shipyard because it was good work in your day and time. Don't you see things have changed? People have more options available to them now. It's a new day. You need to support your son instead of knocking him down all the time."

"Yeah, but— "

"Otis, do all of us a favor and keep your thoughts to yourself. Nobody cares about what you feel. Let me be clear where I stand. I am very happy for Aaron and I hope he makes it with Septi. He's excited about her coming to brunch, so don't ruin it for him. I suggest you go and pick up the flowers now." Lillie Mae walked out, slamming the door behind her. She hated that Otis was always so hard on Aaron. He was their only child. So what if he didn't turn out to be all his father had hoped for--it was his life. She certainly didn't understand why he would be so upset about their son dating Septi.

Otis was not happy about picking up the floral arrangements, a job he had taken upon himself for many years. This year, things felt different. He wished they weren't hosting brunch. He returned home minutes before the first guests were scheduled to arrive.

* * * * *

"These floral arrangements are beautiful, absolutely exquisite," exclaimed Lillie Mae. Upon removing the cellophane wrappings, she placed an arrangement on the dining room table, one in the foyer and the other in the living room. "Otis, where are my roses?"

Otis sheepishly replied, "They sold out."

"Otis Jones, it's Easter. After all these years, it's odd that the florist would have run out of roses. I guess there's a first time for everything." She knew her husband was being spiteful -- he hadn't brought her roses because he was upset with her for supporting the idea of Aaron seeing Septi. Lillie Mae decided not to push the issue with the roses--she had a very special brunch to host and there was no time to fight with Otis. He was being very stubborn today.

Otis saw the disappointment on his wife's face. He suspected she knew he had lied about the roses being sold out since they both knew each other so well, but he didn't care. He was angry with her for supporting the idea of Aaron and Septi being a couple. He had his reasons why these two should not be together and that was all that mattered.

Aaron paced back and forth from the foyer to the dining room, feeling nervous. The guests had started arriving and there was no sign of Septi. He was worried that maybe she had gotten cold feet and had changed her mind about coming to brunch. "Anabay, have you spoken to Septi today?" he asked, entering the kitchen. He picked up a spoon and dipped it into the big bowl of potato salad that Anabay was scooping into a redbird crystal serving bowl. Lillie Mae loved to show off her beautiful crystal from Germany whenever she entertained.

Anabay shook her head "no" and raised her eyebrows upward, letting Aaron know she suspected something was up between him and Septi, especially since he hadn't said anything to her about them being an item.

"Aaron, get out of the potato salad!" Lillie Mae shouted. "You know I hate it when you pick in my food while it's being prepared."

"Sorry, Moms, I'm a little nervous. Septi hasn't answered her telephone for the last hour."

"Aaron, just relax. I'm sure she will be here," Lillie Mae reassured.

"I can't believe you two are an item,"Anabay giggled, "Lord, have mercy."

"Anabay, you better stop calling on the Lord's name in vain," Lillie Mae said, opening the oven door and pulling out her thirty-five-pound Butterball turkey. Why are you so surprised about Aaron and Septi? She's one lucky woman, I can tell you that." Lillie Mae spoke as any proud mother would.

"I'm surprised because I always thought they didn't even like one another," Anabay answered.

"Well, things happen," Lillie Mae responded.

"I wish you two would stop talking about me like I am not here," said Aaron.

The doorbell rang.

"Maybe that's her, Aaron. Why don't you go answer the door so your daddy won't have to get up," suggested Lillie Mae. "He's not feeling well."

"What's wrong with Uncle Otis?" asked Anabay. "I better go get Delbert. You know my son--he'll talk him to death."

"No, leave him. Delbert will be a distraction for Otis. He's just getting old and cranky, that's all."

Aaron greeted Pastor Tisdale, the invited Deacons, Deaconesses, and other church members as they arrived.

"It sure smells good in here," Pastor Tisdale commented, rubbing his stomach. "I'm ready to throw down!"

"Not so fast," Aaron heard, as he was about to close the door. He turned around and there was Septi, standing in the doorway.

"You look amazingly beautiful," he blushed, giving her a big wet peck on her cheek.

"Thanks, Aaron." Septi was happy Aaron liked the lime green booty pants she was wearing and her pink and black two-piece sweater set.

Aaron paraded her into the dining room where the guests were sitting. "Everyone, Septi is here," he proudly announced.

"Just in time for blessings of the food. Sister Lillie Mae, you sure know how to prepare a spread. Young Lady, take a seat next to your future father-in-law," Pastor Tisdale instructed Septi to sit next to Otis, who was sitting at the head of the table.

Septi felt embarrassed. Pastor Tisdale had referred to Otis as her future father-in-law, yet she barely knew the man. She wondered what in the world had been said about her relationship with Aaron before she arrived to have caused the preacher to make such an assumption. She cut her eyes at Aaron, letting him know she was not comfortable with the pastor's remarks. As far as she was concerned, she and Aaron had a friendship and were nowhere close to being in a relationship leading to marriage. Besides, she was there to handle some business with Anabay.

"Pastor Tisdale, please do the honors and bless the food," Otis said.

"My pleasure. May we join hands and bow our heads. Lord, bless the hands that prepared this scrumptious spread before us. May we break bread and drink together for the nourishment of our bodies, in Jesus's name. Amen. Let's eat and, as James Brown would say, pass the peas." Pastor Tisdale was known for cracking dry, witty jokes.

"How long have you two been seeing each other?" Pastor Tisdale asked, looking directly at Septi while biting down on a chicken leg and smacking his lips. "This sure is some good crispy, golden fried chicken, Sister Lillie Mae! You have sure enough put a hurting on this 'almighty gospel bird'! Colonel Sanders can't touch you!"

"Thank you, Pastor." Lillie Mae was grinning from ear to ear.

"Not long, Rev. You really preached a fantastic sermon this morning," Aaron quickly responded, trying to deflect the conversation away from him and Septi. He didn't like being the topic of the conversation, especially when it was about his personal life.

Pastor continued talking. "I must say, you two make a handsome couple. I sure hope you can cook, young lady.

Aaron's used to his mama's fine cooking. You can cook, can't you?"

"Yes, I like to think I can." Septi's voice quivered as she squirmed in her chair. She could not believe her cooking ability was a subject of conversation at an Easter Sunday brunch. The reverend was really getting on her nerves. She made a quick eye contact with Anabay, who smiled back.

"Reverend, I have to agree with Aaron. This morning's service was very moving." Lillie Mae wanted to redirect the conversation away from Aaron and Septi. She knew Otis was not thrilled about them seeing each other and she didn't need Pastor Tisdale to keep reminding him. "Please, everyone eat up. There's plenty of food here."

"Thank you, Sister Lillie Mae. I did preach up an appetite. I'm sure enjoying this food." Pastor Tisdale cleared his throat and reached over for another piece of fried chicken. "You know, speaking about my message this morning, I try to gear my message to the youth-- after all, they are the ones who are left to take over when us old folks are no longer afforded a home on this earth. That's why we must teach them well. You know what I am talking about, Brother Otis?"

"Yes, sir, I know exactly what you're talking about. That's why I encourage my son........."

"Anabay, you're being awfully quiet—you haven't said two words since you sat down," Lillie Mae quickly interrupted. She saw where Otis was trying to steer the conversation and she wasn't going to allow him to start in on Aaron about working down at the shipyard at her dining table in front of all their guests.

"I'm too busy enjoying this food," Anabay replied.

"What about you, Delbert? Are you enjoying the food?"

"Yes, Aunt Lillie Mae."

"Your son is well behaved, Sister Anabay. You are training him well," Pastor Tisdale commented.

"Thank you, Pastor."

"Teaching starts at home with the parents. That's why I encourage all young couples to come out to Couples Prayer Service every Wednesday night at seven thirty. Aaron, you and Septi should consider attending. It makes a good foundation for a long relationship. After all, families who pray together, stay together. My late wife and I were together for twenty-five years and our love was still fresh. Prayer kept us on the path to a happy marriage."

"It's a lot of truth in what you speak, Pastor, but my son and Septi will not be needing any of your services," Otis interjected.

"Otis! Behave yourself," Lillie Mae demanded, giving him her look.

"It's OK, Moms. Pops can't help himself when it comes to me. He always got to say something negative. Why should Easter Sunday be different from any other day?"

Septi sat nervously, wishing she hadn't shown up. "Perhaps I should leave."

"Sit down, Septi," Otis demanded.

"Y'all please excuse my husband -- he's been feeling a bit poorly lately." Lillie stood up, "Otis, can I speak to you in the kitchen?"

"No, you may not and I feel just fine. I don't need you making excuses for me!"

The tension was so thick, one could have sliced it with a spoon. Everyone was on edge. Everyone, except for Reverend Tisdale, had stopped eating and were sitting, staring ahead in silent bewilderment.

"Brother Jones, something is eating at your spirit. I felt it the moment I arrived in your home. This is perhaps not the best day for you to vent, for this is a day for good friends and family to commune and celebrate our Savior, Jesus Christ. Let's finish this lovely dinner in peace and harmony. I 'll be happy to counsel you later about your issues."

"I don't need no damn counseling!"

"Otis Jones, you will not disrespect Pastor! What has gotten into you?" Lillie Mae was petrified.

"It's all right, Sister Lillie Mae. Brother Jones, we all see that something is deeply bothering you. We're all friends and family here, so go ahead and speak your piece," urged Pastor Tisdale.

"Pastor Tisdale, please do not encourage my Pops."

"Shut up, Boy, and listen! This is my house," Otis shouted. "Thank you, Pastor, for setting the platform for me to put an end to this bullshit!"

"Otis, this is enough! I'm not sitting here any longer, allowing you to carry on like this in front of our guests! It's Easter for God's sake! It's obvious you're sick! I suggest you go upstairs and I'll call your doctor right now," Lillie Mae said sternly.

"Lillie Mae, why don't you sit down and stop running your damn mouth for once in your life! You have always lived your entire life pretending everything is fine. Everything can't be alright all the time, so sit down and shut the hell up and stop fucking pretending," he yelled at his wife.

Lillie Mae sat back down at the table in total embarrassment. Although what Pastor Tisdale said about being among family and friends was true, people would certainly talk. Church folks were notorious for gossiping. She knew once this squabble got out, she would not be able to show her face in church for a very long time.

"Oh, hell no, Pops! You can't speak to Moms like that!"

"Aaron, I would advise you not to open your god-damn mouth! You're nothing but a mama's boy still latched to the titty! I should have put my foot down with your sorry ass a long time ago," Otis fired back.

Septi didn't know what this was all about. She could not imagine being the cause of this much family friction.

Anabay picked up Delbert's plate. "Come on Delbert—you can finish eating in the kitchen."

"Mommy, what is latch to titty?" asked Delbert.

"Just come with Mommy into the kitchen, Delbert."

"Anabay, this has nothing to do with you but I don't want you to miss what I'm about to say. So, I would appreciate it if you came back. You need to hear this."

Lillie Mae became numb listening to Otis's ranting. They had been married for over forty years and not once had he ever acted out like this. She didn't know if she would ever be able to forgive him for this. "Otis, please don't do this," she cried out. "Get a handle on yourself."

"It's OK, Moms. I'm a man, I can handle it. Let the old man speak. I'm sure by now everyone at this table knows or has an idea about how my father feels about me."

"I am begging you, Otis, please don't do this. You're not well." Lillie Mae continued pleading with her husband.

"Yeah, let the old man talk! You got a lot of damn nerve! I'm sorry to call you my son!" Otis shouted. "You're a fucking loser! I feel sorry for your sorry ass! You don't even know which end is up!"

"Otis!" Lillie Mae cried out, tears streaming down her face.

"Lillie Mae, I'm telling you once again, shut the fuck up! If you had listened to me and joined forces with me, this could have been handled in a different way. You pushed me to this point." Otis was wound up and beyond the point of no return. It didn't matter anymore, the truth had to be told.

"Deacon Jones, are you sure you want to do this? You might have a lot of regrets come morning. Why don't you and I talk about it in private? You need to pray about whatever is eating at your spirit before you say something that might hurt your family," reasoned Deacon Thomas.

"I'm good, Deacon Thomas," Otis said quickly, brushing him off.

"Pastor Tisdale, no disrespect to you or anybody else at this table but I have prayed about this and I have no choice in the matter," said Otis.

"Aaron, as your father, I don't need you to ask me any questions. I'm going to ask you and Septi to stop seeing each other romantically. Please, son, I'm begging you," Otis pleaded.

"Pops, you're not making any sense. What is it to you that we see each other? You just don't want to see me happy!" Aaron was totally perplexed.

Septi hesitated, but finally managed to say, "I'm confused. I'm not sure where you're going with this, Mr. Jones."

"Septi, don't sweat it. It's my Pops being his usual self. In his world, I'm never good enough. He never wants to see me happy."

"Boy, this time you're wrong. I am very sorry, but it has to be this way."

"Well, I'm not going to stop seeing Septi just because you demand it. That's never going to happen. You can forget about it. I'm a grown-ass man and I choose for myself who I date. Got that?"

"I 've tried to avoid having to tell you guys. Now you leave me no choice," shouted Otis.

"Tell us what?" Aaron shouted back.

"Septi is your fucking half-sister! I'm her daddy! You satisfied now? Now you know the truth! You satisfied?" Otis continued shouting.

"Otis, what are you talking about?" sobbed Lillie Mae.

"You know what, Pops? You are a fucking sick-ass man," shouted Aaron. "You would stoop that low to make up some shit like this just to have your way!"

"Otis, please, why are you saying this?" Lillie Mae cried.

"Lillie Mae, I'm so sorry. I swear I never wanted to hurt you. I had planned on carrying this secret to my grave. Septi's mother is your niece, Belle, and I'm her daddy."

"Oh, my God, Otis! How could you?" cried Lillie Mae.

"Mr. Jones, you've obviously made a mistake! My mother's name isn't Belle, it's Bella," Septi spoke up. "My father is Septimo Bruno. He's Italian. I'm named after him. My parents live in Italy."

"I'm your daddy, Gal. Your mama may be calling herself Bella these days, but her birth name is Belle Bailey and she is Lillie Mae's niece. She changed your name too. Your birth name is Shirley Belle Bailey.

"Shirley Belle Bailey! No way in hell! Now, I know you done lost your god-damned mind! My mother would never give me a country ass name like that! I can't take any more of this shit! You need serious help, Mr. Jones." Septi was livid.

"Gal, I'm speaking the truth. Belle blackmailed me into giving up my parental rights to you when you were a baby so your stepdaddy could adopt you."

"I don't believe you! You are a god damned liar! There's no way in hell--you're my father! You are one sick, twisted, deranged man to be making up all this shit!" Septi was shaking and her eyes were overflowing with tears.

"Ask your mama to tell you the truth, Little Lady. I've been paying her child support since you were born, even though I had no legal obligation to do so. Remember when you used to get those anonymous money orders when you were in college? Well, that was me, sending you a little extra," said a wild-eyed Otis.

Aaron could no longer control his anger. He felt his fists tighten up. All he could see was red--he no longer cared that Otis was his father. "You're a fucking dog! I'm going to kill you!" he shouted out before flipping the table over and lunging towards Otis.

"Oh no!" screamed Anabay. "Somebody call 911!"

Chapter 31

Web of Lies

Septi sat on the edge of her queen-sized sleigh bed like a zombie in a trance trying to understand how this beautiful Easter Sunday ended up being the worst day of her life. Feeling shocked and confused was putting it mildly. She was literally dumfounded and speechless.

She needed to know the truth as soon as possible, and only her mother could give it to her. Could it be true? Was Otis Jones, a man she barely knew, her biological father instead of Septimo Bruno, the man whose name she carried and whom she loved and adored?

The events of this day were so traumatic and overwhelming, there was no way she could even begin to process what Otis revealed. With trembling hands, she picked up the phone on her nightstand and dialed the number to the International Operator. It was six o'clock in the evening in Newark, so in Italy, the time would be around 1 o'clock in the morning. It flashed in her mind that the ringing of the telephone would probably wake up her parents, but she had to know the truth now. Besides, if they had been lying to her all her life, they deserved to be awakened out of their sleep. Hell or high water, she was going to demand the truth.

Septi secretly hoped her mother, Bella, would answer the telephone because she was in no mood to make small talk with her father. Only Bella could answer her questions, after all, Bella was the one who had given birth to her and therefore, she damn sure would know who the sperm donor was.

Just as she had hoped, Bella answered the telephone, sounding sleepy, "Buon giorno."

"Buon giorno, Madre," Septi replied, in a serious, flat tone.

"Septi? Darling, is everything all right? It's been a while since we've heard from you."

The sound of her mother's voice irritated her to the point where she could no longer control herself. In a firm voice, Septi dug right in for the kill, "Who is my biological father, Septimo Bruno or Otis Jones? And don't you dare lie to me!"

A moment of silence ensued for what seemed like an eternity to Septi. In her heart of hearts, she knew the answer. Tears streamed down her face, and her body trembled.

Bella finally uttered the words, "Otis Jones is your biological father."

"Otis Jones!" Septi screamed. Never in her life could she have ever imagined the depth of pain she was now feeling–like a knife was being twisted deep into her heart. She shouted out, "Mother, who the fuck are you?

I hear your real name isn't even Bella – it's Belle and that my birth name was Shirley Belle Bailey! He was your uncle by marriage! How could you have sunk so low? You slept with your aunt's husband and had his baby!"

"Darling, I'm sorry. I never wanted you to find out about Otis," cried Bella. "Life can be complicated and sometimes things happen that we have no control over."

"Are you fucking kidding me? Have no control over? You're full of shit, Mother. Nobody held a gun to your head and made you fuck your aunt's husband! Didn't you think I deserved to know Papa adopted me?

"Septi, you don't understand. Awful things always seem to happen to the women in our family. It's in our blood. Please know that I love you very much. Everything I did, I did for you. I wanted to protect you from the family curse….."

"Give me a fucking break! Mother, you're the one who has cursed my life! I can't listen to you anymore! You can't even take responsibility for what you've done and all the lies you've told! You have no idea what you have done to me! Buona notte, Madre!" Septi slammed down the telephone receiver so hard, she broke a fingernail. "Damn it, damn it,"she screamed. Tears were flowing from her eyes with no end in sight.

It infuriated Septi when Bella tried to blame a family curse for all her lies. No way in hell was she going to let her off the hook based on some old wives' tale. She couldn't bear listening to another word out of that woman's mouth.

Septi realized that she now had the hard task of figuring out exactly who she is. For all of her years on earth, she believed she was the biracial child of a black mother and an Italian father. Septimo Bruno had been an excellent father to her and he indeed was a good man, although he tended to be on the docile side. Bella was a good wife and mother, but she was the dominant spouse. Septi surmised that Bella was the one who concocted the web of lies and Septimo went along with her because he loved both of them very much. She placed one hundred percent of the blame on her mother.

She began reflecting on all the difficulties she had endured as a child growing up in Queens, NY--being teased and taunted for not always fitting in, being called names like half breed, zebra or mutt. All this grief because her parents had made a conscious decision to allow her to grow up living a lie. It now seemed so unfair.

Septi didn't know if she would ever be able to forgive either of her parents, especially her mother. Everything she knew about Bella was a lie, even her name. Bella hadn't lied about being born in Virginia, but she lied about having any living relatives. She told everyone her parents died when she was a small child and that she grew up in an orphanage. "Goddamm you, Mother,

Goddamm the both of you!" Septi yelled out, throwing a picture frame containing their pictures across the room.

Sooner or later, she knew she would have to come to grips with Otis Jones being her biological father, but she just couldn't wrap her head around this thought. She loved Septimo Bruno so much and as she matured into womanhood, it was with pride that she presented herself to the world as half Italian. She spoke Italian fluently and absolutely loved Italian food. But, it was true. Otis Jones, that tall country-ass black man from the South was her real daddy.

"Oh, my God! Oh, my God!" Suddenly, the realization that she had been intimate with Aaron pierced through her veil of consciousness. "Oh, my God. he is my half-brother--and he is also my cousin," she verbalized, detangling the blood relationship. Septi jumped up, ran into the bathroom and started vomiting and dry heaving. She lay on the bathroom floor curled up in the fetal position, crying her eyes out for hours. "Damn, damn, damn! I have committed incest! My life is ruined! I will never feel clean again!" She was feeling ten times worse than when she learned about Kandy being an inmate.

The ringing of her doorbell temporarily jolted her out of her misery. She glanced at her wristwatch and saw that it was nine o'clock. She had forgotten that Anabay and Delbert were coming to spend the night with her.

Anabay knew Septi was devastated and she wanted to be available for her best friend. She and Delbert waited patiently at the door.

Septi finally opened the door, looking disheveled with swollen, bloodshot eyes, Anabay immediately knew her friend hadn't gotten the answer she had been hoping for, from her mother. Uncle Otis had spoken the truth-- he was her father.

"Hi, Aunt Septi," Delbert said, yawning.

"Hi, Cutie. Come on in," Septi responded.

Anabay didn't say a word--she grabbed Septi and embraced her. Septi sobbed quietly in her arms as they stood, holding each other. Anabay whispered to Septi, "I'm going to put Delbert to bed, and then, you and I can talk. I'm here for you."

"Delbert, give Aunt Septi a big hug good night. It's time to go to bed," instructed Anabay.

"Good night, Aunt Septi. Aunt Septi, your eyes are red."

"Delbert, that's enough. March your little self into the bedroom right now, young man," commanded Anabay.

*****

Anabay returned and sat on the sofa next to Septi, who was looking depleted and somber. Both women were thinking the same thing, 'How in the world did an Easter Sunday Brunch, which is supposed to be a pleasant get-together for friends and family, turn out to be the platform for life-changing events.' This particular Easter Sunday had started out so beautifully yet ended up in tragedy.

In between sobs, Septi said the words, "Otis Jones was right. He is my biological father."

"Oh, Septi, I'm so sorry. I was hoping it was all a big mistake. I know how much you love your father." Anabay hugged Septi in an attempt to console her. "It's all right. Everything's going to be all right. We're going to get through this together. I'm here for you," she kept repeating these phrases.

Septi was absolutely mortified and inconsolable--in her state of mind, nothing would ever be all right again. She continued sobbing heavily, barely able to relay the conversation with her mother to Anabay. She really broke down crying hysterically when she said, "The worst part of it all -- I have been fucking Aaron, my own brother."

"Septi, you're going to be all right. We will get through this together," Anabay kept repeating her mantras, while holding Septi and rocking her back and forth.

"Anabay, how can you sit here and tell me everything's going to be all right? Did you not hear what I just said? Don't you get it? I have committed incest with my brother. How nasty is that? It's a sin! I have given my brother my most prized possession! He has seen and touched every crack and crevice on my body! How in hell am I supposed to live with this shit?" Septi was inconsolable.

"None of this is your fault, Septi. You didn't know and neither did Aaron. With time, prayer and forgiveness, you can and you will overcome this."

"I feel so dirty! It's so disgusting and nasty! I have committed incest! I don't understand why God is punishing me like this! What did I do to deserve this?" She continued sobbing hysterically.

"Septi, God is not punishing you. Sometimes bad things happen to good people. Life is like that, you know. We are not always in control . . . "

"Anabay, please stop. Now you are beginning to sound like my lying-ass mother. She had the nerve to say that shit to me -- that things happened beyond her control. Trying to tell me everything she did was to protect me from some phantom family curse."

"Septi, you do realize that we're first cousins, don't you? I can share with you what I know about the curse on the Bailey Women. I grew up hearing about it every day of my life."

Septi looked at Anabay in shock. She could not believe Anabay was attempting to defend her mother by telling her about some mythical curse. She would not accept any justification for Bella's selfish, deceitful, self-serving decisions and lies. "No thank you. I don't want to hear about that old Southern bullshit. You can believe in a stupid, dumb-ass curse if you want, but I never want to hear the word 'curse' mentioned to me again," she shouted, angrily.

"Septi, calm down! I didn't mean to upset you. I'm just trying to shed some light on why your mother may have made the decisions she did."

"I am angry as hell! You know what? My mother is a bitch and I don't care if I ever see her ass again. Because of her, my whole life has been a lie and now my life is ruined. And what about poor Aaron? His life is definitely ruined. I feel so bad. Oh, my God, can you imagine the guilt he must be feeling tonight? My mother caused all of this shit."

"Septi, you do know you're going to have to face Aaron."

"I can't face him and I'm sure he doesn't want to see me either."

"Septi, get a grip. Everything always works itself out, you will see."

"You make me sick Anabay--you're always so damn optimistic. Did you not hear me? Aaron and I fucked. He is the only man who has ever hit my g-spot. My half-brother gave me the best orgasm I've ever had in my life and you want me to believe everything's going to be all right? You've got to be fucking kidding me! How in the hell do you expect me to live with that shit? It's not Aaron's fault--it's his daddy's fault for fucking his wife's niece. He should have kept his dick in his pants. Look, Anabay, I just can't handle any more of this tonight. I appreciate you being here with me but right now I need to be alone. I hope you're not offended." Septi stood up.

"I understand, Septi. Let's go to bed and deal with tomorrow when it comes. One good thing has come out of this fiasco though--you and I are first cousins in addition to being best friends. I love you, Septi. Come here and give your cousin a big hug."

"Thanks for all your support, Anabay. See you in the morning."

"Septi, I hope you don't mind but I need to make a few phone calls. I want to make sure there weren't any problems closing the restaurant tonight."

"I don't care. Do what you have to do."

Anabay made her calls but the last one was to her home. The phone rang and rang but no one answered. She thought to herself, 'Where in the world is Kandy? He left on Thursday night to visit his mother in her new nursing home. He said he would be back tonight.'

Anabay retreated to the bedroom deep in thought. Belle was probably the pretty young girl standing next to her mama in an old picture she found tucked away in a Bible. When she had asked who the girl was, Bet replied the girl was nobody of importance. Her mama and her sisters were a strange bunch. They were all so different and they seemed not to care about keeping in touch with one another.

Her attention then reverted to poor Aunt Lillie Mae, who was in the hospital in intensive care after suffering a heart attack. Her heart just couldn't handle Uncle Otis's betrayal with her niece and the embarrassment of her son and husband physically fighting in front of church folks.

Anabay couldn't get the image of Aunt Lillie Mae lying on the floor, holding her heart and gasping for air, out of her mind. She kept trying hard to speak but her words were too muffled to understand. Before they hoisted her onto the gurney, she did manage to grab Anabay's hand and pull her in close. Anabay could have sworn she heard her aunt say the word 'curse' before she lost consciousness.

How ironic. Now Septi's mother, Belle Bailey, was talking about the stupid family curse. Maybe there was some truth to the curse after all.

Anabay got on her knees and prayed for Aunt Lillie Mae, Uncle Otis, Septi and Aaron. She also prayed for her aunt, Belle Bailey, and her husband, Septimo Bruno. She turned off the lamp on the nightstand and drifted off to sleep.

Zenora Knight

Chapter 32

Damn You!

Septi woke up to the sound of Anabay's voice speaking on the telephone. 'Damn, it's six o'clock in the morning. Who in the hell could she be talking to?' Septi thought to herself, reaching for her robe lying at the foot of her bed.

"Look, you are not being very nice right now!.... Where is your compassion?.... My family is going through a lot right now and I'm going to stay here with Septi for as long as she needs me.... I really don't care whether you like it or not.... Have a good day," Anabay said, hanging up the phone on Kandy. She couldn't stand his attitude sometimes, everything had to revolve around him. "Oh, my God, Septi! You scared me to death! I didn't hear you walk in."

"You were too busy talking to your fiancé," Septi replied sarcastically. "Anabay, please tell me you didn't tell my business to that man. You know how I feel about him, and how he feels about me."

"Of course not, Septi, I wouldn't do that," Anabay said, lying through her teeth because she had indeed told him everything. "Where do you keep your coffee? I'll make us some."

"It's on the top shelf in the middle cabinet. I gather he's upset with you for staying over here last night."

"You know how men are. They're nothing but big babies, especially when they can't have their way. I'd better hurry up and get ready for work," Anabay said, desperately wanting to divert the conversation away from Kandy. "I have to take Delbert with me to the restaurant. There's no way I'm going to impose him on Uncle Otis today."

"He can stay here with me. I'm not going anywhere. I need time to pull myself together. I'm going to take the rest of this week off and use up some of my sick time."

"Wow, Septi, it would help me a lot if you could keep him. Are you sure you don't mind?"

"Anabay, you know me--I don't say things I don't mean. Delbert cheers me up. Having him around will help me keep my mind off my own problems and, besides, we're family now."

"Thanks, Septi. I really appreciate you doing this for me. I'll send over some food from the restaurant so don't worry about fixing anything to eat. You are a lifesaver."

*****

It was eight thirty when Anabay arrived at the restaurant and the place was hopping, with a full breakfast crowd. After greeting the staff, she settled into her office and began reviewing the restaurant's receipt tally from Easter Sunday. She tried to concentrate but her mind kept flashing back to everything that had occurred within the past twenty-four hours. Without realizing it, she drifted off to sleep only to be awakened by a knock on the door. "Come in," she called out, trying to sound normal.

"Hey, Baby. I just came by to make sure you're alright. I didn't like the way you sounded this morning," Kandy said, sitting down.

"Oh, Kandy, the only thing I can do is pray that everything will turn out all right. Yesterday was unbelievable," Anabay sighed.

"Yeah, sounds like some rough shit went down, especially for your girl, Septi," he said, grinning. "Tell me that part again. Did you say she found out her boyfriend is really her brother?" Kandy burst out laughing.

"No, I will not tell you that part again! I don't see what you find so funny! My family is in a crisis! We are all devastated! Poor Aunt Lillie Mae is in the hospital fighting for her life!"

"Calm down, Baby, I didn't mean any harm by it. I was just trying to lighten things up. I'm your man. Of course, I feel and share in your pain. Is there anything I can do to help?" he asked, trying to sound sincere.

"No, there is nothing you can do. It's in God's hands now. What time is it, anyway?" Anabay asked, looking up at the clock on the wall. "I can't believe it's eleven o'clock already. Excuse me, I'll be right back. I need to have the kitchen prepare and deliver food to Septi."

Kandy remained seated, eyeing the wad of cash on Anabay's desk and plotting on how to get his hands on at least five hundred dollars. He leaned back in his chair, laughing on the inside about Septi's dreadful dilemma and thinking to himself, 'It couldn't have happened to a better bitch.'

When Anabay returned to her office, he stood up and wrapped his arms around her. "Come to Daddy, Baby, and give me a kiss. I really missed you last night."

"If you missed me so much last night, then where were you when I called at eleven o'clock?" Anabay asked, looking him dead in his eyes.

"I was knocked out asleep. I was so tired from my trip -- I didn't hear the phone ringing."

"Whatever," she replied, letting him know she wasn't buying his explanation.

"Baby, I've been thinking. You're going to be staying with your friend for a couple of days and that's not fair to me. Can we have a quick fuck right now?" Kandy was playing the sex card. He knew Anabay hated having quickies, especially at work, and would probably give him some money and rush him out of her office.

"Kandy, I am not in the mood for any nonsense! You need to leave right now!" She was clearly irritated.

"I have needs too. What am I supposed to do?" he asked, still playing the game. "You put everybody before me."

Someone knocked on the door.

"Come in," Anabay said, responding to the knock on the door.

"Miss Anabay, the food you ordered is ready. What's the address you want it delivered to?" asked DeAndre, one of the workers in the restaurant.

"The address is 555 Central......."

"Miss Ana, why don't you let me deliver the food. Lunchtime is busy. I don't mind helping out," Kandy interrupted.

"That's OK, DeAndre. He can deliver the food. Kandy, promise me that you won't say one word to Septi about anything I told you. She's a very private person."

"How ironic! She, of all people, has the nerve to not like people in her business, yet she's in everybody else's, especially yours."

"Kandy, promise me," Anabay demanded.

"I promise. I may not show it, but my heart really breaks for Septi and her brother. Miss Ana, I could use a few dollars. My funds are getting low. Would you mind spotting me five hundred dollars?"

He had caught her off guard. What could she say? There was no denying the big stack of bills sitting there in plain sight, so Anabay counted out five hundred dollars and handed it to him. She was not in the habit of cursing, but she was thinking to herself, 'I'm sick of this shit. I'll be glad when you get the fuck out of my office and out of my life.'

*****

'Misery loves company,' Kandy thought, ringing Septi's doorbell. He could hear footsteps walking towards the door.

Septi looked through her peephole and saw him. "What the hell do you want? Anabay isn't here. She's at the restaurant."

"No shit," he responded, sarcastically. "She asked me to deliver this food to you. Now, open the door. This box is heavy."

Septi reluctantly opened the door. "Sit the box on the kitchen table."

"Can I at least get a hello," Kandy said, strolling in and placing the box on the kitchen table. He turned to face Septi. "Anabay told me you two are first cousins and you guys didn't even know you were blood kin until yesterday. Man, that's messed up!"

"Look, Keith, or whatever your name is--I don't need this right now. Please leave." Septi knew there was no way he was being sincere. He was up to something, she could feel it.

"What do you mean, whatever my name is? You know my name--Keith Jackson."

"Whatever," Septi replied, rolling her eyes. "Please leave. I have things to do. Thank you for bringing the food over. Now get out! Get out right now!" Septi shouted, walking towards the door.

He grabbed her by the arm, pulling her back away from the door.

"Don't fucking touch me!"

"You need to calm your ass down. Where is Delbert?"

"Why do you want to know?"

"Just answer the question--where is the kid? I want to make sure he's OK before I leave."

"He's sleeping. Now leave." Septi was beginning to feel uneasy. Why wasn't he leaving and why was he so concerned about where Delbert was? She knew he had a criminal record. Fearful thoughts begin flashing in her mind.

"Good!" Kandy turned and marched into the living room.

"What do you mean, good!" She was baffled.

He grabbed Septi's waist from behind and pulled her down onto his lap, on the sofa.

"Keith, let me go! Let me go!" She squirmed, trying to break free of his grip.

"I'll let you go when you calm down. Look, Septi, I just want you to know how sorry I am for what happened between us. I'm hoping we can bury the hatchet, especially now--since you and Anabay are cousins."

"That's not going to be possible. I hate you. Now let me go," she yelled, breaking free of his grip.

"Septi, look! My dick is getting hard as a mother!" Kandy was squinting his eyes and rubbing his crotch.

"So, what the fuck does it have to do with me?" Septi rolled her eyes at the sight of the bulge in his pants.

"You always have this effect on me. You know I love fucking you, don't you?" He was observing her reaction and her body language.

"I want you to leave now! You're one sick bastard!"

"Just hear me out. I feel really sorry for hurting you the way I did. It made me realize--if I hadn't cut you off from this good dick, you would still be my friend instead of being my enemy." Kandy had a big smirk on his face. "The way I see it, this is enough dick for both you and Anabay." His eyes rolled back into his head as he continued massaging his crotch.

Septi stood there listening to him with a forced frown on her face but truthfully, the full-grown bulge in his pants was turning her on.

He was inhaling and exhaling deep breaths through his mouth like a patient in a doctor's office having a chest exam. "Girl, my dick is so hard--I'll jackhammer a new hole in your ass. Let me fuck you," he whispered. "I miss that sweet pussy of yours. It's always so wet and juicy. Just let me taste you."

Septi continued standing, mesmerized by his words and the site of his erection. Her pussy was wet and throbbing.

He reached up and pulled her down onto his left knee and they began kissing, passionately. With his right hand, he quickly disrobed her and explored her body. The sounds coming from Septi as he gently suckled her breasts confirmed to Kandy—he had hit a homerun. He stood her up and pulled down her silk ivory panties, all the while kissing her upper thighs and the front of her vagina. Septi willingly laid down on the sofa and parted her legs for him. He used his tongue to outline her vagina lips before plunging his tongue deep inside her. "I'm thirsty," he whispered. "Mmmmmm."

Septi's nipples were hard as rocks and her pussy was pulsating and throbbing like a migraine headache. There was no denying it--she loved having sex with him. He always brought out her kinky side and Lord knows, she loved herself some dick, especially his. His was a perfect fit for her. Kandy was giving her exactly what she needed at this moment--her troubles had completely disappeared. With her neck bent back and her eyes rolled to the back of her head, Septi was deep in ecstasy, moaning and making hissing sounds.

Kandy had Septi right where he wanted her. He knew she was the type of woman that required constant sex and now that Aaron was completely out of the picture, he felt she would become more miserable and would start making trouble for him and Anabay. Women like her can become real vicious when they're unhappy. He figured that if he started giving her a little, that would make her happy and he could trap her into becoming his side piece, at the same time. She wouldn't utter one word to Anabay, for fear of hurting her cousin and destroying their relationship.

Septi was drunk with pleasure, absorbing the bliss Kandy was bestowing on her. "Get the fuck off me, you goddamn piece of shit!" She began kicking her legs and pushing his head from in between her legs. She had snapped back to her senses.

"You schizophrenic or something? What's up with you? One minute you oohing and cooing and the next minute you screaming get off me," Kandy said, wiping his mouth.

"I don't want you! I hate you! You're a fucking dog! Get the fuck out of my house!" She continued shouting, while scrambling to put her robe back on.

"I guess only brotherly love can satisfy that hot box of yours these days. Tell me, Septi, is it true what they say, brotherly love is the best?"

Septi stood with her hands folded, narrowing her eyes at him.

"Damn, Girl, I heard about Aaron tapping that ass of yours! You must feel like shit! You don't seem to have any luck when it comes to men," he laughed, while straightening his clothes up.

"If you came here to rub that in my face, it's not going to work. I already feel ashamed and dirty, but not as dirty as I felt, laying down with your ass!"

"You got a lot of fucking nerve! Laying down with me ain't shit compared to you freaking your own brother!"

"Why don't you tell me if this is true or not, Keith? Is it true that jailhouse sex is the bomb?"

He was taken aback by her question. "I've heard some of the guys where I work say this is the case. What's your point?"

Septi was so mad, she was breathing fire. "You know what? You don't have a soul! The only thing you've got going for yourself is a big dick! Now get your jailbird ass out of here before I call the police and have you thrown out!"

"Did I hear your right? You calling me a jailbird?"

"Cut the crap! I know everything about your sorry ass, Keith Jackson, or shall I call you Kandy? You're nothing but a fucking street hustler! A thug! You've got a notorious reputation and an extensive criminal record! I know all about your fat-ass wife and your five kids! I've even been to your house and talked to Justine!"

Kandy was boiling mad. He started walking towards Septi. "Bitch, you had me investigated?"

"I investigated you myself after I saw you with your family down at my job. I'll bet Anabay doesn't know about your family, does she?"

He jumped up in Septi's face, pointing his finger. "Bitch, you better keep your goddamn mouth shut if you know what's good for you! I don't play!"

She slapped his finger away. "I'm not scared of your punk ass! I'm going to tell Anabay everything! I'm going to tell her all about how you were screwing me behind her back and about your wife and kids! I'm going. . . "

"She won't believe you!"

"Oh, yes, she will! Did you forget, Dumbass--I work for Social Services? I have documented proof! I'm not going to let you make a fool out of my cousin anymore and use her up, like the rest of your women! Anabay has no idea what a dirty, low-down dog you really are!"

Kandy went in for the kill. He grabbed Septi and pinned her to the wall. "I ought to break your neck! You have just fucked with the wrong guy!"

She started screaming, but he quickly covered her mouth with his hand. Septi observed his eyes roaming around the room like he was searching for a weapon of some sort. She felt relieved when she heard Delbert's footsteps running down the hall.

Kandy had no choice but to quickly let go of his grip on her.

"Aunt Septi, I want to watch cartoons. Hi, Uncle Keith."

"Hey, Buddy, how you doing?" Kandy replied, rubbing the top of the little boy's head.

"I'm fine. Aunt Septi, can I have some more cereal?"

"No, Delbert, you already had cereal this morning. Your mommy sent us over some food from the restaurant. I'll fix you something to eat as soon as Keith leaves."

"Alright," said Delbert, looking disappointed.

"I'm leaving now," said Kandy. "Delbert, see you later. Septi, would you mind walking me to the door?"

"I have to fix lunch now. You know the way out. Good bye, Keith." Septi turned her back to him and walked out of the room.

Kandy walked out, slamming the door behind him, with a sick feeling in the pit of his stomach. His future with Anabay was clearly at risk. "Damn it! Shit! That bitch is going to fuck up everything for me!" He was so angry he punched the wall.

After lunch, Septi lay back on her couch, reflecting on her encounter with Kandy and how brave she had been, standing up to him. She thought about him pleasuring her with his tongue, and how good it had felt. She was happy with herself for stopping him before he stuck that big, hard dick of his in her. She thought about how Anabay had lied to her face about telling her business to him.

"I'm going to confront her about it tonight," Septi declared to herself.

*****

Anabay returned to Septi's apartment around ten o'clock that night.

When Septi opened the door, Anabay was standing there, sobbing uncontrollably. "Anabay, what's wrong?"

"Aunt Lillie Mae died."

The two women embraced each other and her plan to confront her cousin evaporated.

Chapter 33

Homegoing Service

"Hey Otis, wear your blue suit today and put on that new white shirt I bought you with your blue and black striped necktie."

"Alright, Lillie Mae, whatever you say," Otis sleepily mumbled, turning over in bed. "Oh Lord," he shouted, jumping straight up. Feeling bewildered and perplexed, he remembered today was Lillie Mae's funeral. 'How is it possible for her to be telling me what to wear?' he wondered.

Otis sat motionless, plagued with guilt. His revelation, about his affair and love child, was the major contributing factor to his wife's untimely, massive heart attack. He was a realist, however, so there was no way he could ever have allowed his two biological children to carry on romantically with each other. The truth needed to be told. Lillie Mae had been a good woman and wife, but she had one big fault--she kept her head buried in the sand, only seeing the good in people. This had been the case with her niece, Belle.

Lillie Mae, being the kind-hearted woman she was, took in her niece, Belle, to live with them. There had been no stability in this young girl's life since the death of her mother, Lillie Mae's sister, Fannie. She had been living on and off with various family members, who passed her around. Lillie Mae was committed to providing her niece with a stable home environment and an opportunity to go to college.

Belle had just turned sixteen when she came to live with them. What a breath of fresh air! She was beautiful, frisky, and headstrong, and Otis and Lillie Mae absolutely adored her. They had been trying, without success, for years to have a child of their own, so Belle became their surrogate daughter.

One year after Belle moved in, out of nowhere, it happened! Lillie Mae became pregnant. Now, their family would finally be complete.

Otis and Belle began spending more time alone now that Lillie Mae was pregnant. They played card games or watched television together, and he often drove her to and from her various school activities. He was lulled by her sweet innocence so he was oblivious at first to her carefully orchestrated plan of seduction. A kiss on the cheek goodnight slowly changed to a quick peck on the lips or she would rub up against him, supposedly by accident. Belle had a lot of other little tricks, like getting dressed with her bedroom door open, not wearing a bra around the house and when she did, her blouses would be buttoned real low.

Otis tried his best to resist her temptations, but after drinking one night with the guys at the shipyard, he returned home to find her sprawled out, naked on the living room coach. He couldn't resist. Lillie Mae was sound asleep upstairs, seven months pregnant with Aaron. Belle was way more experienced for her age than Otis ever imagined--she knew tricks most grown women never heard of. He couldn't get enough of her tight, young body. After that night, they had sex every chance they got right under Lillie Mae's nose for about a year, until Belle announced her pregnancy.

Otis remembered being a nervous wreck during this time, unable to eat or sleep. Belle was in love with him, wanted to have his baby and she didn't give a damn about Lillie Mae or Aaron. She was dead set on breaking up his marriage and on a daily basis, she threatened to expose their affair.

Otis ended up doing what most married men do, he lied and told Belle he was going to divorce Lillie Mae but he needed time to put his affairs in order. He finally convinced her to move into an apartment he found for her in the Bronx and promised to financially support her and their baby.

It was love at first sight for Otis, when he laid eyes on his baby girl, Shirley Belle. He loved everything about her--holding her, feeding her, burping her, changing her. She was a good natured baby with big brown eyes. She was his heart.

He continued sleeping with Belle for about a year after the baby was born, until she wised up and realized he wasn't leaving Lillie Mae. Otis will never forget how cold she was to him, the last time he visited her in the Bronx. She told him it was over, she never wanted to see his ass again and that she had found a real man to step up to the plate and love her the way every woman deserves to be loved. She told him that he meant nothing to her except green dollars and that if he didn't honor his financial obligations, she would tell Lillie Mae everything, for sure. She slammed the door behind him and shouted out, "You can't fuck anyway. Mail me my money by the first." She cut off all contact with him— wouldn't take his calls or open the door for him.

Two years later, Belle requested a face-to-face meeting with Otis during which she presented him with legal documents, relinquishing his paternal rights to their daughter. She was now happily married, and her husband wanted to adopt Shirley Belle. Otis hesitated at first to sign the papers, until Belle threatened him. She said if he didn't sign, she would tell Lillie Mae about their affair and love child. Otis truly loved his wife and the life they had built together, so he gave up his rights.

Belle also made it clear to Otis--he was not off the hook for child support. If he so much as missed one payment, she swore to him, she would tell Lillie Mae everything. It was blackmail, plain and simple, but he was caught in a trap. Otis paid child support until his daughter graduated from college, even though she had been adopted by another man.

Belle chose not to have any further relationship with Lillie Mae, except sending occasional holiday cards with no return address. Lillie Mae never even knew her niece had a child until this past Easter Sunday. Belle managed to always stay in contact with Otis, however, to make sure he stayed current on his financial obligations.

It was ten o'clock in the morning and various family members and friends had begun assembling in the parlor, waiting for the cars from the funeral home to arrive and transport them to church for the eleven o'clock service.

Aaron slowly descended the stairs, dressed in a black suit and wearing black sun shades to hide his red, puffy eyes. He knew it was inevitable--one day he would have to say his final goodbyes to his parents. It was life, but he had no idea it would be this soon and so suddenly. He loved his mother so much--she was his best friend. She was the only one who ever believed in him and loved him unconditionally. Everyone greeted Aaron warmly with hugs and kisses when he entered the parlor.

* * * * *

"Come on, Delbert, Mommy needs you to walk faster." Anabay was panicking because Uncle Otis wanted everybody to leave from his house at precisely ten o'clock.

"I'm tired, Mommy. I don't feel like walking. Pick me up." Delbert whined and tugged on his mother's arms.

"Delbert Jones, you are a big boy. You're wearing a three-piece suit now. I am not picking you up. Now, come on."

"OK, Mommy. I'm a big boy."

Anabay breathed a sigh of relief when the house came into view and the funeral home's stretch limousines were nowhere in sight.

"Let me ring the door bell, Mommy."

"Go on ahead."

Ding-dong, ding-dong.

Aaron opened the door, looking exhausted. He picked Delbert up and hugged him and then he embraced Anabay, sobbing. "Anabay, I just can't believe my Moms is gone. It just don't feel real."

"I know, Aaron. Aunt Lillie Mae was a wonderful woman. We all loved her and we're all going to miss her. She will always be in our hearts," Anabay responded, trying to remain emotionally strong for her cousin.

"Thanks, Anabay. Moms loved you and Delbert, too. You were the daughter she never had. Come on into the parlor. Some people have been waiting anxiously to see you and Delbert."

"Anxious to see me and Delbert? Who could that be?" Anabay was puzzled.

Upon walking in, her eyes immediately locked on Claudale's brothers, Sammy Lee and John Henry Jones. The last she saw them, they had been teenagers. She was pleased to see that they both had grown up to be quite handsome young men. They rushed over and embraced her, and of course, they made a big to-do over Delbert. Both said he was the spitting image of Claudale.

Three black stretch limousines pulled up in front of the house at ten thirty. Anabay answered the doorbell to find a fat, dark-skinned man, dressed in a black suit, standing there.

He rushed in past her, without properly introducing himself, and started shouting out commands. "Good morning. Folks, it's time to rock and roll. We need everybody to line up so we can get this show on the road. Time is money here. No C. P. time today, folks."

Anabay was taken aback by this man. 'Insensitive, obnoxious jerk!' she thought to herself. 'Surely the funeral home could have sent a better representative. He's the one who's late and now he has the nerve to be rushing everybody else.'

Before she could open her mouth, Aaron butted in. "Family, it's time to go. Get your things. Come on, time to go."

"Where's Uncles Otis," asked John Henry. "He's not down here."

"Jesus Christ, don't tell me Pops ain't ready. I don't believe this sh--." Aaron caught himself before saying the full word.

"Calm down, Aaron! He's probably still getting dressed. I'll let him know it's time to go," Anabay said, walking towards the staircase.

Upon reaching the top landing, Anabay could see that his bedroom door was ajar. She knocked and walked in, not waiting for him to respond. Otis was sitting in his recliner, fully dressed, staring out the window.

"Uncle Otis, the family cars are here. We have to leave now."

"Oh, Anabay, I'm having a hard time getting myself together. I keep thinking about Lillie Mae." His voice was low and hoarse. It was obvious from his red, puffy eyes and his swollen eyelids, that he hadn't slept well in days.

Anabay felt sorry for him. "I know, Uncle Otis. It's hard to believe she's gone."

Tears were welling up in Otis's eyes. Anabay grabbed his hand and escorted him down the stairs and out the door to the waiting limousine. Aaron and Delbert were already seated inside.

*****

The people in the funeral procession were exiting their vehicles when church bells chimed at the eleven o'clock hour.

The fat black man jumped out of the lead car holding a bullhorn. "My name is Willie Brown and I am the assistant funeral director for the W.T. Funeral Home. I want to extend my deepest sympathy to the family and friends of the late Mrs. Lillie Mae Jones. Now, I need everyone to line up according to your relationship to the deceased. Father and son, sisters and brothers, grandchillens, aunties and unks, and other extended family members. I want y'all to line up in pairs--that would be two for those of you who don't know how to count," he said, holding up his index and middle finger and letting out a loud chuckle.

'This man is really a jackass,' Anabay thought to herself. 'I'm going to write a letter to the funeral home and complain about him.'

Aaron's eyes watered. He was thinking about all the love his mother had given to him -- his entire life. He, too, was struggling with feelings of guilt. She would still be alive if he hadn't invited Septi to Easter Brunch. That's when the shit hit the fan. His father, a supposedly stand-up guy, announced that he was Septi's father and that Septi was the product of an affair he had with his wife's niece.

Aaron remembered his mother talking about her niece, Belle, and about how she had tried to help the young girl and how Belle had suddenly turned and wanted nothing to do with her. He remembered Lillie Mae saying Belle broke her heart. Lillie Mae never understood why that was, until last Sunday. To break it all down, Aaron had been dating and sleeping with a woman who was both his half-sister and his cousin. The very thought of it made him feel ashamed and nauseated. He didn't know if he would ever be able to muster the courage to face or speak to Septi again. His father's big confession had changed all of their lives forever.

Otis and Aaron stood next to each other, the closest they had been since Easter. Aaron could barely contain the anger he was feeling towards him. He wished his father was lying in the coffin instead of his beloved mother. To distract himself, he adjusted his sunglasses and stared straight ahead.

"Aaron. Aaron. Boy, you hear me taking to you?" Otis whispered.

"What is it?" Aaron pulled his sun shades down from his tear-filled eyes onto the bridge of his nose and looked into his eyes. Otis's voice irritated him. He wondered, 'What could he possibly have to say that's so important –that it can't wait until after the service?'

Otis took a deep breath and swallowed hard. "I want you to know, before we enter this church, I am your father, not your mother. She ruined you. I am not going to take care of you like she did, so it is up to you whether you sink or swim."

Aaron stood there clenching his fists and biting down on his lower lip, speechless and completely floored by Otis's audacity. All of his life, his father had done nothing but put him down every chance he got. Now, today of all days, he couldn't even allow him to mourn his own mother in peace without hurling an insult his way. As far as he was concerned, Otis was nothing but a hateful, old yellow-ass man who deserved a good ass kicking. But, out of respect for his mother, Aaron knew he had to maintain his composure.

Pastor Tisdale walked up and stood in front of the family line. "Attention everyone. I just want to say: Father God knows your hearts are heavy and he knows you don't understand. He knows some of you are angry, but he also wants you to know he does not make mistakes. He will take care of you. You must trust in the Lord. Join hands."

The ushers opened the church doors and Pastor Tisdale turned his back to the family, facing the pulpit. "All rise," he commanded in a deep, husky voice. The congregation stood to their feet. "Let the church say Amen." Pastor Tisdale led the family into the Sanctuary, reciting the 23rd Psalm. "The Lord is my Shepherd, I shall not want. He maketh me to lie down in green pastures, he restoreth my soul . . ."

Lillie Mae had touched the lives of many people. The church was packed to capacity with family and friends. Her body was lying in an open, bronze coffin surrounded by a sea of flowers, all types and colors. She was dressed in a lilac chiffon dress with a matching crystal encrusted lilac pillbox hat. She looked peaceful, like she had closed her eyes and drifted off to an eternal slumber.

Aaron and Otis approached her coffin first, for their final viewing. Otis bent over and kissed his wife's face and patted her white gloved hands. He was quiet but tearful. Aaron sobbed loudly and uncontrollably. He kissed his mother and proceeded to sit down next to his father in the designated family section.

Anabay and Delbert were next in line to say their final goodbyes. Anabay was a bundle of nerves as she approached the coffin, with tears streaming down her face. It hadn't dawned on her until this very minute that Delbert was only five years old and perhaps, he might react badly to seeing Aunt Lillie Mae's body. She wished Kandy could have come with her today. 'I surely could have used the support,' she thought.

"Mommy, why is Aunt Lillie Mae sleeping in the box?" Delbert asking, pulling on her hand.

"Aunt Lillie Mae is with God now, Baby. Just like your daddy." She burst out crying.

Delbert started crying out loud, too. "I don't want Aunt Lillie Mae to be with God! God is mean! Tell her to get up, Mommy! Get up, Aunt Lillie Mae! Get up!"

Anabay's heart ached for her son. He was too young to understand the cycles of life and death.

An usher intervened and escorted Anabay and Delbert to their seats next to Aaron and Uncle Otis. After the last family member viewed the body, Aunt Lillie Mae's coffin was permanently sealed. There wasn't a dry eye in the church. All remembered how much love she had shown to all who were fortunate enough to cross paths with her.

The service proceeded on with readings from both the Old and the New Testaments followed by a solo of Precious Lord from Sister Childs, the superstar of the Gospel Choir. The next order of business was the reading of the obituary by Anabay, who struggled to fight back tears. She read a special poem she had written, titled 'Heartfelt Sorrow.'

Pastor Tisdale led the church choir, singing Lillie Mae's favorite hymn, "May the Work I've Done Speak for Me." His singing always brought the house down to its knees. When the lyric, "When I'm resting in my grave, there is nothing more to be said" was sung, Otis became emotionally unleashed. He wailed at the top of his lungs, "Lord, have mercy on me. I'm so sorry." The church medical team rushed in and whisked him out of the chapel temporarily, so he could compose himself.

Aaron felt no mercy for his father. He hoped every day going forward, Otis would be reminded of what he did to his mother.

Pastor Tisdale adjusted his robe and walked up to the pulpit. "Father God, I pray that you wrap your arms around this family today. They need you, Lord. As it is stated in Matthew 5:4—Blessed are those who mourn, for they will be comforted." Pastor always did his finest preaching at funerals. There was joke in the community, if you're not sure about making it into heaven, hire Pastor Tisdale, he'll preach you into heaven. His church was known for having real emotional, throw-down funerals, with people crying and fainting, and having to be carried out of the church. Sometimes the mourners would even throw themselves into caskets or graves. It was 'Show Time' for Pastor Tisdale.

"Church, open your Bibles to Job 14: 14. I'll give those of you who are struggling with your Bibles a few minutes," he chuckled lightly. "If a man dies, shall he live again? All the days of my service I would wait, till my release have come. Well," he said, "Just last Sunday morning, Sister Lillie Mae came to church. Yes, she was sitting in the congregation, just like you all are doing right now, hmm." He paused. "She went home and prepared brunch, hmm," pausing again. "She didn't know it was going to be her last day here, on her earthly home, church," he raised his voice, making sure he had the attention of all. "I said, I . . . want you to hear me now" . . . lowering his voice. "I . . . but I want you to hear me now. Hmm . . . The difference with Sister Lillie Mae --- she was a clean and godly woman who . . . lived . . . her life each and every day for the Lord. When he called her home, she was ready. Yes, Sister Lillie Mae was ready! She wasn't worried, because she lived ready, waiting on the Lord. Church, can I get an amen? How many of you here today can honestly say you're ready to go home if the Lord called you home right now?"

After an hour-long sermon, Pastor Tisdale commanded the congregation to rise up for the benediction. The choir sang the closing hymn, "Going Up Yonder."

Everyone was crying, even little Delbert. The pallbearers hoisted up the casket and proceeded out the church behind various church members carrying flowers. Pastor Tisdale walked behind the procession followed by the family.

*****

Anabay was standing outside talking to the church clerk about the repast when she felt a tug on her arm. She turned around and, to her surprise, Septi was standing there dressed in a black pant suit with a long black sheer veil covering her face. Through the veil, Anabay could see she had been crying. "Septi! You came!"

They embraced, holding onto each other.

"She was my aunt, too. Oh, I forgot! She was also my stepmother," Septi said, frowning. "I'm sorry I never got to know her like you did. From what everyone says, she was a real sweet woman. I blame my bitch of a mother for everything. She has ruined my life. I'm sorry, Anabay. I don't mean to carry on this way, especially on a day like this."

"It's OK, Septi. I'm happy to see you," Anabay squeezed her hand. "I can't begin to imagine how much courage it took for you to come here today. I know Uncle Otis and Aaron will appreciate that you came."

"I only came to show my support to you and Delbert. I can't face them. Why do you think I have this veil on?"

"You're going to have to face them one day. You're not at fault. You shouldn't feel so ashamed."

"Easier said than done. Anyway, the service was beautiful. Pastor Tisdale sure is a handsome man for his age and he can preach his ass off! He's got a set of windpipes on him! He's single, right?"

"Girl, please. I know you're not sweating Pastor," Anabay giggled, lightly elbowing Septi.

"I'm kidding. Anyway, I'm heading back home now."

"Why don't you come with us to the cemetery and to the repast? It's at the restaurant and you know the food is going to be awesome."

"I wish I could but I'm not up to it. Besides, everybody's going to be whispering about me."

"Septi, if you found the courage to come here to the funeral, surely you can find the courage to face people. I doubt seriously if anyone is going to be whispering about you. All they know is -- Aunt Lillie Mae had a heart attack. I'm not taking 'no' for an answer. You can ride with me and Delbert in the family car."

"Are you out of your mind? You're really pushing it now. That's not going to fucking happen," Septi responded in a raised voice.

"Septi, lower your voice. All right, perhaps riding with us in the family car is too much, but you're coming, you hear me? I'll find you a ride. I'll ask Brother Glover Davis."

"Where is Delbert anyway? Septi asked, changing the subject.

"He's in the car."

"How's he doing? I saw the way he was crying. I felt so sorry for him.

"He's too young to understand."

"You didn't expect him to, did you?"

"No, of course not. I know he's going to be asking for Aunt Lillie Mae and I'll have to keep explaining to him that she is in heaven. That's all I can do."

Septi leaned down and peeked into the limo's window. "Look, he fell asleep."

"It's been a long week. He's tired."

"Anabay, why don't you let me take him home with me? You can pick him up after everything is over."

"I wish I could, Septi, but Claudale's brothers are here and I know they want to spend time with him. Besides, I want you to come with us."

"I'm not going, so please stop asking me!" Septi spoke firmly, letting Anabay know she meant 'no.' "And I'm taking Delbert with me. His uncles can see him another time. He's tired," she insisted.

"Are you sure you don't mind taking him?"

"Don't be silly. You know how I feel about Delbert. You need to officially make me his godmother." Septi opened the limo door, scooped Delbert up into her arms and kissed him on his cheek.

"Thanks, Septi." Anabay was relieved Delbert was going home with Septi. She hoped Claudale's brothers wouldn't think she was being selfish.

"Don't mention it. I'll see you later."

"Attention everybody," Willie Brown shouted through his bullhorn. "Whoever is accompanying us to the cemetery, please go to your cars and start your engines and don't forget to turn your emergency lights on. Once you see the family cars pull out, fall in line. We're going to drive by the Jones' home and then we're going to get on the Garden State Parkway South. It's about a twenty-five-minute ride to the cemetery. No time to be driving on E--you know who you are." He cleared his throat and chuckled.

'So annoying! I'm definitely going to write that letter and complain about him to the funeral home,' Anabay thought.

Willie Brown waited for everyone to get into their cars before jumping into one of the two white Chevy El Caminos carrying the flowers, and pulled away from the curb, followed by three black family limos. The procession was approximately three miles long.

It was quite a somber ride in the first family car. Aaron sat in the back with his head buried in his hands trying to deal with the realization that his mother was gone. He thought about how unfair life could be sometimes.

He was trying to wrap his mind around his mother's last words, "The Curse." He could count on one hand and still have fingers left over, the number of times he had heard the story about the family curse. He hadn't realized his mother believed in it, that is, until last Sunday, when he heard the words from her mouth. The notion of a family curse deeply troubled him. He wanted answers.

Anabay sat in the back seat directly across from Aaron. She looked out the window the entire time, not wanting to make eye contact or small talk. She wondered what was going to happen between Aaron and his father. Everyone knew Lillie Mae kept the two of them civil. She wondered if she was at fault for introducing Aaron to Septi. She regretted not talking to her aunt about the alleged curse. Now it was too late.

Otis rode in the front seat with the driver. There was no pretending. He didn't want to be near Aaron. As far as Otis was concerned, he had said everything he needed to say to his son before entering the church and he meant every word. Otis looked straight ahead, occasionally reaching for his handkerchief to wipe his teary eyes and runny nose. "How could this have happened," he asked himself, repeatedly.

What one does in the dark often comes to light, but Otis had been careful. He had done everything in his power to make sure his infidelity and love child never came to light. He vowed to take his secret to his grave. He never imagined it would come back and bite him in the ass with a vengeance, like it did. Now, his wife, the love of his life, was dead because of it. 'It's that damn Aaron's fault,' he convinced himself. 'That boy has always been a pain to me from the day he was born.'

Otis's stomach was full of butterflies as the procession turned into the gates of the Rose Hill Eternal Rest Cemetery and drove on the winding roads before coming to a complete stop.

Willie Brown was the first to exit the car, with his bullhorn. "Please exit your cars and bring your umbrellas. It looks like a cloud is approaching."

What seemed to be a beautiful early spring day was now overcast with angry-looking clouds. The driver looked at Otis, whose legs were trembling uncontrollably. Tears flowed down his face. "You all right, Mr. Jones?" he inquired, placing his hand on Otis' forearm to steady him.

Otis sighed deeply. "Yes, son, I'm good," he whispered.

Everyone exited their cars and walked down the grassy slope to the tent-covered freshly dug grave surrounded by all the floral arrangements and chairs for the immediate family.

"Mommy, Mommy!"

Anabay turned around at the sound of Delbert's voice and saw Septi and Delbert walking beside Brother Davis. 'Septi is an amazing woman,' she thought to herself, waiting for them to catch up to her.

"Pick me up, Mommy. I'm tired."

"Delbert Jones, look at you. Your shoes are muddy! I told you to be a big boy," Anabay reminded him.

"I don't want to walk, Mommy," he pleaded, whimpering.

"Come, let me pick you up, Sweetheart." Septi stepped forward.

"OK." He reached his arms out.

"Septi, you are spoiling him. He's going to dirty your pantsuit," Anabay warned.

"It's fine. He's tired." Septi picked up the weary child.

Pastor Tisdale was standing at the head of the casket. "May we gather around," he said, holding his Bible firmly. "Death reminds us all that this place we call home is not our home but a temporary dwelling. We are all only passing through. For everything there is a season, and a time for every purpose under heaven; a time to be born and a time to die; a time to weep..." (Ecclesiastes 3:1-2, 5).

Thunder was rumbling and the sky grew darker. Pastor Tisdale prayed and committed the body to the earth and asked everyone to place a flower on the casket. "This concludes our service. The family will thank you at a later date. The family will greet you at the repast being held at SisBros' Southern Cuisine. I understand there's going to be quite a spread in memory of Mrs. Jones."

"I heard she could throw down," Willie said, surprisingly without the aid of his bullhorn.

Aaron wanted to see his mother's coffin lowered into the ground, so he stayed seated in his chair by the graveside.

"Aunt Septi, I want to say hi to Cousin Aaron," Delbert said, loud enough to get Aaron's attention.

Septi whispered in his ear, "Delbert, let's go to the car. It's lightning and it's going to rain."

"No!" he screamed. "I want to say hi to Cousin Aaron now!" He kicked at her sides with both of his feet.

Septi wished she had listened to Anabay and not picked him up. She had no choice but to take him to see Aaron. Delbert had made a big scene, making it obvious if she had ignored him and his loud demand. With Delbert in her arms, she slowly walked towards Aaron.

"Hi, Cousin Aaron," Delbert called out as they approached.

"Hey, Miss Hollywood!" Septi heard a voice shouting out from behind her, causing her to stop in her tracks and turn around.

Aaron looked up.

Pow! Pow! Pow! Pow!

Gunshots were heard.

"Shots being fired! Run!" Someone yelled out.

Everyone started screaming and scattering for cover, to their cars and behind tombstones.

Delbert flashed into Anabay's mind. "Delbert! Delbert!" she cried out hysterically. She took off running back to find Septi and Delbert. Her heart dropped at the sight of Aaron kneeling over somebody on the ground.

"My baby!" She grabbed Delbert from Septi's arms and sat on the ground clenching her son's blood-covered body in her arms. "Somebody help me! Help me!" she screamed and cried.

Aaron was next to her, holding a wounded, semi-conscious Septi in his arms.

"Help me! Help me!" Anabay continued screaming and crying at the top of her lungs. "Somebody shot my baby! God have mercy!" She heard her mother's voice whispering in her ear, I tried to warn you. "Mama, why? Why, Mama? Why the Curse?" She wailed in pain, holding on to Delbert for dear life. She could feel his little body shaking and twitching and finally, his life slipped away. His lifeless body had to be pried out of her arms. She fainted.

Zenora Knight

Epilogue

"Hey, Babycakes, it's time to rise and shine. It's been two years already – you've got to snap out of it. The woman I fell in love with wouldn't give up and lie around feeling sorry for herself like you've been doing. Where's the spirit of my country girl who wouldn't let anyone or anything keep her from leaving Fort Mitchell? You are the strongest person I know. What happened to our son was not your fault. Delbert is fine. He is happy here with me, and Aunt Lillie Mae, and your mama too. You will see him again-- not now, but some day. Thank you for giving me a son. I'm going to take real good care of him. Don't you know, that within yourself, you have everything you need to succeed and to be happy. But first, you must forgive yourself and everyone else involved. Now, pick yourself up, and go on and live that fabulous life you were born to live. I will always love you."

Anabay could feel Claudale's lips on her cheek.

"Honey, one more thing," he began to say, "About the curse. . ." Then, he vanished.

Anabay was aware of the sound of her own voice, crying out, "Please, Claudale, don't leave me again. I need you." Suddenly, she woke up from her deep sleep. She was sweating, her heart was beating fast, and all of the muscles in her body felt paralyzed as she lay in her bed, trying to calm herself down.

It was only a dream, she told herself—but so vivid and real. She felt its truth to the bottom of her soul. She closed her eyes in a wordless prayer. What happened next could not be captured in words. Anabay felt a protective warmth flooding her body and spirit. Her religious background told her--this must be what it means to be touched by the Holy Ghost. She lay very still, like an infant cradled in the hands of the Almighty. She had no other explanation for the experience, or way of describing it.

Immediately afterwards, she knelt down and prayed. "Thank you, Jesus!" she breathed. "I am terribly wounded by the death of my son, but I know he is with you. With your help, I will do my best to go on living."

Anabay stood up slowly, drenched in sweat, and immediately reached for her pink leather journal. She wanted to make sure she recorded everything while it was still fresh and vivid in her mind. Her psychiatrist, Dr. Weinberg, had asked her to write down her feelings each day.

In trembling handwriting, she penned this entry: "Today is exactly two years to the day my son, Delbert was killed. As a mother, the pain and the grief has been enormous, beyond words. Burying my husband was one thing, but no mother should ever have to bury her child. Most days I cannot get out of bed or lift a finger. I have become a depressed, non-functioning human being. The thought of taking my own life is never too far removed. I just haven't had the courage to do it. My mama tried to warn me about the family curse. I feel guilty because Delbert is dead because of the curse. Up until last night, I had no more fight left in me, no reason to go on. But the Lord showed me mercy and blessed me, allowing Claudale to visit me and assure me that Delbert is fine. Now, I have peace, knowing my baby is with God. I think I can do this thing called living."

She wondered why Claudale wasn't able to tell her everything he started to say about the curse. He wanted to tell her something, but what? She spent the rest of her day meditating and praying for strength and making telephone calls to address some of her long overdue affairs. She made a decision that tomorrow would be her last appointment with Dr. Weinberg.

*****

Anabay woke up the next morning at seven o'clock sharp, feeling refreshed and well rested for the first time in years. She reached for her diary and wrote: "I feel pain at this moment, but this day is different. I know I can face the world. I am determined to pick up my broken pieces. I will not let sorrow consume me. I have received confirmation from Claudale himself, that Delbert is happy in heaven and being well taken care of by those nearest and dearest to my heart."

After writing, praying and meditating, Anabay showered and looked for something to wear to her eleven o'clock therapy session. She selected an eggplant colored pantsuit and matched it with a pink V-neck sweater.

After dressing and brushing her hair back in a ponytail, she went downstairs to the kitchen where she knew her uncle would be sipping coffee and reading his newspaper. "Good morning, Uncle Otis. Today, I am going to my appointment alone."

Uncle Otis was shocked to see her standing there dressed in a color other than black, ready to go to her appointment. He usually had to argue her into keeping her appointment with Dr. Weinberg. But today, she wanted to go—and on her own. 'This was a good sign,' he thought to himself. He wondered if he could trust her out of the house by herself. Was she really getting better, or was this just a desperate escape from the four walls of her room? He decided not to stand in the way of what appeared to be progress.

Anabay kissed him on the cheek and left the house, basking in the warmth of the sunshine on her face for the first time in two years. Upon arriving in downtown Newark at the Broadway Building, she took the elevator to the 12th floor.

"Good morning, Edna," Anabay greeted Dr. Weinberg's secretary.

Edna was floored. This was the first time Anabay had uttered one word to her since becoming a patient at the office. Not only that, she was smiling, had on makeup and was dressed very nicely. She looked completely different from the old Anabay—the broken woman with sad, blank eyes. "Have a seat, Mrs. Jones. I'll let the doctor know you're here."

Edna sprang from her chair and ran directly into Dr. Weinberg's office. "Doctor, you have worked a miracle on Mrs. Jones! I knew you could bring her back. Wait until you see her!"

"Edna, calm down! What on earth are you talking about?"

"Mrs. Jones! She has come back to the land of the living! Wait until you see her-- you're going to be so happy! I'm so glad you stuck with her!" Edna was so excited.

Dr. Weinberg looked perplexed and didn't quite know what to say. "I guess I'll have to see with my own eyes. Send her on in, then. I'm ready."

Dr. Weinberg was a psychiatrist who specialized in bereavement counseling. He had taken Anabay on as a patient as a favor to a colleague at Newark Beth Israel Hospital, who felt she needed more than traditional grief counseling. After hearing her story, he was hopeful he could help this young woman. But, after two years with little or no progress, he frankly didn't know what mode of treatment might work. Trying to engage her in conversation was fruitless—she rarely said a word--so his only resort had been to write prescriptions for anti-depressant drugs in an effort to at least ease her suffering.

Her story was one of the saddest he'd heard in his three decades of practice. Someone had shot and killed her five-year-old son at a relative's funeral. When her baby took his last breath, she had been holding him in her arms. After this traumatic experience, it was lights off, no one home for Mrs. Jones. Her heart still beat and she took regular breaths, but she was literally dead to herself and others. Tucked away in her bra, she carried her son's blood-stained bowtie wrapped in a white silk handkerchief.

Dr. Weinberg couldn't get his first meeting with Mrs. Jones out of his head. She stared him down with blank, bloodshot eyes and responded to all his questions with one-word answers. In her trembling hands, she clutched that white handkerchief and repeatedly mumbled about being a cursed woman.

After that initial appointment, he regularly saw her every two weeks. She never had much to say other than to repeat her beliefs -- everything was her fault, her mother had been right, she was cursed, the Bailey women were all cursed. Whenever he tried to get her to open up about the details of her family's mysterious curse, she froze up and shut him out.

Dr. Weinberg met privately with her uncle, Otis Jones, and her cousin, Aaron Jones. They revealed that Anabay was slipping away as a person. She had forsaken the restaurant in which she was a part owner and spent her days lying in her bed with the blinds closed, either sleeping or crying. Sometimes she would spend hours rocking in a chair, writing letters to her deceased son or reading the Bible. She had abandoned her home and didn't even have the strength or energy to pay her bills. Her uncle said he had paid her bills for several months but stopped since she was obviously in a downward spiral. Otis rationalized he had worked too hard for his money to continue trying to help someone who absolutely had no desire to help herself. Her cousin Aaron felt she was a big strain on the family and her needs would be better met at a nursing home or psychiatric hospital.

Dr. Weinberg was a tough-minded doctor who kept his word to stick by his patients, especially through their worst times. He certainly didn't want to see a young woman like Anabay confined to a facility of any kind. But, in spite of his vow to continue having therapy sessions with her, his patience began wearing thin. He was particularly concerned by her insistence that she and all the women in her family were cursed. The whole idea of curses sounded to him like something medieval.

Edna dashed back to her desk just in time to answer the telephone. "Dr. Weinberg's office. How can I help you?" She spoke in a sing-song, clear professional voice.

"Good morning. This is Otis Jones. Did my niece arrive?" From the sound of his voice, Edna knew he was anxious and nervous.

"Yes." Edna detected that Otis didn't want Anabay, who was seated nearby, to know he was checking up on her.

She had been doing this job a long time and most of the time she knew what people wanted before they spoke.

"As soon as she leaves your office, can you or the doctor call and let me know how the appointment went? It's her first day out alone and I'm worried about her."

"I certainly understand and I will definitely give the doctor your message."

Edna turned to Anabay, "Mrs. Jones, please follow me. Dr. Weinberg will see you now." Edna wanted a quick glimpse at the doctor's face when he saw the 'new' Anabay.

"Hello, Dr. Weinberg," Anabay greeted him, walking into his office.

Edna had been right. Dr. Weinberg was indeed surprised to see Anabay so upbeat. This was a very different Anabay -- from the tormented soul he had been treating.

"Mrs. Jones!" Dr. Weinberg stood up from behind his desk and walked around, extending his hand to her. "You look . . . well, just wonderful today. Please sit down. You must share with me what's going on." He sat down on the edge of his desk across from her.

"Thank you, Dr. Weinberg. You are not going to believe it, but something unimaginable happened to me. Now, I want to live again."

"Well, please share with me." He couldn't help from focusing on the dramatic change in her mood and appearance.

"If I talk about it, I'll become emotional. Please read these two pages--I tried to explain it there." She dug in her tote bag, pulled out her journal, and flipped through a few pages before handing it to the doctor.

"Do you mind if I read out loud? I think it would be healing for you," he suggested.

"I would prefer for you to read it to yourself. I don't want to get weepy," Anabay responded, her eyes starting to well up with tears.

"Trust me, hearing your written words back can be healing. We will take it slow." Dr. Weinberg began reading, pausing intermittently to observe the expressions on her face.

"Continue reading," Anabay said, wiping teary eyes.

"Amazing, Anabay! This is really very profound. I, myself, am not a religious person, but that doesn't mean I think less of your faith. Obviously, you've had a spiritual epiphany. Look at you. You are a completely transformed woman. Do you truly feel you can work through your grief and go on with your life, as you've written in your journal?"

"Dr. Weinberg, for the first time since the loss of my son, I feel like trying. I am not whole, but remember, it's only been one day since Claudale paid me a visit and told me Delbert was with him. Claudale said I should go on with my life." Anabay's voice cracked, as she wiped away more tears and blew her nose.

Dr. Weinberg picked up the thread of the conversation. "You never really told me in detail what happened to your son. I did some research of my own. From what I gather, an ex-con was gunning for your best friend and accidentally killed your son. It clearly wasn't your fault, Anabay. But I know from our sessions, you feel guilty. Was it because you brought him to the cemetery?"

Anabay composed herself and looked Dr. Weinberg square in his eyes. "No. Here's the entire truth. I feel guilty because I exposed Delbert to a very bad man who ultimately was responsible for his death. Everyone calls him Kandy, but his real name is Keith Jackson. I met him at the prison where I was working. He was an inmate. It was shortly after my husband died and I guess I was lonely and vulnerable. I completely ignored all the warning signs and got involved with him. He turned out to be nothing but a criminal, a dirty low-down player, a sex addict and a con man. I'm so ashamed of myself."

Dr. Weinberg looked at his notes. "But according to the paper, a man named David Owens was the gunman. What's the connection to Kandy?"

"It's a long story, but the short of it is, Kandy wanted my best friend and cousin, Septi, dead because she had threatened to expose him to me. In his sick way, he had plans for living off me by taking the profits from my business. All the while, according to Septi, he had been having sex with her. Septi said she thought he and I were just co-workers. When she found out he was involved with me, too, she cut it off with him. But, he never stopped trying to get back in the bed with her. To make matters worse, Septi found out he was married with five kids." Anabay paused, catching her breath.

"Are you saying Kandy put this David fella up to killing Septi?" asked Dr. Weinberg.

"It all came out in court. Juice, that's David's nickname, said Kandy hired him to get rid of Septi."

Dr. Weinberg scratched his chin. "I don't recall reading about anyone else being arrested other than this David guy. Was the other fellow, Kandy, arrested too?"

"What you have to understand about Kandy," Anabay confessed, "He is slick, manipulative, and evil. He knows how to cover his bases. Juice claimed he offered to pay him five thousand dollars--money he planned on getting from my restaurant--for killing Septi. But, it was Juice's word against his--there was no proof beyond a reasonable doubt. He told investigators that when they were in prison, he and Juice used to fantasize about women all day, every day and that when he got out, he hooked up with Septi almost immediately but Juice couldn't get the time of day from any woman. So, according to Kandy, Juice became crazy with jealousy, to the point he shot Septi to teach him a lesson. But, I believe Juice."

Dr. Weinberg interrupted. "So, is Kandy a free man right now?"

"I'm not sure. I heard he violated his parole and was sent to prison to finish out his sentence."

"Do you think you'll be able to keep him out of your life?"

Anabay sighed deeply. "Entirely and absolutely. I have an order of protection against him, as does Septi. I think we've both seen the last of him."

"How is Septi emotionally and physically? I read that she was also injured in the shooting," probed Dr. Weinberg.

"She was shot in the leg and her shoulder," Anabay answered, "but she has recovered and is doing fine. I know she feels guilty that Delbert was killed by bullets intended for her. She has been reaching out to me, but I have been so under water with my own grief, I didn't have the strength to get back to her."

Their conversation paused for a long moment before Dr. Weinberg broke the silence. "Anabay, you know you can't fully move forward until you fully forgive yourself and Septi for what happened. That means getting back in touch with her. Soon."

"I know, Doctor," Anabay said, burying her face in her hand. Then she looked up again. "I plan on going to see her. I need to tell her that I don't blame her and that I love her."

Dr. Weinberg smiled. "That will be marvelous therapy for her and for you. Reconnecting with people you love is a big step in finding the strength to live again."

Anabay returned his smile as best she could. "I'm a work in progress, Doctor. I'd like to see if I can walk on my own legs again. You have been my rock for the past two years. I truly believe God sent you to me, whether you're a religious person or not."

They both chuckled.

"But now," Anabay continued, "I want to put my life back together. I know it will take time, and I may be back to see you."

Dr. Weinberg nodded. "You can return any time, Anabay. You're one of my true success stories."

She stood up and extended her hand to the doctor, then opted to give him a big hug instead.

"I wish you the best, Mrs. Jones. If you need me, you know where to find me," Dr. Weinberg said, opening the door for her.

"Oh, Mrs. Jones, one more quick question. In our sessions, you referred often to a curse of some kind, on the women in your family."

"The Curse," she whispered, barely parting her lips.

"I'm wondering," he said slowly, "how you feel about it now that you've found a new measure of personal strength and a brighter outlook on life."

Anabay was quiet for a long moment. She touched her fingertips together and looked earnestly at her Doctor. "I'm not sure. Everything's still very raw in my mind."

"May I share with you my thoughts about a curse?" Dr. Weinberg asked.

"Yes."

"I think people who believe they're cursed are indeed cursed because when anything negative happens to them, it is seen as part of the curse. But," he continued, hoping she was truly absorbing what he was saying, "If you don't believe you're cursed, then you're not—life is life. No one knows what's ahead for each of us. Sometimes life throws us a real loop, knocking us down to our knees. We have to find the courage and strength to get back up and keep on living."

A long silence ensued between the two of them.

"Having said all, I've just said, do you truly believe you're cursed or was it just a delusion because of your depression?

Anabay turned around, "You tell me, Doctor." She winked and walked out the door.

"Goodbye, Edna."

"Bye, Mrs. Jones."